continued . . .

Titles by Lori Foster

THE WINSTON BROTHERS
WILD
CAUSING HAVOC
SIMON SAYS
HARD TO HANDLE
MY MAN, MICHAEL
BACK IN BLACK

Anthologies

HOT CHOCOLATE
(with Suzanne Forster, Elda Minger, and Fayrene Preston)

SINFUL
(with Maggie Shayne, Suzanne Forster, and Kimberly Randell)

WILDLY WINSTON

THE POWER OF LOVE
(with Erin McCarthy, Toni Blake, Dianne Castell, Karen Kelley,
Rosemary Laurey, Janice Maynard, LuAnn McLane, Lucy Monroe,
Patricia Sargeant, Kay Stockham, and J. C. Wilder)

CHARMED
(with Jayne Castle, Eileen Wilks, and Julie Beard)

DOUBLE THE PLEASURE
(with Deirdre Martin, Jacquie D'Alessandro, and Penny McCall)

TAILS OF LOVE
(with Stella Cameron, Sue-Ellen Welfonder, Kate Angell, Sarah
McCarty, Donna MacMeans, Dianne Castell, Patricia Sargeant,
Ann Christopher, and Marcia James)

OUT OF THE LIGHT, INTO THE SHADOWS
(with L. L. Foster and Erin McCarthy)

DOUBLE THE HEAT
(with Deirdre Martin, Elizabeth Bevarly, and Christie Ridgway)

Writing as L. L. Foster

SERVANT: THE AWAKENING
SERVANT: THE ACCEPTANCE
SERVANT: THE KINDRED

BACK IN BLACK

Lori Foster

BERKLEY BOOKS, NEW YORK

THE BERKLEY PUBLISHING GROUP
Published by the Penguin Group
Penguin Group (USA) Inc.
375 Hudson Street, New York, New York 10014, USA
Penguin Group (Canada), 90 Eglinton Avenue East, Suite 700, Toronto, Ontario M4P 2Y3, Canada
(a division of Pearson Penguin Canada Inc.)
Penguin Books Ltd., 80 Strand, London WC2R 0RL, England
Penguin Group Ireland, 25 St. Stephen's Green, Dublin 2, Ireland (a division of Penguin Books Ltd.)
Penguin Group (Australia), 250 Camberwell Road, Camberwell, Victoria 3124, Australia
(a division of Pearson Australia Group Pty. Ltd.)
Penguin Books India Pvt. Ltd., 11 Community Centre, Panchsheel Park, New Delhi—110 017, India
Penguin Group (NZ), 67 Apollo Drive, Rosedale, North Shore 0632, New Zealand
(a division of Pearson New Zealand Ltd.)
Penguin Books (South Africa) (Pty.) Ltd., 24 Sturdee Avenue, Rosebank, Johannesburg 2196,
South Africa

Penguin Books Ltd., Registered Offices: 80 Strand, London WC2R 0RL, England

This is a work of fiction. Names, characters, places, and incidents either are the product of the author's imagination or are used fictitiously, and any resemblance to actual persons, living or dead, business establishments, events, or locales is entirely coincidental. The publisher does not have any control over and does not assume any responsibility for author or third-party websites or their content.

BACK IN BLACK

A Berkley Book / published by arrangement with the author

PRINTING HISTORY
Berkley mass-market edition / February 2010

Copyright © 2010 by Lori Foster.
Excerpt from *Mad, Bad and Blonde* by Cathie Linz copyright © by Cathie Linz.
Excerpt from *Something About You* by Julie James copyright © by Julie James.
Cover photograph by Queerstock. Cover design by Rita Frangie.

ISBN: 978-0-425-23298-9

BERKLEY®
Berkley Books are published by The Berkley Publishing Group,
a division of Penguin Group (USA) Inc.,
375 Hudson Street, New York, New York 10014.
BERKLEY® is a registered trademark of Penguin Group (USA) Inc.
The "B" design is a trademark of Penguin Group (USA) Inc.

PRINTED IN THE UNITED STATES OF AMERICA

10 9 8 7 6 5 4 3 2 1

To Tammy Helton

Sales Account Manager

West Chester, Ohio, Marriott

I know I speak for everyone in saying how much we appreciate all that you do to help organize our annual "Reader and Author Get Together." The hotel accommodations are fabulous, the food provided is delicious, and the atmosphere is always friendly and welcoming. What started out as an uncertain effort to bring together readers, authors, editors, agents, and publishers has grown into a heartwarming event of major proportions, and the hotel has contributed greatly to our success. Because of your terrific management and assistance, we're able to continue with an affordable event, and at the same time make significant donations to very worthy local causes.

Thank you for being so good at what you do.

~Lori Foster

www.lorifoster.com/community/readergettogether.php

CHAPTER 1

G ILLIAN Noode stood against the back wall of Roger's Rodeo, the popular bar where many fighters hung out. She was close enough to observe him, but not close enough to get noticed. Yet. At least, not by him. Plenty of other men had already given her the once-over, showing appreciation for her trim black skirt, her low-scooped white blouse, and strappy sandals. A few had even tried to strike up a conversation. Though tempted, she'd politely declined.

She'd come here for a reason, and Drew Black was it.

Dressed in well-worn jeans and a comfortable black T-shirt bearing the logo of the SBC fight organization, the president of the extreme sport sat at the polished bar. Currently, he was in close conversation with two long-haired lovelies whose bloated busts defied believability. No woman *that* slender had breasts *that* large.

But Drew showed no signs of disbelief. Like a king of his own making, he openly ogled their bounty. Thrilled with his appreciation, the girls played with their long hair, flirted, and *giggled*.

Gillian fought a gag.

From the many interviews and television spots she'd watched, as well as her current scrutiny, Gillian surmised that Drew Black had a fighter-type physique, sculpted with honest muscle rather than the steroid-induced kind. He wasn't quite as shredded as the actual fighters, who made workouts and a healthy diet a regular part of their routine, but he looked strong and capable.

Obviously his ego demanded that he stay in shape. After all, he was often surrounded by younger men in their prime, elite fighters with rock-hard bodies and astounding ability.

Drew Black intrigued her beyond the job at hand.

As an entrepreneur he showed great intelligence; no one could have accomplished what he had without a lot of smarts. He'd taken a mostly dead sport, banned in many states, and turned it into an astounding success.

And motivation? The man had it in spades. He couldn't possibly sleep more than six hours a night, given his enthusiastic workload and insane social calendar.

Good looks, great body, intelligence, enthusiasm, and money . . . Drew Black would be quite the catch if he wasn't such a sexist, foul-mouthed jerk with the tact of a mountain goat.

With her external analysis now complete, Gillian moved closer, just a short way down the bar. She could hear Drew's deep voice—not that she expected much enlightenment from his conversation.

But Drew surprised her.

"Will you call me?" bimbo number one asked him with a pout.

Lacking malice, he gave a low and mellow laugh. "No, I won't."

Look-alike bimbo number two said, "How about me?" She toyed with his ear in a way that made Gillian twitch. "I can promise you a *really* good time."

"I just bet you can." Drew took her wrist and moved her teasing hand away. "But I have to pass."

Gillian raised a brow. She'd expected him to suggest a threesome, and instead he'd rejected both of them.

Interesting.

The bimbos combined their whining complaints and attempts at persuasion until Drew appeared to get annoyed. "Girls, what the fuck? C'mon, I have shit to do and it doesn't include having my ears ring. Go find something— or someone—else to do, okay?"

"But Drew, we waited a long time to get to talk to you," Bimbo One whined.

Drew leaned around the woman to eye his male companion. "A little help here, Brett?"

Gillian recognized the other man as a fighter. Grinning, he held up big, capable hands. "Sorry, Drew. I have a girl waiting at home."

"We aren't at your home, damn it."

He smirked. "Yeah, well, Spice doesn't like to share me."

Drew pulled back. "Spice? What the fuck kind of name is that for a female?"

"The kind that suits her." Unruffled by the implied insult, Brett finished his drink. To Gillian, it looked like juice. She gave Brett points.

"Look," Drew said to the closest bimbo, "you're too fucking young and, frankly, too damned pushy."

"We have to be pushy to get near you. You're just so popular—"

"How about I give you a couple of tickets to the next SBC fight instead? Good seats. How's that?"

The girls bounced with enthusiasm. Gillian couldn't take it. She asked the bartender for a martini. By the time she'd been served and taken a few fortifying sips, Drew was alone at the bar with Brett.

"You're brutal, Drew."

"Did you see those girls? Not only were they phony from head to toes, the damn giggles were wearing on my nerves." He worked his shoulders, as if releasing tension. "Jesus, I do have some standards, you know."

"Yeah? Like what?"

"You want the whole list, huh? Well, it doesn't apply here, but she has to be less than forty. Older broads are too independent."

Brett laughed. "Those two together weren't forty."

"No, but young and *not stupid* don't have to be exclusive."

Brett grinned. "So what else?"

"She has to be childless, because let's face it, the whole kid thing is a major pain in the ass. No way am I fucking anybody's mother. And before you say it, yeah, I know, those two are still children themselves."

Brett saluted him with his juice.

"On top of being good-looking and sexy, she has to have a modicum of intelligence—at least enough that I can carry on a conversation with her. And no squealing. God Almighty, I detest broads who squeal."

Brett commiserated. "They were squealers."

"Can you imagine how loud they'd be in the sack, riding out a big O?" Drew laughed. "I'd need fucking earplugs."

Brett grinned. "Braggart."

That nasty mouth of his, Gillian thought as she shook her head. *Riding out a big O.* Who talked like that? The things Drew said, the crude language he used, were not befitting to the force behind the fastest-growing sport in history. That mouth had gotten him into trouble, whether he realized it yet or not.

It was her job to clean up his act, to make him a more presentable figurehead for the SBC franchise.

Daunting, but maybe not impossible. She always enjoyed a challenge.

The trick would be to beat him at his own game, to always keep the upper hand, and to grow a skin so thick that her feminist core wouldn't be damaged in the process.

She'd also have to remember that he was a grade-A jackass toward women, albeit a sexy one, so it'd behoove her to keep her emotional distance. Trusting him, in any way, would be a mistake. She could not let herself be drawn to him.

Sadly, he was the first man she'd found exciting in a very long time.

He was the *last* man she could ever get involved with.

Picking up her glass, Gillian moved down the bar and slid onto the vacated seat beside Drew. Slowly she crossed her legs. While sizing him up, she removed the olive from her drink and bit into it.

Both men stared at her, not so much because of her looks, which she knew to be average, or her figure, which was a little more voluptuous than currently popular. But because she'd invaded their space—and was now staring back.

Drew swiveled around on his stool to face her fully. Without a word, he checked her out, lingering on her legs, her cleavage, and then her mouth.

When his gaze finally crept up to hers, he said in a low voice, "Hello, there."

Oh, men were *so* easy. Smiling in triumph, Gillian held out a hand. "Hello."

A very warm, firm hand, twice the size of her own, enveloped her fingers—and held on. "I'm Drew Black."

"Of course you are." Still smiling, she retrieved her hand from his. "Gillian Noode."

"Nude?"

Of course he wouldn't let that one slide. With a chastising look, she spelled, "N-o-o-d-e."

His mouth quirked. "Hell of a name."

"Yes, and I've heard every joke there is, from every grade-school boy out there." She reached beyond Drew to the fighter. She'd heard Drew use his first name, but she liked proper introductions. "And you are . . . ?"

He took her hand gently. "Brett Bullman, ma'am."

Unlike Drew, who shaved his head, Brett had shaggy brown hair a little too long, a little too unruly. Gorgeous green eyes showed good humor.

He also had a name familiar to her. "The Pit Bull, right?"

His mouth twisted with chagrin. "I hear that's what they're calling me."

"I've read about you, Brett. You're touted as a self-taught phenom taking the fight scene by storm." Gillian tilted her head at him. "You don't like your nickname?"

He shrugged with indifference and shared a friendly smile that had surely melted many female hearts. "Long as the contenders know who I am, I don't care what they call me."

She lifted her glass at him. "You've certainly earned some respect."

"Maybe. The thing is, I haven't really been challenged yet." He gave a nod at Drew. "Hopefully we'll correct that."

So it was a business meeting. "And I'm interrupting. Shame on me." She stood to leave. She could wait for their negotiations to conclude. "Congratulations on your recent success."

"Thanks, Ms. Noode. But please don't leave on my account. This was just a meet-and-greet, really, and we're all talked out now anyway. I was just finishing up my drink."

Drew agreed. "I'm all yours, honey, so why not park your pretty ass back up on the stool so we can get better acquainted?"

Gillian's teeth locked, but her smile didn't falter. To Brett she said, "Call me Gillian, please."

He nodded. "All right, Gillian."

"When is your next fight?"

"It's still being set up. After that last win, I got noticed by the SBC and recruited by a great team." He shrugged. "I'd prefer to train with them for a while first. But if Drew wants me to fight now, I wouldn't turn him down."

"No more going it alone, huh?" Gillian had read that Brett had taught himself the finer points of MMA—mixed martial arts—success by watching taped fights and then practicing the moves in his own makeshift gym.

His grin personified charm. "No, ma'am. I only started out that way because I didn't know how to go about getting the right training." He flashed her that white-toothed smile again. "But I'm always open to learning from more experienced guys."

Drew lounged back, elbows on the bar, and copped an attitude over being ignored. "We have to finesse a contract yet, so we can't get ahead of ourselves. But I don't see any problems there. I'll figure out some key promotion, then probably give him a fight on pay-per-view. I just want to decide on the best way to build him up a little more first."

"I find it fascinating how this all works. Thank you for explaining." Gillian turned back to Drew but did *not* reseat herself. "So, Drew." She let out a big breath. "I suppose we really should talk."

"You heard Brett. I'm all talked out." His brown eyes challenged her. "But hey, you got something more physical in mind, count me in."

Gillian might not have an extensive romantic background, but neither was she obtuse. Drew was sexually attracted to her. After he'd sent off the young bimbos, she felt marginally flattered by that. But not enough to play the fool. "I'm sure nothing more than talk will interest you."

A brow went up. "The hell it doesn't."

This time her smile was snide. "But I don't meet your many requirements, Drew."

His gaze went over her again, slower this time, lingering in a way meant to discomfort her. He paused on her chest. "Honey, I think you fit the requirements just fine."

Rather than feeling offended by his near-tactile scrutiny, Gillian felt . . . warmed. And that annoyed her. So he was confident. And take-charge. He *did* possess a raw type of sex appeal.

But it was so raw as to be dangerous.

She put an arm on the bar and propped her chin on a fist. "But Drew, I'm forty-one," she lied. "That puts me well beyond your age stipulation."

His mouth twitched into a grin and he took up the game with practiced ease. "You sneaky broad. You were eavesdropping on us."

"Guilty. But you see, on top of being elderly, I have five . . ." She paused for effect. "No, let's make that *six* children."

"You're a terrible fibber." He turned his head to study her waist in the snug skirt. "I'd put you at no more than thirty-three tops. And any idiot can see those are not the hips of a child-bearing woman."

Brett gave a choking cough and made a point of looking at the ceiling.

"Hmmm." Gillian leaned in closer to Drew. "Perhaps you're right." She gave him a quizzical frown. "But why ever do you think I'd lie about such things?"

"Modesty?"

She pursed her mouth as if in thought. "Or *maybe* I stretched the truth to deliberately disqualify myself based on your list of suitable criteria. You know"—she waved a hand—"to avoid your personal interest."

Drew got closer, too, so close she felt his breath on her lips. He stared at her mouth. "Ah. So you assumed I'd be personally interested, did you?"

"Accurately, it seems. After all, you did suggest certain things you'd like to do."

"To you. Yeah." His gaze locked on hers. "If you need more details, they involve you baring yourself and getting a little sweaty. So what do you say?"

Good Lord. The man showed no decorum at all. "Ummm . . . no. Afraid not." For her own peace of mind, Gillian moved away from him again. "You were probably too hasty in sending away the enthusiastic groupies who, I'm sure, would have been much more accommodating."

"But they didn't interest me." His appreciative attention held her captive. "They were too artificial for my tastes."

"The laughs?" she guessed.

"The boobs." He nodded toward her cleavage and smiled. "I like things a little more natural."

Gillian fought a blush even as she felt defensive toward womankind. "I don't see much difference between their breast implants and the bright red lipstick I'm wearing. Both are meant to make a woman more attractive."

"Yeah, but one is surgery, and the other"—he closed the space between them to whisper—"can be licked off."

Shocked at both his audacity and her innate response to it, Gillian straightened and pulled away.

The man had no shame, no sense of social boundaries!

She was out of her league, so she'd have to play it a little safer.

"Now don't run off," Drew said. He touched her wrist on the bar with a light fingertip. "Things were just getting interesting."

Gillian shook her head. "You might be willing to bend your rules, but I'm afraid I'm not. And mixing business with pleasure is considered my number one no-no."

Caution replaced some of his amusement. "Good thing we don't have any business together then, huh?"

"But we do. That's why I'm here."

"What are you talking about?" His expression went from seductive to annoyed. "If we have business together, I sure as hell don't know about it."

"I'm here to inform you of it." It was evil of her, but Gillian felt gleeful at the opportunity to set him straight. She put her shoulders back and smiled. "I've been hired as your new publicist slash handler, slash . . . well, miracle worker really. And I daresay that with a lot of hard work on your part as well as mine, I'll succeed in transforming you into a man fit for polite society."

Drew came to his feet. His face tightened and his brows came down. He didn't shout, but, given his expression, he didn't need to. "What the fuck are you talking about? I never hired a publicist."

"Slash handler, slash miracle worker," Gillian clarified again.

Brett pushed away from the bar. "Maybe I should give you two some room to talk."

Sotto voce, Gillian said, "You may be right. It'll be safer from across the room."

Brett eyed her. "You don't look worried."

Lifting one shoulder, Gillian said, "I get paid the big bucks to tackle the tough jobs." She swung her gaze back to lock on Drew's. "And the owners of the Supreme Battle Challenge are very big payers."

His jaw tightened. "No fucking way."

Slowly, letting her lips form the word precisely, Gillian said, "Way."

DREW felt his left eye twitch. She had to be fucking with him. No way would Loren do this to him.

As he dug out his cell phone, he pointed a finger at her. "Stay put."

She fashioned an affronted look at the order, then, with a twitching smile, she shrugged. The blasé roll of her shoulders did interesting things to that impressive rack of hers. Oh, yeah, this lady was all real. Silicone did not jiggle like that.

His skin heated.

Then, as if to exacerbate his libido further, she slid that delectable tush back up on the bar stool and picked up her drink.

Drew stared from her shoulders down her spine to that heart-shaped ass that looked downright kissable.

Red-eyed and feeling more than mean, he forced himself to turn away. If he hadn't, he'd have gone back to seducing her instead of what he needed to do, which was take care of business.

Brett eyed him warily. "You okay?"

"Just fucking dandy."

"Okay then." Brett turned to leave.

Damn it, he hadn't meant to run him off. Brett was a real up-and-coming fighter. Crowds loved him. He had a kick-ass presence on the Web already.

And other fight organizations wanted him.

Drew caught Brett's arm. "Hey, I'll call you as soon as I get something concrete set up."

Brett nodded. "I'll be training. Whenever you say, I'm ready to go."

After one more glance at Ms. Fancy-pants sitting all prim and sexy at the bar, Drew walked out of the main bar area and into a hallway. It was a little quieter here, making the phone call easier.

He hit speed dial on his cell, listened to the fourth ring, the fifth. A glance at his watch showed it was only a little after ten P.M. Loren had probably left the office hours ago.

In a grumbling, irritated voice, Loren picked up on the sixth ring. "Make it work with her, Drew."

Son of a bitch. Loren had obviously expected his call, because he knew Gillian would be talking to him tonight. "No fucking way, Loren. It ain't happening. I don't need a damned babysitter, and you know it."

Exasperation sounded in Loren's tone. "Drew . . ."

"I fucking well built this company without any help from some stick-in-the-mud, prim-and-proper skirt getting in my way."

"No one is disputing that. But it *has* grown, so—"

"I never heard you complaining when I put in seventy-five-hour weeks and more, or when your investments more than fucking doubled."

"It's not entirely my idea, Drew. There are other factors at play."

"Like what?" He'd crush whoever was responsible for doing this to him. He'd annihilate . . .

"Listen up, Drew." The new voice on the phone was more feminine, but no less powerful. "You're doing this, so suck it up and be a man about it."

Fran. Drew pinched the bridge of his nose. Fuck, fuck, fuck. He should have known that if Loren was still in the office, Fran was, too. He pictured the two of them waiting around for his call, knowing damn good and well how he'd react, and it ratcheted up his anger even more.

Loren's sister was co-owner of the SBC, and while

Drew appreciated her business savvy, he detested dealing with her. In most cases, she wasn't nearly as manageable as Loren. "Frannie, listen . . ."

"You know I loathe that name, Drew. You use it just to annoy me."

Yeah, he did, but Fran was the type of ballbuster woman who just naturally brought out the worst in men like him. Drew dropped his hand from his brow and began to pace.

He disliked cajoling, but with Fran instigating this, he had little choice. "Fran, come on. We both know you're a smart gal with a keen mind for business."

"Agreed."

Like most women, Frannie loved a compliment. "So you damn well know that it doesn't make sense to mess with success, right?"

Catching on to him, she sighed. "You are such a pig, Drew."

Drew could almost see the satisfied smile on her striking face. "That's harsh, Frannie, even for you." Not that he gave a fuck what Fran Ferrari thought of him. *Except that she had the power to shit-can him on a whim.* Drew held a sliver of ownership in the company, but the controlling shares went equally to Loren and Fran.

If he wanted to keep his position as president of the organization and spokesperson for the sport, he had to win her over.

"You're not only a pig," she said, "but you're proud of it."

Okay, Drew thought, continuing to call her Frannie had maybe exacerbated things.

"However," she went on, "Gillian Noode is known for her talents in cases like these."

"What the hell does that mean?" *Cases like these.* So now he was a damned case?

"She has a reputation of taking pigs and turning them into silk purses."

"Great. Just the image I want." The president of a hardcore sport could not be seen as a fucking silk . . . *anything.* "Put Loren back on."

She didn't. "I suggest you work with her, Drew, because I've had it with you. And don't think to bully Gillian, either. I'm paying an outrageous fee to an elite company for her to conform you, enough that Gillian will soon be able to establish her own business in a big way. She's motivated enough to ignore any efforts on your part to get rid of her."

Ah, Drew thought, grabbing hold of a possible lifeline. *So Ms. Noode needs this job, does she?* Gaining his compliance would help her to obtain her own goals.

Loren came back to the phone. "Sorry, Drew, but Fran is right. With every new fight card, we go more mainstream. We want the networks to pick us up. But sometimes, and I'm only saying sometimes, your temper and . . . colorful way of speaking shed a bad light on things."

"That's bullshit and you know it." He could be as circumspect and tactful as the next guy. But those attributes hadn't gotten him where he was today. "Lose the babysitter and I can show you—"

"It's too late for that, my friend. This is Fran's project, so you and I both might as well go along with her until she has her way."

"Thanks for nothing," Drew said, and he disconnected the call.

Through the open doorway to the main barroom, he could still see Gillian, now surrounded by men. She laughed at something, and it made his muscles tighten. The woman had a teasing way of looking at men that made them stupid. The guys around her acted like a bunch of lapdogs, waiting for her attention.

Just then, she looked toward him, saw him standing there watching her, and she had the audacity to *wink.* She knew his balls were in a wringer on this one.

But what she didn't know was that he was a master manipulator. He hadn't gotten where he was now by being a wimp or by backing away from a challenge. Thanks to Fran's bragging, he knew this job was important to her, and he knew why.

That information could be used to dissuade her, no two ways about that. And in the process, he'd get what he wanted—*her*—and his freedom to run the franchise as he saw fit.

When he smiled, slow and triumphant, her eyes widened before she narrowed them again. With little more than a word, she sent her entourage away and left the stool to approach him.

He met her halfway. The noisy confusion of the live band, and the loud drone of conversation, blared around them.

And still, being only a foot from her felt somehow intimate.

Drew could smell her light perfume and the warmer scent of her skin and hair. Her glossy black hair picked up the low lights in the room and her blue eyes shone with amusement. He appreciated the moue of her sexily painted mouth.

Standing a half foot taller than her, Drew looked down into her face and waited, leaving it up to her to speak first.

Trying for a confidence that wasn't there, she said, "I trust you got everything straightened out?"

"Yeah, I did." Unable to stop himself, he brushed his knuckles over her cheek.

Such a simple touch, but it charged him. "We need someplace more private to talk."

Alarm stiffened her shoulders, but she brazened it out. "Yes, of course. I have a game plan I'd like to go over with you anyway. Why don't we meet over lunch tomorrow and we can discuss everything?"

"I'm busy." He took a step closer and leaned down on the pretext of ensuring she'd hear him. "Make it dinner, and I'll be free."

At his nearness, she caught and held her breath.

A telling reaction, that. She'd picked up on the same chemistry he felt. That'd make things easier.

And hotter.

With his mouth almost touching her ear, he whispered, "Gillian?"

"Oh." She shivered, then leaned away from him. "Yes, dinner is fine."

Sensitive ears. Where else was she sensitive? He couldn't wait to find out.

"My place, then." Drew took out a silver card holder from his pocket, flipped through it for his more personal card, and handed one to her. "My address is on there. I'm sure a sharp businesswoman like yourself can find her way there. Six o'clock. Don't be late, Gillian."

She tried to protest, no doubt preferring they meet at an impersonal restaurant, but Drew had already turned away. On his way out the door, he smiled.

He'd give Ms. Gillian Noode a week, no more, and she'd be packing it in for easier game. But before then, he'd have her, and he'd show her such a good time, she'd give up the challenge with no regrets at all.

CHAPTER 2

Brett walked past Ms. Noode, where she stood motionless, staring at . . . nothing. He put a hand to her back.

"Ms. Noode? You okay?"

She blinked and focused on him. "What? Oh, yes. I just got outplayed, that's all. But no worries, I'm better at this game than that chauvinist jerk thinks."

Brett had no idea what she was talking about, but he assumed the jerk was Drew Black. "He's not so bad once you get to know him."

"Ha!" She stowed the small business card she was holding into her purse before turning to him. "I need to go now. There are plans to formulate."

She was so serious, Brett had to fight a smile. "Yes, ma'am. Did you want me to walk you out?" Roger's Rodeo was a nice enough bar, in a nice enough area. But a parking lot was no place for a lady alone.

"I don't want to put you out."

He looped his arm around her. "I was leaving anyway."

She went along without further argument. "That's very sweet of you, Brett. Thank you."

At the exit, he asked, "Did you have a wrap of any kind?"

"Not tonight. The weather is just beautiful, isn't it?"

"Not bad." For late March, the temperatures had been mild even through the night. Even in this commercialized area, spring flowers bloomed everywhere, filling the air with sweetness.

They stepped outside to a full brilliant moon—and feminine chaos.

"Oh, my word." Gillian got jostled by a gathering crowd of women.

Frowning, Brett took notice of one particular woman. Blonde hair bounced around a pretty face dominated by big brown eyes. She wore no makeup that Brett could see. All serious business, she was handing out stacks of flyers to the other women, who all talked at once.

"What do you suppose is going on?" Gillian asked.

"Don't know." He reached out and snagged a flyer for himself. No one paid any notice to him. He skimmed the words—*WAVS: Women Against Violent Sports*—and laughed. "Drew isn't going to like this."

"What is it?" Gillian accepted the flyer he handed to her. She read it quickly, then let out an exasperated breath. "My job just got harder, didn't it?"

Brett barely heard her. He and the petite blonde had locked gazes. She was small enough that she'd barely reach his chin. Not exactly a good physical fit, but the lower parts of him didn't seem to care.

He smiled and gave her a nod.

Color rushed to her face and she jerked around, giving him her back as she talked to a redhead. Brett didn't mind the snub because it afforded him a quick survey of her hips in the slim, faded jeans.

Cute. Real cute.

Gillian elbowed him. "Really, Brett. Men are *so* easy."

Drawn back to her, he laughed and took her arm, urging her across the street. He'd come back and talk to the blonde after he saw Gillian safely to her car. "And you think women aren't?"

"Not in the same way, no."

"Amen to differences."

Gillian smiled, too. "It doesn't bother you that she's protesting your sport? What did the flyer call it? Human cockfighting?"

"She doesn't understand it, that's all. No big deal." A lot of folks were misguided about the level of dedication it took to compete in MMA fighting. It wasn't just one discipline of fighting but a complex, complementary set of combat techniques including boxing, kickboxing, martial arts, grappling, and wrestling.

He sure as hell wouldn't let a feminine fear of the sport keep him from pursuing a woman who interested him.

"You plan to explain it to her?"

"Why would I?" They reached Gillian's sporty RX8, and Brett waited for her to unlock the door.

"You don't feel defensive about it?"

He shook his head. "Everyone has a right to his or her opinion. Doesn't matter to me."

"Well." She slid into her seat. "You show admirable restraint. If it was me—"

"You'd be bristling, I know." He braced a hand against the roof of the car and leaned down toward her. Grinning, he said, "I saw you get all miffed about a supposed insult to those groupies trying to get a free pass at Drew."

She lifted her chin. "It was an insult."

"The comment about their implants? Just a fact, nothing more." He tapped the roof of the car and stepped back. "Man has a right to his preferences."

She peered across the street toward the protesters. "Such as a preference for that one?"

Brett looked, too. She was short and slim in a very sweet package. "Yeah."

Gillian laughed as she shook her head. "Good luck, then.

But you know, as soon as she finds out that you're a fighter, you'll be at a disadvantage."

Probably. "If she doesn't ask, I won't tell her." Brett closed her door. "Drive safe, now."

Still smiling, Gillian started her car and drove away.

Heading back over to the cluster of women, Brett saw the little blonde take note of his approach. Visibly flustered, she made herself busy real fast.

The act didn't deter Brett; at least now he knew that she was aware of him, too.

He'd always been partial to little gals, and this one, with the mulish set to her mouth and her determined air, especially intrigued him.

Rather than scare her off by being too direct, he asked the group, "You ladies enjoying the night air?"

Almost as one they turned to look at him and went mute. A few twittered. One smiled at him. And another said in a low, throaty tone, "Well, hello, there."

The redhead, in a protective gesture, stepped in front of the blonde who interested him.

Brett grinned. He'd always enjoyed female attention, and now was no exception. "Hello back atcha."

The blonde stepped out from behind the redhead and huffed. "Excuse me, but we're trying to work here."

"So I see." He held up the flyer. "Got a protest planned, do you?"

She planted her hands on her hips and tipped her head back to stare up at him. "Do you care?"

"Nope." Roger's Rodeo had more than adequate security. If the women got too rowdy, they'd be shown the door. "Just curious."

The smiling female sidled up close to him. "Audrey organized us tonight just to hand out the flyers. But we do hope to stage a protest soon. Would you like to join us?"

"Well, now, I don't know." He glanced back at the blonde. "You're Audrey?"

She hesitated, but finally nodded. "Yes. Audrey Porter." She held out a hand.

Brett engulfed it in his own. Small, soft, with short, clean nails. "Nice to meet you, Audrey. I'm Brett Bullman." He watched her face for any signs of recognition, but saw none. Huh. So Audrey protested the sport without knowing the competitors. Interesting. Not that he was a headliner . . . yet. But he soon would be, especially after he signed with the SBC and won his first fight there.

He smiled at her. "You're the one in charge?"

As if seeking courage, she glanced around at the other women. "Yes."

He held on to her hand. "Did you plan to go inside to hand out the flyers, too, or just out here?"

"God, no," the redhead rushed to say. "We wouldn't go in there." She looked as though the idea horrified her. "Fighters hang out in there."

She said *fighters* with the same disdain she'd give to demons. Brett smothered a grin and nodded. "Yes, ma'am, they do indeed."

"It could be dangerous," she insisted. "They really are brutal specimens."

"They can be." In a fight, a mixed martial arts fighter could take as well as give major punishment. "I have a solution. How about you ladies wait out here, and I'll escort Audrey inside so she can hand out more flyers? You'll be double-tagging the customers. What do you say?"

"Absolutely not!" the redhead said.

Audrey sputtered. "No, I couldn't . . ."

But the other women supported his cause with enthusiastic encouragement.

Ignoring the nays, Brett nodded. "Great. Give us twenty minutes." Teasingly, he said to the disgruntled and surly redhead, "You can hold down the fort until I return Audrey, can't you?"

"Of course, but there's no way Audrey will—"

"It's okay, Millie," Audrey assured her friend.

Then she handed Brett her stack of flyers. "I'm only going in if you give a flyer to *everyone* in there."

"I'll do my best." Tugging Audrey in his wake, Brett got

her away from the clinging Millie and just inside the lobby of the bar, near the coat check. Suddenly she dug in.

Over his shoulder, he saw her wide eyes as she looked beyond him into the crowded, dark, noisy bar. Music blared, strobe lights flickered, and people laughed. Roger's Rodeo had great atmosphere, but Audrey looked like he wanted her to enter a brothel.

To be heard, he moved closer to her. "Something wrong, Audrey?"

Her slender fingers contracted on his before she pulled her hand away. She twisted her hands together. Swallowing, she glanced up at him. "I have a confession."

Damn, but Brett wanted to kiss her. Bad. Right here, right now. He could give her all kinds of things to confess.

Instead, he leaned one shoulder on the wall in a deceptively casual stance. "Yeah? What's that?"

"I've never been in a bar."

Unbelievable. He missed a few beats there before asking, "Never?" When she shook her head, he asked, "Why not?"

A preoccupied couple stumbled out, and it was obvious the woman was tipsy. Her date held her up, laughing with her, nuzzling her neck while she tried to stroke him.

Audrey looked aghast. She stared so hard at the couple that Brett caught her chin and brought her attention back to him.

"They must have been celebrating." He smiled.

"Oh." She turned to get one last look at the couple before they stepped outside. "A little too much celebrating if you ask me."

Brett preferred not to judge. Over the years, too many people had drawn conclusions about him, and found him guilty by association. He hadn't liked it, so he tried not to do it.

Besides, to him, Audrey looked more fascinated than repulsed. Had she lived such a sheltered life that she'd missed out on some fun?

He planned to find out. "You don't visit bars because . . . ?" he prompted.

Again flustered, she frowned and said, "I don't drink."

Nice. Brett had few aversions regarding women, but smoking, too much drinking, and cruelty of any kind were dead turnoffs for him. "Me, either."

His admission surprised her. "But . . . then what are you doing here?"

"There are other things to do at a bar besides get hammered, especially at this bar, which is more like a club, ya know?"

Suspicion inched her back a step. "What else do you do here?"

Laughing, Brett leaned down to her to say, "Little Audrey, it's not a whorehouse, if that's what you're thinking. Nothing wicked going on, I promise." He put an arm around her and got her moving again.

People jostled them, danced around them, and along the way Brett handed out the flyers. A few of the fighters he'd met gave him a funny look, but they accepted the paper when he held it out, especially after they peered around him to see Audrey.

Despite some misconceptions, most fighters were not dumb louts. Fighters in the SBC were more often astute than obtuse, and with one look at Audrey they surmised exactly why Brett was passing out her info.

By the time Brett got them to the other side of the room, he was out of flyers—which meant he now had both hands free. He tugged Audrey over to watch the antics on the mechanical bull for a while.

In no time, her eyes went wide with exhilaration and curiosity.

When one fellow got tossed hard, Brett felt Audrey's gasp and gave her a short, quick hug. Bending close to her ear, he whispered, "He only hurt his pride."

They shared a smile, and Brett said, "Come on." He got her as far as the hallway, then she resisted going any farther.

"I should get back out front . . ."

Brett held her elbow in a light grasp. It was quieter here,

but music from the band filtered in, overlain by the drone of laughter.

He glanced at his watch. "We have a few minutes yet. Let me show you around the rest of the bar." When she balked, he added, "That way, if you stage a protest, you'll already have the lay of the place."

After biting her bottom lip, Audrey agreed.

He wouldn't mind nibbling on that soft, plump lip, too—but it was too soon for that, so Brett showed her the billiards room instead. Next he let her peek in on the arcade, and he then took her to where they served food on the upper level.

In awe, Audrey walked to the railing and looked down on the crowded barroom floor.

"I had no idea the bar itself was so . . . huge."

Leaning back against the rail, Brett watched her. Colored lights from below flickered over her face and in her eyes. She looked . . . mesmerized. And hot.

"Wanna come back with me sometime?"

She jumped as if he'd goosed her, and then she turned those big eyes on him.

Oh, yeah, Brett thought. He had to have her.

"Research," he fibbed, remembering that he had to play it cool. "The more you know about the place, the better. Early evening during the week, the fighters are scarce. We could come on a weekday, and you could plan things out then. Like where best to stage your protest, what day of the week, and what time. All that."

When she still looked wary, he lifted both hands, palms out. "No obligation or anything. Just thought I'd offer to help."

"I don't know." Her brows pinched down as she studied him. "Why would you want to help?"

Pushing off the rail, Brett stepped closer to her and again, he put his fingers to her chin, lifting her face. "I think you're cute as hell, Audrey Porter, and I want to get to know you better."

Her chin tucked in. "Are you serious?"

"Oh, yeah. You have no idea how hard it is not to kiss you right now."

"Not to . . ." She couldn't even finish.

"Kiss you." He brushed a thumb over her bottom lip, then dropped his hand and took a step back. *Damn.* "But I can tell you're not ready for that yet, are you, Audrey?"

She snapped her mouth shut and scowled at him. "No, I am not."

"Then I'll just practice patience." Brett held up a flyer. "But this is important to you, right? So for now, I'm okay with just helping out. For you."

Giving him the same study she'd give a two-headed toad, Audrey put a hand in her hair. "This is nuts. How am I supposed to respond to all that?"

"How do you *want* to respond?" Before she could answer, Brett said, "Don't think about what you should do. Just tell me what you want to do." He tried a persuasive grin. "Come on, Audrey. Fess up. You know you want to."

She gazed over the rail again—and nodded. "I'm very curious, I admit."

About the bar, or maybe about him, too? Brett hoped for the latter.

When she turned back to him, she caught him looking at her backside, and she started scowling again.

Brett grinned without shame. He wanted her, and he wouldn't pretend otherwise. But because he didn't want her to change her mind, he retreated a little. "What time do you get off work?"

"Depends. I'm a photographer, and if we have a big shoot to do, it can run over. But usually nine to five."

"A photographer, huh? Like in a studio?"

She nodded. "Picture This."

He'd seen the kitschy studios in malls. "Those places are everywhere, right?"

"Just like fast-food chains." She made a face. "If I can save enough money, I hope to have my own, classier place someday."

That disclosure surprised Brett. "A great goal. I'm sure you'll get there."

As if she only then realized that she'd shared a dream, she straightened. "Anyway, Mondays are usually light, Fridays are insane. The rest of the week is somewhere in between."

So she didn't work weekends? Good to know. And since he usually stayed in the gym till five, her hours meshed with his. "Let's say six o'clock, Monday. Can I pick you up?"

"No." She laughed as if the idea were absurd, then caught herself and cleared her throat. "I'll just meet you here. Out in front of the bar, I mean."

Rather than push his luck, Brett nodded. "Already looking forward to it." After handing out the rest of her flyers to the diners, who set them aside without really looking at them, Brett walked her back out front to rejoin her friends.

To the women waiting, he made a show of holding up his empty hands, proof that he'd kept his word. Impressed that he'd given out all the flyers, the ladies made a show of congratulating him. Millie moved protectively to Audrey, as if she'd just returned from war, and spoke quietly with her. But Audrey must have reassured her, because after a quick and private conversation, Millie relaxed with a smile.

That one, Brett decided, was a true mother hen. But it didn't bother him; since he'd grown up without it, he'd always considered protectiveness to be a good quality. And if Audrey had friends who cared so much for her, it spoke of what a good person she was.

Brett bid them all a good night and headed for his truck. He'd have some questions to answer later, if any of the guys bothered to read the flyer. Though even if they didn't look closely, he didn't know how anyone could miss the headline:

STOP THE VIOLENCE. BAN THE SBC NOW!

Imagining Drew's reaction, Brett couldn't help but

chuckle. Joining the SBC had already been interesting. Now, with Audrey Porter in the picture, he had even more to look forward to.

GILLIAN arrived at Drew's impressive home at six o'clock sharp. She had to knock twice before he answered, and then he came to the door looking as if he'd just stepped out of the shower. Naked except for a medium-size towel that barely reached around his hips, he held the door open for her.

She gaped. She looked at her watch, frowned, and made her attention go to his face—instead of his chest or shoulders or, God forbid, his tight abdomen. "You did say today, at six, yes?"

"Yeah, yeah, six. Come on in. I had some shit run over so I'm behind a little. No big deal."

She maintained her position on the other side of the door. "If you need to reschedule . . ."

Loosely holding the towel together with one hand, he reached out and grabbed her arm to haul her in. "Quit acting like you've never seen a naked man before." He secured the door behind her. "I didn't buy that shit about you being in your forties, but you're sure as hell not a blushing schoolgirl, either."

He turned away from her, and Gillian saw how the towel parted over his hip, down to his thigh. Her mouth went dry. "This is not at all professional."

"Screw professional. Do you know what my schedule is like? No? Well, Loren does, and he still let his pain-in-the-ass sister sic you on me. So if we're going to do this, we're going to have to make it work. If you can't do that . . ."

He left the question open-ended so that Gillian was forced to either agree to his unorthodox manner or call it quits.

She couldn't quit, though, not with so much at stake. Feigning an air of indifference, she gestured at his towel.

"Flounce around buck naked if it pleases you. It's no matter to me."

He barked a laugh. "Flounce? Yeah, I bet you'd love for me to lose the towel, wouldn't you? Admit it. And here you pretend to be so proper." Shaking his head, he didn't give her a chance to correct him or take umbrage. "Grab a seat and take a load off. I'll be right back. And Gillian?"

She met his gaze with a raised brow.

"No peeking."

Rolling her eyes, she gave him her back and strolled across the room to take a seat. When he disappeared from sight, she let out the breath smothering her.

For one heart-stopping moment, she'd thought he would drop his towel, and she'd been very undecided on whether to leave, or stay and get an eyeful.

Her pulse still sped and she felt too warm. Moseying into the dining room, she set her purse and briefcase on the table and then removed her black linen-blend jacket. For hours, she'd agonized over what to wear, but in the end, she decided not to let Drew Black influence her wardrobe choice.

She liked dressing feminine, so she'd opted for a sleeveless, scoop-neck, sheath dress with a tailored fit. It hugged her in all the right places, emphasizing her waist, and ended just below her knee. The black and white pattern of the dress went well with her dark hair. Black pumps were always businesslike, and these were heeled enough to give her needed height in dealing with Drew.

To keep herself from picturing Drew getting dressed, she looked around at what she could see of his house.

His front door opened into a spacious living room with high ceilings and lots of natural light. He had enormous plants, traditional furniture, modern art . . . altogether it looked great. Very stylish. She wondered if he'd decorated on his own or hired someone.

She was just about to peer into the kitchen when music started, and she turned to see Drew standing a few feet away, dressed in worn jeans and an open, casual white shirt, bare feet braced apart. As he stared at her, he buttoned up the shirt.

Gillian's mouth went dry again. What was it about barefoot, jean-wearing men that was so . . . elemental, so macho? "I hope you didn't rush on my account."

His gaze slid over her, hot and personal, studying her throat, bare shoulders, and cleavage, before it tracked down to her legs.

One side of his mouth quirked up. "You're making this really easy, you realize."

"This?"

Rolling his sleeves up to his elbows, he approached her. When he stood right in front of her, he said nothing, just kept looking at her while he finished with his shirt.

"Drew?" Damn him, he left her *so* unsettled. "Really, I don't—"

With his voice deeper than usual, he asked, "Do you ever wear your hair down?"

Her jaw loosened. "I don't see—"

"Because I bet you look sexy as hell loosened up a bit, don't you, Gillian?"

Her stomach fluttered and her breath caught. *Get a grip, Gillian.* Standing her ground, she thrust her chin up and glared at him. "You are outrageous."

"I know. But it's still true. You look hot all spruced up, but I'm betting you look even better freshly tumbled."

He found her sexy? *Freshly tumbled?* Gillian shook her head to clear it. "Enough of that, Drew. We have business to discuss. Important business."

"That we do." He looked into her eyes, and his were so dark, so filled with purpose, that she felt herself falling. "But we've got all night, don't we?"

All night. What did he mean?

He said nothing more, but Gillian was so aware of him, her every nerve ending started to tingle.

As he reached around her, she found herself leaning in—and caught his small smile.

"Have a seat."

The fog cleared. He'd . . . pulled out a chair at the table for her? And she'd thought . . .

Heat rushed into Gillian's face, but she tried to pretend it hadn't. Her voice trembled, ruining her crisp tone when she said, "Thank you."

"My pleasure." He circled around to a fancy bar situated in the corner of the dining room. "Drink?"

"No, thank you." Obviously she needed her wits about her to deal with him.

"I ordered dinner. It'll be here in an hour. If you're hungry now, I could grab something to snack on."

She shook her head. "I'm fine. Thank you." In fact, given her overboard reaction to him, she'd do well to get this done and skip dinner completely. She tried a smile. "Maybe we can get started?"

"I'd love to."

Now why did that sound so sexual? Maybe it was that expression of his that accompanied the words.

She started to speak, and he said, "Fran told me they're paying you well."

Sensing a trap, Gillian went still. Cautiously, she masked her expression and took the time to consider her response. She did make a ton of money, and she had no reason to be embarrassed about it.

She put her shoulders back. "With my record of success, I now earn a top-of-the-line wage." Without modesty, she added, "That's because I'm the very best at what I do."

Ignoring what she said, Drew slouched in the hard seat and studied her. "*Outrageous*, I think is how Fran described it. She said she's paying you an outrageous amount of money."

Unwilling to let him bully her, Gillian got out her paperwork, set it neatly aside, and folded her hands on the tabletop. "Your point?"

"You don't want to lose this job."

"Ha!" An understatement, but surely he had more at stake than she did. "*You* can't afford the repercussions if I should quit."

"Touché." His gaze warmed. "So we both want this . . . arrangement to work, agreed?"

Bantering with Drew Black was like playing with fire—tricky, and she could get burned so easily. Warily, Gillian said, "I suppose that's a fair statement."

So much satisfaction showed in his expression, Gillian felt like running. *I will not let him get to me.*

The corners of his mouth curled up. "The thing is, if you quit, or if you can't handle the heat, Fran will just find herself another broad to harass me. But she won't shit-can me, Gillian. She and Loren might not want to admit it, but they need me."

Gillian feared he was right. Even while ranting about his less-than-sterling qualities, Fran Ferrari had extolled his business virtues. "I can see that *you* believe it." His conceit knew no boundaries.

"I *know* it. They might have funded this venture, but I'm the one who made it worthwhile. I'm the one who took a floundering organization and turned it into a multimillion-dollar enterprise."

Very true. She gave a blasé shrug. "So?"

"So when it's all said and done, I'd prefer to work with you."

She would not be flattered by that. Raising a brow, she asked, "The devil you know?"

"The devil I've already met." His gaze dipped to her mouth, then her breasts. "A sexy devil."

She started to remonstrate with him, and he cut her off. "But if you hightail it out of here, I'll still be around, make no mistake about that. Fran and Loren might want me reformed, but they still want me."

Gillian gritted her teeth. "Again I ask—what's your point?"

"I have a deal for you." He sat forward, hands flat on the tabletop. "You can take it or leave it, and to hell with consequences. But make your decision knowing the consequences will be worse on you than on me. I might get stuck with a woman less appealing than you. But you"—he rose from his seat—"won't be able to meet your financial goals."

What did he know of her financial goals? Damn Fran for broadcasting her private business. What she wanted, how long she might have wanted it, was not his business.

Rather than let him know that he'd gotten to her, she pretended it didn't matter. And it wasn't easy, because now that he was standing, Gillian felt almost vulnerable in her seat.

She tapped her fingernails on the tabletop. "Are you going to get to the deal anytime soon?"

He grinned and walked around to prop a hip on the table by her chair. The side of his calf brushed her knee. "You think my cursing and my temper are the root of all evil, right? No, don't answer. I'm not an idiot. I know how women like you think."

Affront made her forget some of her determination. "Women like me?"

"Yeah." His voice went deeper. "Women who want to homogenize the sexes. You pretend disdain for men who act like men. You want us to be all smooth and glib and proper. But deep down"—he leaned toward her—"at night, in your bed, you know damn good and well you want a real man."

Gillian opened her mouth, but nothing came out.

"You want a guy who's comfortable in his own skin. A guy who is different from a woman, in every way."

As heat rose beneath her skin, she sputtered. "You . . . are so full of it." And maybe a little right. But it was her dreaded secret, and she would never admit it to him.

He let that go. "You want me to control myself in public? No problem. Half the shit I do is just for effect anyway. But if I suck it up and censor myself, then you have to put up with me being *me* . . . in private."

Oh, now that was too provocative for her to stay seated. Gillian slowly stood before him. "What, exactly, are you saying?"

CHAPTER 3

LOOKING down into her wide eyes, seeing the flush
on her skin, Drew almost forgot that this was part of
a plan. He almost forgot that everything he did right now
was to achieve an end goal.

He'd just told her that he did outrageous things for
effect. The SBC audience appreciated his "man's man"
attitude; the more he cursed and ranted, the cruder he
acted, the more they loved it.

He'd lay bets that right now, standing so close to him,
Gillian wouldn't remember that.

Ramping up the machismo, but keeping his stance
relaxed, he said, "I want you, Gillian Noode, and I'm not
going to pretend otherwise."

"But that's . . ." She started over. "You can't just . . ."

"But I do. How and where doesn't matter. Hell, the dining table here would work for me. I'm not picky or all that
traditional."

Hot color scalded her face. It was anger, not embarrassment. *"No."*

"When was the last time you got laid?" He touched the

pearl at the end of her chain necklace, resting almost in her cleavage. Damn, but her skin was warm and so silky . . .

"None of your business."

"That long ago, huh?" He toyed with the pearl, just to brush the backs of his fingers over her skin again and again. "When was the last time you even had a date?"

She grabbed his wrist to stop his teasing. "I get asked out all the time."

"But you don't accept." Drew wasn't certain how he knew that, but he did. Gillian seemed so set on business, she probably didn't leave herself any time for dating. "Do you?"

She still held his wrist, which left his hand all but resting on her, just below her collarbone. After several beats of time, she shook her head. "No, I usually don't accept."

"Why not?" He toyed with the pearl again, the caress far too personal, far too intimate. To his surprise, she dropped her restraining hand.

After a very deep breath, she said, "I'm choosy."

Not all that choosy. Hell, she was here now, with him, letting him tease her. "Know what I think?"

"You think? Really? Wow, I'm so impressed."

Drew almost laughed. Damn, but she had an acerbic wit. He liked it. "I think you hang out with refined gentlemen who just don't do it for you." Using the chain, he tugged her closer. "You want a real man, don't you, honey?"

"Do you mean a misogynistic jerk? You are referencing yourself, aren't you?"

Misogynistic? "Ah, now Gillian, you have me all wrong. I adore women."

She scoffed. "To serve your needs."

"Yeah, I like sex as much as the next guy. If you gave it a chance, you might like it, too."

"I like it fine!"

Now he did chuckle. "Well, that's good, because here's our deal." He released the necklace to slide his hand around her nape. "You tell me the first image-improving gig you want me to do, and I'll give it my best shot."

She stared at his mouth and replied in a whisper. "Perfect. I have an appearance set up for you with—"

"*After* I get to kiss you." He brushed his thumb on the side of her throat. "No tongues or anything. Yet. I'll just kiss you . . . here."

"You . . . *what?*" She strained away from him, not so much to escape, but to stare up into his face with utter disbelief.

As if explaining it, he said, "I want to kiss you. Just here, on your throat." Again, he brushed his thumb over her racing pulse. "Three seconds. I'll let you count, okay? After that, you tell me what it is you want me to do—for the image, I mean, not sexually. Today it's only a kiss. No more. I insist."

"You insist?"

"Yeah. Hell, I'm ready to go, but I don't want to rush you." He held back his grin when her eyes narrowed. "It's a good exchange, Gillian. Surely a hard-core business broad like you isn't afraid of one little three-second kiss on her throat, right? And then you have the power. You tell me what to do first, and whatever it is, I'll do it."

Now she shoved out of his arms and moved several feet away. Facing him, she crossed her arms and glared. "This is outrageous even for you."

"Yeah, I know. But this is private—and that's the deal, remember? In private, I get to be me. Out in public, I'll tone it down as per your specifications." He winked.

Surprising him again, she paced while saying, "I can handle this, no problem." With a glance up at him she admitted, "I'm even a little curious, to be truthful." She looked away again. "But this might cross the line of business ethics."

"You think?" It damn well crossed the line in a big way, and they both knew it. "I won't tell if you don't."

She stopped to glare at him again. "If I agree—"

His heart started pounding hard. No way had he expected that.

"What would your next demand be?" She waved a hand. "As you said, a kiss is easily forgotten."

"Now there's a challenge."

"But I have a four-month period planned for rehabbing your reputation. It can't be a kiss one day, and then . . ."

"What?" Drew wanted her to say it, just to watch her face when she did.

She didn't balk. With a shrug, she said, "And then sex the next time. I won't bargain that far, so don't even consider it."

"Deal. We'll keep things fully clothed. How's that?"

She gave one brisk nod.

"But I have a condition. Whatever it is you want me to do can't start for a few days. I'll need time to rearrange my schedule. And I want to know up front everything you have planned." With a little warning, he could rearrange the less desirable appearances without her ever knowing.

"Of course." She nodded toward her briefcase. "I have a detailed strategy all mapped out. Once we put our heads together and compare time frames, I'm sure we can make everything work."

"Then it's a deal." Drew started for her, and even though he didn't want to admit it, the thought of tasting her skin left him edgy and taut.

She held up a hand. "I have a condition also."

Damn it. He should have known. "Let's hear it."

"When in public, whether on arranged publicity or not, I want you to refrain from using objectionable four-letter words."

And so it begins. For Drew, a word was a word. He couldn't see why everyone got so hyped up over it. "Like? Give me an example of what you consider objectionable."

Suspicion tightened her features. "Drew Black, you know exactly what I'm talking about."

"Sorry, I don't." Would she say it? He hoped so. Gillian Noode could use some loosening up. He was just the man to help her with that. "Be more precise."

"Fine." Proving she had plenty of backbone, she said, "I'll compile a list for you and present it to you at our next meeting."

Drew couldn't help but laugh. "Gillian, you little prude. You can't even say it, can you?" He eased closer, coaxing her. "Come on, lady. Let me hear you say it. Whisper it in my ear if that helps."

Seconds passed, and then a devilish light shone in her bright blue eyes. "All right."

"Really?" His pulse thrummed in excitement. Damn, he was getting easy when something like this turned him on. "Well, come on then."

Wearing the slightest of smiles, Gillian sashayed up to him, put her small hands on his shoulders, and went on tiptoe. Her breasts pressed into his chest.

With her lips all but touching his ear, she breathed, *"Fuck."*

She eased back to her heels and looked at him.

Ridiculous as it seemed, he felt the stirrings of a boner. "I like how you say that."

"Thank you." She looked very pleased with herself, as if she'd somehow put him in his place.

That wouldn't do.

To keep her close, Drew put his hands on her waist. "What I'd really like is to hear you screaming it. In bed. You know, as in, 'Fuck me, Drew.'"

Her smug expression faded beneath embarrassment. She moved away from him—and he felt like a jerk.

"Gillian . . ."

She didn't let him speak. "*Hell* and *damn* aren't too horrible, if used in moderation and in certain situations within a defined audience." She kept her back to him as she put a lot of distance between them. "But you'd do well to avoid *son of a bitch* and *bastard*, too. Oh, and calling women *broads*." Turning back to him now that half a room separated them, she shook her head in a pitying way. "That term is so Neanderthal, Drew, it has hair on it."

Tension spiking, Drew rubbed the back of his neck.

Somehow, his plans had gone awry in a big way. He needed to get things back on track. "Fine. So now that I know what I can and can't say, what's first on the agenda?"

She seated herself at the table again and shuffled through her papers until she found a brochure. She handed it to him.

"What's this?"

"I've been in contact with the director of this local group. They work with troubled teenage boys. Many of them have horrid home lives. They need something to aspire to."

Huh. Not a heinous task at all. Drew could see the merit in giving at-risk kids some guidance. Some of the fighters had joined the sport to harness their anger over an abusive background. Some had gotten into it to escape the trappings of poverty. The SBC was a family that supported, encouraged, and rewarded.

"Good idea."

She looked nonplussed for only a moment. "The director has agreed to let you do a presentation. It's imperative that you get across the more positive aspects of your sporting organization."

"Want me to hunt around for something good to say, is that it?"

"I didn't mean it like that." Shifting in her seat, she presented him with an earnest expression. "Do you think maybe you're a little sensitive about the subject, given the effort you've put into making the sport a success?"

More like he was sensitive around her, given her attitude toward him, namely that he needed to change to meet standards. But that wasn't her fault, really. She was just doing a job. He'd have to remember that.

Drew leaned on the wall. "What do *you* consider the most positive features of the SBC?"

Dead serious, as if she'd been championing the SBC from its inception, she recited a list to him. "For starters, I'd talk about the dedication and hard work that it takes to learn the various disciplines. This isn't just one sport, it's a combination of many sports meshed together for the greatest effect."

"True." He liked it that she understood the complexities of mixed martial arts. Alongside the guys who'd joined to escape the streets, he had Olympic contenders and All-American wrestlers. He had the best of the best. "What else?"

"The boys could use some encouragement toward caring for their health by avoiding drugs, cigarettes, and alcohol. You could remind them about the benefits of keeping up with a good diet and routine exercise. And they should understand the motivation necessary to stick with something until you're successful."

"Not every fighter is successful." Like any sport, only the very best got title shots or gained any real fame.

"Of course not. So you could talk about how they learn from their experiences and move on as wiser, better men. But also cover the tolerance to accept the learning curve inherent in any sport. I watched some DVDs, and a lot of those guys get the crap beat out of them, but they stand up and shake hands and later, in interviews, they say they already know what they did wrong and how they will correct it for the next fight."

Drew realized that he enjoyed talking to her. That was rare for him. Sure, he enjoyed chatting with the women he dated, but this was different. Gillian was different. He spoke with her as he might . . . a fighter. Only this was better, because she looked a whole hell of a lot better than any dude.

Grinning at his own observation, Drew said, "Every good fighter learns as much from a loss as he does from a win."

"There, you see? You'll be perfect for this if you present it that way. I think you'll be a wonderful speaker to teach them about respecting others, especially those who try to guide you and train you so that you can improve yourself."

"Huh. I'm impressed, Gillian." He pushed off the wall

and walked over to her. "You do seem to have a handle on the finer points of mixed martial arts."

The praise must have pleased her, given her smile. "Barely, but I'm trying to learn."

And doing a good job of it. Drew stopped before her. "When did you want me to speak to the group?"

"When is the soonest you'll be free?"

Together they went over his schedule and, assuming it would work with the director of the club, decided on Monday. Then, while she had her paperwork out, he looked over the other media appearances she had planned for him.

One particular group, WAVS, made him scowl. Women Against Violent Sports was composed of a bunch of uppity biddies who protested everything they didn't understand. The group, and especially the ringleader, Audrey Porter, had become a thorn in his side. Not that long ago, he'd lost his cool in an online interview video, calling Audrey's second in command a few choice words for misquoting him. He didn't remember the woman's name, only that she'd tried to malign him and the sport in the worst possible way.

Unfortunately, the video had flown around the Internet at the speed of light. Damn near everyone had seen it . . . but apparently not Gillian or she would have been on his ass about it. No doubt the unkind things he'd said to that woman would make Gillian's hair stand on end.

Drew wasn't particularly proud of what he'd done, but he also figured anyone who dished it could damn well take it, and the uptight broads at WAVS liked to dish it with great regularity.

He decided to say nothing to Gillian for now. When she got around to lining up a date with the annoying group, then he'd clue her in on the past history so she'd understand just how badly that meeting might go.

After giving him a copy of the schedule, filled with a dozen appearances over the next few weeks, Gillian filed away her own copy. He'd have to do a lot of shuffling within his personal agenda, but what the hell? He thrived on chaos.

When she finished up and closed away her laptop and briefcase, he drew her around to him. "Now."

She blinked twice fast. "Now . . . what?"

"My turn." As Drew touched her neck and brushed her soft hair over her shoulder, his voice went husky in anticipation. "You ready?"

"Really, Drew." She tried to scoff, but her lashes kept fluttering and her lips trembled. "No preparation is needed. It's *only* a kiss, and only on my neck."

We'll see, he thought. "Okay then." He leaned in and breathed against her skin. "When I kiss you, you can count to three for me. When the time is up, let me know."

"Got it."

So soft and husky—she could deny it all she wanted, but her voice gave her away; she anticipated this as much as he did.

Dragging out the suspense, Drew got close enough to breathe in her scent but didn't yet touch her. He kept his hands at his sides, but he was so much bigger than her that he still surrounded her by his size and strength.

He liked that.

Gillian wasn't a frail woman; she had curves galore, but she was small boned and delicate compared to him.

He brushed his lips over her and felt her involuntary gasp. Opening his mouth, he took a soft love bite, soothed with his tongue, and then sucked against her skin.

Holding perfectly still, even her breath held, Gillian didn't protest.

She didn't count either. But then, hell, Drew got so drawn into tasting her, enjoying her, that he forgot that this was meant to tease, to keep her from getting the upper hand.

With a soft moan, she tipped her head more and her hands came up to clutch at his shirt. Drew slipped his arms around her and drew her in close.

Yeah, that felt right.

She pressed against him, trembling, and Drew realized that things had gotten out of hand. He couldn't, *wouldn't*, finish this tonight, so there was no point in further teasing her, or himself.

As he lifted his head, he pressed hers to his shoulder and whispered, "Three."

She stiffened, but he was quick to run a hand up and down her back. "Don't get prickly, because I sure as hell forgot what I was doing, too."

She tucked in her chin so that her forehead was against his pecs. "I . . . I don't know what to say." But then she pushed back from him. "I'm sorry."

His eyes widened. "Are you kidding me? For what?"

"For letting that get out of hand." She smoothed her clothes with shaking hands and tried to infuse a hoity-toity tone to her next jibe. "We all know that your behavior sinks to unreasonable depths on a regular basis, but I'm supposed to—"

"Be better than that?" He crossed his arms. "Better than me?"

"I was going to say more professional."

"Yeah, I just bet you were." So pissed that he could barely contain himself, Drew glared at her. That she would cop this attitude now, when only moments before he could have . . .

Inspired, he dropped his arms and indulged in an evil smile.

"What?" Alarmed, Gillian took a step back. "What are you thinking?"

"You want me, Gillian Noode. Wallow in denial all you want, but it's still true. And know what? You're going to have me."

"What? *No*, I most certainly am not."

"Oh, yeah, you are. Probably sooner than you think." When she looked ready to run, he held up a hand. "Even you have to know I don't force women."

"I never said you did."

But still she looked at him as if he might sprout horns. Drew shook his head. "We'll continue playing these games for now, because I don't mind waiting. But mark my words, lady, your time will come."

Gillian put her shoulders back in a display of affront. "I've had enough of your bullying."

"Yeah, well, if you're not going to eat dinner with me, then it's time for you to go anyway."

Her mouth fell open. "Would you honestly expect me to sit through dinner now?"

Shrugging, he said, "Why not?" He looked her over. "Afraid you won't be able to resist me that long?"

Jerking around, she grabbed up her belongings, all the while muttering to herself. Drew appreciated the picture she made; even all fired up, she still moved with feminine grace.

Holding her laptop and briefcase like a shield, she faced him. "I'll call the director of the boys' group tonight. Given his enthusiasm the last time we spoke, I'm sure Monday will work, but either way, I'll be in touch."

"'Course you will." He couldn't resist teasing her again. "And you know, you don't have to pretend that it's all for the job, either."

She actually growled, then she stormed around him for the door. Right before she reached it, Drew said softly, "Gillian?"

Maybe expecting an apology or some such nonsense, she paused with her hand on the doorknob. Over her shoulder, she looked at him. "What?"

"I just thought you should know something."

One brow lifted.

"I marked you."

Brows beetling in puzzlement, she said, "Excuse me?"

"You have a killer hickey on your neck." He winked. "Next time we play that game, maybe we should pick a body part that's not so visible."

In less than the three seconds he'd originally planned for the kiss, she was out the door and had slammed it behind her.

Drew laughed. Damn, he liked her.

Worse, he wanted her.

Now what?

* * *

GILLIAN stood in the back of the auditorium as the excited director of the boys' home introduced Drew as a "very special surprise" to the audience of squirming, defensive, disgruntled youths. As she'd half expected, the director had jumped at the opportunity to have the infamous Drew Black as a guest, even on short notice, and he'd quickly rearranged the schedule for the day.

Drew took it all as his due, and now he looked perfectly at ease on the stage. He'd worn an SBC T-shirt and jeans, and it was the perfect choice to fit in with the youths.

While Gillian listened to the director revering Drew in his drawn-out introduction, she fingered the colorful scarf wrapped around her neck.

For as long as she could remember, she'd bruised easily. With the sensual way he'd devoured her neck . . . well, as Drew had stated, he'd most definitely marked her. Not since her college days had she had a hickey. Though no one could see the mark, thanks to the scarf, she still felt conspicuous and . . . wickedly risqué.

Ridiculous.

But every time she remembered the touch of his mouth there, his hot breath, the way he clutched her to him . . . she got chills followed by flashes of heat and the unmistakable churning of desire.

She wanted Drew Black, more than she'd wanted any man in a very long time. He seemed to know her, really know her—as a woman, and as a sexual being.

Not that she'd been sexual lately.

For far too long, she'd been too particular to get sexually involved. She'd had casual dates that didn't even rate a kiss, much less intercourse. The interest necessary for that level of intimacy just hadn't existed for her.

But now, it was impossible not to imagine how someone like Drew, so free of social inhibition, might be in bed.

From the stage, his gaze met hers, and even with so much distance between them and thirty rowdy young men waiting impatiently to be entertained, she felt ensnared by his provocative intent. It was all Gillian could do not to bite her lip. Shifting her feet, she squeezed her thighs together. A deep breath had her breasts straining the front of her blouse.

And looking at Drew, at the quirk to his mouth and the glimmer in his eyes, she saw that he *knew* how he affected her.

Luckily, the director joined her, giving her the excuse to look away from Drew to indulge a quiet whisper.

"Thank you again, Ms. Noode, for bringing us such a terrific speaker."

Was that an assumption? "You've heard him before, Mr. Darwich?"

"On televised interviews and online. He can be . . . colorful. But he's also a brilliant, motivated businessman."

"Such accolades," she teased.

Mr. Darwich grinned. "I admit I'm a fan, both of Mr. Black and the SBC."

After that, they quieted to listen to Drew. He had a presence about him that demanded attention. He spoke with experienced authority, in a way that kept the young men listening.

About twenty minutes into his explanation of how the SBC worked, and about the rules that applied, one of the boys spoke out.

He asked, "How much do fighters make?"

"As with most things in life, that depends on how hard they work and how good they are. But that sort of goes hand in hand in most cases—the harder you work, the better you get."

"That ain't no answer."

Drew shrugged. "I can give you a range." He named two figures that were worlds apart, setting more boys to grumbling. "A new guy barely makes anything, especially if he's fighting in a nontelevised bout. If he has to cover his own expenses and doesn't have any sponsors . . . yeah, it'd be tough to make ends meet. The stars, the guys who have earned the right to title shots—"

"Like Havoc, or Sublime."

Drew nodded. "Yeah, like them. Those guys make top dollar. On top of that, sponsors are paying them more than most people make in a year, just to have a photo of them wearing their boxers or using their razor."

That launched a few jokes, and Drew grinned with the boys.

"Yeah, it's freaking nuts, isn't it? But that's what dedication can get you. And let me tell you, fighters like Havoc, Sublime, and Handleman, they're smart and they're not afraid of staying up late, getting up early, working harder than the other guys work to get what they want. Usually within a few training sessions, I can see who has the heart and talent it takes, and who doesn't."

A wiry young man stood. "Dude, I could be a fighter right now." He flexed a scrawny arm, very impressed with himself. "Why don't you give me a shot?"

Unfazed, Drew smiled. "For one thing, you're not eighteen yet."

"So?"

"So you can train, but you can't yet compete in the SBC. If you really have what it takes, you could get involved with a gym, get some experience. I know fighters who've been training since they could walk. But as to how good you are right now, let me tell you, dude, no way in hell am I taking *your* word for it."

The group laughed, making risqué jokes at their friend, heckling him good-naturedly.

They quieted when Drew again spoke. "You don't know how many guys think they can cut it, but then they get into training and a coach works them over for hours. Most are ready to quit. This shit is not easy. I know the really good guys might make it look like it is. That's why they're the really good guys."

The boy copped an attitude. "Man, I've been busting

heads on the streets since I was ten. I tell ya, I can fight. Ask anyone."

Drew shook his head. "You think street fighting impresses me? It's stupid. Beyond stupid."

The kid subsided, but Drew didn't cut him any slack.

"You guys are young, and you think you're invincible or you just don't care. I don't know which it is. But unsupervised mixed martial arts means that someone could get seriously hurt. You—or a friend of yours."

His impact astounded Gillian. The boys all looked enrapt as Drew continued.

"You know how many serious injuries or deaths we've had in the SBC?" He put his index finger and thumb together to make a zero and held it up. "None. I want to keep it that way. That's why the fighters are well trained, why we have rules, and why we have special equipment."

"Wasn't always that way."

"Hell no, it wasn't. When I took over, the sport had been banned in damn near every state. Getting a pay-per-view was impossible. But I turned it around, and now we're the fastest-growing sport there is. I took it from a failing business venture to a multimillion-dollar organization. You know how I did that?"

He didn't wait for a reply.

"By being smart. Anyone can be tough and dumb, and that pays jack-shit. But be tough and smart, and it's worth big bucks. So don't confuse what we do with barroom fighting. Our sport is not spontaneous and it's not dirty. You have to be trained, in shape, smart, and fast and you have to have heart." He searched the crowd. "You guys know what heart is?"

When they mumbled in uncertainty, Drew left the mic and walked to the edge of the stage. "Heart is getting back in there when you've just puked your guts up or taken a fist to the face or, worse, to the gut. It's twelve-hour days of cardio, boxing, wrestling, jujitsu." He scanned the crowd of faces. "It's not drinking, not smoking, no Big Macs or ice cream."

A few guys protested that. Obviously they liked their fast food.

"There's little time for girls, or family."

More complaints, these a little louder, and Gillian didn't think it was the prospect of little family interaction that had set them off.

Drew strolled out into the audience. "This is not a career choice for candies, let me tell you. You have to have a stand-up and a ground game. And you absolutely have to be in shape. I'm talking gas in the tank. I've seen more fighters lose because their cardio sucked than I've seen knockouts. It's pathetic." He moved among the boys. "But most importantly, a fighter has to be smart."

One boy said, "You don't have to be a genius to throw or take a punch."

"Maybe not," Drew agreed. "But raw power is only going to get you so far. You think any of the top fighters are dummies?" He looked around at the boys, and with a crooked grin he added, "I sure as hell wouldn't call any of them dumb."

Robust agreement erupted.

"A fighter has to remember hundreds of moves until they're automatic. He has to be able to analyze his opponent, figure out a game plan, and adjust accordingly during a fight. But he also has to be smart enough to manage his career, to make good decisions along the way."

Another boy stood. "You talk tough, but you ain't no fighter."

Not in the least offended, Drew agreed. "Hell no. I don't want to diet all the time and run twice a day. And when I don't get much sleep, it's because I've stayed out late, not because I have an injury or too many bruises to count." Sotto voce, he said to the crowd, "Those guys are *tough* as nails, no doubt about it."

When the boys stopped laughing, Drew put his hands in his pockets and started strolling among them again. "I'm not a fighter, and I know it. So that means I had to find something else that I'm good at." He glanced toward

Gillian. "I'm good at running the SBC. I'm good at understanding fighters, and I'm an incredible businessman."

"And real humble," someone called out, igniting more chuckles.

He released Gillian from his gaze and laughed with the boys. "Hey, I've got the background to prove it, ya know? The thing is, there's always a choice. No matter how bad shit seems, no matter how others try to drag you down. Every one of you is good at something, and you should know it. There's nothing wrong with recognizing your talents. If it's fighting, then come see me when you're eighteen and I can recommend some good camps where you'll get the best training. If it's business management, then Mr. Darwich can probably recommend some classes—"

Boos erupted.

"What the hell?" Drew said. "You telling me you guys are too wimpy to cut it in school? Do you know that at least fifty percent of the SBC fighters have a college degree? A lot of them have more than one degree."

Gillian drew in a breath at Drew's cursing—not out of disapproval, but rather admiration. Drew had analyzed his audience and knew the second he started to lose control of things. Just as he said a fighter should react during a fight, Drew had adjusted accordingly to keep them engaged. A few choice curse words had left the boys with a feeling of association, an affinity.

More questions were asked and answered, and through it all, Drew really reached the kids. By the time Mr. Darwich rejoined him back on the stage for a final thank-you, the boys were all pumped up and excited and making plans.

Then Drew stunned her, and them, by saying that, with Mr. Darwich's approval, he'd like to donate an entire library of SBC DVDs. Most of the DVDs were taped fights, but some of them were instructional videos by the fighters themselves.

And for that, Drew got a standing ovation and raucous cheers.

Gillian applauded, too.

Drew Black had surprised her—again. Every minute that she knew him proved him more outrageous, and more considerate, than any man should be.

CHAPTER 4

As they left the group home and walked out to the lot where Drew had parked, Drew caught Gillian's arm. She turned to him with a brow raised.

He took up the pace beside her. "So what's the verdict?"

He needed reinforcement? Did her opinion really matter to him, or was he only concerned about his position as president of the company? Either way, she didn't have the heart to leave him wondering. "Two thumbs up."

"Seriously?" Skepticism beetled his brows. "I don't lose points for slipping in a few curses?"

"Not at all." He deserved to hear the truth. "I wouldn't have changed a thing. Your methods worked. The boys listened to you."

"Yeah?" Pleased, he shrugged and said, "Thanks."

As she again started away, he asked, "Where are you going?"

"I parked in a lot down the block."

Puzzled, he looked from her, to where she indicated, and back again. "Why?"

To avoid this very situation. She hadn't wanted to be tempted to leave with him. And he was tempting, too much so. He affected her too strongly for her to test her own powers of resistance.

She fudged the truth by saying, "I wasn't sure if the lot would be full."

"Yeah, lot of traffic at a boys' home, huh?" His dubious expression gave little credence to her lie. "Well, it's too bad you insisted on driving yourself. We could have . . . chatted on the way over here."

Gillian pasted on a very practiced smile. Drew had offered to pick her up, but being alone with him, even while traveling for business, was out of the question. "I had to drive because I have other commitments tonight, but—"

"Yeah, me, too."

She stalled, and her rehearsed spiel about keeping things professional dissipated like a weak mist. "What do you mean? What are you doing?" Good Lord, she sounded far too curious, and far too . . . possessive. To cover up her reaction, she gave him a severe look of warning. "I trust you won't be getting into trouble."

"Nothing for you to faint over." He paused beside a sleek black BMW, leaned back on the fender, and crossed his arms over his chest. "I'm going to Roger's Rodeo. Supposed to meet some folks there for drinks and conversation."

"Business?"

"Not really, no. But if you're worried about it, you could join us and keep an eye on me firsthand. What do you say?"

She really wanted to, but . . . she'd already laid claim to other plans. *Drat.* "I wish I could, Drew, but I'm needed elsewhere."

"Needed, huh?" His gaze dipped to her chest and remained there. "As in sexually, you mean? 'Cause if that's the case, I have some needs of my own—"

In self-preservation, Gillian smashed a finger over his mouth. If he continued like that, she'd never be able—

His hot tongue touched her finger and he drew her into his mouth.

"Drew."

Catching her wrist so she couldn't pull her finger away, he licked her again.

It felt . . . *sinful.*

"So." He wore that *Got you* look and continued to hang on to her wrist as he kissed her palm and then the inside of her wrist. "What is it you have going on tonight, Gillian?"

As if he wasn't doing the most sexually suggestive things to her, as if she wasn't breathless because of it, he casually waited for her reply.

Gillian curled her fingers into her palm and tried to still the racing of her heart. There was nothing she could do about her trembling voice. "You may not take such liberties."

"Of course you're right." Moving away from the car and bending his knees just a little, Drew met her gaze at eye level. Speaking oh so softly to her, he said, "Know what I think you should do about it, Gillian?"

The way he kept using her name was as effective as his touch. "I am *not* quitting."

"Good." He straightened and, still holding her wrist, stepped closer. "I don't want you to. Not anymore."

He didn't? "Then . . . what?"

Close to her ear, his jaw brushing her cheek, he whispered, "I think you should come by my house tonight so we can get all this sexual tension out of the way. What do you say?"

Yes. "No." As much to convince herself as to deny him, she shook her head. She had a job to do, an important, well-paid job that would enable her to start her own company wherever she wanted. "It wouldn't be ethical."

Putting his fingers under her chin, he lifted her face. "And *ethics* are the only thing keeping you out of my bed?"

How could she answer that without further exacerbating the situation?

When she said nothing, his eyes darkened. "You're

telling me that you're as attracted to me as I am to you? If we weren't working together, you'd be saying yes instead of no?"

"Drew . . ." Floundering, Gillian lifted her shoulders. "The fact is that we are working together and getting personally involved with you would discredit me to my employers."

"Well, damn, woman." He cupped her face and caressed her cheek with his thumb. "I'm going to have to see how I can remedy the conflict."

Gillian started to say something—she had no idea what—and his cell phone rang.

After a hesitation where he visibly struggled with himself, responsibility won out and he glanced at the caller ID.

"Damn it, I'm sorry. I need to answer this." Taking a step away from her, he said, "Give me just a second," and he opened the phone.

Still unnerved, unsure what to do, Gillian stood there. Maybe she *should* just get the sexual tension out of the way. After all, they were both adults, both free of romantic commitments. If she lost this opportunity to explore the hottest sexual attraction she'd ever experienced, wouldn't she regret it later? How much harm could it really do . . . ?

No. Putting a hand to her brow, she turned away from Drew. What in the world was she thinking? She was a rational, reasonable woman. She was not a woman influenced by base desires.

At least, she hadn't been that kind of woman before meeting Drew Black.

Drew's voice rose with an edge of urgency, reclaiming her attention.

Judging by his expression and tone, it was not good news. It'd be best if she excused herself now and gave him some privacy for his call.

But when she gave a short wave and started to ease away, he reached out and caught her hand. He didn't look at her, and frustration showed in his stiffened shoulders and the set of his jaw. But his hold on her hand was gentle, a request rather than a restraint.

Gillian subsided, willing to wait for him to finish the call.

"Yeah, I'll be there in . . ." He glanced at his watch. "Ten minutes or so, give or take traffic." He returned the phone to his pocket, drew her close, and kissed her, but it was a quick kiss of frustration. And then he just frowned at her.

Gillian sputtered. "What . . . ?"

"I like you, Gillian Noode. Hell of a predicament, isn't it?"

"I, ah . . ."

Releasing her, Drew ran a hand over the back of his neck. "I don't suppose you could change your plans tonight?"

If she had any sense, she'd take him to task over that careless kiss; the man truly knew no boundaries. But at the moment, a bad foreboding got the better of her.

Gillian let out a breath. "What's wrong, Drew? What have you done now?"

"What have I done?" Affronted, he fried her with a look. "Not a damn thing. But one of my fighters . . ." He drew up short, shook his head in stubbornness. "Never mind. It's not your problem. Forget it."

"No, wait." Guilt left her flustered. "I'm sorry. I shouldn't have just assumed . . ." Trying again, she cleared her throat. "Was there something you wanted me to do?"

"Besides have sex, you mean?"

It didn't take him long to recover, obviously. Mimicking him, Gillian said, "Never mind. Forget it."

Drew laughed. "I'm sorry. That was bad even for me."

"The apology loses something when you're so amused by it."

He wiped away his grin and held out his arms. "Behold, a serious man. Dead serious, actually. I don't have time to explain, but one of my fighters is having a meltdown and I need to go get him before the cops are called. I just thought . . . that is . . ."

"You'd like company?" For whatever reason, the idea that he wanted her with him during a difficult time softened Gillian. "Is that it?"

"I wouldn't mind another rational person going along for the ride, yeah."

So he did value her input. She more than softened; she went all mushy, and she was not a mushy person. "Then of course I'll go with you." Man, she was easy. "Along the way, you can tell me what's going on."

"Thanks. Let's get going."

Gillian walked around to the passenger side of the BMW. Like a true gentleman, he opened her door and waited for her to be seated before striding around the hood to the driver's side.

As he started the engine, he asked, "Don't you need to call someone?"

"For what reason?"

"To cancel your plans."

Oh, yeah. Her *plans*. "It was a group gathering," she hedged. "My absence won't stall things." Anxious to change the subject, Gillian settled into her seat. "So what happened to the fighter?"

"It's pretty fucking stupid, if you ask me." They left the parking lot and entered the thoroughfare. "Dickey Thompson's girlfriend broke things off with him, and he's having a damned meltdown, I guess. He went to a tattoo parlor to have a design put over her name."

"He had his girlfriend's name tattooed onto his body?"

"Yeah, right over his heart. Do you believe that shit? Some of these guys . . ." Drew shook his head. "But I guess the little lady doesn't like being left at home while Dickey's away for a fight or training, and he doesn't make enough yet to afford taking her along."

"I don't recognize his name."

"He's newer. Got a lot of potential, but a lot of baggage,

too. He has to get his damned head together. I tell you, girl-friends fuck up more fighters than steroids ever could."

Trying to sort things out in her head, Gillian asked, "And Dickey called you?"

"He doesn't really know too many people in the area, so he gave my name and number to the tattoo artist." The repercussions of that struck Drew with new fury. "Which means that now some fucking tattoo artist has my fucking cell phone number." He squeezed the steering wheel. "I just might strangle that little prick."

"Is he little?"

"Physically? Fuck no."

At the continued foul language, Gillian lost her patience. She touched his biceps. "Drew, I know we had an agreement about you being you when we're out of the public eye, but once we reach the tattoo parlor—"

"Don't worry about it. I won't embarrass you."

Did he really think that was her only concern? She wasn't such a delicate flower that a few words meant that much to her. She was more worried about him damaging his already flogged reputation. "It's admirable that you're available to the fighters when they need you."

"Don't get the wrong impression. Usually I'm nowhere around when shit like this happens. And don't think I excuse his dumb-ass behavior, because I don't. I'm not a damned coddler."

Droll, she shook her head. "No, Drew, I doubt anyone would accuse you of coddling."

He shot her a quick look, then tried to relax. "Know what really pisses me off?"

Inexplicably, Gillian found herself amused with Drew's mood. Like a surly bear, he growled and snarled . . . but he was still going after Dickey to help him.

Drew Black's bark, she realized, was much worse than his bite.

Smiling, relaxed despite his sizzling temper, she said, "Tell me."

"We got interrupted."

Alarm bells went off in Gillian's head. She could think of nothing to say.

Holding the steering wheel in an edgy, frustrated way, Drew picked up where they'd left off as if there'd been no interruption at all. "Let me get this straight. If we weren't working together, we'd be burning up the sheets?"

How could she have forgotten, even for a second, how unpredictable the man could be? Gillian fidgeted in her seat. "It's . . . more than our working relationship, Drew."

"What, then?" Again he glanced at her, at all of her, before returning his attention to the road. "And don't tell me you don't want me. I have plenty of bad credentials, but obtuseness isn't one of them."

More fidgeting. "No . . . I mean, yes, I do want you."
Good Lord, why would she admit such a thing?

Gillian rushed into explanations. "But let's face it, Drew, you're known as a womanizer, and I don't want to be just another notch on your belt."

All of his tension seemed to have eased away. "How do I know I won't be a notch on your belt?"

She gave him a long look.

"Lady, you know how to tease. Admit it. You look at a guy and you have him drooling in a heartbeat."

Warm pleasure spread through her. Did he really think she could be so effective in seduction? "I don't see you drooling."

He made a rude sound. "I'm more interested in figuring out how to have you than daydreaming about it. And speaking of that, let me make sure I understand the scenario. You don't want your personal or professional reputation *tainted* by being with me. Do I have that right?"

Hearing him say it aloud like that made it sound really . . . *horrid.* Gillian's face went hot at her lack of sensitivity. "Drew . . ."

"Just work me with here, okay?" Far from wounded by her reservations, he asked, "What if I swear not to tell anyone? It could be our own, very private fling. No one has to know, right?" He took a left into a busier business area. "And Gillian, for the record, my word is good."

She believed him. He might be many things, but he wasn't a liar. Drew told you what he thought, no holds barred. He had no reason to lie.

"Think about it—an exciting, illicit affair without repercussions of any kind. Sounds tempting, huh?"

Her thoughts scrambled and her heart pounded hard. Was she actually considering this?

Yes, she was.

Drew didn't let up. "Why not live a little, you know? I'll make it worthwhile, scout's honor."

"You were never a scout."

"How would you know?"

Another misconception on her part? "Were you?"

"No."

Of course he wasn't. Drew Black would never be able to follow rules. Could she handle that? Gillian bit her lip in indecision.

"Come on, Gillian," he encouraged. "What do you say?"

She drew in a deep breath. "I say . . ." She looked at Drew and gave up. "If no one will know, then there's really no reason to wait until we aren't working together."

His expression was priceless, a mixture of surprise, anticipation, and red-hot heat. Then his mood darkened as he put on his turn signal. "Talk about fucked-up timing." Pulling into the small lot behind the tattoo parlor, he parked and killed the engine.

Before Gillian had time to blink, he unhooked her seat belt and pulled her half over the console to kiss her silly.

By the time he finished with her, the windows were steamed up—and so was Gillian.

With his mouth still touching hers, he said, "This will probably take a couple of hours."

Gillian held on to his shoulders. "This?" His expensive sports car wasn't really big enough for making out. She felt the parking brake dig into her side.

Humor lifted the corners of his sexy mouth. "Dickey, remember?" He smoothed a tendril of hair behind her ear. "That's why we're here."

"Oh." She tried to straighten away from him, but was too off balance.

Drew set her back in her seat. "But I like how you think. And hey, if it's hours you want, come home with me after we take care of this. I'll need to take the edge off first, but then, hey, I can last as well as any guy."

What had she gotten herself into? Drew Black was more than she could handle.

But she couldn't wait to try.

WITH the collar of his leather jacket turned up against the damp evening wind, Brett stood out front of Roger's Rodeo. After the last few days of nicer weather, there was now a decided nip in the air. Black storm clouds obscured the moon and stars, leaving the neon lights of the establishments and the street lamps to glow through the thick humidity.

The flannel he'd put on over a T-shirt wasn't doing much to keep out the cold.

A few feet down from Brett, a woman leaned against the wall and enjoyed a smoke. Her short leather jacket was meant more for looking good than protecting her from the weather. The glow of her cigarette showed in between ribald comments spoken a little too loudly about what she'd like to do to him. She was drunk and easy to ignore, but her smoke irritated Brett as it carried on the wind.

For him, there was a fine line between bold enough to be sexy, and so brazen that it became a turnoff. Courage from drink was always a pain in the ass. And he couldn't abide kissing women who tasted like an ashtray.

Audrey Porter, with her moral crusade, intrigued rather than annoyed. Brett liked women dolled up or dressed down. He liked it when they fussed with their nails and makeup, and when they went natural. He liked them sexy in short dresses and comfortable in worn jeans.

Until he set eyes on Audrey and knew that she pushed every single one of his buttons, he'd never really thought about preferences.

Just as the lady down the way sidled up to Brett, determined to strike up a conversation, a small car pulled up to the curb. Beneath the light of a street lamp, Brett could see Audrey in the passenger seat. Tonight she had her hair in a high ponytail and thin gold hoops in her earlobes.

Anticipation sparked in his gut and before the hopeful woman vying for his attention could get a word out, Brett said to her, "Excuse me," and went to the car to open Audrey's door for her.

Behind the wheel, Millie waved to him. When she was smiling and happy, she really was cute, Brett thought.

"Hello, ladies," he said. "Looks like you just beat the storm."

Audrey stared at him with nervousness, and that endeared her to him even more. She didn't say anything, just froze with her hands on the seat belt latch.

Brett leaned in and unhooked it for her. "I see you hitched a ride."

"My car is being serviced," she blurted out. "New tires, long overdue. I thought I'd have to cancel, but Millie was nice enough to chauffeur me."

"Not a problem," Millie said. "I was going out anyway. What time should I come back for her?"

Audrey started to reply, but Brett beat her to it. "How about I bring her home and save you the trouble? We really don't know how long we'll be, and I'd hate to interrupt your plans."

"You wouldn't be interrupting," Millie told him. "I'm just meeting at a restaurant with some friends. I'll be in the neighborhood anyway—"

Brett took Audrey's arm and urged her out of the car. "But hey, if it works out, I might be able to talk Audrey into staying late." Now with her standing at his side, he put his hand to the small of her back. Even through her jacket and sweater, he felt the vitality of her. "What do you say, Audrey? Okay if I drive you home?"

Put on the spot, she stalled, then nodded. "Sure. That should be fine. Thank you."

Millie asked, "Are you sure?"

Brett didn't know if he should be amused or annoyed. If either of them really considered him untrustworthy, why accept his invitation in the first place?

"I'm sure." Audrey leaned down. "Thanks again, Millie. See you tomorrow?"

"Noon. I'll be there." When Brett shut the door, she gave a friendly wave and put the car back in gear.

Audrey shivered in the brisk wind, giving Brett the perfect excuse to pull her protectively against his side. "Where did spring go?" he asked her as he led them inside.

"The weather report said it's just a temporary cold front. It should be nice again by Wednesday." She wore a puffy down jacket with skinny jeans, black ankle boots, and a black turtleneck. Her fair skin and blonde hair made a striking contrast against the dark sweater.

She hadn't exactly piled on the makeup, but Brett could see a hint of lip gloss and her lashes looked darker, longer, surrounding her deep brown eyes.

When she cleared her throat, he realized that he stood there staring down at her.

"Is there a place for us to put our coats?"

Shaking himself, Brett grinned. "Yeah, sorry." He helped her out of her jacket and, along with his, gave it to the coat check. "I got distracted looking at you."

"Why?" She put her palms to her cheeks. "Is something wrong?"

"Not a thing." Running a hand along her ponytail, Brett took in the sleek softness . . . he'd love to see her hair fanned out on his pillow as he made love to her. "You look terrific tonight."

Her shy smile flickered. "Thanks." Indicating her jeans, she said, "I wasn't sure what to wear, but I figured jeans went everywhere."

Because he couldn't help himself, Brett put his hands on her slim waist. "On you, jeans look especially sexy."

Her eyes widened, but she didn't move away.

Bending down, Brett put a butterfly-soft kiss on her cheek. Her scent, that of shampoo, woman, and fresh air, left him feeling like he'd had one too many drinks. She gave him a buzz, and he liked it. For only a moment, he lingered, relishing her closeness.

But unwilling to push his luck, he straightened, took her hand, and headed into the main bar area. "Are you hungry?"

"I could eat."

Honest. He liked that. Too many women picked at their food. Audrey was slight, but he had a feeling it was a fast metabolism that kept her that way, not a perpetual diet. "Let's get some food first then."

"First?"

Weaving around couples on the dance floor, Brett waited until they'd reached the other side of the main room to speak again. "We'll try everything tonight, okay?"

Speechless, her lips parted, but she said nothing.

This time, Brett gave her a quick, very unsatisfying kiss on her mouth. Staying close so she could hear him, he teased her. "Get your mind out of the gutter, woman." He rubbed his thumb over her bottom lip. "I meant pool, dancing . . . the bar activities."

Even more flustered now, Audrey stared up at him and seemed to melt. Her eyes darkened and her lids grew heavy.

Taking Brett by surprise, she went to her tiptoes—and kissed him.

A real kiss. A *hot* kiss.

Her fingers sank into his hair and her lips moved over his with barely restrained hunger.

Not one to pass up an opportunity, Brett wrapped his arms around her and turned so that she had her back to the wall. He had a feeling that public displays of affection were not the norm for Ms. Audrey Porter. In this position, with one hand braced on the wall beside her head, and her small body tucked in close to his, he protected her from view of anyone else in the place.

Taking over the kiss, Brett cupped her face in his free hand and leaned into her so that she felt all of him—and so that he could feel her.

Her breasts were on the small side, but so rounded and firm that he had to struggle not to touch her there. Even through her bra and sweater, he felt the stiffening of her nipples, and it tested his resolve in a big way.

She tipped her hips in against him, curled her fingers in his hair, and the perfect fit made his heartbeat heavy. Audrey was small and delicate and so soft and sweet, he wanted to take her right here, right now.

When he teased her mouth with his tongue, she opened for him, even turned her head a little to accommodate the deepening kiss. Hot with both need and frustration, Brett groaned.

Never had he expected this.

Hell, he'd been hoping to steal a real kiss when he took her home. *If* he got to take her home. But to have her initiate things right here in the middle of the bar . . .

Before he got any more carried away, he slowed things down, easing away from her by small degrees, kissing her jaw, beneath her ear, and then pressing her head to his shoulder so they could both catch their breath.

Her hands clenched in his shirt and he could feel her heartbeat galloping.

"Damn, woman." He kissed her temple, and wanted to go on kissing her. But now, here, wasn't the time or place, especially since he teetered so close to a boner. "Hell of a nice surprise."

Stiffening, Audrey put her forehead to his sternum.

He could feel her shaking and, hoping to soothe her, he coasted his hands up and down her narrow back.

"I'm sorry."

Brett did a double take. "What's that?"

She levered back to look up at him. Expression stricken, cheeks hot with color, she cleared her throat. "I said I'm sorry. I was out of line."

Was she kidding him? One side of Brett's mouth kicked up. "Honey, you don't hear me complaining."

"But . . . but I'm giving you the wrong impression."

The impression he got was that she wanted him *almost* as much as he wanted her. "Yeah? How so?" Brett couldn't wait to hear what she had to say. By the second, this got more interesting.

"I'm not that . . . that easy."

Already knowing that, he shrugged. "Never said you were." She appeared so distraught, Brett wanted to get her alone and someplace quiet. Unfortunately, no such place existed in the bar.

Brett touched her chin and lifted her face. "It was just a kiss, Audrey. One hell of a kiss, but still . . ." He grinned.

"It's just that . . . well, ever since I agreed to meet you here, I've been thinking about this." She bit her bottom lip. "About kissing you, I mean."

Good to know. "Me, too."

Skeptical, she frowned a little. "Really?"

Hadn't he been plain enough yet? "Hell yeah. I've thought about kissing you, and a whole lot more."

Groaning, she covered her face. "But that's just it. I shouldn't have kissed you like that because I'm not going to do . . . well, *a whole lot more*."

She was so damn cute. Charmed, Brett cupped a hand around her neck beneath that adorable ponytail. "Don't sweat it, Audrey. I'm not a guy who pushes, okay?"

Gasping, she dropped her hands to stare at him. "But that's *all* you've done is push!"

True enough. Brett couldn't help but laugh at her

outrage. "Yeah, to get to *know* you, sure. But I meant I wouldn't push you for sex." Hard as it'd be—in the literal sense—he meant what he said. For him, no meant no, period. "You want to kiss, we'll kiss. You know I enjoyed it. A lot. But anytime you call it quits, we're done. Got it?"

Still she hesitated.

"Look, I don't want you to be afraid to kiss me, or touch me, or do whatever you want. I'll go on record right now as saying an enthusiastic *Hell yes*."

She blushed at his sincerity.

"But it's up to you, Audrey. Always. Deal?"

After a second or two, she nodded. "Thank you for understanding. Believe me, I normally don't go around attacking men."

He bent his knees to see her face. "Tell me you enjoyed the kiss, too."

Her voice lowered. "I did. Too much, probably."

"Great." With heartfelt sincerity, Brett told her, "Feel free to attack me anytime you want."

She almost laughed. *"Brett."* She did smack his shoulder, then left her hand there, caressing him—until she caught herself. "God, this is awkward."

Drawing her closer, he looped his hands at the small of her back. "Shouldn't be." He loved it that she wanted him. "Not with me."

"But that's just it! I hardly know you. I definitely don't know you well enough to . . . to get so intimate. I don't know what's wrong with me. Except, well, you obviously know how good-looking you are."

A compliment or an accusation? Again, Brett grinned. "I do, huh?"

Realizing how that had sounded to him, she rushed to explain. "I didn't mean you were conceited or anything. I just meant . . . well . . ." She lifted her shoulders. "How could you not know? I saw that woman trying to get your attention outside. Every woman in here keeps looking at you."

Brett resisted the urge to test her theory by glancing over his shoulder at the crowd. Right now, the only woman who mattered was her. "That's an exaggeration."

"Not really." She studied his face and then his upper body. "I haven't been on a date in forever. Years, actually."

"That long, huh?" He didn't have a single doubt that men had asked her out, so why wasn't she dating?

"I've been totally focused on work, and on organizing WAVS. But don't get the wrong idea about our group. We're not a bunch of wallflowers."

"Didn't say you were." But he found her defensive mode intriguing. It must be a touchy spot with her.

"Two of the women are in serious relationships. One is divorced. And Millie . . ." Audrey flapped a hand and smiled with affection. "She dates all the time. She's actually outgoing with men, just not in crowds. She's more of a movie-and-quiet-dinner type."

He couldn't have cared less about Millie's social calendar. "So what's the story with you? A woman as pretty and nice as you should have her pick of men every night."

The compliments flustered her; Brett could tell that she didn't think of herself that way.

"I just . . . haven't been interested, I guess. But then suddenly you're in the picture, and you really are nice and *so* incredibly good-looking and . . ."

Brett bent down and kissed her again. "So you lost your head, huh?"

She loosened up enough to laugh. "I told Millie this would happen."

Had she told Millie that she wanted him? Oh, to be a fly on the wall for *that* conversation . . . "Millie's a worrier, isn't she?"

"Sometimes." Audrey moved one hand to his chest, just laying her hand there, sort of testing things. "We're close, and she feels protective."

Brett would have happily reciprocated, but he had a feeling that if he started pawing her chest, she'd run off.

Her dark-eyed gaze went from his mouth up to look into his eyes. "I can't really blame Millie for how she feels. Since this place caters to the SBC, she has good reason to mistrust what goes on here." Audrey let out a breath. "And so do I."

CHAPTER 5

AUDREY felt a new tension in Brett and wondered at it. With her hand on his chest, she absorbed the hardness of him, the bulge of muscle and pure strength. She guessed him at over six feet, which meant he towered over her.

Usually the disparity in their sizes would have intimidated her. With Brett, it was exciting. He was by far the boldest man she'd ever met, but he had a genuineness about him, a gentlemanly "down-home" air that made everyone feel comfortable with him. Even Millie had commented on what a nice guy he was, and Audrey valued her insights.

Brett caught her hand and flattened it on his chest, keeping her still. "You have some kind of history with the SBC?"

Memories overwhelmed her, and she looked away. "One day, I'll get the rest of the world to see the sport for what it really is."

He frowned, but let that go. "Millie has the same beef as you?"

"Not really." She shrugged. "We've been friends for

a couple of years now, ever since she joined WAVS. We hit it off immediately. It was like we'd known each other forever. She's been a wonderful friend—and that's why I blame myself for what happened to her."

Concerned now, Brett said, "That sounds ominous."

After a deep breath, Audrey nodded. "Drew Black attacked her."

Stunned, Brett took a step back. "No way. Sure, everyone knows that Drew is far from perfect, but I've never once heard about him hurting—"

"No, of course not." Audrey shook her head. "Sorry. I didn't mean that he'd attacked her physically."

A small boisterous group joined them in the hallway, so Brett put his arm around her and started her again toward the stairs for the restaurant.

On the way up, Audrey said, "But he was vicious to her all the same, and believe me, that hurt her."

At the landing, Brett steered her toward an empty table close to the railing. He looked grim. "What happened?"

After taking her seat, Audrey looked over at the barroom below. As Brett had promised, it wasn't nearly as busy tonight as it had been on the weekend. From what she could tell, there were fewer fighters present, too. To Audrey, they stood out from other men. Most of them were tattooed, loud and rowdy, big and buff. Despite the lack of a sports crowd, there were still plenty of people milling about.

Quietly, she recalled that awful scenario involving Millie and Mr. Black. "As one of the spokeswomen for WAVS, Millie posts articles and information about the SBC on various bulletin boards, and on her own blog. Sometimes other outlets pick up the info, too. She did an interview with a small local paper that later got posted on the Internet. It wasn't really a big deal, but she . . . had a few minor facts wrong."

When the waitress came by, they ordered drinks—a diet cola for Audrey and an ice water for Brett.

She was wondering about the water when Brett said, "I take it Drew reacted badly?"

"That's putting it mildly." Temper sparking with the memory, Audrey curled her hands into fists on the tabletop. "Rather than just correct her, Mr. Black demolished her in the cruelest ways possible. He called her awful names, cursed her, and maligned her intelligence. The whole conflict hit the Internet and Millie was publicly humiliated."

Recognition showed on Brett's face. "The online blowup. That was Millie?"

She gave a humorless laugh. "You see? Everyone has heard of it."

"I've seen it, yeah. If you follow the sport at all, it would have been hard to miss."

He reached across the table and took her hand. Smoothing his thumb over her knuckles got her to relax her fist.

"Drew was harsh, but Audrey, you have to admit that Millie got more than a few minor things wrong."

Audrey's jaw loosened. "You're *defending* him?"

"Not what he said, but his reasons for saying it, yeah. Millie put the SBC in the worst possible light, and she accused Drew of unethical business practices."

"That's not how she intended it!"

"That's how it came off." He kept her hand when she would have pulled away. "Drew Black's temper is legendary. The thing about Drew, though, he doesn't really attack first. But if anyone wrongfully criticizes the SBC, as Millie did, he goes rabid."

She was not in the mood to hear anyone explain away Mr. Black's faults. "Millie has always been shy in large groups, and how he treated her . . . she's still in WAVS, but never again will she be a spokesperson for us. In fact, I have to do all the interviews now myself because no one else is willing to risk the wrath of Mr. Black. As far as I'm concerned, he's a foul-mouthed bully and a complete jerk."

"Foul-mouthed, yeah. No one can deny that." Appearing frustrated, Brett let out a breath. "But you'd have to know Drew to understand—"

Aghast, Audrey freed herself of his touch. "Do *you* know him?"

Rubbing the back of his neck, Brett sat back in his seat and scrutinized her. "I've met him a few times, yeah. And like most, I'm familiar with him and his role in the SBC."

As his tone sank in, her eyes widened. "You actually like him."

"I respect him. And the sport."

He caught her before she could push her chair back and bolt. Audrey struggled for only a second, but relented when he wouldn't release her. She didn't want to cause a scene. "Let me go."

"Come on, Audrey. Give me five minutes, will you? Please."

She saw no point. "You *know* how I feel about it, Brett."

He made a display of releasing her hands and holding his up. "Yeah, I do. But I don't know *why*. Stay for dinner, talk to me about it. Make me understand your angle."

"I don't have an angle." But she didn't want to leave. Brett Bullman was the nicest, sexiest guy she'd ever met. And he wanted her.

Millie had insisted that she needed more of a social life. She'd encouraged her to get to know Brett, to add balance to her life of work and WAVS. Not since her brother passed away had she dated anyone, and while she hadn't summoned the interest to find involvement, she did miss the romance, the comfort of wanting and being wanted.

Brett was not only nice, he was by far the most gorgeous man she'd ever met. And he liked her. Should she really let a difference in perspective get in the way?

Maybe if she stayed, she could convert him to her way of thinking. If she walked out, he'd never see the SBC for the brutal, bloody street fighting that she knew it to be.

The waitress brought their drinks and flipped open a pad to take their orders.

Brett watched Audrey, leaving it up to her. As he promised, he didn't pressure her.

She took a calming breath—and asked for a burger and fries.

Relaxing, Brett ordered grilled chicken and a side of steamed veggies.

When they were alone again, they sat in silence for some time. Finally Brett leaned forward and propped his elbows on the table. "I'm glad you decided to stay. After dinner, maybe I can talk you into a game of pool." He took her hand. "And then dancing?"

Not since college had she danced with a guy. "I'd like that."

"And what about the mechanical bull?"

She laughed with him. "Now you're pushing it." No way would she attempt that bone-jarring feat. But if all went well, she wouldn't mind kissing him again. Imagining it made her stomach jumpy, and her toes curled in her boots.

Brett's expression sharpened. "I know what you're thinking, Audrey, because I'm thinking it, too. Soon as you're ready, just say the word."

She couldn't help herself. Brett Bullman was walking, sweet-talking temptation. She drew in a breath and said, "Now would be good."

GETTING Dickey settled took a lot longer than it should have, especially since he came around enough to offer up a lot of protest. He wanted his keys, he wanted to go find his girlfriend, he wanted to tear up the streets . . . he wanted to do a lot.

But Drew stood in his way.

He had no problem with fighters partying hard, and if that included getting smashed, no big deal. Far as Drew was concerned, the guys worked damned hard, and they deserved to let off steam—unless it affected the SBC.

If Dickey made an even bigger ass of himself, it'd come back on the sport. Even more importantly than that, the dumb-ass could end up injuring an innocent. No way would Drew let him drive when crocked. And with his judgment impaired, Dickey could get caught up in a street fight. Even plastered, he'd annihilate an untrained man.

But Gillian didn't want Drew to just knock him upside the head. No, she wanted him to be understanding.

What do I look like? A fucking babysitter?

Dumb as it seemed, Drew didn't want to disappoint her. Luckily, the tattoo artist wasn't unreasonable. He apologized for bothering Drew and assured him he was a big fan of the sport. As such, he'd hesitated to call the cops, and he had no interest in contacting the papers for a big scoop.

For that, Drew was damned grateful, enough that he promised the guy a couple of expensive floor seats at an upcoming fight. The last thing the SBC needed was more bad press.

For years it felt that with every two steps they took forward in mainstreaming, someone wanted to knock them back one. It infuriated Drew, as much for the effort and dedication of the fighters as his own time and energy spent building the organization.

Every sport had its pitfalls; on occasion, an athlete fell from grace with a DUI or a disorderly conduct. Some chump wouldn't pay his child support or his taxes . . . shit happened, in football, baseball, basketball—hell, in every professional sport. No one approved of athletes shirking responsibility or behaving badly, but let it happen in the SBC, and politicians went right back to comparing them to human cockfighting.

"Did he show up here hammered?" Drew asked the tattoo artist. If Dickey had driven there drunk . . .

"Nah. He had a buzz going on when he came in, but he wasn't wasted like this. I tried to talk him out of the tattoo, but he was pushy about it." The guy held up a fancy silver flask. "He guzzled this down after I finished his tat."

"What a dumb-ass." Drew took the flask and put it in his pocket. "Did he pay you?"

"Not yet."

At the moment, Dickey sat in a chair, his head back,

his eyes closed as if in pain. Pathetic. Drew couldn't imagine letting a woman twist him up like that. If Dickey's ladylove didn't understand the importance of what he did, the necessity of training at different camps, then to hell with her.

But Dickey apparently disagreed, given his morose posture.

Shaking his head, Drew decided against searching out Dickey's wallet. "How much does he owe you?"

The artist sounded apologetic as he named the price.

The fancy tattoo design, used to cover up Dickey's girlfriend's name, had cost a pretty penny.

Drew ponied up his credit card without too much grumbling. "Give yourself a twenty percent tip for being discreet."

"No way, man, that's okay." The artist held up his hands and shook his head. "You don't have to—"

"You fucking earned it, dude. Don't worry about it." He nodded toward Dickey. "I'll make sure he pays me back."

After they settled up, Drew bullied and badgered Dickey out to his car. But what to do with Dickey's ride?

"I can follow you in his car," Gillian offered.

"Fuck that." It looked ready to storm, and besides, Drew wanted Gillian with him. "I'll have it towed."

Propping her hands on her shapely hips, Gillian rejected that idea. "No, you will not. I'll drive his car to wherever you're taking him, and then you and I can leave from there together."

God save him from independent, outspoken women.

A cold wind cut through Drew. He watched Gillian pull her wrap tighter around her and he wanted to rage at the way things had unfolded. "Night of your life, huh?"

Despite the dropping temps, she gave him a sultry look. "That remains to be seen."

Okay, maybe he liked independent, outspoken women. "Is that a dare, Gillian?" He caught her upper arms and saw her smile as he pulled her in close. "By God, I think it was."

She looked at his mouth. "Possibly."

They were out in public, but other than Dickey, who paid no attention, there wasn't anyone around. Deciding it was safe enough, Drew kissed her. But he felt the chill in her lips and the way she trembled, so he cut things short.

For only a moment, Gillian put her icy nose to his neck. Then, with renewed purpose, she pushed back and held out a hand. "Do you have his keys?"

Since he knew he wouldn't win, Drew dropped the keys into her palm. "Stay close, okay? I'm not entirely sure where the dumb-ass is staying, and I don't want to lose you."

"Drew," she chided. "You should stop calling him that. He might hear you."

Ignoring that lame bit of advice, Drew said, "You still have my cell number just in case?"

"In case what? Good grief, Drew. I *do* know how to drive. Now, unless you're dragging your feet out of performance anxiety—"

Laughing, he kissed her one more time and even dared a quick swat on her voluptuous behind. He could barely wait to get his hands on all her lush curves. "Sounds like I have a few points to make tonight. I promise I'll do my best."

With both hands, she rubbed that sweet ass. "Paybacks are hell."

Enjoying her, Drew grinned. She had such a great sense of humor; that had been evident from the first moment he'd met her. "Is it naked payback? Because, honey, I could get into some naked payback."

She gasped and looked around for a rock, presumably to throw at him. Pretending to believe the threat, Drew hustled into the car. It occurred to him that he'd laughed more with Gillian in the few days that he'd known her than he did with most people in a month.

That realization threw him, but with Dickey giving drunken complaints nonstop, Drew didn't want to dwell on his reaction to Gillian.

It took damn near a half hour before they finally pulled into Dickey's motel. The damp night air felt charged with electricity and smelled of rain. Hoping to get out of there before the storm erupted, Drew dumped him in his room to sleep it off.

Unfortunately, Dickey didn't want to stay put. Even as Drew turned to leave, he started hunting for his keys.

"Forget it," Drew told him. "You're going to sleep it off, and the keys are going with me."

"But it's my fucking car!"

His patience had ended some time ago. "Two choices, Dickey. I can sit outside and wait for you to *try* to leave, then call the cops and let them arrest your sorry ass. Or I can take the keys. Decide quick, because I've had more than enough of you already."

Behind him, Gillian murmured in disapproval, *"Drew."*

Drew did not want her to be a part of this. "Wait outside," he told her without looking her way.

She hesitated.

"Now, Gillian. I mean it."

When he felt her retreat, he really wanted to clout Dickey.

Dickey stumbled toward him. As a six-foot-four heavy-weight who was all muscle, he could intimidate most people.

At the moment, Drew only saw him as a drunk.

Pointing at Drew, Dickey said, "Just because I fight for you—"

"Used to fight for me, dumb-ass." Stepping up to him, Drew met his temper. "You think I'm going to let this shit slide? *Think again*. You need to go home until you've grown up a little."

Mouth falling open, Dickey stared at him. "You're dumping me?"

"For now, you bet your ass I am. Show me you can get it together, and we'll talk again then." Drew held up the keys. "But these are going with me, and if you have any fucking sense at all, if you *ever* want to fight in this sport again, you'll keep to this room until you're dead sober."

Drew pocketed the keys and turned to leave. When Dickey was ready, he'd have a long, heated lecture ready for him. Maybe, *maybe* if Dickey seemed like he'd learned a lesson, Drew would give him another chance.

But tonight, right this minute, his first priority was to get Gillian alone.

As they left the motel room, a boom of thunder shook the ground and lightning splintered the sky in a bright display. They raced for his car, but the skies opened up in a stinging deluge just before they got in.

In seconds, they were both soaked.

Using a tissue from her purse to pat her face, Gillian looked out the window. "Wow. What a downpour."

Anxious to be on their way, Drew adjusted the heat and then drove out of the lot. "I'll have you out of those wet clothes in no time." Saying it amped up his lust. Jesus, he had it bad.

Gillian glanced at him. "You need to swing by the group home first, so I can get my car."

She *had* to be kidding. "Tomorrow." The familiar tat-tat-tat of hail began pelting the roof.

It didn't deter Gillian. "Uh, no. I need my car tonight, Drew."

"Why?" Trees bent under the force of the escalating wind. He'd always found storms sexy as hell. He couldn't think of a better way to spend the night than having sex with Gillian. "It's not like you're going anywhere tonight except to my place, right?"

"I don't have any other plans, no. But when I'm ready to leave your place, I want to be able to."

Her tone sank in and he shot her a look. What the hell? Did she expect him to screw her and then kick her out of bed? Sounded like. "I wouldn't mind if you spent the night."

That startled her. "Thank you." She smoothed wet hair

off her face. "I might take you up on that. But if I decide otherwise—"

All he wanted to do was get her under him, and it sounded like she was already planning on leaving him. "Hell, I'll give you my keys, okay?" The determined set to her posture irked Drew. "If I do something to piss you off that much, you can just take my car."

In a show of stubbornness, she folded her arms over her chest. "I appreciate the offer, but I want *my* car."

Slowly, Drew let out a breath. "Look, Gillian, I'm not real good at this 'pretty please' shit, but I'm trying all the same, so be reasonable, will you? The weather is crap and it's getting late. I swear to you, if something happens and you want to leave, I'll take you, or you can take my car. I have another in the garage so it's not a big frigging deal, okay?"

It was dark inside the car, with only the bluish glow of the lights on the dash for illumination.

"You'd let me drive your BMW?"

"It's just a car. No big deal." But Drew saw her indecision.

Trying for a solution, he added, "Want me to have your car towed to my place?"

"*No*, of course not." She shifted, showing a hint of indecision.

"Look, I'd rather do that than see you get soaked in this downpour or have you worry about it." More thunder boomed, almost immediately followed by a thick, blinding bolt of lightning. "Seriously."

She relented with ill grace. "Oh, all right. But I am taking your keys. And so help me, Drew Black, if you give me cause, I *will* leave in your car and you better not try to stop me."

Damn, but she amused him. "Wouldn't dream of it." He thought of everything he wanted to do to her and with her. It would take half the night and leave her exhausted. The woman wouldn't be going anywhere, whether she realized that yet or not. "Are you wearing panty hose under that skirt?"

She gawked at him. "I swear, the way your thoughts leap around is mind-boggling."

"No leaping, not really. I've been thinking of undressing you since I first saw you today. Hell, from the moment I met you, I've been thinking about what's under the lady-like clothes."

Sputtering indignation turned into a reluctant laugh. "Outrageous, as always."

No sense in denying that one. "You look great, by the way."

"Thank you."

Since she hadn't yet replied, he prompted, "Panty hose?"

With a roll of her eyes, she confirmed that. "Yes."

"Hate the things," Drew told her, "but I'll overlook them for you."

"Gee, Drew, that's really big of you."

"I take it you don't have stockings?" A man could fantasize.

Such a caustic look should have left him melted on the seat. "Tell you what. You try wearing a garter and nylons to see just how that works out for a hardworking businessperson, and then I'll follow suit."

"Uh . . . no, thanks." He was so turned on, forming coherent words took an effort. "Uncomfortable, is that it?"

She sniffed. "They show under close-fitting clothes, and they're far more time-consuming."

"All that? I had no idea." Imagining Gillian naked except for stockings and a garter left him shifting in his seat. "I suppose you could go commando."

One brow lifted in query.

"You know. Sans underwear altogether. Naked underneath." A mental image accompanied the words, nearly doing him in. "Bare assed." *Easy access*—but he kept that to himself.

"I get it, Drew. You can stop explaining."

To his surprise, she considered it. He held his breath, waiting . . .

"Maybe tomorrow."

Oh, hell. That did it. "Damn it, woman." He shifted again. "Now I have a boner."

Her light, teasing laugh exacerbated the situation for him. "Bully for you."

The foul weather kept him from driving any faster; he wouldn't risk her safety in any way. She already thought the worst of him. No reason to give her fuel for her disdain by driving like an idiot.

They turned down his street and with his thoughts in a riot of lust, Drew said nothing else. He pulled up the driveway, but when he tried the garage door opener, nothing happened.

"Power must be out." He put the car in park. "Stay put. I'll be right back."

In the time it took him to jump out of the car and open the garage door manually, he got soaked clear through to his skin. The icy rain did nothing to cool his need. The sooner he got them both undressed, the better.

When he slid back in beside her, she gave him sympathy. "Poor Drew." She touched a light fingertip to his dripping jaw, down over his throat, and then his shoulder. "You're drenched."

"Not for long." He parked the car in the garage with a jerk. Damn, but he'd never been this anxious to bed a woman before. It was nuts. He had to get a grip or he'd blow things, and she'd end up thinking him an unskilled dolt.

In a heartbeat, he got out and closed the garage door again, shutting out the worst of the storm and leaving them in total, absolute darkness. Normally, he would have dried the fine leather of his car seats, but right now, he just didn't care.

Fumbling his way over to her door, he opened it. "Let's go."

With a smile thick in her voice, Gillian asked, "In a hurry, are you?"

Her teasing had to end. Drew found her arm and pulled her in close to kiss her long and deep. While she softened against him, he moved his hands from her back to that lush ass and snuggled her in tight against his erection.

Perfection.

Against her mouth, he whispered, "I'm on the ragged edge, lady, so unless you want me to have you right here, right now, in a cold garage on the hood of my car, you better stop taunting me. Got it?"

In the darkness, Drew couldn't see Gillian's face, but he heard her heavy breaths and felt her faltering nod. "Yes . . . okay."

Pulling her behind him, Drew led the way into the house. "Watch your step."

"Don't you have a flashlight?"

"Good idea." He had started to go straight to the bedroom, but he wanted to see her. All of her. A flashlight would help with that.

He stopped at the hallway. "Wait right here. Don't move."

"Hurry."

"Yeah." He bumped into a chair, cracked his shin on a table, and then he found the kitchen and felt around until he located the right cabinet. The utility light shone brightly, making his return to her much easier.

Leaning against the wall, Gillian stood with one knee slightly bent, her head back, her hands flat on the wall beside her generous hips. Through her open wrap, her wet clothes clung to her body.

Unlike the model-slim babes with inflated boobs who usually came on to him, Gillian had real curves in all the right places. She wasn't vain, but neither was she shy about her appeal. Her confidence was almost as sexy as that voluptuous body.

When she opened her eyes and smiled at him, Drew shook himself. *Get a grip, already.*

Several deep breaths helped him to slow down. A little.

Small talk required more patience than he had left. Leading with the light, he again took her hand and started down the hall for his bedroom.

With her heels clicking on his hardwood floors, Gillian laughed behind him. "My, my, Drew, you really are in a rush, aren't you?"

"I'm sporting mahogany here. Of course I'm in a rush."

In a laughing, throaty purr, she murmured, "I'm flattered."

Finally in his bedroom, Drew set the flashlight on the nightstand like a lamp and turned to her.

Already she had shrugged out of her wrap, stepped out of her shoes, and untied the scarf from around her neck. Knowing he'd marked her left him burning with deep satisfaction.

When she caught him watching her, her hands paused on the fastenings to her skirt. "Well, don't just stand there," she playfully ordered. "Clothes *off.*"

God help him. "Yes, ma'am." Keeping his attention glued to her, Drew stripped off his jacket and started unbuttoning his shirt.

CHAPTER 6

GILLIAN made a neat little pile of her clothes, folding each piece and placing it on a chair. When she stood in only her skirt and a pale, lacy bra, Drew couldn't help but stare. The bra, despite the underwire, didn't seem adequate to hold her bountiful breasts.

Gillian didn't mind.

Smiling, she reached up under her skirt and rolled down the panty hose. Thick shadows enhanced everything.

Outside, the storm raged, with rain battering the windows and the wind howling in fury. Every few seconds, lightning flashed with a blinding, strobe effect.

Knowing that he watched her every move with rapt attention, Gillian shimmied out of the skirt with a provocative lack of haste. His hands curled into fists, his cock strained behind his fly.

Gillian's panties were made of the same lace and matched her bra. She looked so incredible, Drew knew he wouldn't last.

"Come here." He sounded harsher than he meant to, but never had he wanted a woman like this.

He took two steps to meet her halfway and, with his hands moving everywhere at once, ravaged her tender mouth. Her skin was damp from the rain, warm and soft. When he slid his hands into her panties, palming her cheeks, squeezing, Gillian bit his bottom lip.

"You have some catching up to do."

He felt her busy fingers at his waistband and groaned. Pushing her hands aside, he shed the rest of his clothes in record time. Gillian tried to touch him, but Drew wanted her naked, too. Right now. He cupped her breasts once, just because he had to, and then unhooked the front clasp between the cups. The bra opened and Gillian shrugged the straps off her shoulders until they dropped down her arms.

Sucking in a shuddering breath, Drew again slid his hands into her panties, this time to push them down her thighs. When they fell to her feet, she stepped free—and *finally* they were both naked.

His hands shook as he covered her breasts, felt her stiffened nipples and her galloping heartbeat. It thrilled him that she was every bit as carried away as him.

"So fucking sexy . . ." Bending, he took one nipple into his mouth.

On a sharp inhalation, she dug her fingertips into his shoulders. Hefting her in his palms, Drew used his teeth to nip her carefully and felt her tremble. He circled with his tongue, flicked, and when she pressed him closer, he sucked at her like a starving man.

Her long, shuddering groan rewarded him, tightening everything inside him, making him throb.

With his other hand he smoothed along her waist, over her hip, and then to her belly.

"Drew . . ." She said his name as a soft moan of eagerness.

He switched to her other breast, and just as he sucked that nipple into the heat of his mouth, he palmed her sex.

Her fingers contracted on his shoulders, digging hard into his muscles.

Slowly, so slowly that it tormented them both, he used his fingertips to explore her, open her. Hot. Damp. He teased along her inner lips until they parted—and pushed one finger in deep.

Crying out, Gillian arched into him.

Damn, but he could feel her pulsing around his finger, feel her wetness, the slick heat.

He withdrew enough to work in a second finger and taunted her nipple again with his teeth.

Clenching around his fingers, she stiffened and trembled. Drew straightened to look at her face. "You're already close, aren't you?"

She nuzzled his jaw, moved against him. *"Yes."*

Pleased with her, he lightly kissed her parted lips. "I want to see this." He brought his thumb up to touch her clitoris.

Her eyes closed and her head fell back. Holding on to him, she moved with him as he worked his fingers in and out of her, teased her clit, and palmed her ass.

Her stiffened nipples rubbed against his chest, abraded by his chest hair. He'd somehow known she'd be hot, but he hadn't expected this.

Panting, she said, "Drew . . . I need the bed."

God, she was amazing. "No," he whispered. "Not yet."

"But . . ." Heat poured off her. Between her legs, her slick flesh swelled. *"Drew . . ."*

He kept up the steady rhythm, pushing her, and as her orgasm overtook her and her legs went weak, she held on to him.

Drew watched her face, how her expression tightened, twisted. Beautiful and real. Gillian wasn't a screamer, but her low throaty moans and gasping breaths were a huge turn-on, as much so as her voluptuous, sexy body.

Spent, she went limp in his arms.

"Now the bed," he decided. If he didn't get in her soon, he'd embarrass himself.

Gillian let him settle her to the mattress, but she wasn't quite aligned with the bed. Instead, she lay crossways.

From the knees down, her legs hung over the side. Raising her arms above her head, she smiled, and it affected him like a well-placed lick.

"God, the things you do to me . . ." Drew said, but she either didn't hear him or didn't care.

Even as he got a condom from the nightstand and rolled it on, Drew wondered what it was about Gillian that had him fumbling in such a rush.

Sure, she was hot. No two ways about that. And he'd just discovered that she was uninhibited and sexual, too.

She had a full-figured, killer body that only an idiot wouldn't appreciate.

Classy, smart, witty, motivated . . . okay, what was there about her *not* to enjoy?

"Drew, don't take this the wrong way."

Forcing his gaze from her soft belly and damp pubic hair to her face, Drew lifted a brow. "What?"

"I'm flattered that you appear to enjoy looking at me. And you're not exactly hard on the eyes, either." As she said that, her gaze dipped over him, stalling on his erection. She squirmed on the sheets, shifting in urgency. "Very impressive, in fact. But I'm a more tactile person, I guess. I'd really like to *feel* you, not just look at you, you know?"

Closing his eyes against her stimulating words, Drew struggled for control.

Gillian didn't let up.

"Seriously, Drew, if you think you could bring yourself down here to me . . . well, that would be very nice."

"You don't know when to quit, do you?" Lost, Drew caught her legs in the crook of his elbows and moved over her. As he spread her supple thighs wide, he wedged his hips in. The flesh of her silky inner thighs against his waist sent blood rushing to his head. The sensation of dominating her turned him on even more.

This, he thought, *is how a woman should feel, giving and sexy and soft.*

Her legs pressed back, exposing her more, making his heartbeat thunder in his ears. He could see all of her. Even in the dim light, he was able to watch as his cock pressed into her, as her sleek, pink lips opened around him.

Rather than protest, Gillian put her head back in a sign of submission. *She* loved it, too, and knowing that was enough to destroy his control.

Immersing himself in the sounds of her heavy breathing, the heat of her, and the intoxicating scent of her arousal, Drew entered her.

And found her wet, but so damn snug.

He hadn't expected that and he closed his eyes for only a moment, struggling with himself. When he opened them again, he sank in a little more and locked his teeth at how she squeezed him so tightly. "How long has it been for you?"

Lifting her head, Gillian stared at him in lust-dazed disbelief. "My God, Drew, do you really want to have this conversation now?"

Hear about Gillian with other men? Was he an idiot? No. He shook his head. "Probably not."

She dropped back again. "I didn't think so."

Jaw clenched, testicles tight, Drew kept up the slow pressure until she held every inch of him. Liking that a lot, he leaned down onto her, pressing her legs back even more, relishing every sensation.

The muscles in her legs tensed; she knotted her hands in the bedsheets and groaned. In this position, he was impossibly deep—and still he leaned down more until he could suck on her jutting nipples.

As soon as he did that, Gillian moaned, arched her back up to accommodate him, and grabbed for his biceps as if she needed an anchor.

Pushed to the limit, Drew pulled back and thrust in again. He felt her womb, felt the clenching of her body, almost as if in pain.

They both gasped.

Holding himself still, Drew asked, "Are you okay?"

She swallowed twice, nodded, and whispered, "Don't you dare stop."

"No, no, I won't." Done with holding back, Drew rode her hard, withdrawing and driving in again, over and over, harder each time. Positioned as they were, every thrust slid his length along her clitoris. She went wild.

Whatever finesse he'd hoped to employ would have to come after he took the edge off, Drew decided. But it didn't matter right now anyway, because Gillian was with him, moving her hips as much as she could in his restrained hold.

She spurred him on with soft moans and harsh groans and the continuous gripping of her body as she neared her release.

Before he'd even realized she was ready, she cried out, her back bowing hard and her inner muscles clamping down.

"Gillian." He said her name just to hear it, just to reaffirm the reality of her here with him, taking him and giving to him and enjoying every second.

It went on and on, pushing Drew over the edge. He needed her mouth, so he kissed her, and he kept on kissing her until he sank down onto her with his own numbing release.

Moments later, depleted, he carefully released her legs and moved to her side. The storm still battered his house, almost matching his heartbeat.

Languidly, Gillian reached over and put a hand on his sweaty abdomen. He covered it with his own.

"You're right, Drew."

He couldn't even breathe yet, and she wanted to talk? Taking a deep breath to help catch his wind, he tried to man up. "About?"

She turned to her side to face him and slipped one leg over his.

That felt nice. Really nice. Curling up with Gillian after incredible sex—yeah, he liked that.

She snuggled into him. "I'm in no hurry to run off."

He didn't quite have the energy to laugh, but he at least managed a smile.

Turning his head toward her, Drew found her silky black hair mussed around her face. Her eyes were heavy, her lips swollen.

So fucking sexy.

And thinking about sexy . . . he remembered the tightness of her, the fit. "So how long has it been for you?"

Incredulity fell over her face before she slanted him a look. "You already knew that my tastes were . . ." She searched for a word and settled on ". . . exacting."

Of course she was—and it flattered him. "But I passed muster, huh?"

Smiling, she ran one finger down his chest. "You do possess a sort of raw appeal."

He turned toward her and smoothed back her hair. It was so sleek, it felt liquid. Everything about her was ultimately feminine, and yet strong. Particularly her sexual appetite.

She pressed her cheek into his palm. It was the weirdest thing, especially since he was well sated, yet far from done.

But right now, with Gillian Noode, maybe for the first time with a woman, he felt . . . tender. Affectionate.

Drew shook his head. No way in hell was he ready to head down that road just because of awesome sex. Okay, it was more than sex, but still . . . "Clean up, food, and then back in the bed."

"Mmmm." She smiled again. "The upcoming order?"

"For the rest of the night." He kissed her hard and fast and rose from the tangled sheets. "You can stay put and I'll play the gentleman if you want."

"Dinner in bed?"

With Gillian, he wouldn't mind *everything* in bed—especially if she stayed just as she was now: smiling, sweet-tempered, responsive to him, and best of all, naked.

He looked her over and wanted her again. Already.

Shit.

Sounding a little hoarse, he said, "Yeah." And then, before he started doing something stupid, like declaring himself to a woman he barely knew but who wanted to change him in every way imaginable, he said, "Relax. I'll be right back."

WITH his heart thumping and his body taut, Brett pushed back his chair and came around to Audrey's side of the table. Startled, she stared up at him. A smile would have helped, but he couldn't quite drum one up around the thrumming of lust. He held out a hand, and when she accepted it, he pulled her to her feet.

"Here?" she asked in a near squeak.

Brett hesitated. Did she regret taunting him? Was she having second thoughts, or did she just enjoy teasing him?

Since he was falling fast, it might be time to find out. Drawing a breath, he said, "Come on."

Leading her back to the stairs, he walked down a few steps then turned to her. They had a few seconds of privacy here, and he hoped it would be enough.

Ah, no, she wasn't teasing him, Brett thought. Looking at her, he saw a reflection of everything he felt. Already Audrey breathed too deep and her brown eyes were wide, darker, and glittering.

She wanted him.

But unlike him, she had reservations that he'd have to help her overcome. Once he did, he felt sure they'd both enjoy themselves for however long things lasted.

Audrey slicked her tongue over her bottom lip. "Our food should be ready soon."

Brett wanted to groan at her uncertainty—but he had promised her. Besides, when they finally got together, he wanted her with him one hundred percent.

Flattening one hand on the wall beside her head and staring down at his feet, he worked to compose himself. When he felt in control again, he faced her. "It's up to you, Audrey. What do you want to do?"

For an answer, she looked at his mouth, and with every second that passed, the tension ramped between them.

Suddenly she was on him again and Brett felt consumed. The sounds of the bar faded beneath the heat of her mouth, her unique scent, and her anxious participation.

The food would wait.

Leaning into her, Brett slid a hand from her waist to her hip—and urged her in for some sizzling, full-body contact. She was so small that one of his hands would cover a good deal of her cute little bottom. His palm tingled at that thought.

When the music suddenly died and the sound of the crowd grew rowdy, Brett didn't understand.

He could hear Barber, the lead musician, making an announcement, but in the stairwell his words weren't clear. And with Audrey clinging to him, kissing him so hotly, he didn't really care.

Until the door to the stairs burst open.

"What the hell?"

Several people rushed through. Brett flattened himself against Audrey to protect her.

"Brett?"

"Shh. Something's going on."

At the top of the stairs, he saw a bouncer directing people into the stairwell, cautioning them to go slowly and in an orderly fashion.

Something had happened. What, he had no idea. Maybe a fire? But he hadn't heard an alarm and he didn't smell any smoke. He took Audrey's hand and pulled her around so that she could go down the stairs in front of him.

She held back. "What's going on?"

"I don't know yet. Let's go." He kept her to his right side, closer to the wall. People jammed into his back, knocked into his shoulder, shoved and shouted.

Audrey, bless her heart, did her best to keep up without a single complaint. She didn't even seem worried.

When they reached the main floor, Brett saw Gregor Marsh. That fighter towered over others, making him easy to spot. Gregor had taken on the task of ushering folks out the front doors, keeping things orderly.

"What's going on?" Brett asked as soon as he reached him.

Without taking his attention from directing the crowd, Gregor said, "Got a bomb threat." He kept one fellow upright when he would have stumbled, and he stopped another from turning back to talk to a friend. In short, he added, "I'm helping Roger get everyone out."

Bomb? Brett rocked back. Of all the things . . . well, he hadn't expected that. Audrey said nothing.

He wanted her out of the place, and fast, so he didn't ask any more questions.

"Got it. Thanks." But before Brett could merge with the outgoing customers, Gregor caught his arm.

"We met the other day, right?"

Brett nodded. "Yeah." With any luck, Gregor wouldn't mention that they'd met in a gym.

"I sent my lady outside, kickin' and bitchin' and none too happy. Tall gal, sweet on the eyes. Jacki Marsh. Havoc's little sister. Can you look after her for me until I get this place cleared?"

Understanding his worry, Brett clapped him on the shoulder. "Got it covered."

"Thanks, dude."

When Brett had to nudge Audrey along to get her moving again, he looked down and found her eyes as wide as saucers. But it wasn't the mention of a bomb that had her boggled. Even as he led her away, she craned her head to stare back at Gregor.

Yeah, Gregor had that effect on lots of people, male and female alike. Even as heavyweight fighters went, Gregor was gargantuan, and solid as steel. To go with his impressive size, he had an abundance of tattoos, shaggy black hair, and ears thickened from his profession. His imposing visage didn't quite match his congenial manner, though.

As he nudged Audrey along, he asked, "You okay?"

She nodded. "Was that guy a fighter?"

"Yeah. A good one, too."

That made her thoughtful, and she said no more as they wended through the throng.

They got bottlenecked at the door as people insisted on wanting their jackets and wraps from the coat check. Idiots. Their jackets wouldn't matter if they all got blown to bits. Two employees of Roger's Rodeo continued to calmly and insistently move the patrons forward.

Finally Brett got them both through the door. Thick black clouds blocked the stars, and rain threatened. People milled about right outside the club, trying to find shelter beneath the overhang. If there was a bomb, how safe did they think they'd be standing so near the building?

For now, he left them to their own fates and started to lead Audrey across the street. Then, from behind them, he heard someone yell out her name.

For the first time, Audrey looked unsettled as she jerked around and searched the crowd. "Millie?"

She couldn't see over the masses, but Brett spotted Millie's red hair as she went on tiptoe, calling out to them again. Somehow she'd gotten hemmed into an alcove and the flow of human traffic wouldn't allow her to get free.

"I heard Millie," Audrey told him. She started to push past, to reenter the club.

"I see her," Brett told Audrey. "She's okay." Now where to take Audrey? Across the street, beyond the parking lot would be his first choice. But a few unfamiliar men stood over there, and he wasn't about to leave Audrey alone with men he didn't know.

Brett was deciding what to do next when, beside them, a tall woman called out orders to the others. She had a fun, eclectic style that seemed at odds with her drill sergeant tone as she instructed people to clear the doorways, to distance themselves from the building, and to stop pushing and shoving.

Seeing that she held her own against the milling, panicked bystanders, Brett yelled to her, "Jacki?"

And she looked up.

Perfect. Audrey reluctantly allowed him to edge her in that direction. As soon as he reached Jacki, he said, "Gregor told me that I could count on you for some help."

"Did he?" Jacki still looked pissed that she was outside and Gregor wasn't. "Doing what?"

"If you and Audrey go across the street, at least to the other side of the cars parked there, then others will probably follow."

"Brett, wait." Audrey strained against him. "I can't go without Millie."

He caught her face. "I'm getting her, okay? But you need to get out of harm's way first."

She started to protest, and Brett's temper kicked in.

"Damn it, Audrey, you'll only get trampled, and I'd like to know how the hell that's going to help Millie."

As if they weren't threatened by a bomb, Audrey scowled up at him. "I'm not stupid, Brett."

"Then let me go get Millie."

"Okay, but hurry it up. She's uncomfortable with crowds."

Which would have been a good reason for her not to dodge into a busy club. Brett looked at Jacki for assistance.

She rolled her eyes. "You guys are all such cavemen, I swear. But . . . I guess it is a good idea."

Someone plowed into Jacki, almost knocking her off balance, and with a feral look she brought her elbow back, causing a guy to yelp. "Well, come on, Audrey. Let's lead the pack."

"Fine." Beside Jacki, Audrey looked even more petite, but she had no problem snagging others along the way. Between the two women, they soon had a small contingent across the street.

With Audrey safe, Brett wedged back into the club, pushing against a slow-moving group of friends who'd had way too much to drink. He found Millie on the verge of tears. Stationing himself in front of her, he caused a block to the now dwindling swarm. Above the din of excited

voices, he could hear Gregor issuing orders to some strag-
glers, and ahead of him, he saw Roger Sims, the owner of
the club, double-checking down corridors and in closets.

Brett pulled Millie out in front of him. When she stumbled, he looped one arm around her and kept her on her
feet. She was almost as short as Audrey, but not as slight of
build. Once outside, he didn't pause.

"Audrey's across the street."

Clinging to his arm, Millie nodded. "Thank you so
much, Brett."

His brain cramped at the thought of a bomb. *Why?* Did
someone have a grudge against Roger or the patrons of the
bar? "Not a problem."

"I tried," Millie told him, embarrassed, "but I couldn't get
out of there. What happened, anyway? Why is everyone—?"

"Bomb threat, I'm told." Maybe Gregor had misunderstood. "But I don't know for sure." He got Millie over to
Audrey and started back for the club.

Audrey grabbed for him. "Where are you going?"

"If Millie got stuck, maybe someone else did, too. If
Roger tries to check every nook and cranny himself, he'll
never get out of there."

Jacki called after him, saying, "It's probably a hoax, but
just in case, none of you should play hero. Tell Gregor I
said to get out of there, and fast."

Brett sent her an affirmative wave and jogged back.
Inside the building, he saw Gregor scouring the rooms
upstairs, Roger downstairs.

"What can I do?"

Frazzled and furious, Roger glanced at him with suspicion. "Who the hell are you?"

From upstairs, Gregor yelled, "Brett Bullman. He's a
fighter."

Roger hesitated only a moment before nodding.
"Thanks. We're about done in here, but if you could get
people to clear the front door and at least go across the
street until the cops show up, that'd be great." He started

to walk away, then added, "Brett? Use force if you have to. Just get them away from here."

"You got it." Brett headed back out. Sirens sounded in the distance. Only about fifteen minutes had passed, but it felt like an hour. As he started people moving, he glanced across the street at Audrey. She, Millie, and Jacki were directing people, encouraging them toward less chitchat and more action.

Something close to pride unfurled inside Brett. Audrey had a good head on her shoulders, and now that she'd gotten her bearings, she reacted with cool control. Other women were huddled together, some gabbing too loudly, a few crying, one lamenting a broken heal on her sandal.

But Audrey took charge.

Roger and Gregor joined Brett on the perimeter just as the police arrived. The officer in charge instructed the others to turn off their radios because radio frequencies could be used to trigger a bomb.

Agog over that information, Gregor looked at Brett and whistled.

Uniformed cops started pushing everyone back even more while other cops shut down the street one block up both ways. The guy in charge joined them. Roger greeted him with an extended hand, introducing himself as the owner of the club.

"Officer Sparks." He surveyed the area. "Tell me what happened."

Gregor looked at Brett again and mouthed the name: *Sparks?*

Brett shrugged; that was irony for you. A guy named Sparks investigating a bomb threat. Not that there was anything remotely humorous about this situation.

Roger paid no attention to the man's name at all. "My bartender got the call and forwarded it to me in my office. I was just about to head home—" As if struck, Roger pressed a fist to his forehead. "I have to call my wife to let her know why I'm late, damn it. She was waiting on me. If she hears about this—"

Gregor said, "I'll call her, Rog," and he already had his cell phone out, using his thumb to press in numbers.

"Thanks." Roger closed his eyes a moment. "Make sure she knows everyone is fine."

Nodding, Gregor turned his back on them to speak quietly to Roger's wife.

Brett could only imagine what Roger felt. He'd not only had a scare, and had his business threatened, but he held responsibility for over a hundred people who'd been inside. Right now, some of the people were grumbling about a wasted meal or a drink they didn't get to finish.

Roger would lose money on this, as well as credibility.

Furious with the situation, Roger brought himself back around. "It was a man, and he said that the place was set to blow, that a bomb had been hidden here with the intent of killing Drew Black and as many fighters as possible."

Brett went still. Oh, hell. This was about Drew?

Gregor closed his cell with a whistle.

Running a hand through his hair, Roger cursed. "I asked the bastard where the bomb was, but he told me to clear the place or a lot of people would die, then he hung up." His hands curled into fists. "I haven't even seen Drew here tonight. Hell, most of the fighters show up on the weekend, not during the week, so it couldn't have been anyone real familiar with my clientele."

Frowning in thought, Officer Sparks asked, "Was Drew Black supposed to be here? Did he have a meeting that someone knew about, and maybe he canceled?"

"Not that I'm aware of, but I don't exactly keep tabs on that stuff." Roger shrugged his shoulders. "My wife is Dean Conor's sister."

"My wife, too," Gregor said. And when Sparks looked at him in confusion, he explained, "Roger's wife is Cam, my wife is Jacki, and Havoc is their brother."

The cop must've been a fan, because he knew Dean Conor's fighting name of Havoc.

"Was Havoc here tonight?" He looked around the milling group of people with hope.

"He's out of town doin' a promo gig," Gregor said.

With sudden perception, the cop looked at him anew. "You're Gregor Marsh, *the Maniac*."

"One and only." Gregor winked at him.

"I'll be damned."

Brett could almost feel Roger's palpable frustration as he gestured in explanation. "There are a lot of fighters that hang out here. You can't take two steps without tripping over one. Dean came to visit, then he opened a gym, more fighters came to town, and my honky-tonk turned into more of a . . ."

"Fight club," Gregor supplied.

"But still a honky-tonk, too," Roger insisted.

Brett wondered what the hell it mattered. He turned to the cop. "I met with Drew here at the club the other day. Like Roger said, on a weekend. But far as I know, he does a lot of his business here. If he had a meeting tonight, I don't know about it. But it's possible."

The officer took that in. "Anyone got his number?"

Roger shook his head, Gregor noticed Jacki waving at him and headed that way, so Brett found Drew's card in his wallet. He read the number to Officer Sparks.

"What now?" Roger asked.

"We'll have to sweep the place, make sure there isn't a bomb before we let anyone back in."

"Not rushing you or anything, but do you know how long that will take?"

"Two to four hours, give or take." The officer looked around at the growing mob. "After the county sheriff's department's bomb-sniffing K-9 team clears the site, we'll do a visual. They should be here soon." He turned back to Roger. "Not sure how late you're open during the week, but it might be a good idea to call it a night."

"I assumed as much." Roger withdrew a stack of vouchers from his pocket. "Do you need me anymore, or can I gather up my people to hand these out?"

"Don't leave," the officer told him, "but feel free to handle your guests."

"Thanks." Roger went off to gather up his employees and explain how vouchers would be given for free drinks, and for interrupted meals and games.

Brett searched for Audrey. Now that patrons from other nearby establishments had joined them to get the scoop, there had to be a couple hundred people or more hanging out. At least with the roadblocks, there wasn't any traffic except for those leaving the area.

He found her sitting on the curb at the corner, a safe distance from the threat and the chaos, talking quietly with Millie.

Millie saw Brett first and jumped up, surprising him with an embrace. "Thank you again, Brett. I can't believe I got stuck like that. Everyone was just so pushy and rushed."

He looped an arm around her shoulders. "When they get scared, people forget manners and common sense all too quick."

Audrey said nothing, and that worried Brett.

Inhaling, Millie launched into more speech. "Not you, though. It was pretty impressive how you just stopped the flow of human traffic. I almost got flattened, but people had to go around you, you were so immovable."

He tipped his head at Audrey, wondering why she wouldn't look at him. "I'm a little bit bigger than you, Millie. Makes it easier for me."

"Your friend, Gregor, was wonderful, too. Very take-charge."

What the hell was going on? Why was Millie so chatty while Audrey sat in stern silence?

Almost in apology, Millie patted his arm, and when Brett looked at her, she whispered, "She knows."

Brett felt his stomach knot. "Knows what?"

Still in a whisper, Millie said, "That you're a fighter. Gregor, too. Jacki told her." And with a wince: "I'm sorry."

CHAPTER 7

A UDREY flinched when she saw the disappointment on Brett's face and the censure on Millie's. He really was a nice guy—but her personal prejudice ran deep. Millie knew that, and she knew why.

Tonight they'd been through hell. Over her shoulder, she glanced back at the group of gawkers. Some were titillated, some frightened, some blasé. None of them had deserved this.

Most were without their coats, having left the building in such a rush. As the air thickened with the moisture from the impending storm, women huddled up to men for warmth.

Audrey would have loved to steal some of Brett's warmth. But he'd lied to her, if not outright, then still by way of omission.

With her arms wrapped around herself and her shoulders hunched, she sat on the curb, shivering. At least Millie still wore her coat, had never taken it off, not when she hadn't planned to stay.

As if she'd read Audrey's thoughts, Millie bit her lip,

and in an effort to break the strained silence, she said to Brett, "I'd only stopped by to say that I was going to take in a late movie. I knew Audrey wouldn't be able to call me, because I'd have to turn off my cell. I just . . ."

She looked to Audrey for help, but Audrey turned away. God, she felt so stupid. Brett had walked her through the bar, handing out flyers to his *friends* . . . she remembered some of the looks she'd gotten, how puzzled many of the men had been.

The joke was on her. Had they laughed behind her back?

Sighing, Millie continued. "I knew you were planning to take her home but I wanted to—"

"He's not," Audrey said with no inflection at all. Now that she knew everything, she had no reason to let him continue with the deception.

Brett put his hands on his hips and glared down at her. "So that's it? From one extreme to the next, just because I'm an athlete?"

"A *fighter*," Audrey stressed, even as heat rushed to her face. Brett knew how attracted she was to him—because she'd thrown herself at him.

"Same damn thing," Brett said right back.

Though Brett's tone wasn't loud, his annoyance couldn't be missed. Several people looked their way, including Jacki and Gregor.

No way would Audrey let him cause a scene. Millie hated crowds, and she especially hated being the center of attention.

A hand to her stomach, Millie seated herself beside Audrey. "I'll drive you home, Audrey, you know that."

No doubt Millie was anxious to get away before the situation got any worse.

Without humor, Audrey laughed. "You've already missed the movie now anyway, right?" She started to stand.

Millie put a hand to her knee, stalling her. "I'll take you home, but Audrey, think about it. It was the club owner,

the workers, and the *fighters* who took charge to make sure
everyone got clear of the building."

As thunder rumbled and the first few raindrops began
to fall, Audrey stared at Millie. "You're defending him?
To *me*?"

The weather worked wonders at breaking up the scene.
Women rushed to their cars with men following behind.
Lightning split the dark sky, prompting police officers to
pull on rain slickers.

Like a different man, not angry but very impersonal,
Brett stared at Audrey as he asked Millie, "Where are you
parked?"

"Just down the street."

"I'll walk you ladies to the car before I go."

Just like that, Audrey thought. With no explanation, no
defense?

Millie gave Audrey a *Do something* look. In a hiss, she
said, "The night should not end this way."

No, it shouldn't. She had a few things to say to Mr. Brett
Bullman. Pushing to her feet, Audrey faced him. "You
played me for a fool."

"No, I just hedged my bets." He glanced up at the sky,
then pulled off his flannel and put it around her. "Doesn't
matter now, though, does it?" He started them toward
the car.

He sounded hurt? But he was the one who'd duped her!
And why walk her to the car now? He had to know she
wasn't going home with him. Not now, not ever.

A little voice inside herself suggested that maybe there
were things about Brett that were true—like the protective
instincts she'd witnessed tonight.

Audrey started to doubt herself.

Until Brett suddenly said, "You weren't too worried
about a bomb, were you, Audrey?"

"What?" She stalled, but Brett kept her moving until
they were close to the car.

Looking suspicious, and disgruntled because of it, he
used his hold on her arm to turn her to face him. "As I

recall, you were more intent on ogling Gregor than on getting out of the building."

She inflated with umbrage.

Yanking herself free of Brett's hold, she squared her shoulders and stared him in the eyes. "Are you accusing me of something?"

Shoving his hands into his pockets, Brett shrugged. Audrey thought he looked cold, standing there in the damp wind in only a T-shirt. But he didn't shiver, he just kept his arms closer to his body, his shoulders slightly lifted.

The wind plastered his shirt to his body, showing off wide shoulders and a solid chest.

Not that she cared about any of that.

His jaw tightened. "Got any men in your organization?"

"Why?" Never would she back down against a slur to her reputation. "No, wait, let me guess. Did a man call in the threat?"

"Are you out of your mind?" Millie finally caught on to Brett's accusations. "You actually think that Audrey placed a bomb threat? Good Lord, you don't know her at all, do you? Audrey would never do such a thing." She harrumphed. "And to think I was defending you!"

Brett didn't look at Millie; his attention stayed focused on Audrey. "Is that a yes or a no?"

Movements stiff with anger, Audrey peeled off his flannel and threw it at him. "There are no men taking an active role in WAVS."

Millie scoffed at him. "The name ought to tell you that. It's *Women* Against Violent Sports."

"But," Audrey said, interrupting her, "in case you want to accuse them, we have been backed by male senators and state representatives, and plenty of supportive men have given us cash donations for printing literature about the sport—literature that *you* helped to disperse under *false interest*."

He dared to laugh, mocking her. "I thought I was pretty damned clear about my interest. And at least I was willing to listen to another opinion, which is more than you can say, right?"

"You didn't give me a chance!"

"Come on, Audrey. What you thought of fighters was pretty clear. What was it Millie called us? Brutal specimens?"

Millie flushed. "I, ah . . ."

"I figured if you knew I was a fighter, you wouldn't give me the time of day. And I was right, wasn't I? The second you found out, you were pissed."

Oh, no. She would not let him turn this around on her. "Because *you* didn't tell me." Audrey's voice dropped, and she couldn't hide the resentment. "I had to find out from your friends. Do you know how stupid that makes me feel?"

His brows pulled down more. He drew a breath. "I'm sorry," he said on an exhalation.

Millie softened.

Audrey wasn't so quick. Too much had happened today for a simple "I'm sorry" to make a dent. "For what, Brett? Not telling me that you're a fighter? Or for accusing me of sending a bomb threat?"

Casting a furtive look around them, he winced. "Bring it down, will you?" He moved closer to explain, "Rumors can get started that way."

Audrey couldn't believe his belated concern. "*You* started them!"

"And I apologized." He ran a hand through his already rumpled hair. "It's just . . . well, you sort of took everything in stride—"

"Oh, right." Sarcasm rippled through her; her ponytail bobbed as she shook her head. "I guess I was supposed to scream in terror and panic?"

He eyed her militant stance.

She wasn't through. "Maybe I should have collapsed, so you could have thrown me over your shoulder and carried me out like a hero?"

"Maybe." At her ridiculous description one side of his

mouth quirked. "I wouldn't have minded. But you didn't need rescuing at all, did you?"

"Neither did you," she threw back at him. "But I didn't sling accusations at you because of that."

"I needed help," Millie reminded them.

Audrey spared her a glance. She knew Millie wanted to help, but this was too personal.

She hadn't known Brett long, but what he thought was important to her. "I'm incapable of something so unethical, Brett."

Appearing regretful, he nodded. "I'm sorry. Again." He glanced back at the police lights and chaos of investigation. "I hope like hell it was only a prank."

"Me, too." Audrey thought of the panic that the threat had caused. "But whether it was or not, it's still unconscionable."

"Yeah." Affectionate once more, Brett again draped his flannel around her. He bent his knees to give her a cajoling smile. "Forgive me?"

She couldn't quite meet his gaze. "Not much has changed, Brett. You're still a fighter." And he'd still misled her.

As if her stubbornness broke him down, he pretended weak knees.

"Come on, girl." Grinning at her, he straightened again. "At least give me a chance to show you that fighters are nice guys, too."

Not moving away from his nearness, Audrey slanted him a look. "I don't know. The way you acted tonight wasn't very nice."

He rubbed the back of his neck. "You're right. I guess I'm not used to women taking threats in stride."

"I'm a tomboy." She always had been. Panicking was not her m.o. Fixing the issue—that was the course she liked to take whenever possible.

It was also how she'd gotten so involved in WAVS.

"Sexy tomboy," he said, and then his grin faded. "The thing is, Audrey, I'm not going to be the only one to consider you. You were just at the club to protest the SBC. And the guy who called in the threat said he wanted to take out Drew Black and whatever fighters he could."

Devastated, Audrey sucked in a breath. "And you thought that was *me*?"

"Or a guy working for you." Shaking his head in apology, he said, "I know how much you dislike him. And thanks to those flyers we handed out, so does everyone who frequents the club."

"You're right." Good God, she could be a prime suspect. Her stomach went queasy. She looked at the officer and thought about going to him now, to get it out of the way. But he was so busy . . .

"It's cold and it's rainy," Brett told her. "Let me take you home."

Audrey weakened, but she didn't give in. Not entirely. "Thanks, but it's been a crazy night. I need some time to think."

His disappointment showed, but still he opened the car door for her. "No pressure. But Audrey? If you change your mind, I'll be at Havoc's gym most days till five."

And with that, he walked away.

Audrey watched him go with a pang of regret and a wealth of confusion. She understood his allegation; she really did. To most, she'd be a likely suspect. But that didn't make it any easier.

It suddenly dawned on her that Millie had gone too quiet.

"Hey." She touched her arm. "Are you okay?"

Millie nodded, but she looked shaken. "It's so stupid, but it still shakes me up to think about that man."

"Drew Black."

She looked away. "I'm sure he has a lot of enemies, but I can't believe the caller named him as a target." Shaking it off, Millie started her car and put it in drive. "One of these days, he's going to get someone hurt."

Or worse, Audrey thought. One day, Drew Black might get someone killed.

* * *

ANOTHER furtive search amplified frustration; Drew Black was nowhere in the crowd. Why hadn't he been at the bar tonight? And where was he anyway? Off fucking with someone else's life?

His plans changed so often, and he was so unpredictable, sabotaging him wasn't easy.

That just meant the challenge of destroying him would be more fun. And in the end the world would be a better place.

A sound disturbed Gillian, but after being utterly sated from hours of rigorous, mind-blowing sex, lethargy made it impossible to focus. Drew slept wrapped around her with one large hand cupping her breast and his chest hair tickling her back. The heat from his big body added to her lassitude.

Heavenly. Unexpected. And probably foolhardy.

But she didn't care. How could she after what they'd just shared? She'd read about superhot sex, and she'd seen made-up examples in the movies. She'd never thought to experience it firsthand.

The sound came again, nudging at her tired brain until she realized it was a cell phone. Not her ring, so it must be Drew's.

She stirred enough to lift her head, and before she could speak Drew snuggled closer and said, "Ignore it."

A glance at his bedside clock showed it wasn't late. Only about eleven P.M. Gillian smiled. They'd started their sexual marathon before dinner, and though neither of them were used to early nights, they'd both been sleeping soundly.

"It could be important."

He shifted, and his mouth touched her shoulder at the same time she felt him press his erection against her bottom.

"*This* is important." The hand at her breast got busy, cuddling, stroking, exploring as if he hadn't already gotten acquainted with her each and every curve.

Crazy as it seemed, desire started a slow burn inside her. "What if it's Dickey?"

"I'll kill him." Opening his mouth on her nape, Drew sent tingles down her spine. His thumb circled around her nipple, then over it, and the already sensitive peak grew taut.

"Drew . . ." Breathless, she caught his wrist. "Wait."

"I hope that's a joke." With her trying to slow him down, he slid his hand relentlessly along her body until he could press his strong fingers between her legs. "Yeah," he said when he felt her heat and the way she tensed in pleasure. "Definitely a joke."

The phone went silent. With that issue resolved, Gillian tried to move to her back to accept more of Drew's attention, but he forestalled that plan.

"No, I like you like this." And then lower, his voice a growl: "I love your ass." He moved against her until his erection slid along her cleft.

"Drew . . ." He was by far the most sexual man she'd ever met. For him, nothing seemed forbidden as long as she enjoyed it, too.

"You like it doggy style, Gillian? Because I do."

"I don't know." She was far from inexperienced, but her bedroom pleasures had always been less than adventurous. Missionary style with the lights low; never with so much chitchat.

"Yeah? Let's find out." He leaned up to look at her. "Stay put while I get a condom." Hastily he rolled to his side of the bed. Lying on her left side, away from him, Gillian let her mind imagine all sorts of things, like how Drew would look as he handled himself, rolling on the condom. She closed her eyes and resisted the urge to turn and watch him.

In seconds, she heard the nightstand drawer open, the crinkling of a condom packet, and then Drew was back.

Arranging her as he pleased, he wedged one arm under her neck and across to her chest to give his hand access to her breasts. Cupping her knee with his other hand, he urged her right leg higher—and then she felt the head of his penis at her sex.

He didn't enter her right away; instead he slid back and forth, each time making her wetter, more aroused. With every glide she wondered if he'd thrust into her.

He didn't.

"Drew . . . ," she warned.

"In this position," he said, his voice rough, "I can get to your nipples and your clit." As he said it, he did it, tugging on a nipple at the same time he found, and lightly pinched, her clitoris.

"Drew."

"I like how you say my name, Gillian." In one long, strong move, he thrust into her.

The shock of so much sensation all at once overwhelmed her and she moaned. But now that he was in her, he didn't start the friction that they'd both need to come. Instead, he just pressed hard into her—and stayed there.

"Now, isn't this nice?"

It was, but . . . "I need you to—"

"Move? Not yet." He kissed her throat, the sensitive spot where her neck met her shoulder, up to her ear. Sounding gravelly and aroused despite his control, he said, "You wrung me out already, so guess what? I can last for hours now." He rolled her nipple, worked her clit with his thumb, and whispered, *"Hours."*

Oh, God, she'd never be able to take it.

His phone rang again, and again he chose to ignore it. But even in a maelstrom of lust, it worried Gillian. "Do you always get this many evening calls?"

He ignored the question and slid out of her, only to drive back in. Hard.

The bed rocked. Gillian gasped. She forgot about the phone.

He did it again. And again. Each thrust was slow and

solid as he almost pulled out of her and then buried himself deep. And with each thrust, he held on to her nipple, her clitoris.

Far too quickly, Gillian felt herself on the brink. When Drew's phone finally stopped ringing, she reached back and clasped his hip, trying to make him move faster.

"Only drawback with this position," he said, "is that I can't suck on your nipples. Later, maybe after we've showered and gotten something else to eat . . ."

How in the world could he talk right now? Eyes closed and skin dewy, Gillian felt the building of a powerful orgasm pulsing through her nerve endings.

". . . I'll get you to sit on my lap, and let me take from you until I get my fill. What do you think, Gillian? Will you let me have an hour or so just drawing off these soft pink nipples of yours?"

The thought astounded, and stimulated, her. Hours? No, she'd never be able to do that.

"Or how about right here?" He caught her small turgid clitoris between fingers and thumb. Tugging gently, he asked, "You like oral sex, honey? Could I maybe sit between your legs, with them real wide, and suck on you here until you—"

Crying out, Gillian climaxed.

She heard Drew chuckle—*chuckle*—and wanted to strangle him. Later she'd get even. Somehow. She'd have to think about that one. But right now, thoughts were impossible.

He held her close as she came. Toward the end, as a great shuddering moan went through her, she felt him stiffen at her back, felt his hand hard on her hip, keeping her steady for his pounding thrusts.

And he joined her.

They both lay panting, limp. Gillian felt him leave her, and he rolled to his back.

Still breathing fast, he rested a hand on her hip. "I like how you moan, but it does me in."

Trying to think of something to say, Gillian fell to her back, too—and his doorbell rang.

Both surprised, they looked at each other.

Gillian recovered first. "Well, aren't you Mr. Popular tonight? First phone calls, and now a visitor."

His eyes closed for the briefest of time, then frustration took over.

"Son of a *bitch*," he snarled as he launched himself out of the bed. "I don't fucking believe this." He stormed into the bathroom and came back with the condom gone and a towel in his hand. He wrapped it around his hips as he headed out of the bedroom.

"Be right back."

He had no shame at all. "I'm not going anywhere." Gillian knew he didn't hear her because he'd already stomped through the door. She started to worry about Dickey, as he was the obvious choice for interrupting, but then it occurred to her that it could be anyone calling. Getting caught buck naked in Drew Black's bed wouldn't be a smart business move. She all but leaped from the bed.

Forgoing underwear, she stepped into her skirt and was still buttoning her blouse when she crept to the hall to listen in.

Peeking around the corner, she saw Drew look out the window first, and then with a muttered *"What the fuck?"* he opened the door.

A solid, uniformed officer stood there. He must have gone prematurely gray, because he looked to be in his late forties but had a full head of silvery hair. "Drew Black?"

"Yeah." Drew leaned out the door to look beyond the cop. "What's going on?"

"I'm Officer Sparks. Everyone is fine, but there was an incident I'd like to discuss with you."

For Gillian, an officer at the door was a monumental thing, so she couldn't believe it when Drew said, "It's a bad time, Sparks. Can you make it fast?"

The officer's face grew stony. "All right, I'll try to cut to the chase, then." His smile wasn't pleasant. "A bomb threat was called in to Roger's Rodeo."

"No shit?" Drew didn't seem particularly thrown by a bomb threat, either. "Anyone hurt?"

"No. We did a thorough check of the building and found nothing."

"That's great." He propped a shoulder against the door frame. "So why are you at my door?"

"The caller specifically named you as the target for the bomb."

Gillian's automatic gasp drew the officer's attention. He leaned into the entrance to look at her.

Oops. Too late to dart behind the wall as she'd like to do. It was unfortunate that she hadn't tucked in her blouse or retied her scarf to hide the love bite on her neck. Chagrined, she stepped out into the open. "Officer Sparks."

The officer did a quick, automatic once-over before nodding. "Ma'am." He averted his gaze.

Attention lingering on her breasts beneath the white blouse, Drew sent her a chiding glance. Raising a brow, he turned back to the officer. "As you see, I'm a little preoccupied right now."

Pen poised, the officer asked, "And she is . . . ?"

Drew repositioned himself to block Sparks's view of her. "She's none of your business."

Shocked at the disrespect, Gillian gaped at him. "Drew, what in the world is wrong with you?"

Sighing loud enough for his neighbors to hear, Drew pivoted around to face her. "He has a notebook, honey." When she just stared at him, he prompted, "For taking notes?"

Neither the officer nor Gillian understood.

"He's investigating a bomb threat," Gillian reminded him. "I imagine he wants to get his facts straight."

"I'm sure he does." Drew didn't budge an inch. "But I'm the prez of the SBC, and someone apparently sent that bomb threat in my name. Given that everything with me goes public, this will sure as hell hit the Net, and probably the local papers and news stations. Even if the good officer is discreet, you know how jammed Roger's place gets. Lots of folks would have gotten wind of this by now."

"Oh." Drew was trying to protect her. Gillian felt like a fool.

"So tell me, doll, do you really want him to write down your name, give details of how he found you, and share with others what it's pretty clear that we've been doing?"

Her cheeks warmed at his deliberate provocation. "Of course not."

Drew smiled at the cop. "There you go. The lady's keeping mum."

If she had something to throw, Gillian would have lobbed it at his head. How dare he put this all off on her? He didn't want their intimate relationship known either. Sure, she had more to lose. But if the SBC owners found out, Drew could end up fired.

Officer Sparks looked between them with disinterest. "I take it one of you is married, huh?"

Gillian gasped, *"No."* How dare he make such an assumption? Holding up her ringless fingers, she gave the cop a good frown. "It's not like that at all."

Drew silenced Gillian with a single look, and when he gave his attention back to Officer Sparks, his smile turned feral. "Neither of us is cheating, but again: it's *none of your business.*"

Thankfully for Gillian's peace of mind, the officer let it go. "Were you supposed to be at the bar tonight?"

Drew shrugged. It amazed Gillian that he was as at ease in a towel as he was in a suit. "Had planned on it, yeah."

"What happened?"

"You're kidding, right?" He referenced Gillian with a shrug of his head. "I found a better way to spend my evening."

The fib left Gillian uncomfortable. Drew had changed his plans because of Dickey. Getting together with her happened after that. But maybe he had a reason for keeping Dickey out of the equation.

"Were you supposed to meet anyone at the bar?"

"Not a set meeting or anything. Just loose plans to hang out with friends."

"Any of those friends maybe want to see you blown up?" Drew laughed.

Asking the question forefront in Gillian's mind, the officer said, "That's funny?"

Cool, rainy air blew in through the open door, but Drew didn't invite the cop in to extend his visit more comfortably.

"Look, in my position, someone always hates me. Threats are made." He shrugged with indifference. "It comes with the territory."

"How so?"

Holding out his arms, Drew said, "The buck stops here, baby." Then, more seriously, he explained the scope of his responsibilities. "I'm the one who decides if a fighter gets a spot in the SBC or if he gets sent home. I choose the venues, not just here in the States, but in the rest of the fucking world, too. Everyone wants us, but not everyone can have us. So someone's always crying foul play."

Officer Sparks stopped writing to listen.

"I deal with overzealous managers and agents, and the athletic commission. On top of all that, I handle a lot of the press. Every pissant so-called reporter who doesn't get a scoop wants to rip my guts out. And then there are the fanatics who think the sport is too brutal or who—"

Holding up a hand, Sparks cut him short. "Got it. You can be public enemy number one."

Drew's smile showed his lack of concern with the animosity. "Yeah, and sometimes I'm everyone's *best* friend. Just depends on what's going on and who's involved. I can't let any of that shit get to me or I wouldn't be able to do my job. I'm sorry that Roger had the hassle, and I hope it didn't ruin the night for anyone, but what the fuck? You can't expect me to take it seriously."

Gillian held back, but it wasn't easy. Whether or not Drew saw any validity in the threat, it scared her.

The cop considered his attitude. "Actually, as long as I'm taking it seriously, I'd appreciate it if you did, too. So tell me, have any of the haters, past or present, seemed the type to issue a bomb threat?"

"Not really, no. But then I don't exactly go out of my way to understand the mental workings of those who give me grief, you know?"

"Understandable. So who knew about your plans tonight?"

"Just some people in the business. Regular folks."

"You know them all well?"

"Well enough that I wouldn't accuse any of them of being bomb happy."

The officer had several more questions, wrote lots of notes, and finally handed a card to Drew. "If you think of anything, even something that might not seem important to you, give me a call."

Drew tossed it onto a table. "Thanks."

Hands on his hips, Officer Sparks turned to Gillian. "If you want to maintain anonymity, I'd suggest you finish dressing and get out of here. The press was showing up when I left. If the owner of the club, Mr. Sims, mentions any details . . . well, you could end up with reporters at the door instead of me." And with that, he tipped his hat and left.

After he closed and relocked the door, Drew surveyed her and groaned. "You're leaving, aren't you?"

Gillian stared at him in wonder. How could he remain so cavalier? "Most definitely. The sooner, the better." Already on her way back to the bedroom, she shouted, "Get dressed and get me out of here, Drew. Hurry it up."

CHAPTER 8

DESPITE understanding, Drew's mood soured with each minute he got Gillian closer to her car and the official end of their . . . well, not exactly a first date. But a notable night all the same. "This was not how I'd wanted the evening to end."

Face silhouetted by weak moonlight, Gillian kept her gaze out the window. "No?"

"Hell no. I had about a dozen more things I wanted to do." He glanced at her. "To you." His gaze dipped over the prim way she'd folded her hands in her lap, how she crossed her ankles, and the contradiction of that ladylike posture with the way she'd been in bed only stoked the fire. "To that smokin' body of yours."

"Drew, really." But she smiled when she said it.

He saw the slight dimple appear in her cheek. Her mouth . . . damn, but her mouth made him nuts. He shifted uncomfortably. Right now her makeup was more off than on, her hair hung loose, and she'd left off the panty hose.

His fingers flexed on the steering wheel. Her passion matched his, and that was saying something. If this bullshit bomb stuff hadn't happened, she'd have stayed the night, and his imagination went nuts conjuring up ideas of what they would have done, the many ways he would have taken her.

Few cars passed them on the road. The storm had blown past and now a sliver of moon struggled past remnants of dark clouds. Drew had the radio playing low, but he could still hear the hiss of tires on wet pavement. With every breeze, raindrops fell from trees and overhead lines.

Suddenly, she turned to face him. "I detest waiting around for a man to make a move."

Taken aback, Drew asked, "Is there a move I missed? Because, hell, I'm willing."

Exasperation changed her expression. "Will I see you again? Other than with business, I mean."

"Well, hell, I hope so!" Was there a doubt on that one? Had she been sitting there stewing, wondering if this was a one-and-only kind of night?

"Given the circumstances—"

"That stupid bomb business?" Drew locked his teeth. If he ever found the guy responsible, he'd make him pay. "Forget about it, will you?"

"Forget a bomb? No, I don't think so." She pulled one knee up onto the seat. "But you'll probably be under closer scrutiny now. There'll be added risk of us getting caught."

Yeah, because God forbid anyone should know how he makes her scream in the sack. Damn it. He'd had plenty of sexual relationships, but never one where the woman was ashamed of herself for sleeping with him.

"I haven't even come close to getting my fill, Gillian, so don't go there." He turned down the street of the boys' home and went on past it toward the empty gravel lot where Gillian had parked her car. "It's not like we don't have reason to be seen together, you know. You were hired to . . . what? Transform me?"

Her gaze shot to him. "If anyone asks, I'm a publicist, which is true. But also a handler and a—"

"Miracle worker, right?" It still burned his ass to think about it. "Isn't that how you first put it?"

"Drew." She reached across the console and put a hand to his thigh.

Dangerous move, lady.

"I said that before I really knew you."

She thought she really knew him now? After one bout of sex? He flicked his gaze over her. "And now?"

She gave him that small smile again. "As a publicist, I think you have some rough edges that we could smooth down just a *little* bit. As a woman, your sexist attitudes make me nuts." She squeezed his thigh. "As someone who's shared your bed . . . well, words desert me."

Drew laughed. "Liar."

"About what?"

"You know I'm not really sexist and it doesn't really bother you that much."

Her laughing reply got cut short when Drew said, "Fuck."

"What?" She followed his gaze through the windshield and saw her small car illuminated in the headlights. "Oh, my God."

Someone had trashed her little RX8. A shattered side window had let in the rain. White spray paint showed stark against the dark green exterior, across the hood and driver's-side door. The words—*Let the damned go to the devil*—sent a red haze over Drew's vision.

"That's a reference to me."

Gillian didn't hear him. When he stopped, she opened her car door. Moving like a zombie, she made to get out.

He caught her arm. "Are you nuts? Stay put and let me call Officer Sparks."

"Wait." She snatched at his cell phone. "We have to think about this."

In her pretty blue eyes, Drew saw shock, confusion, and hurt. He could tell that no one had ever personally attacked her before and she didn't quite know how to deal with it.

"Read what it says, Gillian. Someone is pissed at you for working with me."

"You . . . you can't know that." But she did stare at her

car to read the sloppily painted message. Slowly, she shook her head in denial. Voice faint, she said, "What does that mean?"

It seemed clear enough to Drew. "I'm the devil someone wants damned."

In quick denial, she said, "Don't be ridiculous." But she didn't look convinced as she continued to stare at the destruction. "Not everything is about you, you know, despite your monumental ego."

Drew appreciated her effort to deflect the accusation, but he knew a real threat—when it was aimed at an innocent like Gillian. "Get real, honey. First the bomb threat, and now someone beats up your car, which was left near a place where you arranged a speaking engagement for me? I just hope whoever did this doesn't know *why* you left the car here. But either way"—he took his phone from her again—"I need to call Officer Sparks."

She groaned and fell back in her seat. "I just know this is going to end up front-page news."

Drew shook his head at her. "Hardly that. I think Sparks can be tactful." When the officer answered, Drew gave him the details. They ended up waiting on Sparks, who arrived twenty minutes later. He took a report, which included getting Gillian's full name and association with Drew, but, as Drew had suspected, not much could be done.

Sparks did caution them to be careful, and he promised that he wouldn't share Gillian's name unless it became absolutely necessary. Right now, it wasn't.

After he left, Gillian wanted Drew to do the same so that she could call for the tow truck—and not be seen with him.

What was he? A scourge? An embarrassment? The devil himself, as the car wrecker presumed?

Gillian's desire to hide her personal interest in him made him nuts, but he still would have obliged if he wasn't worried for her safety. Instead, he called an associate who had a tow truck and asked him to take the car to a garage. No other explanations were necessary.

"Just that easy?" Gillian asked with wonder.

Drew paced around her car, even though he'd already done that with Officer Sparks and even though there wasn't enough light now to see much. "When you're as high profile as I am, it's good to make affiliations with people who don't ask questions. I've worked with that garage before, too. They're good. Your car will be in good hands."

Drew left the key hidden in a designated spot. "Tomorrow you can give the garage a call, tell them it's your car, and you can take over from there with no one the wiser on your social life."

Pleased with that plan, Gillian said, "You're a handy man to know, Drew."

Actually, knowing him was what had gotten her car trashed.

Feeling powerless, he escorted Gillian home.

They rode in silence with her worrying and him stewing until they reached her driveway.

Gillian unhooked her seat belt in a rush. "You don't need to get out."

Because she didn't want to risk anyone seeing her with him. The insults were starting to get under his very thick skin. "Am I allowed to sit here until I see you're safely inside?"

For answer, she craned her neck to look out the rear window, the side windows. "I think it's okay. No one is up and about right now anyway."

Drew's smile started to smart. "Then it's safe for me to do this." Catching her before she could suspect his intent, he brought her closer and stole her gasp with a scorching kiss. As always, she melted in seconds, and soon she had her fingers knotted in his shirt as she tried to get more of him.

The silly woman forgot all about her fear of discovery—but Drew didn't. No matter his reputation, he was a damned gentleman, and she'd made it clear that keeping their relationship under wraps was crucial to her.

Feeling a little like a cad now that he'd made his point,

he released her. Or at least he tried to. When he freed her mouth, Gillian kissed his chin, his throat, and when she took a small love bite of his shoulder, he jumped.

So did his dick.

Better to get this over with now before he lost all reason. Setting her away from him, Drew took a deep breath, but it didn't help all that much. With any luck, he'd get her out of the car before she noticed his boner.

"Gillian?"

"Hmmm?"

He touched her face. "Get some sleep, and think about me."

Big blue eyes blinked at him, widened, and then narrowed. "Those two things do not go hand in hand."

He wasn't sure of her meaning. "Come again?"

"If I think of you, I'll never get any sleep." Leaning in for a soft, quick peck, she destroyed most of the rancor he'd felt; her smile took care of the rest. "Thank you for all your help today, and for being so discreet."

Again, Drew stopped her. He did not want this newest turn to scare her away. "We should cool it for a few days, just in case anyone is keeping track. But I'll be in touch later."

"Okay." She reached for the door.

He stopped her. Again. *Fuck*. "No arguments?"

"I'm not keeping tabs on you, Drew. But I do know you have some out-of-town business coming up this week."

Oh, hell. He'd forgotten all about that. Yes, he kept an insane schedule, but it was so unheard-of for him to forget any of it that he just sat there, staring at her.

She misunderstood his silence. "You're meeting with producers, right? Something about doing a piece on a fighter's background."

How the hell did she know that? He hadn't told anyone, not even Brett Bullman, the fighter they hoped to "uncover."

At his silence, her uncertainty showed, but she tried to put a brave face on it. "It's fine, Drew. Really. I had hoped to meet with you prior to your leaving, to discuss your chest-beating, profanity-ridden style of negotiation, but I suppose that, for better or worse, that's you."

Another fucking insult! Right now, after realizing he'd *temporarily* forgotten a major commitment, he was just out of sorts enough to snap. "How the hell do you think I've survived this long without you spoon-feeding me dialogue?"

As if he hadn't spoken, she continued with her tone now prim, proper, and very detached. "All in all, I'm convinced that, especially in particular forums, your instincts are your best guide." She opened the door. "But I would ask you to remember our deal. You agreed to no public profanity, and I would consider a negotiation with producers to be quite public."

Drew opened his mouth to correct her—and she slammed the car door.

Stubborn woman. Jaw tight, he watched her dig out her keys as she sashayed along the walkway to the front door. She unlocked the door, went inside, and shut it again without a single glance back at him. Lights came on inside. More lights. Drew waited, but everything seemed to be routine.

Just to be sure, he called her on his cell.

She answered with exasperation. "*What*, Drew?"

He meant to say that he was only making sure she got inside okay. Instead, he heard himself say, "We could do dinner the night before I leave." He winced at his own neediness, but it was too late to retreat now. "You know, to go over dos and don'ts."

She hesitated, but then said, "That would be nice. Thank you."

He let out the breath he hadn't known he was holding.

Then she said, "And Drew?"

Caution rose. "Yeah?"

"I'm already thinking of you." She ended the call with a click, leaving Drew smiling, hard, and fucking well enchanted. So even though he'd acted like an ass, Gillian didn't hold a grudge? Good to know.

She wasn't an easy woman, but she wasn't difficult, either.

He liked that about her. Hell, he liked everything about her.

No way in hell would he sit idle while someone fucked with her property. He'd find the guy responsible. As he'd told Gillian, a man in his position needed special associations. For Drew, that included a top-notch investigative group.

DREW stood in the sidelines of Havoc's busy gym, waiting for Brett Bullman to finish up. He paced, cursed to himself, and generally emanated a *Fuck off* vibe to anyone who thought to speak with him.

For more than a week, things had been great. With negotiations, with Gillian, with life. He'd fulfilled a lot of travel obligations, but it didn't tire him, especially not when he had Gillian to think about—and thinking of her had turned into his favorite pastime.

Then Brett had to go and mess up his mojo.

How the hell could Brett refuse?

Most fighters would be all over this type of over-the-top publicity. But as soon as Drew thought it, he saw Havoc talking to Simon Evans, both of them now coaches as well as fighters, sweaty from sparring, and he remembered how private those two had been, too. They were each well known with a broad fan base, but they didn't hog the limelight or seek out attention. Low-key, that described them. Damn good at what they did, confident in their abilities, and secure enough that they never had the need to prove anything—except in a fight.

Fighters could be so damned difficult.

Drew started pacing again. Many of the guys had left for the locker room to shower and change, but not Brett.

Tireless and dedicated, he stayed in the ring, going full steam. He'd been at it for hours, switching up sparring partners several times, and now he went toe to toe with Gregor on his ground game.

He didn't run out of gas.

Amazing. Brett Bullman was the real deal, a natural athlete with a rock-solid work ethic and enough heart to take him to the top. The SBC could capitalize off Brett big time, if he'd only get on board with the program.

Done talking, Simon and Havoc walked over to coach Gregor and Brett as they went through practiced moves, both in stand-up positions and on the ground.

Intrigued with possibilities, Drew watched.

As one of the most gargantuan fighters in the sport, tall, broad, all muscle and core strength, Gregor should have been able to outpower Brett. Gregor was in a weight class over Brett, and he was no slouch. He might be goofy at times, but in the ring, Gregor turned it on and went after his opponent with single-minded intent.

Didn't matter this time.

Brett fended off every attack and launched his own with success. Brett had the kind of speed usually only seen in lightweights. From previous bouts he'd seen on the Internet, Drew knew that Brett was rock jawed, shaking off punches that would have put most down for the count, and his punches landed like sledgehammer blows.

Gregor couldn't best him.

Getting caught up in the excitement, Simon and Dean continued to yell instructions. But now, hoping to even up the fight, it was only Gregor they coached.

Their encouragement had no visible effect.

Brett was a fucking wonder boy.

Only recently had Drew learned about Brett's background. He came from a home so broken it bordered on abuse. As a kid, he had lived part-time on the streets, and then somehow put himself through college. After he saved a little money, the crazy s.o.b. decided to teach himself to fight.

And apparently when Brett decided to do something, he succeeded.

Not many knew about the piss-poor parents he'd had and the neglect he'd suffered. Brett kept that all real private. But the fact that he'd schooled himself off DVDs of other fights wasn't a secret. He'd divulged that much after a win, when the commentator asked him about his training.

Now, even though Brett lacked exposure, he'd made the rounds through smaller venues, annihilating all competition until he'd become an Internet phenom.

Fans loved him.

When they learned of his past and all he'd overcome, they'd love him even more.

After some promotional buildup, Drew wanted to put him in the ring with the best, and he knew, even if Brett didn't win, he'd put on one hell of a fight that the audience would eat up.

With the right press, Brett's first big SBC fight could break the record at the gate.

His was a great human-interest story. It epitomized the sport: how the strong survived, how motivation and heart could never be discounted.

But Brett, damn him, wanted no part of it. Not that Drew would accept his decision. Giving up hadn't gotten him where he was today. Pushing, working deals, convincing others to go along with his marketing schemes . . . that was key. One way or another, he'd get Brett on board.

Finally Simon called a halt to the bout. Gregor spit out his mouthpiece, pulled off his headgear, and bent over with his hands braced on his knees, sucking air.

For half a minute, Brett paced the mat like a caged lion. After he'd worked off the adrenaline, he walked over to Gregor with a smile—and thanked him for "helping him out."

Gregor, still winded, feigned a sucker punch to Brett's jaw, laughed, and then slapped him on the back.

Brett never even flinched. Leaning on the ropes, he talked to Simon and Dean. After asking questions, shadowing a few moves, and taking more instruction, he called it quits.

Brett had that killer instinct that would take him to the top. And he was one hell of a nice guy, to boot. Women would love seeing his background. Men would be inspired—

"He's not going to go for it, you know? You might as well forget it."

Drew hadn't even heard Simon approach. He acknowledged him with a scowl. "Did he tell you that?"

"I heard him tell *you* that."

Someone knocked over the bar to a weight set, making a terrible clatter on the concrete floor. Drew glanced up and found a woman standing there, her eyes rounded and her attention glued to Brett.

Simon leaned around Drew to see her. "Who is that?"

"Hell if I know." Turning back to Brett, Drew watched him as he headed for the shower.

The son of a bitch knew he was there to talk to him, but he was trying to dodge him!

Drew started to go after Brett, but Simon forestalled him.

"Don't be an ass, Drew. Let the man shower off the sweat."

"Is there a back door?"

"Not from the showers, no." Amused, Simon shook his head. "You're relentless."

Taking that as a compliment, not an insult, Drew rolled his shoulders. "A shitty upbringing like his is a fucking fantastic angle, and you know it."

The girl had snuck closer, and at Drew's language, she made a sound of disapproval.

Drew eyed her. Great. Now he'd have Gillian bitching him out about his language again. A gym should be sacred from delicate female ears, damn it.

Simon stepped around him. "Can I help you?"

With a sort of wide-eyed, slack-jawed concentration, her gaze went all over Simon. But then Drew had expected no less. The ladies had fawned over Simon from day one. That was why his fighting name had become "Sublime," something Simon would never shake off.

Right now Simon wore only black boxing shorts, and as physiques went, he was no less than gifted. His hard training had a hand, but a prime draw from the gene pool had played a part, too.

Drew snorted. "Cat got your tongue?"

She snapped to attention—without taking her gaze off Simon. "I was hoping to speak to Brett."

"He just hit the showers," Simon told her. "He'll be out soon. You're welcome to wait."

"Oh . . . okay. Thank you."

Drew studied her with new interest. "Are you Brett's girlfriend?"

"No, I . . ." Her eyes widened again. "Ohmigod. You're Drew Black."

At her tone, a mix of revulsion and awe, Simon crossed his arms and grinned.

The poor girl didn't know which way to look.

If he'd met her before, Drew didn't recall it. No big deal that, because as prez of the SBC, a lot of women tried to align themselves with him. He forgot most of them.

Shrugging at her, Drew said, "Guilty."

To which she replied with sharp disdain, "Most definitely." And then to Simon, "I'm sorry about knocking over that . . . bar thing."

"No harm done."

"Okay, then . . . I'll just wait over there." She pointed to the far side of the gym, well away from them. "Thank you, again."

The second her skinny little uptight butt cleared hearing distance, Simon started laughing. Leaning in close to Drew, he whispered, *"Ohmigod, you're Drew Black!"*

Drew fought a grin. "Shut the fuck up."

Simon slapped him on the shoulder. "I don't think she's a fan, Drew. I think her shock was based more in horror."

"Like I give a shit." He paced around again. "What's keeping Brett?"

"A desire for cleanliness?" When Drew didn't share his sense of humor, Simon gave up on him with a pitying shake of his head. He left for the locker room.

A few fighters emerged, freshly showered and dressed in street clothes. Since Drew still stood there, not looking very busy, they paused to speak to him.

Pasting on his patented smile, Drew joked around, encouraged them, bitched about this and that, and then bid them farewell. Off to the side of the front door, he saw the little blonde looking very uncomfortable as she waited for Brett.

She kept sending him cross looks as she, too, paced. With each step, a ponytail bounced and swished. The late March day had brought a taste of early summer, with clear skies, moderate temps, and no wind, so the girl wore light clothes. A cotton football jersey hung loose over skinny jeans and frayed canvas sneakers.

With a jaded scrutiny, Drew decided she was probably cute enough to entice Brett. Too bad she seemed to have an aversion to him already, or he might have enlisted her to help him sway Brett to his way of thinking.

Drew caught himself and scowled. *Screw that.* Never before had he needed a woman to help him accomplish jack-shit. It was Gillian's bad influence, making him think such things.

And now that he'd thought of her, that familiar coil of desire tightened inside him.

Their damned dinner before his departure had ended without a recap of their sexual escapades. He hadn't exactly asked her back to his place, and she hadn't exactly turned him down.

It was more like both of them were being circumspect. But damn it, he already craved a repeat. Soon.

Somehow he'd have to work it out.

Finally, when Drew's patience neared an end, Brett pushed through the locker room door. Hair still wet, dressed in jeans and a plain white T-shirt, he headed across the gym with single-minded determination.

He didn't look at Drew, and when he got close, he beat Drew to the punch, saying, *"No."*

Unacceptable. "You're giving up a great fucking opportunity."

Without breaking stride, Brett shrugged.

Drew followed him. "This is your chance to make a big entrance, damn it. The public will fucking *saint* you once they know everything you've overcome."

Through his teeth, Brett said, "I don't want to be sainted."

"We can use your background to build up the hype like never before. I'm talking network coverage. ESPN. The whole shebang."

His expression darkening even more, Brett said again, *"No."* He pushed through the front door, and Drew went after him.

Outside the gym, the setting sun painted the skies crimson and nearly blinded him. Drew held up a hand to block the glare.

Brett pulled on mirrored sunglasses and kept going.

Drew halted. He'd be damned before he'd chase after a new fighter. Putting his hands on his hips, he shouted to Brett's back, "For God's sake, man. Everyone has a bad relative or two."

Brett froze with his back to him; his shoulders went rigid.

At least he had his attention, Drew thought. "People will relate to what you went through. The drunken father, the mother in prison—"

Brett jerked around. In a deadly low tone, he said, "Shut up, Drew."

Uh, yeah. Drew took Brett's measure and knew he was truly enraged. Maybe he shouldn't have mentioned his parents' situation . . .

"I mean it, Drew." Brett inhaled, seeking control. "My past and everyone in it is off-limits."

"It's the perfect angle."

"Find another fucking angle."

Drew took a turn reaching for control. "This is the one we can capitalize on. So make up your mind: do you want to be part of the SBC or not?"

Shoving the sunglasses to the top of his head, Brett came closer. He was definitely angry, but mostly astounded. "You're telling me that if I don't do this, you won't give me a contract?"

Not really, but if that'd work . . .

Drew sized him up. In one hand, Brett held his gym bag. His other hand was fisted at his side. But he knew fighters well enough to gauge things. Brett Bullman wasn't the type to start brawling in the street. A major factor in any fighter's success was great control. Brett had it in spades.

He might walk away, but he'd worked too damn hard for this to ruin it by pulverizing Drew.

Confident of his position, bearing his own annoyance, Drew put his hands on his hips. "How bad do you want this, Brett?" His expression didn't change. "I can make you a fucking star. I can get you sponsors out the ass. I can make your name synonymous with the sport so that—"

"Not happening." Shaking his head, Brett leaned in to say, "No one dictates my personal life to me, Drew. Not you, not anyone." He settled back again. "If it requires you digging around in my past for me to get signed on, then I guess I don't want the SBC all that much after all."

And to Drew's astonishment, Brett turned and walked away.

He barely noticed the little blonde trotting after him. Feeling like an ass, Drew was about to go after Brett, too, when from behind him, Gillian said, "Gee, Drew, that went well."

CHAPTER 9

D REW swung around to see Gillian standing right behind him.

Surprise faded under appreciation.

Wow.

Wearing slim-fitting dark blue designer jeans, lethal high-heel strappy sandals, and a body-hugging sweater with little white pearl buttons up the front, she looked like a fashion statement. She'd opened enough of those pearl buttons to show off some tantalizing cleavage.

"Gillian." Drew couldn't keep his gaze from going all over her. "What the hell are you doing here?"

"Offering sarcasm, of course." She started tsking at him. "Drew Black, whatever has gotten into you? You were *threatening* Brett."

Running a hand over his head, then rubbing the back of his neck, Drew said, "More like coercing, but yeah, it didn't work." Again he looked at those jeans, how they showed off her voluptuous hourglass figure. She personified sexy. Could a woman be more enticing?

Smiling over his attention, Gillian put one hand on a hip and struck a pose for him.

With business at hand, Drew tried to hide the instantaneous combustion of heat inside him. He glanced back at Brett. "Now I'm going to have to go after him, and I hate when that shit happens."

Gillian's smile did wonders for his bad mood. "You dug that hole yourself, and you know it." She tipped her head to study him. "But before you remedy things, I want to talk to you, and I do not want you to overreact."

Oh, hell. Anticipating a situation that might put him over the edge, Drew stepped closer and whispered, "Are you commando today?" He remembered her promise about skipping her underwear, and today, with those sexy jeans clinging to her ass, would have been the perfect timing. "If so, I make no promises about not overreacting."

Her laugh mocked him. "Don't be silly, Drew. Now stop staring at my clothes and listen to me."

"It's the body under the clothes, babe." Again in a whisper, he growled, "I would so do you right now."

"Drew!"

"I would." And lower still: "I've missed doing you, Gillian."

Color tinged her cheeks, but whether from embarrassment or interest, Drew couldn't tell.

"That's enough." She glanced around, specifically toward where Brett and the petite blonde chatted. "Now behave, please, and listen to me. This is important."

"You have my attention." Hell, she'd had it from the first second he saw her.

As if from nervousness, Gillian's tongue slicked over her lips. "You're aware of the organization WAVS?"

Wariness crept up Drew's spine. He had hoped that Gillian wouldn't hear about his questionable verbal demolition of one of the WAVS' spokeswomen. Wondering how much she knew, he said, "I am—but I didn't think you were."

Gillian leveled a look on him. "I was hired to give your

reputation a boost, so of course I've researched you and everything that concerns you. Right now would be a good time for me to remind you about your promise to behave in public. No cursing, no shouting . . ."

Drew waved that off. "The shit with Brett just spilled out of the gym, that's all. Besides, there isn't any press around to overhear me."

"Maybe not, but a secondhand account from a passerby can't be ruled out."

"A secondhand account of *what*?"

Gillian sighed. "You see the lovely young lady who's speaking with Brett?" She touched Drew's arm. "That's Audrey Porter, none other than the founder of WAVS—"

"Oh, shit." The last thing he needed was some wacky broad taking advantage of a tense situation. He doubted that she or anyone else could talk Brett out of fighting, but anything Brett said might end up plastered on the Internet. So far the WAVS group had been a big pain in his ass. He didn't want to feed them stuff to gossip about.

Drew started in Brett's direction.

"Drew Black, stop right there!"

Halting in midstep, Drew did a slow about-face. That Gillian would dare to take him to task on a public street left him thunderstruck. He was incredulous more than enraged, but the two emotions must have looked the same, given Gillian's wary expression.

"Now Drew . . ." She quickly moderated her tone until it almost sounded cajoling. "I'm trying to keep you from digging that hole deeper."

"By ordering me around?" Mere inches from her, he crossed his arms. "That could maybe work in bed. Hell, I might even enjoy it." His eyes narrowed, and he left no room for negotiation in his tone. "But you have to stay out of my business."

With a sound of exasperation, Gillian took his arm and pulled him back a few feet for added privacy. "I'm sorry," she said as soon as she felt they wouldn't be overheard. "I don't want you to lose your job, and another vicious attack on anyone in WAVS will most definitely make news. Fran won't like it, and you know what that means."

"Yeah, another woman bitching at me."

Anger flashed in her eyes. "Maybe if you'd behave like a civilized human being, instead of an ill-bred beast, women wouldn't find it necessary to *reason* with you."

Her voice rose with every word. Was that what she called reasoning? Because they were on a public sidewalk, and because she had a very real aversion to anyone knowing they were an item, Drew couldn't grab her up and kiss her.

But he wanted to. Bad.

Eyeing her heaving breasts, he asked, "Are you free?"

The change of subject threw her. "What? When?"

"Now." Drew shook his head. "Five minutes from now, actually, after I make things right with Brett."

"Are you joking?"

"No, so hurry up and make up your mind. Brett could leave any minute, and I don't want him filling that woman's head with trash talk about me."

"Warranted trash talk, but . . . yes, I'm free." Bearing no signs of her previous annoyance, she tipped her head and looked at his mouth. "What did you have in mind?"

Desire put a death grip on him. "Oh, honey, if you knew what I was thinking . . ." With new motivation to get the current mess settled, Drew held open the door to the gym. "Go on in and make yourself at home. I'll be done in a minute." And with that, he turned, calling out to Brett at the same time.

AFTER that awful confrontation with Drew, Audrey almost didn't announce herself. Only her need to reassure Brett kept her from slipping away unnoticed. "Brett?"

At the sound of her voice, he jerked around and stared at her. "Audrey?" Stunned, he dropped his gym bag by a big black truck and pulled off the mirrored sunglasses. "What are you doing here?"

Though she'd watched him fighting and knew he'd taken some hits, Audrey couldn't stop staring at him. He'd worn protective gear part of the time, and still he had bruises and mat-burn everywhere. The bridge of his nose looked swollen, and there was a purple swelling beneath one eye.

Tension hummed from his body; his muscles looked bigger, pumped up.

He didn't appear happy to see her.

Her confidence waned. "I . . . I wanted to talk, but . . ."

"Now's not really a good time."

Acknowledging that, she nodded. So should she just say good-bye and walk away? She tried to smile, but it fell flat. "I'll just . . . um . . ."

Propping his hands on his hips, Brett dropped his head to stare at the ground. He seemed to be struggling with himself. Mouth grim, he looked up at her again.

And Drew Black called out to him.

Brett's narrowed gaze went beyond her, and he muttered low, "Shit."

"Hold up," Drew called. "Give me just a minute, okay?"

Stride forceful, Brett met him partway. "No, it's not okay. I'm done."

"No way in hell do I believe or accept that." Drew half smiled. "Come on, Bullman, you're too fucking good to let me run you off over one disagreement, and you know it."

"Lady present," Brett admonished. "Watch your mouth."

They both looked at her, and Audrey felt horribly conspicuous. "Oh, no, that's fine. I'll give you two some privacy—"

Reaching out to snag her arm, Brett kept her from moving away. "Stay. Drew can check his language for short periods." His smile taunted. "Isn't that right, Drew?"

Offering his hand, Drew said, "I'm completely domesticated when need be. Drew Black, and you are . . . ?"

As if he didn't already know. Audrey put up her chin and took his hand. "Audrey Porter."

After all the Internet buzz, he had to know her name, but he didn't acknowledge it.

"Great. Nice to meet you, Ms. Porter." He dropped her hand and turned back to Brett. "Why don't we work this out? Man to man. I'm sure we can find a compromise—"

"No compromises." Putting his head back, Brett looked down his nose at Drew. "If my fighting skills aren't enough for you, I'll look elsewhere."

"Like where?" Exasperated, Drew's brows pulled down. "You know other MMA sports associations can't compete with the SBC. They can't give you the same exposure, or the same level of pay."

"True." Brett folded his arms over his chest. "But I can beat anyone you have, and you know it. The way I see it, whoever I go with can set up some blockbuster publicity by pitting their organization against the SBC."

Drew went blank. "A challenge?"

"Made publicly." Brett stared him in the eyes. "You'll be almost forced to accept. And the exposure will be good for me, and for whatever organization I'm with."

Nonplussed, Drew rocked back on his heels. "That's fucking brilliant."

On a long sigh, Brett reminded him, "Language, Drew."

"Oh, right." He scowled at Audrey, as if the slipup were her fault. "Sorry." Then back to Brett, "But it is. Brilliant, I mean."

Audrey could see Drew's mind working, and it maddened her. Did Drew Black *ever* stop maneuvering?

"Except," Drew said, working through details aloud, "I want you in the SBC. I can crush the competition—not that there's much there, you know. You'll be way better off with us, trust me. But I like your approach. I can see it working."

Relaxing a little, Brett draped an arm around Audrey's shoulders.

Absorbing his touch, her eyes closed for only a moment. He was so warm, his arm heavy and solid. Being near him like this satisfied something deep inside her, something she didn't know was hungry until she'd met Brett.

Being away from him recently had been awful. She

hadn't known him long, but she'd missed him as if he'd always been a necessary part of her life. Never before had that happened to her. Long ago, she'd dated, and she'd even had a few more serious relationships.

But she hadn't felt like this, the way she felt only with Brett.

Relishing the familiarity, Audrey looped an arm around him, too, then slid her hand into his back jeans pocket and leaned into his side.

Brett went still in surprise. She felt his muscles clench, his arm tighten. Glancing down at her, he studied her and came to some decision.

"Is that it, Drew?" With sudden urgency, he tried to wrap up their discussion. "I need to get going."

"What?" Drew focused on them again. "Yeah, as long as you're not still pissed, we're good. Let's set something up. I'll call you, okay?" And before Brett could specify terms, Drew added, "Private life is private, got it. I'll do up a contract and get in touch."

Brett considered it, but finally nodded. "All right."

Pointing at him, Drew said, "This is the real thing, Brett. You need a manager, you know that, right? Talk to Havoc or Simon about it."

"Already did."

Drew grinned. "Great." He looked over his shoulder at the gym, and impatience showed in his hurried speech. "Okay, then. Glad we could get that settled. You two take care, now."

As he walked away, Brett shook his head. Turning to her, he smoothed a hand over her hair, wrapped her ponytail loosely around his hand. "You okay?"

He looked so intent and serious that Audrey wasn't sure what he meant. He was the one who'd sustained bruises in practice, and who'd just been in a confrontation with Drew Black. "I'm fine. Why?"

He waggled her head a little. "You have a history with Drew. I wasn't sure if seeing him would upset you."

"Oh." She scowled at Drew as he paused at the street,

checked the traffic, and then jogged over to the gym. "I don't think I'll ever like him, but he doesn't intimidate me, if that's what you mean."

His half smile made her heart flip. "Fearless, huh?"

She lifted her chin. "I would never back down from a bully." Touching a scrape on his chin, she asked, "Brett, are you sure you want to fight for him?"

Dismissing her concerns, he said, "It's not really for him. It's for the SBC." He caught her wrist and tugged her along to his truck. "And what he said is true. If I want to make this a career, and I do, then the SBC is the best way to go."

Audrey bit her lip. "What he said about your past—"

"Forget it." He stopped by the passenger's door. "Did you drive here?"

Audrey had heard enough to know that Brett had not had an easy life. An alcoholic father and a mother who'd earned prison time . . . she couldn't imagine. He was such a nice man, and so polite to women, that she had assumed he had great role models around to influence him.

Thinking of how his past still hurt him left her hurting, too. "I took a bus."

"Car in the garage again?"

"No, but I was sort of hoping you wouldn't be busy, and we could—"

Leaning down, Brett kissed her. Against her mouth, he murmured, "Yeah, we can."

Oh, God, already her heart beat double time and her pulse fluttered. She fisted her hands in his shirt. "I missed you, Brett."

Pausing, his green eyes going dark, he groaned and kissed her again. They were shielded behind his truck, but still in a public location. But it didn't matter.

Audrey put her arms around him and ran her hands up his broad, hard back. He was so solid, it left her breathless. She loved the feel of his hard body beneath the soft cotton T-shirt.

For his part, Brett turned his head a little and kissed her

more deeply. His tongue sank in, stroked and, with near desperation, he slid his hand up to her left breast.

Audrey froze, but Brett didn't.

He groaned again as he cuddled her, held her breast in his palm, and found her nipple with his thumb.

Her knees felt shaky. "Brett . . ."

Jerking away, he said, "Let's go somewhere, Audrey." Heat colored his high cheekbones. "Right now."

He needed her, so she wasn't about to deny him. She breathed so hard, she could barely form a coherent reply. "My apartment is . . . is close."

At her agreement, his jaw clenched. "No misunderstandings, Audrey. I want to have sex with you."

For reasons she didn't understand, his clarification made her lips twitch into a smile. "I know."

He opened the truck door and said, "Get in."

While she fastened her seat belt, he jogged around to the driver's side. Once behind the wheel, he asked, "My place okay instead?"

"I guess." She studied the severe lines of his expression in profile. "Why?"

"Spice is waiting on me."

She went still. "Spice?" Who the heck . . .

"My cat." He put the truck in gear and pulled onto the road. "She's a possessive thing and misses me when I'm gone. She knows when I'm due home, and she's always at the door, waiting. She's been home alone all day already."

Audrey couldn't take it in. "You have a cat? Seriously?" Somehow that didn't fit the picture of a big, buff athlete like Brett.

"You don't like animals?"

"I do, but . . ." A big dog, now that would have seemed more commonplace for a man of Brett's abilities.

"She's been with me since she was a tiny puff of fur." He held out a hand, palm up. "She used to be able to sit right there, in my palm. I think she only weighed a few ounces."

From sexually amped up to talking about his cat with

such deep affection, Brett Bullman was an amazing man. "Where did you get her?"

"Found her." A memory tightened his hands on the steering wheel. "I was working as a bouncer in a bar, and after close, I helped clean up the place. I stepped out back to an alley, to dump some trash in the bins back there, and there she was. Thick with fleas, eyes all gooey, barely able to walk."

Her heart clenched. "Oh, how awful."

"Someone dumped her there. If I'd found the guy . . ." He let that threat drop off. "I wrapped her up in my shirt and took her into the bar." Flashing a grin, he said, "The owner had a fit, but what was I going to do?"

"You took care of her?"

"Well, yeah. I wasn't going to just let her die." He shifted his shoulders in discomfort. "I have no use for idiots who mistreat animals."

Remembering some of what she'd heard Drew say, Audrey rested a hand on his thigh. Had Brett ever had a pet as a boy? "How long have you had her?"

"Five years now." He chuckled with the memory. "I smuggled that cat into the bar every night, and I fed her during my breaks, when I should have been doing my papers."

"Papers?"

Another shrug. "For college." He glanced at her and explained. "I worked at the bar nights and weekends to help pay my way through school. Took me a little longer that way, so I didn't get my degree until I was damn near twenty-three."

Working nights, weekends, and college classes? Not many could handle that. Audrey couldn't help but wonder why a man with an education would choose to be a fighter. "What was your major?"

"Business." Sheepish, he grinned again. "I had thought to do some kind of suit-and-tie gig. I don't know, just . . . because. To prove I could, maybe, you know? And if I didn't make it as a fighter, I'd have that to fall back on. But

I'd always been an athlete, and I like being physical, so MMA is a good fit for me."

There was so much she didn't know about him. "Who taught you to fight?"

"I did." Covering her hand on his thigh with one of his own, he smoothed his thumb over her knuckles. "I'm analytical. Always have been. It's why I'd be good in business and in sports. I can look at things and see why they do or don't work. I'd watch a fight, see what moves the fighters used, and then copy them."

The discoloration under his eye worsened. "I can't imagine why anyone would enjoy getting hit."

That brought a gruff laugh from him. "It's not that I like getting clobbered. But I do like fending off a hit. I like testing my strength and endurance. After a fight, win or lose, I feel more alive."

"I watched you in the gym."

He shot her a surprised look. "I'm sorry I didn't notice you."

"It was . . . brutal."

"That was just practice, Audrey."

"You're still beat up."

He laughed. "Woman, you're insulting my ego. I am not beat up. But with any sport, you get banged around a little during practice and sparring. Believe me, I got worse than this in high school and college sports."

Audrey was so attuned to what he told her that she almost missed it when he turned toward an impoverished neighborhood. He caught her quick look around and apologized.

"Sorry. I haven't been in town long enough to look for more permanent housing. The place where I'm staying is close to Havoc's gym, lets me have Spice, and stays out of my business." Flexing his hands on the wheel, he said, "If you'd rather not be here—"

"I'm with you." Smiling with sincerity, she smoothed a hand over his shoulder. "I feel totally safe."

That gave him pause. "I'm glad." He pulled up in front

of a four-family brick house and parked on the street. Turning toward her, he used his pinky to smooth back a few strands of hair that had escaped her ponytail. "I wouldn't let anyone hurt you, Audrey."

"I know."

He looked beyond her and grinned. "There, in the second-story window? You can see Spice." He opened his door. "She's waiting for me."

Audrey looked out the passenger window and saw the cat's silhouette on the inside sill. When Brett opened her door, she stepped out. "Does she like visitors?"

"Haven't been any since we moved here, but she's a social creature. She won't mind you."

So he hadn't brought any other women to his home? Given how she already felt about him, Audrey was glad to know it.

Several young men, maybe in their late teens and early twenties, loitered on the poured concrete porch, smoking and drinking beer. Brett only nodded to them as he led her to the door.

"Dude, when you fightin' again?"

He paused with a theatrical groan. "I told you guys, I don't know yet."

"Been forever, man. Why's Drew Black draggin' his damned feet?"

"Yeah," another one said. "If the man had any sense, he'd get you out there."

After an apologetic smile to Audrey, Brett turned to the young men. "Drew's a businessman, and the SBC is a business. That means everything has to be legal. Takes a little time, you know?"

One of the older boys drew on his cigarette, then flicked the butt into the yard. "There's a fight going down at the club on Saturday. You should enter."

Hearing that stole Audrey's breath. An unsanctioned, unsupervised brawl meant that things could easily get out of hand. There'd be no one to enforce fair play, no rules. *No holds barred.*

Her vision narrowed and her chest hurt. Boys could get hurt, or even . . . killed. She had to do something.

Stepping away from her, Brett went deadly serious in an instant. "What club?"

"Paulie's, down on Minton Street. Out in the back alley after closing." He pushed away from a porch roof column. "If you enter, I'll bet on you."

"Me, too." Saluting with a beer can, another young man said, "You'd kill 'em all."

"Brett," Audrey breathed, barely able to get a word past the restriction in her chest. He couldn't be thinking of taking part in something so—

He took her hand and squeezed her fingers. "Cops don't know about this?"

One of the boys snorted. "Hell no." He threw his beer can like a basketball into a broken flowerpot in the yard. "The 5-O would break that shit up."

"Right." Brett looked at each of them. "I'll have to pass, but you guys have fun."

Groaning complaints followed Audrey and Brett into the foyer. When Audrey started to speak, he shook his head and gave her a look. "Not here."

Numbness pervaded her limbs on the climb to the second story. Somehow she had to stop the fight. She just wasn't sure what to do yet.

How offended would Brett be if she called the police?

"Take a breath, Audrey. It'll be okay. Trust me." He dug keys out of his pocket and stopped in front of a thick wooden door. A rhythmic "pat, pat, pat" sounded from inside his apartment.

"That's Spice scratching on the door," he told her. "Let me grab her so she doesn't slip out on me."

One hand on the doorknob, he bent before pushing the door open—and scooped up a slinky multicolored cat who meowed her pleasure with ear-splitting delight.

Brett moved into the apartment and held the door open for Audrey. "Come on in."

Almost robotic, Audrey stepped in. He closed and locked the door behind her.

Her thoughts skittered about until Brett cupped the back of her neck and drew her in for a warm, soft kiss.

Blinking at him, she tried to decide what to say.

He smiled and lifted the cat up to his chest to scratch under her chin. "Don't worry so much. I'll take care of it."

"It?"

"The fight." He nudged her toward a seat, then dropped down beside her. The cat left his lap to investigate her.

Audrey liked animals, so she stroked the cat's back and was rewarded with a deep, rumbling purr.

Stretching an arm out along the back of the sofa, Brett settled in close to her. She hadn't noticed when he got out his cell phone, or when he'd put in a call.

With the phone to his ear, he kissed her temple, her jaw. Someone answered his call, and he eased back from her to say that he wanted to report an upcoming illegal fight at a nearby bar.

He must have been put on hold, because he went back to seducing Audrey.

"Street fights can be dangerous," he said between light kisses that left her skin tingling. "Someone drinks too much and decides he's Superman. Drugs blunt pain so you don't realize how badly you're hurt, or how much you're hurting someone else. There aren't any medics on hand to monitor things."

She knew that only too well.

Just then, his call was picked up again, and Brett leaned forward to relay the details of the fight. He chose not to give his name, but did share what he knew. He thanked the officer on the phone and, after shutting off the call, put the cell phone back in his pocket.

"Thank you."

"What?" He settled back in the seat again. "You think you're the only one who doesn't like street fighting?" He drew a hand along the cat's back, then transferred it to her waist.

She felt caged in—and liked it. "So you don't approve?"

"'Course not." Somehow he got his hand under her shirt, to her bare skin. His thumb stroked along her ribs, almost touching the bottom of her breast.

Voice low, somehow soothing, he said, "Those fights are nothing like the professional bouts put on by legitimate MMA organizations." He nuzzled her jaw. "The cop on the phone said he'd check into it."

Just like that? No arguments, no misunderstandings. She should have known, should have trusted him. Brett wasn't a thickheaded lout with no understanding of danger.

The cat let out a loud "Rowwrrr," making Brett chuckle.

"Stay put while I feed her, and I'll be right back."

As soon as he said it, Spice launched herself off Audrey's lap and loped into the tiny kitchenette. Brett followed, leaving Audrey with the opportunity to familiarize herself with his home.

When they'd first entered, she'd been under a barrage of emotional memories. Seeing those young men with their cocky attitudes and reckless disregard for danger had hit home in a big way. Their love of bloodshed could be deadlier than any of them guessed.

But she didn't want to dwell on the past right now. She wanted to focus on Brett and how unique it felt to be with him like this.

The sofa was cushy beneath her, threadbare on the arms, but clean. One old leather lounge chair sat in front of a modest television with a crate beside it for an end table. There were no lamps, just old-fashioned ceiling lights.

A modern, covered cat box dominated one corner of the room.

A trunk holding gym paraphernalia sat in the other corner, along with a set of weights on the floor.

The kitchenette was separated from the TV area by a two-seater bar. No room for a dining table. Down a short hall she saw two doors, and she assumed one would be his bathroom, the other . . . his bedroom.

Leaving her purse behind on the sofa, she wandered

toward the hall. A small distance away, Brett spoke with the cat just like he would a baby. She found it endearing that he pampered his pet as easily in front of her as he did alone.

All in all, his home was ultraorganized, clean, sparse, and barren of even a single photograph.

Based on Drew Black's comments about his childhood, he might not want any mementos. More than anything, Audrey wanted to make a difference in his life. She wanted to ease the bad memories from his past, to help heal any hurts he might still suffer.

She wanted . . . to love him.

Feeling far too brazen and wicked, Audrey went down the hall and opened the first door. His black-and-white-tiled bathroom smelled of shaving cream. She breathed in the scent, and her desire tightened.

Already Brett had made a difference in her life. Without even knowing her past, he had helped alleviate the pain of memories. By being himself, he made her doubt her perceptions about fighting and the motivation of fighters. She had a lot of reevaluating to do.

But for now, she craved to know more about him, physically, emotionally.

Intimately.

Heart thudding in slow, heavy beats, Audrey went to the next door and pushed it open. A full-size bed dominated the room, accompanied by a dresser and one nightstand. Fading light spilled through a window on an opposite wall. He'd left it open enough to keep the air cool.

Brett had tidied the room by smoothing out the sheet and a colorful, worn quilt. The dresser held some change, a few receipts, and nothing else.

Drawn to the bed, Audrey went into the room. She sat on the edge of the mattress and put her palm on one of the two pillows, where she imagined Brett would lay his head.

When she heard the door click shut again, she looked up, and Brett stood there, watching her. Saying nothing, he walked to the dresser and took out his wallet, his keys. He turned back to her and, still silent, reached over his shoulder for a fistful of shirt. He pulled it off over his head and dropped it to the floor.

God Almighty, the man had such a fine body.

Audrey's pulse sped up when he unbuckled his belt and slid it free of the loops in his jeans.

If he shed his pants right here, right now, she'd probably embarrass herself with her enthusiasm.

To her mingled disappointment and relief, he didn't. He took off his shoes and socks and came to stand by her, his bare feet braced apart. One hand touched her chin, and the other hung loose at his side.

She was eye level with the most remarkable set of abs she'd ever seen *and* a definite erection beneath his fly. Her mouth went dry.

CHAPTER 10

STROKING his fingertips over her jaw, her lips, Brett
gentled her nervousness and her racing need. He
stepped closer and leaned toward her to remove the band
holding her hair in a ponytail. It slipped free, and he moved
his fingers through her hair.

"So pretty."

She'd always been a tomboy with no interest in fashion,
makeup, or the latest hairstyle. But Brett made her feel
feminine—and more. And because he still stood there,
taking his time, her natural modesty waned.

Putting both hands flat on his abdomen, she explored
his taut skin and the incredible warmth of his body. A tantalizing trail of dark hair led from his navel down into the
waistband of his faded jeans.

The muscles tightened beneath her palms, and his hands
stilled. She heard his indrawn breath before he deliberately
relaxed again. Cupping the back of her head, he tilted her
face up to meet her gaze.

"Whatever you want, Audrey, I'm game."

Such an offer.

She knew exactly what she wanted, she really did. It had never appealed to her before, but now, with Brett . . . *definitely.*

Just thinking it tightened her womb and made her nipples stiffen. Biting her bottom lip, she popped open the snap on his jeans. His nostrils flared, his mouth firmed, but he didn't move.

Freeing herself of his gaze, she gave her attention to her task. Carefully, without haste, she dragged down his zipper. Through snug black boxers, she could see the size and shape of his straining penis. She dragged the backs of her knuckles over him and felt the tension in his body tighten.

He locked his knees and cupped her head in both hands.

Audrey pushed his jeans down to midthigh and at the same time, leaned forward to breathe in the rich musk scent of his arousal. Forehead against his abdomen, she put her lips to his erection.

Brett gave a low, muffled groan and his hands clenched in her hair, but quickly loosened again. "Damn, Audrey." He caressed her hair, encouraged her. His deepened voice, the way he touched her, even the way he held himself, told her how much this excited him.

And that excited her. For the first time, she understood the power women had over men—and she loved it.

Anxious to further explore this new aptitude, Audrey pushed down his boxers, too, then pressed him back a step. With the enticing image of supplication in her mind, she slid off the bed to her knees before him.

A short, hungry sound came from deep in his throat, and Brett again stiffened his knees.

Excitement left her trembling. He was so hard, throbbing, and thick. A drop of precum glistened on the head of his erection, tempting her.

She wrapped a fist around him, holding him still in one hand while with the other, she palmed the taut muscles of his rear. Everything about him was perfect and masculine and so stimulating to her senses.

She licked her lips as she looked at him and, impatient, Brett urged her forward.

Audrey didn't think about what he might expect, or how to tease him further, or even about the proper way to do it. This was her moment of pleasure; she gave in to her own hunger and, after one long lick that ran along his length and ended at the crown, she drew him deep into her mouth.

His harsh groan vibrated in the quiet of the room.

Wildly excited by the taste of him, Audrey enjoyed his rich scent and his reaction. He guided her, groaning anew each time she drew him in, shaking as she pulled back. She put both hands on his backside and let him have her mouth, let him dictate the depth and speed and—

"God, that's enough." Brett went rigid, fighting himself more than her. Breathing hard, he started to pull back.

But Audrey didn't want him to.

This was her first time taking a man in her mouth, and she wanted everything.

She clenched her fingers in the muscles of his butt and slicked her tongue around him.

"Audrey . . ."

He sounded in pain and, loving it, she licked him again, swallowing more of him.

For two seconds of suspended time, he hesitated, and then he gave up. His big hands curved around her head and he drew her in close again, eased her back, brought her in again.

Each time, his breathing rasped, and Audrey felt him throbbing in her mouth.

"Audrey," he growled as she took him deep. "Suck on me. *Hard.*"

That command was almost enough to push Audrey over the edge, too. Feeling wickedly sensual, she did as he instructed, and he lost it. Fitting his thumbs into her hollowed cheeks, he let himself go.

His taste was unique to her, hot and salty. When his release ended, he dropped his head forward and petted her in a leisurely, affectionate way, stroking along her hair, her cheek. Audrey didn't want to let him go. But now when she licked, he flinched as if it were too much, so she finally eased away and rested her cheek against his hip.

He reached down for her arm and tugged her to her feet. Green eyes glittering, warm with emotion, and soft with release, he stared at her.

Audrey licked her still-tingling lips.

Smiling crookedly, he touched his thumb to the corner of her mouth. After another beat of time, he shook his head on a small laugh. "I have to tell you, Audrey, that was one hell of a nice surprise."

He sounded gruff, and Audrey blushed. "I'd never done that before."

Maybe he could tell, because he didn't question her. He just bent for a kiss and then tumbled her into the bed with him. "Now I need a minute to recoup."

He'd sprawled on his back with his jeans and shorts still at his knees. Audrey scrambled up. She couldn't imagine ever tiring of looking at him. Now his penis was semisoft, and for whatever reason, that appealed to her, too.

While she cuddled him in her hand, she bent to kiss his chest, those sexy abs, the tops of his thighs. She went off the bed to stand at his feet so she could finish stripping him.

He came up to his elbows, and that position sent new muscles bunching and flexing.

She sighed.

Shaking his head at her, Brett laughed and said, "You, too, hon."

Distracted with his body, now fully bare before her, Audrey glanced at him in confusion.

"Take off your clothes, Audrey. I want to look at you, too."

In all honesty, she admitted, "I don't look as good as you."

His wicked grin and mussed hair only heightened his physical appeal. "Let me be the judge of that, okay?" And when she didn't immediately start stripping, he sat up and drew her between his knees.

The man had no modesty at all, but then, looking like he did, why should he?

She, on the other hand, didn't enjoy the idea of being exposed, especially with comparisons at hand: him looking like a God, and her oh so average.

In one easy, practiced move, he pulled her shirt up and off over her head.

Cool air touched her skin; the heat of his gaze burned her. "This is awful." Even with his fascination plain, Audrey wanted to cover herself, to hide her purely functional bra and modestly sized breasts.

His attention smoldering, he asked, "What is?" Holding her shoulders, he looked at her from the waistband of her hip-hugger jeans to her belly, ribs, over her white cotton bra, to her shoulders and finally her mouth, and her eyes.

Audrey shook her head but couldn't escape the lock of his intensity. A deep breath didn't really help. "Wanting you like this. It's not something I'm used to."

"Yeah?" Spreading his fingers out, he trailed his hands over her chest, around her breasts—which exacerbated her need—down her body, around to her derrière and back again to the snap of her jeans. "How does it make you feel? Tell me."

He expected her to think while he undressed her? To be able to speak? She wasn't experienced enough for that.

Deciding she should be proactive, Audrey toed off her sneakers and started to shove down her jeans.

"Now, Audrey." In one swift move, Brett turned her and tumbled her onto her back on the mattress. "Let me."

He stood to the side of the bed but leaned forward and braced his arms on either side of her shoulders. He was so damn big, so tall, that he surrounded her with ease.

"First, though, answer my question."

Never had a man looked at her like this, all concentrated and intimate and . . . connected. She couldn't be this close to him without touching him, so she put her hands on his rock-solid shoulders, and she felt a deepening of need.

A master of understatement, she murmured, "I don't feel like me."

"What's different?"

How to put it so that he'd understand? "I'm not a woman who gets this . . ." *Turned on.* ". . . Preoccupied. Or this bold." He only waited, still looking down at her, until Audrey felt forced to elaborate. "I've never been completely naked in front of a guy before."

Slowly, his sexy mouth lifted into a wolfish smile. "Let's start there, then, okay?" He levered away from her to unzip her jeans and drag them, with her panties, down her legs.

Audrey gulped, but said nothing. If she got naked, they could finally get going. Without thinking about it, she said, "I can't wait to feel you inside me."

His gaze shot up to hers. His nostrils flared. "Woman, I'm trying for a little patience here. But when you say things like that, well, you blow my control."

Shifting her legs, almost squirming in her hunger, Audrey said, "But I don't want you to be patient." And then, because she couldn't stand it, especially with how he looked at her now, she added, "I ache, Brett."

All humor left him. He came down beside her and took her mouth in a kiss that almost did it for her. Man, oh, man, he knew how to use that mouth of his, kissing her in a way that made her feel the sensual effects of it everywhere.

Arching into him, Audrey tried to feel all of him against her. Still kissing her, Brett pressed her onto her back again. Against her lips, he said, "Let's take care of this ache of yours, okay?" And then his hand was there, between her legs, exploring, prodding, every touch inciting her . . .

He opened her and pushed a finger deep.

Her short nails sank into his shoulders and a groan ripped from her throat. Never had she known this kind of arousal. It defied description, and in some ways, it scared her. Feeling like this left her vulnerable to hurt.

What if Brett was only playing with her?

What if this was a one-night stand? She needed to get her fill of him while she could. She needed memories to carry her through after he left her.

And right now, she needed reassurance almost as much as she needed release. "Brett?"

He kissed her cheek, her jaw, her throat. Lifting to watch her face, he worked a second finger into her. Heat flushed her skin and left her breathless. Smiling, he lowered his head to draw on one nipple.

Like a bundle of sizzling sensation, her body felt alive and sparking everywhere.

When his thumb came up to toy with her clitoris, every pleasure amplified and concentrated until she knew she would snap. Her body bowed, a raw groan reverberated from deep inside her, and her muscles all trembled.

The climax raged through her, ebbing and intensifying until it finally, by slow degrees, faded away, leaving even her bones lax.

Brett released her and moved away, but he was back in what felt like a nanosecond. His weight settled over her as he positioned himself between her legs. Holding her face to kiss her, he pushed into her.

She'd been celibate so long; she'd *never* been with a man like Brett. He surrounded her, covered her, slowly filled her, and she loved it.

Yes, *this* was what she wanted. Lethargy left her, replaced with rekindled lust.

While waiting for her to get with the program, he moved slowly, gently. After a shuddering breath, Audrey opened her eyes and saw the strain on his gorgeous face.

He kissed her. "You feel damn good, honey."

Lacking the words to convey her emotions, Audrey wrapped her legs around him and squeezed him tight. Brett raised up to his elbows to maintain eye contact and accelerated his pace. As they moved in rhythm, his chest hair abraded her nipples and his warm breath quickened against her lips. Heat from their bodies mingled; his color deepened—and suddenly another climax took her. She couldn't control the sounds she made, the way her body moved.

But it didn't matter.

Her reaction pushed him over the edge, and he joined her with a harsh groan. Watching him come, knowing he was a part of her, nearly made Audrey cry with over-whelming sentiment.

Little by little, the maelstrom faded and Brett, still breathing hard, sank down onto her.

Her legs slipped away from him, but he didn't move. She relished his weight as it pressed her down into the bed.

Stroking his sweat-dampened back, Audrey thought of her intimate relationships in the past. Sex had been some-thing she'd indulged in out of curiosity and, on occasion, affection.

Before Brett, she hadn't known this red-hot desire.

But now what? Should she excuse herself, get dressed, and leave before he asked her to go?

Drawing in a fortifying breath, she decided on being proactive again. "Brett?"

He kissed her shoulder, her throat, and worked up to his elbows again. More slumberous than she'd ever seen him, he searched her features and smiled. "You look great freshly tumbled, Ms. Porter."

That made Audrey chuckle. "You always look great."

Leaning down, he took a love bite of her collarbone, her shoulder—and fell to his back next to her with a hearty sigh. Eyes closed, unaffected by his nudity, Brett said, "I'm starved. You want to eat?"

"I don't know." She'd never really looked at a man after sex, with his erection softened, a spent condom in place. Brett's naturalness fascinated her. "I don't know what we're doing here."

He looked at her. "What do you mean?"

She licked dry lips. "You drove me here. I don't have my car. I mean, I could take a cab—"

"No." He frowned at her, and then asked, "Are you in a hurry to leave?"

Trying a different tack, Audrey asked, "How late did you want me to stay?"

That deepened his frown. He hesitated, but then rolled up to one elbow beside her. "I get up at the crack of dawn to jog. I get back here around seven A.M., and then I only have a few hours before I head to the gym."

If she stayed, it'd be a huge imposition on him. Audrey tried to make this easier for him. "Then we should make it an early night."

In deep thought, he cupped her breast in his big hand. "Or you could stay the night and I'll take you back on my way to the gym."

He wanted her to stay! "I don't have a toothbrush here."

That blurted response amused him. "I think we're to the point where we can share mine." Kissing her again, he stroked his tongue over hers to accentuate his point. "But if you want to go home, I'll take you. I mean, if you're not comfortable here."

The way he said that made her wonder at his meaning. "Why wouldn't I be comfortable?"

"It's not the best neighborhood." Almost on cue, a police siren sounded.

Before Audrey could formulate a reply, Spice started scratching at the bedroom door, and Brett exited the bed in a rush. "Be right back."

He left the bedroom door ajar, but Spice followed him. Audrey scooted up to lean against the headboard. She pulled the soft quilt up to cover herself.

Brett returned, sans condom, and went to the dresser to pull out a pair of dark, snug boxers. He sat on the bed beside her hip, and Spice leaped up to join him.

Smoothing a hand over Audrey's thigh, he thought for a second and then glanced up at her. "I don't want you to think that I stay here, in this cheap apartment, because I can't afford anything better. Truth is, I get well paid for fighting. But I grew up poor, so in a lot of ways, I'm more comfortable here than I would be somewhere else. Especially while I'm training. But mostly I stay here because I'm socking away a lot of money."

It pleased Audrey that Brett wanted her to know his thoughts, but it worried her that she'd somehow led him to believe that the material stuff mattered to her.

"I like you, Brett, wherever you live. You don't owe me any explanations." Where he lived would never be the issue. *What* he did . . . his participation in the bloody sport still left her floundering in conflicting emotions.

"I want you to understand, that's all. I want you to . . . I don't know, see me as more than a fighter, maybe." He scratched the cat's ears, prompting Spice to a loud purring that resonated in the small room. "I know how you feel about it, Audrey."

For the first time, she regretted her attitude about his chosen sport.

Brett didn't quite look at her as he defended his career. "I fight because I like it and I'm good at it. More than any other sport, it challenges me to be my best, physically and mentally. But it's not who I am, it's just what I do. I don't want you to judge me as *only* a fighter. Do you know what I mean?"

"I think so." And because she really was starting to understand, Audrey added, "Fighters are individuals. They can't be stereotyped. *You* can't be stereotyped."

Her statement lifted his scowl. "Exactly. I've met some who are bullies, and some who wouldn't hurt a fly outside the arena. Family men, die-hard bachelors, partyers, and loners. Dropouts and guys with multiple college degrees. Mostly what successful fighters have in common is that we work hard and prefer being physical to sitting behind a desk. But that's it."

For Audrey, Brett was unlike any man she'd ever met, much less other fighters. Not that she personally knew any other fighters. "Most of them aren't as talented as you."

He gave her that quirky smile again. "You might not be the best judge of that. I'm good, and I know it. But in fighting, one mistake can give you a loss, and every fighter can get caught. I'm training with some guys now that are pretty damned good, and that helps. They're icons in the sport, and I'm lucky to get to train with them."

"But they're excited about you."

He laughed. "What makes you say that?"

"I overheard Drew Black and another fighter talking at the gym." The fighter Drew had spoken with was gorgeous enough to render her awestruck. But he didn't blow her away like Brett did. "They said—"

"No." Already shaking his head, Brett stalled her. "Just forget anything you heard Drew say. You got that?"

Irritated, he set the cat aside and left the bed.

Before he could take more than two steps, Audrey scrambled out from under the quilt to stop him. He heard her and, still irked, glanced back. Slowly, he turned to fully face her again, and his expression changed from cool to hot.

With him now looking at her, she forgot whatever she'd planned to say or do.

Brett took his time studying her body.

Being naked in front of him was getting easier, mostly because of how much admiration he showed.

She shifted her feet in nervousness. "I'm sorry."

His gaze shot up to hers. "For what?"

God, this was difficult. "I've never had a naked conversation before, Brett." He said nothing to that, so she cleared her throat and tried again. "I'm sorry for upsetting you."

Scoffing, he went back to looking at her breasts. "I'm not upset."

"You look upset to me."

He let out a breath and forced his attention away. "Get some clothes on before I forget to feed you."

Putting her shoulders back, Audrey stood her ground. He made her sound like a pet he had to care for, and she didn't like it. "Maybe I should just go after all."

Hands on his hips, his exasperation plain, Brett studied her.

The tension grew unbearable, and Audrey was just about to locate her clothes to dress and leave when he closed the space between them.

Without a word, he kissed her—and kept on kissing her.

She knew they should talk, but right now, more sex worked for her.

"Stay," he requested in between soft, devouring kisses.

God, with him she was *so* easy. "All right." Later, tomorrow or the day after, they'd sort through problems and conflicts. For right now, being with him was enough.

CHAPTER 11

WEARING one of Drew's soft and faded SBC T-shirts and her panties, Gillian joined him in the kitchen. "You ordered the pizza?"

Barefoot, dressed in unsnapped jeans and nothing else, he leaned on the counter and took in the sight of her. "Yeah. Twenty minutes." He tracked her every step as she went to his fridge to help herself to a drink. "You're so damned stacked, you're straining the front of that shirt. I can even see the outline of your nipples."

Gillian glanced down. True enough. The shirt hung on her everywhere, except across her bountiful breasts.

Gazing at Drew over the top of a cola as she took a long drink, Gillian made note of his heated stare. Her nipples tightened, and in return, his eyes narrowed.

Over the last several hours, they'd had sex. *Twice.* Intimate places on her body continued to throb from extended, intense foreplay.

And still Drew looked at her like he couldn't get enough.

He did that a lot, Gillian realized, and it never failed to flatter her. She was used to men treating her with lady-like respect. But Drew treated her as a sexual being, like a woman he wanted to do hot, nasty, pleasurable things with nonstop.

Before meeting him, in theory alone, she would have found that base concept appalling and unappealing.

But now, in actuality, well, being the recipient of all that heated male attention . . . she loved it.

Gillian closed the refrigerator and sauntered over to the table to sit. Propping her feet on another chair, she smiled at Drew. The shirt barely kept her modesty intact. "I'm a full-figured woman, Drew, but then, you already knew that."

His heated attention took in the length of her legs. "Yeah."

So much appreciation in one small word. Drew Black could be ruthless, as demonstrated by his altercation with Brett. A history of sexual conquests also proved his sweet-talking abilities; women fell all over him.

But in most things, and most situations, Gillian could never doubt his sincerity.

He made her feel sexier than she'd ever thought possible. "Down, boy."

"Not likely." He met her teasing gaze. "You're too stacked for me to stay down long."

She couldn't help but smile. Drew was generally blatant about his feelings. What got him in trouble most of the time was the fact that his mouth worked in time with his thoughts, giving voice to anything that entered his mind.

In her case, most of what he said filled her with pleasure. But in other circumstances . . . he really needed to learn to censor things a bit.

One thought led to another. "Do you think you'll be able to work things out with Brett?"

"Definitely."

No hesitation at all. Drew didn't know the meaning of uncertainty.

"It looked like he and Audrey Porter were involved. Isn't that awkward?"

"I have no idea." He stretched, a man without a care. "Their relationship was news to me."

How odd; a fighter and a woman heading up a group against fighting. "Aren't you worried about it?"

His rude snort let her know what he thought of that idea. "No."

"Oh, come on, Drew." That had to be a conflict of interest for Brett. Actually, for Ms. Porter, too. "You're not even a little worried?"

"*Hell* no." He folded his arms over his chest. "Why should I be?"

"What if he tells her something that she can use against the SBC?"

"Like what? There isn't anything. Hell, we're golden right now."

Right, except for Drew's volatile temperament and foul mouth, the arguments against the sport were diminishing.

He shook his head at her. "You act like we're some underground blood sport, with fights to the death or something. For years now we've been a legitimate mixed martial arts sports association. We have the best athletes in the world."

Warming to his topic, he pushed away from the counter and paced in front of her. "These guys all have extensive combat sport training. Hell, they train for up to six hours a day. We have State Athletic Commission approval for all fights, *and* we've never had a serious injury."

Her mouth twitched. She remembered him telling the kids at the boys' home the same thing. "Our ideas of serious must vary, because Drew, I've seen some pretty nasty boo-boos."

He rolled his eyes. "A broken bone or dislocated joint. No big deal. Hell, these guys play hard enough to get that hurt on a weekend."

"One fight that I saw, a young man had a gaping cut on his forehead. Blood was everywhere."

"Head wounds bleed like a son of a bitch." He waved off her concerns. "Believe me, a few stitches is not considered a severe injury. Now, if he was blinded or suffered brain trauma or something like that—yeah, that'd fuck up our good record for sure."

He was so passionate about the sport that an idea occurred to Gillian. "I'm going to set up a talk between you and the local members of WAVS. If you told them everything you just told me, maybe they'd be less inclined to—"

"Fuck that."

Gillian took in his outraged expression and sighed. "If you gave that group even a tenth of the attention you give to the fighters, it'd have to promote goodwill."

His brows snapped down. "Working with fighters is my livelihood. The bitchy dames in WAVS are just a fucking irritant."

Gillian set aside her cola and frowned at him. "Enough with the colorful adjectives already."

"What?"

Irate, she waved a hand, saying, "Fuck this, and fuck that. Expand your vocabulary just a little, would you *please*."

"It's only a word." But he grinned over her disgruntlement. "And I kind of like hearing you talk dirty."

How did he manage to make everything sexual? "You're being stubborn, Drew."

"I'm being realistic." He came to lean over her chair, his hands braced beside her hips on the seat. "Do you have any real concept of how crazy busy I stay? Hell, I travel more than I'm here."

"Because you micromanage everything." This close to him, Gillian could see the striations in his dark brown eyes. Whether seducing her or defending his much-loved sport, Drew Black packed a lot of intensity, and so much intensity in one man left her flustered. "I've been meaning to talk to you about that, too. There's no reason for you to oversee every little thing. If you would just—"

"Woman, damn." His forced laugh had an edge to it. "I

do know how to run my own business, you know. How the hell do you think I got along before you showed up?"

"As I recall, you were on the verge of being fired."

That reminder shot his good humor, and his jaw tightened. "Actually, smart-ass, I'm on the verge of taking this sport to prime time." He looked at her mouth. "And when I can finagle some free time, I'd rather spend it getting sweaty in bed with you, instead of trying to convert a bunch of prissy-ass wallflowers who faint at the sight of blood."

She preferred that, too, but his cynicism wounded her on a fundamental level. She wasn't exactly a fan of WAVS herself. Fanatics never appealed to her, and from what she'd seen, they touted radical views. But she hated to hear Drew continually degrade an entire group of women. After all, *she* was a woman, and throughout her career, she'd met plenty of men who discounted the concerns of women. "You really resent them, don't you?"

"If someone negated all your hard work, twisted your every motive, and always painted you in a bad light, wouldn't you resent them?"

Of course she would. "I realize the fault doesn't lie entirely with you."

"Gee, thanks for the endorsement, baby."

Trying to hide her smile, Gillian leaned forward and gave him a brief, apologetic kiss. "They don't really understand the sport, Drew, which is all the more reason why you should try to resolve things."

He shook his head at her. "I'm impressive, Gillian, I know, but even I can't do everything."

Hand over her heart, she feigned a gasp. "Say it isn't so."

He straightened away from her. "You know I'm working on a big contract for Brett and juggling misbehaving fighters like Dickey Thompson. I've had three trips to L.A. in the past month and another to Canada. I'm negotiating a shitload of deals from sponsors and finessing a new cable show. On top of that, as Officer Sparks warned us, rag-mag reporters are trying to make more out of that damn bomb scare than was there."

His schedule sometimes left her exhausted, but a man like Drew needed to stay busy. "I'm not sure a bomb threat requires embellishment."

"You know what I mean. Someone blabbed that I was supposedly a target, and now every groupie reporter out there wants the inside scoop on my 'death threats.'" He huffed. "Those WAVS broads are probably having a party over it."

At the very least, they probably felt vindicated. Why hadn't Drew told her about this before now? "Who's been in contact with you?"

"Nobody big. I don't think CNN gives a shit, you know? But people from the fighter magazines have called, and a few cable news programs. I accepted a couple of interviews for that, by the way. After we eat, I'll give you the dates and times."

Gillian's feet dropped from the seat to the floor. "Drew!" It was *her* job to handle all his press right now. She wanted to control the outgoing message by handpicking only the places that she knew would improve his image.

If he sabotaged her efforts, she couldn't do her job.

As if it didn't matter, he said, "*Playboy* magazine called, too. They want to set up something."

Her jaw loosened, then clenched. Fury stirred. Through her teeth, she asked, "Anything else?"

"Yeah. Some of the online MMA sites are talking about it. You know how gossip-worthy news goes viral. Next thing you know, it'll be the hot topic on every message board out there, so I offered a firsthand account, just to keep the record straight."

Struggling to maintain a calm façade, Gillian came to her feet. She was suddenly very aware of not being appropriately dressed with him, but she wouldn't let that hold her back on something this important.

Stiff with indignation, she said, "You will make out a list."

One of his brows went up. "I will, huh?"

His infuriating attitude ramped up her annoyance another notch. "I want to know each and every reporter you've spoken with, so that I can contact them myself. After I've spoken with them, *I'll* make a final decision on which appointments you'll keep, and which ones I'll cancel." Her hands tightened into fists over the task ahead. Thanks to Drew, her workload had just doubled, and her carefully thought-out plan was awry. "From now on, I will vet any and all interview situations and choose only the—"

"Too late." He tweaked her chin. "I already said I'd do them, so I can't back out now."

Gillian's eyes widened. He'd not only disregarded her order, he'd *tweaked* her chin. Of all the condescending, obnoxious gestures he could have made, that had to be the worst. It reeked of superiority.

The doorbell rang, and Drew said, "About damn time. I'm starved." He swatted her butt as he passed. "*Someone* wore me out. Not saying any names or anything."

Gillian stood there, flummoxed, mute. Definitely, a slap on the butt was worse than a chin tweak. He'd smacked her hard enough that she could feel the imprint of his hand, tingly and warm, on her backside.

Disbelief melded into fury.

She'd kill him.

Almost heaving in her agitation, Gillian turned to stare toward where Drew had gone. At the very least, she'd make him wish he was dead.

Was it their intimate relationship that made him think he could overrule her business acumen without even the consideration of a discussion? She'd been hired to do a job, damn him, and despite his outrageous provocation, she would succeed.

Dire thoughts of retribution flickered through her mind—until she heard a conversation that sounded nothing like a pizza delivery. Straining her ears, she paused to listen.

Those raised voices were definitely not part of idle conversation with a deliveryman.

With an unsettling sense of déjà vu, Gillian went to investigate. Staying out of sight, she eavesdropped and recognized Dickey Thompson's voice.

Oh, crap.

Here she was, once again caught in dishabille inside Drew's home. What could Dickey want? Drew claimed he had that situation all taken care of, but to Gillian, it sounded like another fire blazing.

"You fucking *dare* come to my house? Are you out of your fucking mind?"

Gillian winced. Drew was truly furious. She'd seen him rage in online video interviews, and heard about his temper in articles, but she'd never personally witnessed him like this.

"I don't have your phone number," Dickey complained.

"That's because you don't need it!"

Gillian peeked around the corner, saw the two men facing each other, and her heart stuck in her throat. Drew wasn't a "little guy" by any stretch, but he didn't match up to Dickey's colossal size.

If he got in a physical altercation with Dickey, it could be devastating on many levels. She might want to kill Drew, but she didn't want some muscle-bulging behemoth to dismember him.

Voice low, Gillian hissed, *"Drew."*

Either he didn't hear her, or he chose to ignore her. Most likely the latter.

Well, maybe she should let Dickey have him. But no . . . *"Drew!"*

Pointing at Dickey, Drew said, "You need to get your shit together, man. There'll be other opportunities, but not if you keep stepping over the line."

Dickey braced his hands on the door frame and leaned in. "That drunken shit the other night was just a fluke. It won't happen again, Drew, I swear it." He pulled in a deep breath and blurted out, "I want an opportunity in the next televised fight."

Without even a second's thought, Drew said, "Ain't happening. Forget it."

Discouraged, Dickey pulled back. "I guess your wonder boy, Brett, is in?"

"That's none of your damned business, but no, not yet he isn't."

Skepticism pinched Dickey's brows. "I don't believe you."

That was the wrong thing to say; it smacked of calling Drew a liar and snapped his barely contained temper. "And I don't give a flying fuck what you believe! Now get the hell out of my fucking house!"

He didn't. Instead, he looked over his shoulder at the street, then back to Drew again. Low, so low that Gillian barely heard him, Dickey said, "Listen, Drew, I didn't just come for that. Some women were talking to me earlier, asking me all kinds of questions about you. I dunno, but I think they expected me to . . . rat you out somehow."

Unconcerned, Drew snorted. "About what?"

"That's just it. I have no idea. But they hinted something about your position being in jeopardy."

Uh-oh, Gillian thought. Had news gotten out about her assignment to pretty up Drew's reputation? Not that she was surprised. Nothing really stayed hidden for long.

"That's bullshit," Drew said.

"I figured. But when I got here, I saw someone across the street taking pictures of the cars in your driveway." Dickey scratched the side of his head. "I'm guessing most know that little compact isn't your car, right?"

Drew ignored the reference to her small rental car. "What are you talking about? Who was taking pictures?"

"I dunno. He took off when I got here. At least, I think he did."

"You're shitting me. Someone was on my property?" Drew shoved Dickey aside and stepped out the door.

"He was across the street, hanging behind those shrubs," Dickey told him as he stormed out.

"Drew!" Forgetting her modesty for the moment, Gillian dashed after him. The idea of anyone snooping around his house left her shaken.

The second Dickey saw her, he said, "Whoa," in surprise, then quickly got out of her way.

"Drew, get in here! Are you out of your mind?" She reached out the door until she could snag the back of his jeans, then she tugged, hard.

He didn't budge.

She looked to Dickey for help, but he held up his hands, and Gillian realized that Drew was never in any danger from this particular fighter. Dickey had no intention of getting physical with Drew in *any* way.

"Drew," she implored without results. "There was a bomb threat against you, you idiot. *Get in the house.*"

"Bomb threat?" Dickey went on the alert.

At her screeched order, she finally had Drew's attention. Glancing at her, he frowned and pried her hand from the waistband of his jeans. With a sound of disgust directed at her concern, he left the porch and went down the walkway to investigate.

"Oh. My. God." Gillian couldn't believe his lack of caution. "Call the police," she told Dickey.

"No," Drew countermanded. "We don't need the cops sniffing around here again."

"Um . . ." Dickey looked back and forth between them. He ran a hand over his head and then asked, "Again?"

THE perfect photograph presented itself as Drew Black himself stood outside in opened jeans. That meddling woman was behind him, wearing only Drew's shirt, proof positive of what they'd been up to. Better yet, next to her stood a disgruntled fighter with plenty of reason to hate Drew.

If the flash went off, escape would be almost impossible.

Was it worth the risk? His heart thundered in indecision. The bomb scare had missed Drew Black entirely, so it was a bust. But this wouldn't be. This would be the perfect picture. It would bring immeasurable appreciation, and good money to boot.

He *had* to do it.

Trying not to make a sound behind the bushes where he cowered, he positioned himself on his knees and aimed the camera.

He had them all three in the shot.

A picture painted a thousand words, and there were many interpretations to the present scene.

He focused . . . and captured the image just as Drew Black started back inside. The flash had him jerking back around again.

With the foulest curse, Drew started toward him.

Panicked, his camera held tightly in his hand, he vaulted out of the bushes. Running as fast as he could, he sped down the walkway. On the opposite side of the cross street, he saw his car where he'd left it parked.

Pushing himself, praying he'd reach his car before Drew Black got hold of him, he ran blindly into the dark street—and headlights flashed on him.

"What the—"

Accelerating, the car slammed into him, tossing him up and over the hood with bone-crushing force. He screamed as the camera flew from his hands and he went airborne. His limbs flopped out of his control. The hard pavement of the street rushed up to meet him, and then . . . he felt nothing at all.

THE car collided with the fleeing photographer, stopping Drew dead in his tracks. The guy's body flipped up and over the length of the car and then slammed into the pavement with a sickening thud.

"Holy shit."

Never slowing, the car sped away. It happened too fast, and the night was too dark, for Drew to get the plates. Within seconds, the car was out of sight.

Limbs grotesquely broken, head cracked open, the photographer lay crumpled in the middle of the road. It was a grisly, macabre scene.

Aware of Gillian and Dickey behind him, Drew turned back. "Dickey, call the cops."

Somewhat stunned by it all, Dickey said, "But you told me not to."

"That was before a man was killed, damn it! Ask for Officer Sparks. Tell him you're with me. Tell him . . . I don't know. To bring an ambulance or something." He caught Gillian before she could get any closer. "Don't."

Trembling, she covered her mouth with one hand. "Oh, God, Drew. *What happened?*"

"Hit and run." A deliberate move, Drew thought. And if he were right, that meant he had bigger problems than an intrusive photographer or reporter. But he'd save that for the cops. "It's . . . you don't want to see him, Gillian, trust me."

"Is he . . . ?"

"Dead?" Drew glanced back at that demolished body. Enough moonlight shone down for him to see a spreading pool of blood beneath the body. "That'd be my guess." He could feel Gillian shaking, and it incensed him. "Hopefully the fucking camera is busted, too."

"Oh, Drew."

She sounded sad that he'd be so callous, but he didn't care. He hated that anyone had upset her like this. And no way in hell would their relationship stay private after this.

"Sparks is on his way." Dickey joined them and looked past Drew to the body. His eyes widened. *"Daaaamn."*

God help them.

"Stay here, Dickey, do you hear me? Don't touch anything. Don't even get close to anything."

By small degrees, Dickey got his attention off the photographer and onto Drew. He scowled. "I'm not an idiot,

Drew. I'm not going to go poking around on the body or anything."

"Glad to hear it. Watch for the cops and come get me if I'm not back when Sparks gets here."

"Where are you going?"

Drew gave him a look. Dickey glanced at Gillian, huddled close to Drew's side, and he made an *Oh* expression.

"Right. I'll wait here." He looked at the body again and winced. "Make it quick, though. Dead people give me the willies."

Drew put his arm around Gillian. "Come on. You need to get some clothes on. At least some jeans, okay?"

As if only then realizing how little she wore, Gillian looked down at her bare legs and feet. She turned big eyes on Drew. "I forgot."

"I know, it's okay." He smoothed her inky black hair. "But I think it aged Dickey a year, seeing you like this. Probably a good thing."

His joke went unappreciated as she followed him back to his house by rote. Drew didn't like seeing her like this, all withdrawn and . . . lost.

And then, out of the blue, she pulled herself together. She stood taller, stronger. Her trembles subsided. "Drew?"

"Yeah?" They walked through his house to his bedroom.

"Someone ran that man over. On purpose."

So she'd come to the same conclusion. "You noticed that, huh?" He was hoping she'd come around the corner too late to see the actual act.

"He was killed." She looked up at Drew, her face filled with worry. *"Murdered."*

"Sure looked that way to me." Drew could tell by her concentrated expression that she was still piecing things together.

"He has photos of me, here with you, on that camera. That last photo . . . I'm in your shirt, Drew. In my *under-*

wear." Distraught and affronted, she stared up at him. "He was . . . spying on you. *On me.*"

There'd be no point trying to sugarcoat it. Gillian wasn't a dummy. "Yeah, afraid so."

Hands in her hair, she strode away from him. "This is just too awful."

Drew watched her with growing cynicism.

She hadn't turned to him for comfort. Instead, she'd set herself apart from him.

He wouldn't kid himself: a ton of significance came with her telling reaction. From jump, Gillian had seen him primarily as trouble, and now she felt she'd been contaminated by her association with him.

Who had the cursed photographer worked for?

"You'll get through it." Drew picked up her jeans and held them out to her. Though he hated it, all he could do at this point was protect her from the danger, and the fallout, as much as possible. "Get dressed, and then stay here in the house. I'll handle Sparks."

"Oh, no." She inhaled deeply and seemed to collect herself before stepping into her jeans. "Forewarned is forearmed. I need to know what's going on so that I'll be better able to control things."

Unbelievable. How the hell did she think to control things now? And how could he keep her safe if she wouldn't stay out of it? "I thought we settled this in the kitchen."

In the process of snapping her jeans, she froze and then slowly brought her gaze up to his. Her blue eyes burned like the center of a flame.

Fascinated, Drew watched her expression tighten into cold fury. Oddly enough, it kind of turned him on. Gillian Noode was a bundle of passion.

"That's right!" As if only then recalling it, she stated, "I'm *livid* with you."

"Really? Why?"

Her back went ramrod straight and in a near screech, she said, "*Why? What do you mean, why?*"

Drew almost smiled. Of course he knew. He'd deliberately antagonized her, almost as a self-preservation mechanism to keep her from getting too close.

But now . . . now everything had changed. Now he damn well intended to keep her under his very close radar.

For her sake.

"Come on, Gillian. Be reasonable." Drew held up a hand to preempt the attack she looked ready to launch. "Whatever has you prickly now, let's agree that it has to wait. I need to get back outside with Dickey."

Trembling with fury, she resisted, and then finally snapped, *"Fine."*

She slipped her pampered, painted toes into high-heel sandals and, still wearing his shirt with her jeans, headed for the door. "Let's go."

Yet again Drew noticed how she filled out his shirt. How could he not? With every step, she bounced and jiggled and just plain looked sexy as hell. He didn't want Dickey seeing her like this, and he sure as hell didn't want Sparks to see her this way again.

He blocked the bedroom door so she couldn't leave. "A bra wouldn't hurt anything, you know."

"Wear one if it'll make you feel better." She all but pushed through him to take the lead. Following behind her, Drew made note of the defiant swish in her gait, and how that delectable ass of hers filled out her jeans. That preoccupation let her get through the front door ahead of him.

For a minute there, she'd been badly shaken by the invasion of their privacy and the residue of danger and death. Every protective instinct in him had taken over.

Now, she was back in control, and as take-charge as ever.

Damn, but he liked both sides of her: the soft, vulnerable lady and the balls-to-the-wall businesswoman.

One thing about Gillian, no matter what, she never bored him. That had to count for something, right?

As he trailed her out the door, Drew paused to grab a

jacket. The evening air had chilled, so he could use that as an excuse to cover up Gillian's impressive rack.

For one of the few times in his life, he felt possessive toward a woman. No matter the deadly conspiracy at hand, he wasn't about to share her.

CHAPTER 12

OFFICER Sparks took statements from each of them separately. An ambulance crew removed the body, and the camera was taken for evidence.

Drew's tolerance wore thin. Gillian held it together, but she looked exhausted. He wanted to pamper her, damn it. He wanted to tell her that everything would be okay—but he wouldn't lie to her. Any assurance right now would be just that—a giant lie.

"So." Sparks looked at Dickey. "What was the purpose of your visit tonight?"

Dickey surprised Drew with his tact. "Just business, to work out details on when I'll fight next."

Unconvinced, Sparks asked, "Is that routine, to visit the president of the company at his house?"

Dickey shook his head. "No." And then, a little chagrined: "Maybe that's why you won't see me fighting anytime soon."

Humility always got to Drew. And it didn't hurt that Dickey was a damn good fighter, albeit with a lot to learn. "Dickey's working through some roadblocks to success, but he's getting there." Drew slapped him on the shoulder, earning a funny look from Dickey.

"As to fighters visiting me at my house, this isn't my only home. Usually I'm in L.A., and yeah, when I'm there I don't mix business with home life. But the atmosphere here is more relaxed. Everyone knows everyone." He gave Sparks a direct stare. "I've had a few of the fighters over. No big deal."

Dickey almost swallowed his tongue over that one.

"Hmmm." Sparks looked down at his notes. "Any idea why a photographer was running from you?"

"Probably because he knew I planned to beat his god-damned ass if I'd caught him."

That irked Sparks. "You threatened him?"

"Didn't get a chance. Like I told you, soon as the camera flashed, I went after him and he ran like a fucking coward who skulks in bushes to facilitate snooping into other people's lives."

Sparks exhibited strained patience.

"Look, I won't lie to you. I was going to smash the fucking camera *and* his face. But he ran like hell around the corner and into the street, and bam, just like that, the car plowed him down."

"On purpose."

Exasperation raised Drew's voice to a near shout. "How many drivers are going seventy, eighty miles an hour on these streets? I didn't even notice the car until the headlights came on, and neither did the dumb-ass photographer."

Sparks looked at Gillian with suspicion. "And you didn't see any of that?"

Arms wrapped around herself, she shook her head. "Not the hit, no. I was a few yards behind Drew, and by the time I rounded the block, it was . . . all over."

"Why were you following him?"

Apologetic, she looked askance at Drew. "I was going to stop him from hitting the guy."

"She was going to *try* to stop me," Drew corrected. "I was plenty pissed, so it's doubtful she'd have succeeded."

A news van pulled up and a reporter popped out with a damned mic already in her hand. A videographer followed right behind her. Two more vehicles pulled up.

Drew sucked in a lungful of cool night air, but it didn't alleviate his rage. "The circus begins."

Sparks ignored them. "And you?" he asked Dickey. "What were you doing?"

He shrugged. "I just followed to see what would happen. That's all."

"Are we done here?" Drew asked. He wanted to get Gillian inside before the inquisition started. As it was, she'd be on some bozo's film, and news cameras were already rolling. No need to add to that.

Gillian put a hand on Drew's arm. "I'm not hiding from them."

This was no time for gumption. "They'll chew you up and spit you out."

Sparks pinched the bridge of his nose and said with resignation, "He's probably right."

Gillian lifted that stubborn chin. "If I run from them, they'll make up their own story anyway."

"And you think that'll be more incriminating than the truth?" Drew shook his head. "You're the one who wants this kept private, if you'll remember."

"Might not matter." Dickey nodded at something behind Drew. "The cavalry arrives."

Puzzled by that, Drew spun around—and found a small contingent of fighters, and their significant others, approaching. They laughed and joked with each other as if they hadn't just stepped into a media frenzy, with cameras already trained on them.

"What the hell is this?"

Dickey leaned in close to Drew. "Diffusion. If they have more to see and talk about, less is said about you and your lady."

Few things in life ever left Drew floored, but this counted. "That's brilliant, Dickey."

He grinned. "Yeah, I know. I called Handleman right

after I called Officer Sparks, and I told him what happened. He rounded up the rest of the guys."

The fighters were deliberately rowdy, causing a stir—and a distraction. They provided confusion as to who had seen what by giving evasive answers and changing the subject.

It worked, to a point.

Then Millie Christian showed up. She didn't have a cameraman or a mic but she had a damned tape recorder, and she made a beeline for . . . Gillian.

Drew tried stepping in front of her, but she couldn't be sidetracked. Making sure the rest of the reporters would hear her, she called out, "Ms. Noode, is it true that you're working to reinvent Drew Black's image?"

A hush fell, quickly broken by excitement.

Someone aimed a camera at Gillian. She didn't panic or shrink away.

Poised, professional even in Drew's shirt and jacket, she said, "I was hired for promotional purposes, in a broad capacity, with many goals in mind."

In that moment, Drew was so damned proud of her.

But Christian didn't let up. Drew remembered only too well how tenacious that witch could be.

Holding out the recorder to catch every word, she asked, "Is it true that you're sleeping with him?"

Drew saw red. But before he could even brace himself for a tirade that would have demolished the stupid woman, Gillian was there, pulling him back with no more than a look.

More attention came her way, but it still didn't notably faze her. "My personal relationships are just that: personal."

Had he ever really thought this WAVS meddler was timid? Right now, she looked like a damned junkyard dog eyeing a meaty bone. Why the hell had he ever felt remorse for ripping her apart online?

Ms. Christian didn't smile, but Drew saw the glee in her eyes—and the fanaticism. Loony-ass broad.

Enjoying the spotlight, Millie Christian pressed her slant on things. "An intimate relationship would bias your task at hand, wouldn't it? How can you coerce Mr. Black into more suitable behavior if you're succumbing to his abuse?"

"No one can coerce Mr. Black, his behavior *is* suitable, and I assure you he has never abused me!"

"He might not strike you, but there are all types of abuse, Ms. Noode. I was referring to the way that he treats women as second-class citizens, how he calls them demeaning names and ridicules them in the business world." Emotion added steam to her outburst. "He is known for using women like paper napkins, only to toss them out with the trash when he's done. And you know he'll be done with you soon enough."

Drew rolled his eyes at her venom, but Gillian didn't have the same reaction.

Her eyes narrowed. "Millie Christian, I presume?"

That took Millie back a step, but she quickly regrouped. "I see that you've heard of me."

"Indeed." Gillian looked her over with the same distaste she'd give to a bug.

"Because of *him*." She pointed the recorder at Drew. "Because of his foul mouth and disrespectful attitude toward women."

"Oh, I don't know," Gillian said. "I believe any source, male or female, who shared so much erroneous information would have garnered the same reaction from him. It wasn't sexist at all, just intolerance for lack of facts."

Drew's eyebrows went up. Score one for Gillian.

"You're *defending* him?" The reporter's red hair nearly stood on end. "But then, I shouldn't be surprised. If you're trashy enough to sleep with him, of course you'd see things his way."

Gillian shook her head as if in pity. "What is wrong with you, Ms. Christian? You sound like a lover scorned, but surely that can't be the case." Her lip curled in a way that Drew had never before witnessed. "I know that for a fact, because Drew Black would never be interested in such a petty, mean-spirited, *stupid* woman."

Millie's face went red with rage. *"You're nothing more than a—"*

With all cameras taking it in, Gillian cut her off and put her in her place.

"Oh, please, Ms. Christian, get a grip. Your vindictiveness and spiteful attitude are not appropriate to a professional interview. You're not asking decisive, pertinent questions. You're just a gossipmonger." Gillian shooed her away. "I'm not talking with you. You're not a professional in any sense of the word."

Millie Christian turned reddened eyes on Drew. Through her teeth, she said, "Tell me, Mr. Black, were you glad when the photographer was killed?"

"Actually, no. His death denied me the satisfaction of beating him down." Drew smiled at her. "And if he'd lived, I could have found out who he was working for."

She sucked in a breath at his honesty. "Just what incriminating scenes will we find on that camera when the film's developed?"

"That's more than enough." Belatedly taking charge again, Sparks stepped in front of her.

But the other reporters were just as keen on a bona fide scandal. They recorded what they could, and the questions were flying like crazy—all aimed at Gillian.

A mic was shoved under her nose. "Are you personally involved with Drew Black, the president of the SBC?"

A second reporter pushed the first aside. "What is the scope of your employed position?"

The first shoved back. "Is Drew Black trying to reform, and why?"

As Sparks herded Millie Christian away, she yelled over her shoulder, "Drew Black's position in the SBC is at risk, isn't it? Have even the owners tired of his crude behavior? Who will replace him?"

"For the love of . . ." Muscling aside the reporters, Drew took Gillian's arm and started dragging her along.

The fighters and their women closed ranks around them, making it impossible for the inquisition to continue. But still the flashbulbs lit the night.

"Jesus," Dickey said. "It was like a damned feeding frenzy."

"Won't matter," Simon said. "It's not like someone from the NFL was caught. This is one time I'm glad we're not more mainstream."

"It'll hit the smaller news venues, mostly online," Dean said. "But I can't see network news picking it up."

Bullshit. Every sports show out there would sink their teeth into the story. Sure, as long as the SBC did great, most chose to ignore it. But something like this?

His fighters weren't dumb; they realized the same thing. But Drew knew they were trying to reassure Gillian, and he appreciated their efforts.

For himself, he wasn't worried. He, and everyone else, knew his value. He was synonymous with the sport, and that made him nearly irreplaceable.

But Gillian . . . this would damage her good name, defame her in the PR world, and affect the jobs she got in the future.

Unless he could figure out a way to fix it.

As everyone packed through his front door to wait out the vultures, Drew's thoughts scrambled. The only solution he could think of was one he didn't want to contemplate.

He looked at Gillian's stricken face, her shattered attempts at dignity, and he knew, for her, he would do it.

He'd quit the SBC.

TOUCHED by some strange emotion, Brett smoothed a hand down Audrey's arm. She dozed against him, her head in the notch of his shoulder, her small hand resting on his abdomen. He wanted her again, of course. It was insane how she stirred him, kept him on the edge, and made him resent his dedication.

She looked so sweet and sexy, curled beside him, and last night . . . well, she'd taken him by surprise with her lack of inhibition. It wasn't a wealth of experience that had made her bold; it was the same churning, irresistible attraction that he'd felt for her the second he laid eyes on her.

Feeling her breath on his skin, the way her long hair trailed over his arm, how trustingly she relaxed against him, filled him with an overwhelming need to claim her the best way known to man.

But he'd kept her up late and didn't want to wake her so early.

Weak rays of sunshine cut through cold gray skies. It'd be a good morning for jogging. Quiet. Peaceful. Unlike some fighters, he didn't mind conditioning. He didn't have to force himself to do it. For him, it was as accepted, as much a part of his routine, as brushing his teeth and showering.

But today . . . today it took a little more effort to leave his bed, only because Audrey was in it.

She stirred but didn't awaken. The room had cooled considerably, so Brett pulled the quilt up and over her shoulder. Curled at the foot of the bed, Spice lifted her head to look at him, blinked her bright eyes, and went back to sleep against Audrey's feet.

Seeing his pet so accepting of Audrey put a funny little twinge in his chest. Other than Spice, he hadn't openly cared for anyone or anything in a very long time. He hoped he was a nice guy, considerate and mannered. But those traits had always come with a purposeful distance.

With Audrey . . . he couldn't quite drum up that same indifference. Already his feelings for her were noticeable beyond enjoying sex or mere companionship.

Whether he was ready or not, she'd crawled under his skin and was making her way into his heart.

As silently as possible, Brett gathered up the clothes he'd need and, with one final stroke along Spice's back, slipped from the room. After he dressed, he wrote Audrey a note and put it on top of her purse, still on the sofa. He chugged down a protein drink and then put on a pot of coffee and set out everything Audrey might need.

Wondering if she'd awaken while he was gone, he slipped out of the apartment.

This early, the neighborhood was quiet. In the impoverished area, most stayed up late and slept in till early afternoon. That suited Brett just fine; he liked that his alternate schedule gave him added privacy.

A blanket of dew clung to everything, even the pavement. Up ahead, fog drifted in and around street lamps still glowing. His sneakers made a satisfying splat, splat, splat with each long stride he took.

He loved jogging.

He'd been jogging since he was fifteen, using it as a way to ease tension, to gather his thoughts, to marshal his anger . . . at his parents, at injustice.

At a lack of viable choices.

But mixed martial arts had given him choices. Plenty of them. As he'd told Audrey, he was a fighter at heart—but he was so much more than that, too. He was first and foremost a survivor. No one could ever take that from him.

He'd gotten through his father's drunken rampages.

He'd muddled through the humiliation of his mother's drug-inspired prostitution.

He'd survived life on the streets, the cold, and the hunger.

Drew called him a wonder boy, but Brett knew that wasn't right; everyone was born with an instinct to endure. What else could he have done? Give up?

Trying to escape his own private demons, and the guilt that sometimes niggled at him, he ran a little harder. The guilt pissed him off. So he hadn't seen his mother in a long time?

He didn't want to see her ever again. For him, she ceased being his mother long ago. She'd allowed his father to vent on him physically during drink-induced fits. She'd relegated him to least importance in their family by begging the bastard to stay. And she'd gone against his pleas by not only drugging away her pain, but selling her body for the money to do so.

No, Brett didn't miss her. He wasn't even sure he pitied her anymore.

Fighters dubbed him "the Pit Bull." Appropriate, he supposed, recalling how his mother used to curse him for refusing to see things her way. Even after his dad had smacked them both around, leaving behind bruises and blood, she'd wanted the bastard to stay.

For her, accepting verbal and physical abuse was better than being a woman alone. Then, when his dad had skipped out, his mother had a complete meltdown; and she became an addict and a whore in less than six months.

A flush of heat, of remembered shame, washed over Brett.

Thanks to his mother, he'd learned that anything and anyone could be left behind. And knowing that had made him a stronger person.

He loved the idea of fighting for the SBC; it had been a goal from the day he started serious training. But, as with everything else in life, it'd have to be on his terms.

Luckily, Drew had backed down from his insistence that Brett's background could be used as a sideshow attraction to pull in viewers.

He put his head down and pounded the pavement in a furious sprint.

When the flush of resentment eased, he slowed again. Last he'd heard, his mom was sitting in jail, and truthfully, it was a blessing. At least while she was incarcerated, Brett didn't have to think about someone killing her with a dirty needle, disease, or just for kicks.

An hour later, with dawn casting hues of pink, orange, and red over the horizon, Brett came back up to his apartment. Sweat soaked his hair, his shirt, but he felt physically good. Loose, relaxed.

He thought of Audrey, either at the table sipping coffee or, better yet, still snuggled in his bed. The now familiar tightening of desire rippled through him.

He opened the front door and found her wrapped in the quilt, sitting on the sofa and talking on her cell phone. She glanced up, her big brown eyes warm with welcome. After a small wave, she went back to talking with her caller.

Brett paused inside the door to look at her.

Her bare shoulders above the quilt looked soft and sleek and pale. Fresh from the bed, her blonde hair flowed down her back in long twining tendrils. Cute bare feet poked out from the bottom of the quilt.

Unable to resist, Brett went behind the sofa and touched his hand to her soft hair, her shoulders, her collarbone. She went still, paused in her talking, and then leaned into his hands.

He needed a shower, but that didn't stop him from brushing aside her tumbled hair so that he could kiss her sensitive nape. A small shiver ran through her.

Damn, she enticed him.

"Millie," she said in a voice gone high and thin, "I need to go now." She stammered and then said, "No! Don't do *anything* until I get there. Yes, I'm serious. Forget deadlines. It'll wait. I won't be"—she glanced back at Brett—"too long." A pause. "That doesn't matter. I want to hear it all for myself before we start posting the story, okay?" She looked at Brett again, over his sweaty shirt and his loose jogging pants. She licked her lips, and her voice went husky. "I'll be quick. I promise."

Brett grinned. By quick, she better mean an hour from now, because he'd have to have her before he drove her back to her place.

After a few more verbal exchanges, she disconnected the call and tossed the phone near her purse. "I left my phone out here and missed a bunch of calls."

Nothing important, he hoped.

Still looking at his body, she said breathlessly, "You need a shower."

"I know." When she finally met his gaze, he held out a hand to her. "Why don't you take one with me?"

CHAPTER 13

ALL her life she'd been a responsible person. For years now, she'd felt a driving sense of duty that kept her from most social endeavors, particularly romantic involvements. She knew she shouldn't leave Millie waiting, especially under the circumstances: Millie claimed to have solid proof of the brutality and corruption in the SBC.

But . . . for once her heart overruled her head.

She stood and took Brett's hand.

As if she'd accepted more than his offering of shared intimacy, his gaze darkened, heated. She felt it, too. They were on a precipice of commitment, and she couldn't be happier—or more nervous—about it.

Walking backward, her hand held securely in his, Brett led the way into the small bathroom. "What do you have going on today?"

Audrey bit her lips, cleared her throat. Knowing what was about to happen, and how new it still was for her, it wasn't easy to think right now. "A meeting with Millie, work, and then just errands." She tried to sound blasé and failed miserably. "Why?"

He towed her into the room and shut the door behind her. With excruciating slowness, he tugged the quilt away from her one-handed grip and held it open wide. His gaze on her belly, he whispered, "I liked sleeping with you last night."

Her heart swelled. "Me, too."

Expression warming, he continued to look at her with the quilt at her back as if it were a barrier from escape. "Want to stay again tonight?"

She couldn't breathe. "Yes." Inhaling, she said again, with more conviction, "*Yes*, I'd like that."

Brett smiled, and it was unlike any other smile she'd seen from him. Dropping the quilt to the floor, he took a step back and peeled off his sweatshirt. "This could become a habit, you know."

Mesmerized by his casual striptease, Audrey croaked out, "What?"

"Showering together. Sleeping together." He shucked off his jogging pants, socks, and shoes and straightened in front of her. With a load of heart-melting meaning, he whispered, "Being together."

For long moments, Audrey just concentrated on breathing, on refraining from throwing herself at him. But she was clear on one thing: "I'd like that, too. If . . . if it became a habit, I mean."

Seeing how she looked at his body, Brett hauled her up close for a devastating kiss. But when she let her hands wander down his torso, he caught her wrists and laughed out an apology. "Sorry. I definitely need a shower before *that* gets out of hand."

He turned on the water and retrieved towels; Audrey stood there watching him, thinking that she loved his heated scent, the feel of his sweat-slick skin over solid muscles. When he had everything arranged, he stepped under the spray and waited for her to join him.

Showering with a man was a unique experience, one of many that she'd had with Brett. In such a short time, he'd given her so much and made her feel more like a self-assured woman and less like a protester on a mission.

Having fun, they took turns washing each other—and it became a special brand of foreplay that tortured her already heightened senses.

"I don't have a rubber in here." Brett kissed her throat, her shoulder. "If I don't stop now, I might not be able to. And neither of us wants that."

She wasn't so sure what she wanted anymore, but Brett had too much planned for his future to take unnecessary risks. Never would she want to be a burden to him.

She stepped away with a smile. "I'll race you to the bedroom."

Brett laughed, and even that, the husky timbre of his humor, excited her. After rinsing, they hurriedly dried and, still damp in places, rushed down the hall like children.

Very conscious of Brett trailing her, Audrey was only a few feet away from his bedroom when he scooped her up from behind and stepped into the room with her held in his arms. She squealed and laughed—and learned that lovemaking could be amusing as well as sizzling.

She hadn't been this lighthearted for a very long time.

Spice leaped from the bed when they came down together onto the mattress, making it bounce.

Rising on his elbows, Brett smiled down at her. "I really like you, Audrey Porter." He stole a soft, quick kiss from her mouth. "Everything about you."

She smiled, too, but she knew it was a lie. As good-natured and accepting as Brett seemed, he *couldn't* like her disapproval of his chosen profession. It was like a giant roadblock in the way of any real, lasting relationship between them, and it almost made her feel ill.

And if Millie had her way and they exposed the ugliness of the sport even more, what would Brett do? Could she let her personal feelings for him get in the way of what she believed was right?

"Hey." Brett tilted his head to study her. "I didn't expect my declaration to make you so gloomy."

"No." Shaking her head and wrapping her arms around him, Audrey denied it. "Your declaration makes me want to cry with happiness, because I *really* like you, too." She pulled him down to her, desperate to take what she could before it all fell apart.

"Yeah? Show me." And with that, he kissed her with the intent of making them both nuts.

There were no more words, and though Audrey knew she shouldn't linger, she couldn't find the strength to hurry things along, either. Luckily, Brett was in a rush of his own, taking her as if his control had left him, as if he wanted her every bit as much as she wanted him.

He was braced on one arm over her, thrusting inside her, pushing her hard while plying her breasts with fascination, when Audrey gave in to an all-consuming climax. Through a haze of pleasure she watched Brett's face, saw his nostrils flare, his jaw lock, and then he, too, came.

When they'd both quieted their laboring breaths, he fell to his side next to her. Audrey stared at the ceiling and relived each incredible moment. How Brett seemed to know exactly what to do, and when, amazed her. He was so in tune to her and her needs that he made her feel very special.

With him, she felt things she hadn't known existed—but not just during sex.

Like . . . right now.

She turned her head to look at him, and there was such a connection to him that it humbled her. "Brett?"

"Hmmm?" He scratched his chest and then turned his head toward her. His small smile was one of pleasure and contentment.

God, she hated this. Best to just get it over with. "Millie wants to do a story."

Maybe it was the way she said it, the dread she felt, but Brett went still and the smile disappeared. "What story?"

Because that one was hard to explain, Audrey said instead, "She called last night, but I didn't hear my phone."

"I know. You left your purse and phone on the sofa." Now frowning, Brett rolled up to one elbow. "What story, Audrey?"

A deep breath didn't help at all. Audrey sat up and wondered where her clothes had gone. She found them crumpled on the floor and gathered them into her arms.

She didn't want to remain naked while explaining this. "Let me get dressed and you can"—she nodded toward the condom—"take care of that, then we'll talk."

After appraising her with a long look, Brett left the bed without a word and headed for the bathroom. Audrey was dressed by the time he returned. He walked past her to the closet and got out a clean T-shirt, then boxers, socks, and jeans from his dresser.

Standing with the clothes in his arms, his feet braced apart, he studied her. "There's coffee in the kitchen."

Nervousness growing, Audrey asked, "Will you join me for a cup?"

Seconds ticked by before he said, "I don't drink coffee, but I'll sit with you."

For some reason, his words felt like a dismissal, so she started edging toward the door. "Okay. I'll . . . be in the kitchen when you finish."

She helped herself to the coffee and was sitting at the table when Brett came in and poured himself a glass of water. "Why do you make coffee if you don't drink it?"

He didn't join her at the table, but instead leaned back on the counter. "Other people do."

He waited without pressing her, but Audrey knew she had no more excuses for not telling him. Millie was waiting on her, and then she had to get to work.

"I don't have all the details yet—Millie will explain everything when I see her. But last night, when she was at Drew Black's house—"

Brett's eyebrows shot up. "She was at his house? Seriously?" He left the counter and pulled out a chair.

"Yes. You see—"

Leaning on the table, he asked, "*Why* was she there? To represent WAVS in some way?"

Disapproval reeked in his tone, and Audrey felt defensive. "Someone—not from WAVS—was taking photos of

Mr. Black and I guess he found out and chased the poor photographer—"

"*Poor* photographer?" He leaned back in his chair. "Unbelievable."

Already on edge, Audrey plunked down her cup and almost spilled the hot brew. "Are you going to let me tell this or not?"

Brett ran a hand through his hair, then gestured grandly. "Sorry. Go ahead."

The beginnings of a headache set in. "The photographer ran away from Mr. Black, and in the process, he got hit by a speeding car and died."

Going still, Brett muttered, "Shit."

Vindicated, Audrey repeated what Millie had told her. "In a response to reporters, Mr. Black apparently expressed a total lack of remorse for the man's demise."

That locked up Brett's jaw, but he kept silent.

Audrey leaned toward him. "It's all very complicated, but . . . my understanding is that the owners of the SBC hired a publicist for Mr. Black, a woman to sort of make him over into a less offensive person."

"That wasn't entirely the plan, but yeah, I already know about her. What of it?"

Audrey's mouth fell open. "You knew?"

"It's not a big deal, Audrey. Lots of public figures have publicists."

"But according to sources—"

"What sources?"

She had no idea. "—This woman isn't just publicizing him, but rather trying to change his image entirely."

Brett shrugged. "Trust me, that's never going to happen. Drew is who he is, and most people either love him or despise him. But I can tell you this: the fans worship him. He made this sport. Hell, some believe he *is* the sport. In my opinion, the SBC is way off in how they're handling this. It's largely due to Drew's image that we've gotten the recognition we have now. Far as I'm concerned, other than the personal conflict you witnessed, Drew Black is fine as is."

Audrey pulled herself together. "How can you say that?"

"I know him better than you do."

Smug, she asked, "Well, did you know that he's *sleeping* with the publicist? No matter how you look at it, that makes for a huge conflict of interest."

His exasperation was made clear with a drawn-out sigh. "Come on, Audrey. Why shouldn't two mature adults get together if that's what they want to do? Their relationship isn't hurting anyone, and if you ask me, it's no one's business."

No one's business. He'd included her in that statement. But how could she ignore this? "Millie was there, and she got the whole thing on her recorder, including the fact that Mr. Black might be replaced within the organization."

Brett straightened. "I don't believe that."

"She says her sources are secure. She . . . well, she interviewed the publicist, too. That's the basis of her story, that Mr. Black corrupts everyone around him and even seduced a woman who he knew was off-limits to him."

That brought out a guffaw. "I met Gillian Noode. Trust me, she's not a weak woman easily seduced. If she's sleeping with Drew, it's because that's what she wants to do, not because she's a victim." He shook his head. "And again, Audrey, how is that hurting anyone? Why does WAVS even care what a publicist does, with or without Drew Black?"

Audrey tried to drum up her earlier convictions. Just weeks ago, she'd have had her verbal ammunition loaded and ready to fire away. But now . . . now she saw both sides, and it made everything so much more complicated.

Her voice rose with the effort to make sense of it all. "The publicist is defending Mr. Black, trying to make him look better than he is. She and the SBC organization are hoping to hide his faults and cover up his brutalities. But Brett, you can't just put a pretty face on the ugly truth."

"What ugly truth are we talking about?"

Oh, God, the way he asked that . . . She did not want their growing relationship to come to a staggering halt, but how could she live with herself if she did nothing, and someone else suffered because of it?

Appearing almost saddened by her attitude, Brett reached for her hand. "Come on, Audrey. Tell me what you have against the SBC, and then we can talk about what really matters."

How did he do that, cut straight to the core of her feelings? He wanted the truth, and . . .

Why not? Talking about it was so painful, but it'd be the easiest way to make him understand why she couldn't just switch alliances. She needed resolution.

Audrey looked at his big hand holding hers with care. Brett was different; she was convinced of that. But one good example didn't change the norm.

She met his gaze—and bared her soul. "Because of the SBC, my nineteen-year-old brother was killed. And believe me, Brett, that's more than enough to make anyone realize what a horrible, bloodthirsty sport it is."

DREW watched Gillian part the curtains with care. For hours now, throughout the night and into the early morning, she'd been pacing with anxiety. Every time she peeked outside, he knew it was with the hope that the nosy reporters had left so that she could escape the invasion of her privacy, the scandal . . . and him.

One by one throughout the long night, the fighters had split, and a few of the reporters had followed them. Only a few die-hard scandal-seekers had remained, but given the relief in Gillian's shoulders, even those must have closed up their tents finally.

"They're gone." Face set in lines of determination, she started to hurry past him, but Drew caught her.

"Where are you going?"

For a heartbeat, she looked so lost, his guts knotted. "I don't know," she finally said. "Home, I guess. I need to get hold of Fran, I need to do some damage control, I need—"

His phone rang, and it so startled Gillian that she yelped.

Eyeing her too-tense posture, Drew pulled out his cell phone, glanced at the number, and shrugged at the inevitability of it.

Knowing Gillian stood there in awful suspense, he put the phone to his ear and said, "Hey, Fran. What's shaking?"

Gillian's eyes sank shut and a cloak of defeat masked her usual confidence.

Fran asked, "Is she there, Drew?"

He watched Gillian. "Who?"

"You know damn good and well who I mean. Gillian Noode. Is she there with you even now?"

"Now, Fran, you know that's none of your damn business." Gillian's eyes flashed open and she stared at him aghast. Shaking her head hard, she tried to discourage him. But what the hell? The damage was done, so why should he go down with a smile?

"My God, she is. I knew when I called and she didn't answer . . ."

"It is damn early still."

"Yet you answered."

Drew shrugged. "Yeah, well, I've never kept regular hours. That's one reason you've been riding my ass, right? To make me conform?"

"*Enough.*" Fran sucked in air to moderate her temper, and then she gritted out, "Put. The phone. On loudspeaker."

Drew rubbed his head. "Fine." Covering the mouthpiece, he said to Gillian, "She knows you're here and she wants to talk to both of us." Before Gillian could assimilate that, he uncovered the phone, hit a button, and said, "Go ahead, Fran. Let the vitriol fly, old girl."

Looking like a deer caught in the headlights, Gillian gasped, "Shut *up*, Drew." Then, remembering that Fran could hear her, she looked ready to sink into the floor.

"Hello, Gillian." Tone clipped and disapproving, Fran said, "I figured I'd find you there, all things considered."

Gillian gave Drew a black scowl and cleared her throat. "Fran, good morning. I was going to call you to set up a meeting as soon as I got home."

"Which would have been when?"

"At a more respectable hour, of course."

Oh-ho! Score one for Gillian for that backhanded censure against Fran's crack-of-dawn phone call. Grinning, Drew feigned a knockout punch as a sign of approval, and said, "Yeah, and speaking of respectable, why don't we set up a meeting for later today, and we can all—"

"Obviously, Gillian," Fran cut in, her voice raised, "this is not how I planned for you to transform Drew's image."

Gillian's backbone came back in spades. "*This* has nothing to do with Drew's image. It's personal and I don't care to discuss it."

"Well, my dear, you should have told that to the reporters who've been calling me through the night, asking for a statement."

Gillian stiffened. "In fact, I did tell them." She struggled for composure. "And as to our business agreement, I have been following a detailed and intelligent plan that I think you'll find is adequately building a more unbiased perception—"

"You're fired."

Gillian's mouth snapped shut.

Drew blew a fuse. "She fucking well did what you wanted her to!"

With ringing sarcasm, Fran quipped, "Oh, certainly, Drew. The transformation is astounding. I hardly recognize you."

Gillian rubbed her forehead. "Drew, enough already. It doesn't matter."

"Bullshit."

Clearly mortified, Gillian straightened her spine and squared her shoulders. "I can see that there's nothing more to discuss, then. Fran, I'll be sending you a list of my arrangements for future speaking engagements I'd lined up for Drew. I believe if you follow through, you can still—"

Drew snorted. "No way. Because I quit."

Stunned silence ensued.

Gillian blinked at him in confusion, and she blinked again when he winked at her.

He could hear Fran breathing. Finally, her voice shrill, she said, "You're bluffing."

"Nope."

"I know you, Drew Black. You would be miserable if you retired."

"Who said anything about retiring?" He gave Gillian a once-over, and she looked so adorable in her uncertainty that he couldn't wait to finish the call. "Your snit changes nothing for me. I'll be doing business as usual."

Gillian didn't understand—but Fran sure as hell did.

"Oh. My. God." And then with ripe fury: *"You're going to another organization?"*

Satisfied with her reaction, Drew propped a shoulder against the wall and smiled. "Now, Fran, we both know I won't have to. They'll be coming to me just as soon as Gillian and I do a press conference explaining that I'm free."

"You bastard!"

After all of Fran's plans to make him over, her attitude that she'd found him lacking . . . well, it felt damn good to have the upper hand again.

And he owed Gillian for that.

"Face it, Fran. You hired Gillian because she was the best. You told me so yourself. And with her representing my interests now, I'm going to come out of this smelling like a rose."

"Gillian agreed to this?"

"You fired her. What do you think?"

As he spoke, Drew took in Gillian's shock. The color had drained from her face, and her entire posture slumped. He saw it in her eyes—how she would try to defend him—so before she could start bowing and scraping on his behalf, Drew took the phone off loudspeaker and put it back to his ear.

"Have a good life, Frannie." He heard Fran start to speak, but he shut the phone on her and slipped it back into his pocket.

Had Gillian really thought he'd let her just walk away? That he'd let her be fired while he stood by and did nothing? Like hell.

Right now, she looked wrecked, not at all her usual poised, classy self. But he'd take care of that.

Drew didn't reach for her. Not yet. He didn't know what she was thinking, if she blamed their affair for the sudden downturn in every direction. All he knew for a certainty was that they weren't done. Not by a long shot. "You okay, honey?"

She shook her head. "You . . . you just *quit*."

Even now, during the proverbial shit-storm, teasing her appealed to him, so he said, "Damn, but you're sharp. Nothing gets by you."

Numbness waned beneath ire. Her impressive chest heaved, drawing his attention. "Are you out of your mind? You *love* your job!"

Drew shrugged. "Yeah, well, Fran was going to fire me anyway. Not permanently, you know, but long enough to manipulate me or punish me—one of those gamey moves women like to use to make men squirm." He pushed away from the wall. "But you know I'm not a fan of squirming."

As if his mood finally penetrated her fog, Gillian took a step back. "Drew . . ."

"Out of bed, that is. In bed . . . honey, you can make me squirm all you want. I'll look forward to it."

Her jaw loosened. "For crying out loud, Drew. I can't believe you're talking about sex right now!"

"I'm horny," he said by way of explanation. "How about you?"

She stopped retreating and took a stance. "Drew, this is serious. When the firm finds out about this, they'll fire me, too. My entire life is crumbling. *No one* is going to want to work with me after this."

Drew couldn't help but snuggle her in close. "Don't be so dramatic. Everything is fine, I swear."

She groaned. "You're an idiot." There was no real venom in her insult, just numb disbelief.

"Yeah, I know," he murmured, being as conciliatory as he thought she needed him to be. "But, sweetheart, I am not a man without resources. Do you think the SBC is the only gig in town?"

She pressed back to stare at him. "I heard what you told Fran, but that was just a bluff, right?"

"Of course not. I wouldn't bluff about something that important."

"But . . ." She slapped away his wandering hands as he tried to cuddle her backside. "You've told me over and over again that the SBC *is* the only gig in town, that it is *the* MMA organization, that no other organization can come close to comparing—"

"Yeah, because I was in charge." Without her realizing it, he started easing her toward his bedroom. He hadn't lied about being horny. Seeing her so vulnerable brought out his inner King Kong. And beyond that, she needed to relax a little so she could get things in perspective.

And once she did, she'd realize that she wasn't done with him, either.

Whatever it took, he would make this right for her— after he gave them both some sexual oblivion. "Trust me, honey, I can build greatness again. I'm not worried about that."

He'd just gotten her to the bed when she recharged, coming around with a vengeance. With her thoughts visibly scrambling, she said, "You're really not worried?"

"Nope." He cuddled a heavy breast. "And you shouldn't be, either. Just think how much nicer it'll be working for yourself instead of others."

"Working for myself." She sort of tasted that before she

began grumbling again. "My God, Drew, you're making this out to be an opportunity!"

"That's exactly what it is." He went to work on her shirt. "Fran knows it, too; that's why she was so furious. And just to rub it in"—or possibly get himself repositioned in the company—"we'll drop in to see her and Loren this afternoon. You can come up with a plan of attack before then, right?"

The shirt coming over her head muffled her reply. Distracted in a mighty way, she pushed away his hands as he reached for her breasts. Drew redirected his efforts and finished stripping her.

She paid little enough attention as her brain worked on strategies. "I suppose I could get a viable plan together. But I'll need the names of the other fight organizations so I can do some quick research on them."

"Not necessary." Drew stripped off his own clothes. "I know everything there is to know about them already, including their lack of profits, what's causing the losses, the faults in their future plans, and what each would need to do to become a contender in the market."

Gillian gaped at him. "You're—"

"Outrageous?"

Eyes wide, she shook her head. "I was going to say *amazing.*"

"You're only just now realizing that?" Grinning, he tumbled her onto the bed. "Luckily, Fran and Loren already know it, as do the fans. Trust me, no one in the SBC wants me working against them."

She put a hand to his jaw. "Most men would be flattened by all of this, you realize."

"All of what?" Right now, he was flattened by how badly he wanted her. Every damn time, he wanted her like he'd been celibate for years.

"Bomb threats and lunatic bloggers, snooping photographers and sudden termination. But nothing fazes you, does it?"

He was fazed all right. But he was a man who liked to

work through problems, not wallow in them. "You must not know me very well if you think I'd go to pieces over this stupid stuff."

Suddenly her eyes flared wide and she straight-armed him, pushing him back enough that she could see his face. "That's it!"

"What?" He caught her wrists and moved her arms up over her head so he could regain the physical closeness. He liked the feel of her breasts against his chest, her soft belly against his abdomen . . .

Struggling, Gillian said, "No one knows you, Drew. Don't you see? It doesn't matter what you say or how you say it. It never has. It's about what you do."

"Well . . . yeah." He wished she'd stop talking and fighting against him. He wanted to be inside her. Bad. "Words are just words. I've always said that."

She managed to get her hands free and tried to scramble out from under him. "I need you to tell me everything good about you."

He caught her by the hips as she was half turned and plopped her onto her back again. "I'm a stallion in the sack."

"Drew, I'm *serious*."

"So am I." He pinned her down and spread her legs with his own, settling between them so she'd have no misunderstanding of his intent. "Give me two hours, and you'll know just how serious I am."

Chapter 14

HUFFING her exasperation, Gillian dodged the kiss Drew tried to give her. Right now, he was making clear thought very difficult. "I can't believe you want to do this now. We have plans to make."

"We'll plan after you're not so tense."

She appreciated his ardor, she really did. But until she resolved a few issues, she'd damn well stay on edge. "I just lost a job, Drew. And I got humiliated in the bargain *and* became part of a scandal. I'm allowed to be tense."

He kissed her throat in a spot that never failed to send shivers over her body. "Nonsense. I have the perfect cure for that. Relax and let me show you."

Oh, for crying out loud. His kisses trailed down to her collarbone—and then lower still. She could actually feel her nipples starting to throb.

One more time, she tried to resist him. "Can't you turn it off for just a little while?"

He licked her nipple, and when she gasped, he murmured, "Not with you around, no."

He sucked her nipple into his hot mouth, and it felt

so good, so stirring, that her fingertips dug into his shoulders—and Gillian wasn't sure if she wanted to push him away or hold him tighter to her.

He teased both nipples until she wrapped her legs around him and lifted her hips, trying to encourage him to haste.

To her frustration, he didn't take the hint. Instead, he moved back up her body and, after a soft kiss to her mouth, he held her unresisting arms over her head. "Are you listening to me, Gillian?"

That particular tone was unfamiliar to her, at least in bed. It was rough and deep and . . . forceful.

The thrill of the unknown sizzled through her. She drew in a tight breath. "Yes."

"In order to get the full effect of this, I want you to stay put, without moving. Got that?"

She licked her suddenly dry lips. "Why?"

Staring into her eyes, he said, "I want you in a supplicant position."

Her independent nature rebelled, and she started to move away. But she didn't get far.

"Ah-ah, Gillian. I want you to trust me." He stretched her out again, and with one hand clasping her wrists, held her that way. "This is for your own good."

Desire battled with uncertainty. "What are you going to do?"

"I think it'll be better if you wait to find out."

She wasn't a wilting flower, but then, neither was she a sexual dynamo. She'd never in her life done anything too risqué, and her experience with powerful men like Drew was nonexistent.

His smile showed cool constraint. "Gillian, you know you're going to like this, so stop resisting."

Oh, God. She swallowed and nodded.

Satisfied, Drew sat up beside her. He took the time to smooth back her hair, fanning it out on the pillow. He trailed his fingertips down her arms and around to her breasts.

"I love your rack."

Gillian choked. "Gee . . . thanks. That's exactly what a woman wants to h—" Before she could finish, he closed his fingertips around both nipples.

He watched her face as he gently rolled, tugged.

Her fingers twisted together to keep her arms in place, and her legs shifted with the growing sensations. Licking a finger, Drew dampened both nipples and then blew on them.

Gillian couldn't help but groan as her nipples tightened almost painfully.

He kept it up for so long, toying with her nipples, playing with them, licking, stroking, sucking, and pulling, that she thought she might come just from that.

But just as the release began to build within her, he retreated and looked at her body again.

Biting her lip to keep from moaning out her disappointment, Gillian watched him. When he half smiled, she *did* moan, unsure of what was to come. She was already so primed, even her skin tingled.

"Drew?"

"Shhh." Clasping her knees, he drew her legs up to bend them and then opened them wide.

Gillian turned her face away, but when nothing more happened, she looked at Drew again.

He'd been waiting for that, apparently, because he whispered, "Better," in approval.

And . . . it was. Seeing his face, what he felt as he looked at her exposed body, heightened her arousal even more.

She was on the verge of asking for his touch when, with one hand, he covered her sex, and with the other he came back to her breasts. She wanted to feel his fingers inside her; she needed to feel that.

He pinched one nipple lightly—and just held her like that. It was excruciating, needing him to do more, but almost unable to bear it.

He pressed his palm to her. "I can feel how wet you are already."

"I'm ready," she agreed. More than ready.

Every so often, the fingers at her nipple tightened or released, rolled or rubbed. By shifting her shoulders a little, she could make it happen, but not to the degree she needed.

He took his gaze off her face to look at her sex, and Gillian held her breath.

When he began lightly petting her, she wanted to melt. It was incredible, but nowhere near enough.

"Open your legs a little more. As far as you can."

She tried to do as he asked—and he rewarded her by sliding two fingers into her, thrusting deep in one smooth move.

Her hips lifted off the bed. *"Drew."*

"Don't move, Gillian. Not until I'm inside you."

She was getting frazzled enough that she snapped, "When will that be?"

He brought his thumb up to her clitoris. "When I'm done having fun this way."

That was all she needed, that one additional touch just there. Her eyes sank shut and her lips parted. It wasn't easy to stay in such an awkward position, especially knowing that he took in her every expression and could see every inch of her. She knotted her hands in the sheets to ground herself and strained to keep her legs sprawled wide.

"Come for me, Gillian." His thumb moved over her; his fingers moved in her.

She felt herself tightening.

"That's it, honey." He sounded as turned on as she felt. "That's it."

The climax slammed through her with startling strength, rocking her body and clenching her muscles so that her thighs closed around his hand. They both groaned.

Just as the release began to fade, he pulled his fingers from her and put them in his mouth. His eyes closed as he licked away her taste. When he opened them again, their gazes met.

He moved between her legs, but not to enter her.

Lifting up, Gillian asked in confusion, "Drew?"

He raised her hips in his hands and, after one long, heated look at her wet sex, leaned down and put his mouth to her.

She dropped back on the bed. His tongue slicked into her, tasting her deeply, and that was enough to set off aftershocks of pleasure. When he stroked over her clitoris, she jerked from the too-intense sensation. But he held her secure, and there was nowhere for her to go, no way to escape the rasp of his tongue and then, all too soon, the gentle suction of his mouth.

She sobbed as the sensations escalated too quickly again. She twisted, alternately lifting to him and drawing away until, faster than she realized possible, another orgasm shook her.

Drew kept her locked to him, taking everything from her, moaning against her as her body quaked.

This time when the orgasm waned, he rushed to get a condom, cursed as he rolled it on, and then came back to her. He hooked an arm through one of her legs, opened her again, and thrust deep. He gave her no time to recuperate, already driving fast and hard, shaking the bed, gasping with each penetration.

"Christ, Gillian . . ."

Overcome by lethargy, Gillian barely managed to get her weakened arms around his neck. Amazing. And yes, outrageous. Wonderfully so.

Not with any other man could she have so completely let go. But with Drew . . . well, she loved him, so much so that it scared her.

Drew's face tightened; his jaw locked.

She knew he was close, she could feel the power building in his body. "Kiss me, Drew."

With a growl, he took her mouth. Even as his release hit him, he continued with a rapacious kiss that left her lips swollen and her heart soft with emotion.

Sinking down onto her, Drew struggled to even his breathing.

Gillian stroked his back, smiled to herself, and whispered, "You were right."

Half a minute passed before he worked up onto his elbows. "Always." He took a few more deep breaths. "What was I right about this time?"

Gillian couldn't help but laugh. The man didn't lack confidence. "I am very relaxed right now. Not a tense bone in my body."

Instead of smiling, he gave her a profound, intense look chock-full of emotion. "Just remember that I'm the one with the cure, all right?"

"Oh, definitely." The way things were going, they would both be tense again in no time.

It was going to be one hell of a day. But thanks to Drew, she at least had a plan. Now that her anxiety had lessened, she couldn't wait to implement it.

"MY brother was such a fan of the sport, and he thought he was so invincible. He badly wanted real recognition, but the SBC wasn't interested."

"How old was he?"

"Bill was nineteen. So young." Her small laugh was one of irony. "I was only twenty—but I always felt way older than him."

It wasn't unheard-of for fighters to be that young while building their careers at smaller venues, on a path to the SBC. Brett wondered if her brother had gone through the right channels, with the right training, or if, like many, he thought he could find a shortcut to fame. "Who did he train with?"

"I don't know. None of us really knew what he was up to. Bill was always a quiet kid who struggled with fitting in. He wasn't the best student or the most popular guy in school. He wanted . . . I don't know. A way to get recognized, I think."

To Brett, that didn't factor in. MMA fighters comprised every personality type imaginable. Some came from wealthy families, some from poverty. Some had known great popularity, where others were total misfits. What the successful ones had in common was talent, training, and heart.

"He was so excited when a small group of organizers invited him to participate in an unsanctioned night of bouts. He . . . he told me about it, and he begged me not to say anything to our parents."

Shit. Brett rubbed her shoulders. "Even at nineteen, he was a legal adult, Audrey, able to make his own decisions. You can't blame yourself."

"I knew it wasn't a good idea, but I believed him when he said it was safe, when he . . ." Tears welled in her eyes. "When he told me he'd be fine and nothing bad would happen."

Now wasn't the right time to point out the gulf that lay between an unsanctioned amateur fight night and the professionalism of trained athletes competing.

Instead, he pulled Audrey over to sit on his lap. "You were there? At the fight, I mean?"

She nodded. "It was so awful, worse than I'd ever imagined. Things were okay at first, even though I flinched over every hit either of them got in. Then the other fighter hit Bill right in the temple, and when it rocked him, he leaped in and kept on hitting him. My brother just sort of covered up, trying to deflect the blows. The announcer called it a 'flurry of punches,' and that's what it was. One strike right after another, over and over again."

If her brother had turtled up and wasn't intelligently defending himself, the fight should have been stopped by the referee. But an untrained amateur ref was as bad as an untrained fighter, maybe even worse since the fighters' safety depended on him recognizing when a fighter was in real trouble.

"Bill collapsed, and while he lay there, unmoving, everyone screamed and cheered in excitement." She looked at Brett with hollow remorse. "The other guy had won."

"What happened to Bill?"

She swallowed hard. "When people realized he wasn't coming to, emergency medical technicians finally came in, and they . . . I don't know, worked on him in some way. I saw that his eyes were finally open and he even stood up, but he was so wobbly." She put a fist to her mouth. "I wanted to go to him, but I didn't want to humiliate him if he was okay."

"And you were only twenty yourself, Audrey." He wanted her to understand the limited expectations for a woman so young. "You were unfamiliar with the fight scene, what was wrong or right."

She lowered her head. "He always complained to me about babying him too much in front of other people."

With his fingertips under her chin, Brett brought her face back up. "But that's what big sisters do, right?" Like *he* had a fucking clue. "They show their love."

She nodded. "But that night, I didn't. That night, I tried to stay out of his way." Her eyes briefly closed. "He had a seizure." More tears welled. "Right there on the mat. Before he could leave the ring, he crumpled and then started jerking in spasms. Everyone was screaming and . . . excited. And by then, I *couldn't* get to him."

The image appeared in Brett's mind, and he could only guess the helplessness and dismay she had to have felt. "Christ, Audrey, I'm so sorry." He put his forehead to hers and wished for a way to take some of her pain.

She dashed the tears from her face and rushed through the rest of the telling. "They took him to the hospital by ambulance, but he didn't get better, Brett. And my poor parents . . ."

Her entire body tensed in remembered heartache.

Again Brett rubbed her back, offering the only thing he could: understanding and comfort.

"They didn't even know Bill was fighting, that he was in danger, and then they had to come to the hospital and see him like that, being hurried off for brain surgery because of a clot on his brain."

Brett had known her long enough now to know how

she'd dealt with it all—she'd taken full responsibility, and in her protesting of the sport, she hoped to atone.

"It was not your fault, Audrey."

She didn't even hear him. Voice now lower, numb with agony, she said, "He lived through the surgery but went into a coma not long after. A few days later, he died without ever regaining consciousness. My parents didn't get a chance to tell him good-bye, and I never got a chance to tell him how sorry I was."

Brett pulled her closer and tucked her head in under his chin. The minutes ticked by, but he could only hold her until she'd regained her composure.

When she finally stirred, it was to look up at him and ask, "Now do you understand?"

He cared about her, Brett realized. A lot. Beyond enjoying her company and the physical compatibility, he was fast falling in love with her.

Hard as it would be for her, he couldn't let her go on thinking that the situation with her brother had any resemblance to the sport of professional MMA fighting. He searched for the right words and decided honesty would be his best bet.

"I understand that, because of your experience, you have a skewed perception of the sport." He smoothed a hand over her hair and kept her close when she would have leaned away. "Yeah, I get that, Audrey. And I know that emotions have a way of coloring things."

"I am emotional about it, but it's also fact."

The tears left her lashes spiked and her brown eyes glistening. "My brother loved MMA. That was clear enough when he explained his plans to me. I know this was an amateur setting, too, but I saw how the crowd got pumped by the bloodshed and how, while my brother was collapsing onto the mat, no one cared." She scrambled from his lap to stand before him, hurt, determined, smothered in guilt. "They were all too busy screaming for the fighter who'd beat Bill nearly to death."

Brett stood, too. "You're a smart woman, Audrey."

She slashed a hand through the air and turned away.

Brett brought her back around again. "What happened to your brother—that isn't the sport any more than a kid jumping off the roof of his garage in a cape is Superman. The SBC doesn't support unsanctioned fights or amateurs trying to emulate professionals. In fact, they go out of their way to try to discourage that stuff."

"If it isn't about bullies and jerks, then why does your president, who represents the sport, need a handler to change his image?"

Ah, hell. It would have to come back to that. "Drew Black is a strong personality, and thank God for it. Most of the fighters are as responsible and caring as anyone else. But, as is the case with most athletes, they like to play hard and negotiate harder. A slick, smooth-talking businessman wouldn't make it a year. Drew . . . he manages everyone and everything around him. Sure, he polarizes some people in the process. They either love him or they hate him, and if you attack his sport, you'll hear from him. On his terms."

She gave him an *Exactly* look of satisfaction.

Brett shook his head. "Honey, Drew isn't the devil. He doesn't beat women or kick puppies. He pays his taxes; he raises a shitload of donations for more charities than I can count; he's not a drunk or on drugs. He's a brilliant entrepreneur with standout leadership quality, who's passionate about his business. He's flawed, like we all are. The difference is that his flaws are highlighted in the media because he's a celebrity of sorts."

He could see that doubt blossom in her demeanor and pressed his point.

"Gillian Noode is a woman hired to do a job. No way should she be a target for WAVS." He put his hands on his hips. "Look at it this way, Audrey. You're sleeping with a fighter who will defend the sport to anyone. Does that mean that a crew of reporters and cameramen should converge on you, dig through your past, and invade your privacy?"

She paled. "No." Shaking her head, she repeated more strongly, "No, of course not. But it's not that easy, Brett. This is Millie's story. She's excited about it and, given her history with Drew Black, she feels totally justified in exposing every aspect of his life. This is the big bomb she's been waiting for to . . ."

"Get even?" Even he hated how that sounded. "And using an innocent woman to do that is okay?"

Audrey wrapped her arms around herself and paced away.

"You realize, of course, why this is important to me."

She glanced at him with empathy. "Your past?"

"My dad caused more damn scenes than a circus elephant on the loose. I could never bring anyone around to our place, even after he split, because I never knew what shape my mother would be in." God, he hated talking about this, but he needed Audrey to understand. "I know what it is to be publicly humiliated."

"You were a child, Brett. No one would ever fault you for your parents' . . . shortcomings."

He almost laughed. Fault him? No, most wanted to put him up on a fucking pedestal for surviving it.

Brett decided it was time to lay it out there. "Bottom line here, honey: I can't be involved with trashing Ms. Noode. I won't be. Not even by association."

Her head snapped up and her brows came down. "Meaning your association with me?"

"Meaning your association with WAVS." He caught her shoulders. "Protest the SBC and Drew all you want, hate him for what you think he is. I can deal with that. Drew can deal with that. But if your group uses Ms. Noode just to hurt Drew, then how can you point the morality finger at anyone else?"

"You're giving me an ultimatum?"

"I'm telling you how I feel. I've been on the hot end of scandal, and it sucks. I can't condone doing that to anyone else. Not for any reason."

"That's not what I do."

"It's what Millie will do if you don't kill this story."

She rubbed her head. "I have to think about all this." Rigid and offended, she turned away. "But for now, I really do need to go or it'll be a moot point, because Millie isn't going to wait on me forever."

Brett hesitated, but damn it, he didn't want to drive her home in strained silence. Pulling her around for a quick hug, he said, "I'm sort of missing you already."

Her frown eased away. In a sincere whisper, she said, "Same here."

CHAPTER 15

WHILE Gillian showered and changed clothes, Drew returned phone calls on his cell and took a self-guided tour around her modest home. They'd made it out of his place with only one return-reporter trying to snag a scoop. The guy wore Coke-bottle eyeglasses and a wrinkled dress shirt, but he knew his MMA. He asked some great questions, to which Drew replied, "I'll be doing a press conference later. Give your card to the lady and she'll let you know the time and location."

When he started to take a photograph, Drew stepped in front of Gillian and blocked him. "None of that or you'll be uninvited. Got it?"

The lanky kid scowled. "For sure you'll call me?"

"And give you dibs on the first question after I've explained things." Drew stretched out a hand. "What do you say?"

The kid accepted his hand.

He had a knack for handling the press—when he didn't let his temper get in the way too much. He'd be tested today, Drew knew, because the first jackass to insult Gillian would get cut out of the loop—for eternity. He didn't give a fuck if it was ESPN. He wouldn't let her be hurt by this.

Since the early morning nooky, she'd been in good spirits. He intended to keep things that way. And thinking about it, how she'd felt and tasted and sounded in her lust . . . yeah. It might have left her relaxed, but it had damn near made him shatter with the effort to keep control.

Taking her like a marauding fiend afterward hadn't really been part of the plan. Not that she'd complained.

In fact, about the only time Gillian complained was when he knew he had it coming. And then she came at him full-go, never whining or teary-eyed the way some women did. Gillian had more than her fair share of feminine wiles, but she didn't use them to manipulate.

Drew could hear the water running in her bathroom, and he pictured her naked, wet, suds sliding over all those full curves . . .

Shit. He needed to think about something else before he joined her in the shower. She needed some time without him pawing at her, and they really did have other issues to deal with. He was first and foremost a businessman, and getting things back on track would now have to be a priority.

As he strolled around her apartment, he made note of everything. Gillian had a nice place, girly like her, but also orderly and functional. High-end pieces filled the place, telling him that Gillian liked the finer things in life. But he didn't have a problem with that. He could afford to give her anything she wanted. With him, she'd never want for anyth—

Whoa. Drew put the brakes on that thought, which encompassed the foreseeable future. Dragging out their relationship was one thing; he loved having sex with her, and her company pleased him.

But was he ready for anything more?

Being with Gillian long term wasn't an insufferable thought. God knew, she looked like a million bucks; any guy would be proud to be seen with her. And in all social settings, she had a classy way of presenting herself that made her stand out from the crowd. She wasn't intimidated by him, even when he lost his temper. And she didn't simper the way some women did.

She was honest but tactful, sincere but strong willed . . . Losing her, now that would be intolerable.

How did she feel about it?

Drew paced into her kitchen and over to a set of balcony doors that overlooked a fountain in the courtyard. Gillian was independent enough that she wouldn't *need* a man. Not for anything.

He was used to fight groupies coming on in droves, but a woman like Gillian was unique. She enjoyed their lovemaking as much as he did, but did she want him beyond the physical?

Maybe he should start with that—find out how she felt—and then he'd figure out his own feelings.

With that decision made, Drew was able to concentrate on his messages. The price of business was that he spent more damn time on the phone than doing anything else.

He'd gotten through four return calls to promoters and sponsors before Fran started calling. Repeatedly.

Knowing he had her in a panic, Drew didn't take her calls and instead let them go to voice mail.

Let her stew, he decided. He was still pissed off over her rudeness to Gillian.

He was on his sixth call, talking to Marcus Gorman, the hard-boiled investigator he'd hired after the bomb threat at Roger's Rodeo, when Gillian came into the kitchen. She'd already dressed and fixed her hair and makeup. She looked sexy, beautiful, and ready to take on the world.

Drew marveled at her serene expression and innate poise. Since knowing him, so much had happened to her, most of it unpleasant. But it didn't get her down. It struck him then that while she was as feminine as a woman could be, she had a fighter's spirit. Beneath her voluptuous curves and silky soft exterior was the core of a champion, with the same unrelenting heart and never-die determination.

Drew laughed, and not only did his caller pause, but Gillian glanced at him with a brow raised.

In that instant, any doubts he'd felt were gone. He knew he didn't want to let her go, not ever.

Silently, she mouthed, *What?*

He covered the mouthpiece and said, "You're beautiful. That's all."

With an exaggerated eye roll and a special little swish to her backside, she turned away. As she began making coffee, Drew forced his attention back to Marcus.

"Sorry. What were you saying?"

"The police found the car that hit your photographer."

"Not *my* photographer." Drew snorted. It was too bad the schmuck had died, but he wasn't about to lay claim to him. "What of it?"

"It was abandoned by the riverbank, and get this— someone had doused it in gasoline and then torched it. All that was left was a heap of metal and the barely distinguishable license plates."

"Any idea who it belonged to?" Not that Drew expected it to be that easy.

"Yeah, but that's a dead end. The guy had reported the car stolen earlier in the night. I have the owner's name if you want it. He's an older guy, retired, and he's never even heard of mixed martial arts. He had the car insured, but he's mostly broken up because it belonged to his deceased wife. She passed away two years ago."

"Damn." Drew turned to Gillian. "Write something down for me, will you, honey?"

"Oh." She opened the drawer he indicated and took out a pen and some paper. "Okay, shoot."

Drew got the man's information from Marcus and shared it with Gillian. She didn't ask any questions, just took down the name and address and then went about her business.

Drew intended to contact the man. He couldn't do anything about the car or the sentimental loss. Drew knew he wasn't personally responsible, but the man had been affected because of some nut-job's vendetta against him, so he'd touch base to see if the man needed anything.

"Is that it?" he asked Marcus.

"Not quite. You know that woman you wanted us to do the background check on?"

"Millie Christian. What about her?"

At the mention of Millie's name, Gillian paused, but not for long. As if she refused to let it bother her, she returned to her breakfast preparations.

"Well, the cursory check sparked some interest, so I went ahead and dug a little more. I figured you'd want that."

"Damn right." Drew watched the innate, feminine movements of Gillian's body as she stood at the counter mixing eggs in a bowl.

Today she wore a vintage-looking dress with a portrait collar that showed off her throat, collarbone, and a tantalizing amount of cleavage. The waist cinched in, emphasizing the fullness of her breasts and hips, and the skirt hung loose to her knees. The light blue color brought out the bluer shade of her eyes. She'd pulled her shiny black hair into a simple twist and fastened it with a clip.

For so early in the day, she looked downright edible. It hadn't been that long since they made love, but Drew was starting to think he could have sex with her ten times a day and it wouldn't be enough to keep the lust at bay.

He turned away from her. "I'm listening."

"Christian has a criminal record a mile long. Dated. Nothing new for a couple of years now, and nothing too serious. Petty theft, harassment, driving under a suspended license, and some drug use. Also, probation a few times, and one court-ordered stint through anger-management classes."

Drew whistled low. "Anger management?"

"It's sketchy, but apparently she flipped out on a friend when they had a disagreement. She slugged her several times in the face and then kicked her when she went down."

"Damn." He could barely picture it. To him, Millie looked like a tall, redheaded frump. "Some friend."

"I thought you'd be interested in all this."

"There's nothing recent, huh?"

"Not for the last two years. The thing is, she moves around a lot. I've had to gather this stuff from three different states. If there is anything more recent, I haven't found it—yet."

"Keep digging. And try to find out where she was last night."

"You think Christian had something to do with that photographer?"

"Makes as much sense as anything else. The woman makes no bones about thinking I'm the devil incarnate." Wouldn't that be a kicker, if it was Millie Christian causing all the trouble? Talk about vindicating himself . . . "How far does she live from where the car was stolen?"

There was a pause and a rustling of papers, and then: "Huh. Less than five miles."

"Interesting, wouldn't you say?"

"I'll get right on this, and I'll let you know as soon as I find out anything. In the meantime, given how things are escalating, I think it'd be a good idea to put a tail on Ms. Christian. How do you feel about that?"

It'd raise his bill astronomically, but what the hell. "Do it. And while you're at it, you have someone you can put on my house to keep an eye on things?"

"I have some very discreet people I work with. Consider it done. What about your lady friend?"

"She's going to be staying with me." And Drew knew he sounded possessive when he said, "I'll watch over her."

"Ah, got it. Okay, then. I'll be in touch."

When Drew turned back around, Gillian had crossed her arms and was watching him.

"Who are you talking about?"

Ignoring yet another call from Fran, he closed the phone. "None other than Ms. Millie Christian."

Gillian shook her head. "No, I got that part, and you'll

explain the details in a minute." Crossing her arms under her breasts, she took a challenging stance. "Who's going to stay with you so you can watch over her?"

Because, in his mind, there was no question about it, Drew didn't balk. "You are."

Her mouth firmed. "I see. And do I have anything to say about it?"

"You want me to go on bended knee to ask all pretty-like?"

That image, usually associated with a marriage proposal, stymied her. "No, no, of course not," she stammered. "But I don't want you making plans that concern me without talking to me about it first."

"Fair enough." He helped himself to a cup of coffee. "A lot of shit has gone down because some lunatic has a grudge against me. It's bad enough that your car got trashed, but you're dead level in the crosshairs now, thanks to the media blast." He sipped his coffee, leaned on the counter, and then gave her a level look. "I care about you."

A slight flinch of her eyes left him guessing if it was inspired by surprise, or dismay.

"No way in hell am I going to let some slimy little psychopath hurt you. And the easiest way to make sure you stay safe is to keep you with me." He took another sip, watching her, gauging her reaction. "Right?"

A flush colored her cheeks. She started to answer, and then suddenly she turned her back on him.

Drew lifted a brow. "Gillian?"

When she faced him again, she appeared more composed, at least outwardly. But he wasn't buying it. He knew her too well to be fooled. He had her on the ropes and he planned to keep her there until he got exactly what he wanted.

Which was . . . everything.

"I suppose it'll be fine since it'll surely be . . . temporary."

Like hell. Drew just waited, curious as to how she'd handle his lack of affirmation on a short-term arrangement.

She didn't know that he had no intention of ever losing her, and once he made up his mind on something, that was that. If she wasn't already won over, he'd ramp up his efforts.

And in the end, she would be his.

GILLIAN felt like a fish on a hook, squirming, gasping, and helpless. Drew, damn him, made no effort at all to clarify things for her, and she just didn't know if his intent was solely to protect her or if, like her, he wanted more.

Subtlety was not her forte. She was a woman used to stating her mind and going after what she wanted.

And, God help her, she wanted the infamous Drew Black.

But she wasn't bold enough to come right out and say so. Too many women before her had made that mistake and been dismissed because of it. If—when—their relationship ended, it'd be because she walked away. Not because he sent her packing.

But in the meantime . . .

Gillian cleared her throat and sought a tactful way to query him on his objective. "So you're proposing—"

He flashed a grin at her word choice.

Face burning hot, Gillian gulped back the rest of what she'd intended to say. Good God, this was *not* a proposal. "Ah, bad choice of words."

He shrugged, still amused, which left her more befuddled than ever.

A little irritated to be in this awkward position, Gillian started again. "What I meant to ask is, how long do you think it'll be necessary for us to . . . to . . ." To *what*? She had no idea what to call their relationship.

"Shack up?" Drew offered.

Jerk. She took a turn shrugging. The base description worked as well as any, and until she could form complete, articulate sentences, she might as well play mum.

"However long it takes, honey." Drew's gaze never wavered from her as he pushed away from the counter. "I'm patient—when I need to be."

That enigmatic statement did nothing to shed light on his purpose.

"I see." But she didn't.

Stopping right in front of her, Drew asked, "Why? Does the idea of living with me bother you? Are you so old-fashioned that you want a ring on your finger first?"

"No!" The shrill denial took her by surprise. Gathering herself, she said, "No," in a much firmer, less horrified tone.

Some vague emotion passed over Drew's face. "The idea of a ring really spooks you, huh?"

Oh, worse and worse. Gillian had never been so flustered over something so simple, but Drew was teasing her with an illusion of what her heart badly wanted.

Time to be logical and reasonable.

"Don't be ridiculous. I'm not in the least spooked." She forced a small laugh. "All I'm saying is that I understand the logic in being extra careful. The world now knows we're sleeping together. The cat's out of the bag on that one."

Drew narrowed his eyes the slightest bit.

"So why take unnecessary risks? Even though my building is secure, I don't relish the thought of being alone."

"Anything could happen," he agreed.

"And we're both mature adults who grasp the reasoning behind . . . cohabiting." She would not use that awful description *shacking up*. "And we both understand that it's on a temporary basis."

"I love logic in a woman."

That tripped her up, but not for long. "Yes, well . . ." Wishing that he wouldn't use the L word, Gillian forged on. "I'm a very capable person, as I'm sure you know. But after the bomb threat, what happened to my car, and the tragic drama of last night, I see no point to foolhardy bravery." Glad to have successfully navigated through those treacherous waters, she released a pent-up breath. "Until we figure out who's behind this nasty business, I'll stay with you."

Drew nodded as if bored by that diatribe. Ever so softly,

he brushed the backs of his knuckles over one breast, and his voice lowered to that sexy rumble. "So it's all about security. The fantastic sex doesn't factor in to your decision?"

Gillian locked her suddenly shaky knees. If he thought she'd deny how much she enjoyed sex with him, he was wrong. "The great sex is an added bonus." She nudged his hand down to her waist. "But understand, Drew, I wouldn't live with any man just for sexual gratification."

Nodding, he drew her closer and said against her mouth, "Just so you know, if you do need a ring, I can get you one, no problem."

Did he really think she was that shallow about appearances? "I can afford to buy my own rings, thank you."

He looked very disgruntled with her, but then her cell rang, interrupting things.

Gillian groaned. She just knew who it was, and she dreaded what would follow.

His expression dark, Drew said, "Ignore it."

But she couldn't. "I'll only be a moment." She sidled out of his embrace and went to the counter to dig her cell out of her purse.

Just as she suspected, it was her boss at the firm where she worked. The second she said hello, the reasoning behind a dismissal began. Gillian had little enough to say in reply beyond, "I understand."

When the call ended, she closed her phone with a click and . . . just stood there.

Never in her life had she been "let go." Her entire life, she'd been an exemplary employee who steadily advanced.

Her status had just changed in a very big way.

But she didn't feel nearly as desolate as she'd imagined—because Drew had given her options.

And speaking of Drew . . . he seethed with concern and tempered anger.

The anger, Gillian knew, was on her behalf. "Well," she said to him with a sincere smile, "I'm certainly glad that's behind me."

"What did they say?"

"In a nutshell, I'm now unemployed."

"Wrong." Drew watched her with caution, as if he expected her to start crying at any minute. "You're working for me now, remember?"

Such an incredible man. "I could hardly forget."

His scrutiny intensified. "How much were they paying you? I'll match it."

Gillian laughed. Amazing that she *could* laugh after everything, but Drew did that for her. "We can negotiate that later. Right now, I want to call Fran and set up a meeting."

"Couldn't we keep her waiting a little longer?"

"No." As she punched in the number, she explained her stance. "Striking while the iron is hot is always a good strategy. The longer we wait to do a press release, the more insane the gossip will be. And we owe it to Fran to get her input before making any decisions. And Drew?"

"Yes, dear?"

She gave him a look for his sarcasm. Fran's assistant answered, forestalling her conversation with Drew.

"Yes, this is Gillian Noode. I'd like to speak to Ms. Ferrari, please."

"Certainly, Ms. Noode." Excitement sounded in the assistant's tone. "Ms. Ferrari asked that you be put right through. One second, please."

So Fran had hoped she'd call? Perfect.

While waiting, Gillian covered the mouthpiece and said to Drew, "When we meet with Fran, you *will* be nice. Is that understood?"

"I hear you." He went back for more coffee, and just as Fran answered, he added, "But as my current number-one employee, you should know that I won't make a promise I might not be able to keep. How nice I am will depend on how nice Fran is."

Drew and Fran were both such dominating personalities that they would always butt heads. Gillian figured that she'd have her work cut out for her. But ultimately, regardless of what he said, she knew that Drew wanted to be with the SBC, so whatever it took, she'd make that happen.

As she'd told Drew when she first met him, she was the best at what she did. She could finesse anyone to her way of thinking.

Now she'd have a chance to prove it.

CHAPTER 16

MILLIE'S agitation was easy to see when Audrey finally met up with her outside her apartment. Spending so much additional time with Brett had her cutting things close, and she didn't have a lot of time to spare before she had to leave for work.

"What took you so long?"

It surprised Audrey to see Millie so disheveled. Her hair looked like it hadn't been brushed yet today, and dark circles discolored the fragile skin beneath her eyes.

"Millie? Are you all right?"

"I'm fabulous," she claimed. "I finally have him, and this time he can't avoid the consequences."

"Drew Black?"

"Who else?" Millie scooped her arm through Audrey's and they headed into the building. "He'll be publicly humiliated now that the SBC is firing him."

"You're sure that they are?"

"Definitely. It should be happening right about now, in fact." She laughed with anticipation. "Long overdue, if you ask me."

Audrey frowned at the gleaming enthusiasm in Millie's tired eyes. She wasn't acting like her usual, quiet self. Instead of vindicated, she seemed almost gleeful with the situation.

"Let's go into my place to talk, okay?"

Millie didn't answer; she just went along with Audrey as they climbed the short stairway to the second-story landing in her unadorned apartment building.

"He's screwing his publicist, Audrey. And the hoity-toity woman didn't even deny it! Now tell me, how is a publicist going to enact change in his public persona when she's become part of the problem?"

Before replying, Audrey unlocked her door and went in. Once she and Millie were both behind the closed door, she dropped her purse and gestured for Millie to join her on the sofa.

"Tell me everything, but we have to make it fast. I'm running late as it is."

Millie's eyes darkened. "So you had plenty of time to spend with Brett, but now that we're on the cusp of breaking a huge story, you're suddenly in a rush?"

Knowing her delay had hurt Millie, Audrey tried not to take offense at her comments. "I told you. I forgot my purse in the living room and I didn't hear the phone ringing."

In mild rebuke, Millie said, "But this morning we *did* connect, and still you kept me waiting."

Guilt washed over Audrey. "I know, and I'm sorry. It's just that—"

Suddenly Millie launched off the couch to stand. "Time is wasting. If I don't break the story, someone else will. They don't have the same details that I have, but it'd still dilute the impact."

Uneasy, Audrey asked, "What details do you have?"

"I know that Gillian Noode jumped into bed with Drew Black almost overnight. I know that she's been staying over at his house, probably screwing him in every room there." She shook her head. "She's obviously a slut. Even last night, when that poor photographer was killed, she stayed with him when any decent woman would have had the common courtesy to show some grief."

Audrey hated this particular attitude from Millie. She'd never seen it before, so she wasn't quite sure how to handle things. "Why do we even have to mention the publicist? I'm not sure I see the importance she plays in all of this."

Tucking in her chin, her expression disbelieving, Millie stared. "You don't see the importance?" She sat down with Audrey again. She even reached for her hands. "This isn't like you, Audrey. What's wrong? Is there some reason you don't want me to do the story? Because if that's it, you know I care too much about you to do anything to hurt you."

Now that was more like the Millie she knew and loved. "I guess I'm . . . starting to look at things a little differently, that's all."

Her smile teasing, Millie asked, "Brett Bullman, right? I know you spent the night with him." She leaned in. "How'd that go? I want details!"

Audrey grinned. "He's . . . well, he's pretty wonderful." Her happiness bloomed. "I'm really falling for him."

"I knew it!" Millie pulled her in for a hug. "I'm so happy for you."

"Thank you. But . . ." She held Millie away. "Now that I know Brett, I realize that I've been wrong about some things."

"Namely that all fighters are not the same, right?" Millie shrugged. "I get that. Brett is an exception—a really nice guy who just happens to fight. But what does that have to do with Drew Black and his whore?"

Audrey winced. "Could we stop calling her that? We don't know what she's thinking or feeling. She could be in love with Mr. Black."

Millie laughed. "Yeah, right, and that'd make her an idiot and a slut."

"Millie," Audrey chided.

Still chuckling, Millie held up her hands. "Sorry. I guess I just can't imagine any woman falling for his bullshit."

Even though the coarse language was unlike Millie,

Audrey didn't want to express disapproval at her friend. Actually, she didn't have time for disapproval. She glanced at her watch and groaned. She'd called in to work and told them she'd be late, but not this late.

"Isn't it enough that the SBC has made it clear that they, too, find Drew Black lacking? They're trying to clean up his blackened image, and he has to be humiliated, right? That should be the focus. I'd like to see you post the facts without involving Ms. Noode."

Millie studied her. "I can kill that part of the story, no problem. But tell me why the about-face? Did Brett somehow change your mind?"

Audrey hoped it wasn't an about-face. She'd never been the type of person who condoned slandering others. But saying so now would seem like an insult toward Millie and would make her feel like a hypocrite. Truthfully, until Brett had made the point, she hadn't really thought how it might impact the publicist to be the focus of such negativity.

Like Millie, she'd lumped together all those associated with the SBC. And now, thanks to Brett, she wasn't even sure the SBC was the bad influence she'd once thought. She really wished she had more time to ponder everything. But things were happening now, and she couldn't very well ask Millie to pass up on everything.

If anyone could handle ugly truths, it'd be Drew Black.

"Brett and I talked about it, yes."

"Aha. I thought so." Millie slanted her a knowing look. "I suppose he'd rather you champion the sport, rather than expose it."

"Actually, Brett hasn't said anything about me exposing the sport. In his mind, there's nothing negative to expose. But he does object to us putting the publicist in the spotlight."

"Why? Does he know her?"

Audrey stared at Millie. Didn't she see that Gillian Noode was an innocent woman, not their enemy? "Brett's met her. But his view is a personal one, since he's had attention drawn to his past before."

"And he hated it?"

Glad that Millie hadn't asked for specifics, Audrey nodded. "He's still sensitive about it, especially since Mr. Black wanted to highlight the more tragic parts as a sort of human-interest draw."

"Wow, poor Brett. Figures the SBC would stoop to exploiting one of their own like that. Drew Black is pure evil. I'm glad Brett refused." She tipped her head. "He did refuse, right?"

Remembering that awful scene, Audrey nodded. "He was willing to walk away from the SBC if Mr. Black followed through in his plans."

"Good for him." Full of concern, Millie whispered, "Is he one of those guys who's managed to turn his life around?"

Audrey shook her head in confusion. "I don't know what you mean."

"Did Brett used to be a drug addict or something like that? Or has he done time for robbery or something?"

"No!" Audrey couldn't imagine Brett ever abusing his body like that, or taking from others. "Nothing like that."

"Then I don't see how the SBC could use him."

"It's just . . . well, his parents weren't the best, I guess."

Millie snorted. "Whose are?" She stood, prompting Audrey to do the same. "My mom was a power-shopper who kept us in debt, and my dad spent too much of his free time working on an old junker he kept in the garage." She moved toward the door. "No parent is perfect, believe me."

"Brett's were worse than that."

"Divorced?"

Audrey looked at her watch again, and Millie was quick to say, "Never mind. You need to go and I need to spruce up my story." She hugged Audrey. "Let's talk tonight after you get off work, okay? And if you see Brett, tell him how sorry I am."

Appalled by that idea, Audrey said, "Actually, it'd be better if you don't say anything at all."

Millie smiled. "I understand. Now go change clothes and get ready for work." On her way out the door, she said, "And have a good day!"

Audrey stood there, a little frozen. There was something in Millie's eyes, some fanatical light, that left her more than a little uneasy. She put a hand to her stomach, trying to quell the sick feeling, but it persisted.

In a rush, she stepped out the door and over to the landing. "Millie?"

From the bottom of the stairs, the door half open, her friend looked back. "Yeah?"

"Let's meet tonight with the others." Audrey licked her dry lips. "Now that we know the SBC is probably going to fire Drew Black, we should come up with a way to really push our point, don't you think?"

Millie's smile looked far too staged. "I'm way ahead of you." She held up the cell phone in her hand. "I was just calling the others for that very reason. Let's say six o'clock. We'll see you then."

DREW saw the crowd of protesters before he finished parking the rental car, and he knew without a doubt why they were there.

Nice.

Gillian could sink her teeth into this tableau with no problem. He couldn't wait to see her reaction. But with the windows up, the air-conditioning and radio on, and her nose buried in assorted paperwork, she hadn't yet noticed them.

She was taking this all very seriously, and he appreciated that, but really, it wasn't rocket science. During their extended flight on a private plane to Las Vegas, and the short drive from the airport, she'd been studying a million and one notes.

"Hey, doll, time to look up and face some reality."

She blinked over at him. "What's that?"

Nodding toward the crowd, he said, "Take a gander."

She twisted in her seat—and stared. Drew figured she was reading one of the many signs held in the air. They ranged from *We Want Drew Black* to *Let's Get Back in Black* to *The SBC Is Drew Black.*

He leaned closer to her. "The gist of it is that they love me as is. They don't want me to change."

"I see that." Awe sounded in her tone. Wide-eyed and disbelieving, she turned back to him. "We'll get mobbed trying to get into the building."

"Nah. They're all very civilized."

"You're taking this"—she gestured toward the friendly mob—"in stride, too, I suppose?"

"'Course I am."

As he got out and walked around to her side of the car, she gathered together her papers. The second he opened her door, she said, "You've seen this before?"

"Picket lines are nothing new, both friendly and otherwise. Every time we go to a new area, it's a process of education. The politicians fuel fear by claiming that we don't have rules, that we'll put on a bloodbath complete with deaths, that we might even see the end of civilization if the SBC is allowed to perform. But the people always counter that." He gestured at the men and women, of all ages, who protested Fran and Loren's stance. "The fans know the truth of things."

"And they love you."

"They love the sport. And I'm a part of it." Grinning, he took her arm. "Come on. Time to put on your happy face and reassure everyone that MMA isn't going anywhere."

For ten minutes they were held up as Drew stood for photographs, signed shirts, laughed and joked. No way in hell would he tell the fans that he might be forced into joining a different organization—unless Fran didn't back down. These people wanted reassurance, and he gave it while dodging direct statements.

By the time they got into the building and on an elevator, Gillian was harried, and he felt damn good about everything.

With one hand splayed over her heart, she said, "That was amazing."

"Yeah." He stood with his arm around her. "I *love* that shit, I really do."

She abandoned her heart to pat his abdomen. "It's nice to have that additional aspect of fan support for our arguments. But Drew, don't start getting cocky. I meant what I said. I want you on your best behavior . . . no, wait. Scratch that. I want you on *better* behavior than your best has ever been. Am I clear on this?"

He gave her a squeeze for her earnest intentions. "Makes you wonder how I got this far without you, huh?"

Her hand knotted in his shirt. "I won't allow you to embarrass me with obnoxious rudeness. If you do, I'm walking out and that's that."

The elevator dinged at the top floor. "Got it. Mind my manners or you're going to be cross. No problem." At the moment, he felt too good to let threats bug him.

They left the elevator and crossed the hall to Fran's office. She had a massive suite of rooms that overlooked the Strip. In the evening, the lights made for a truly impressive show.

Drew strolled into the outer office with Gillian and politely waited while she informed the assistant of their arrival.

Neither of them sat, and within a minute an assistant showed them into Fran's office.

Loren rose from a padded black leather wing chair off to the side, and Fran came out from behind her desk.

The mood was solemn, tense. Screw that.

Before greetings could be spoken, Drew said, "You've got some outraged fans out there. And I hear they've been calling, e-mailing, clogging the message boards, all in all kicking up a fuss." He grinned, ignoring Gillian's shock as she went rigid beside him. "Now the ball is in your court. And Frannie, despite appearances, I'm sure you remember what to do with a ball, right?"

* * *

SHOCKED silence clogged the room. Gillian locked her teeth and her knees, and then she elbowed Drew. Hard.

Her aim was good—right in the guts.

He oomphed, bent forward, and wheezed, "Damn, woman. A simple 'Shut up, Drew' would have sufficed."

Fran and Loren stared in slack-jawed amazement.

Gillian said, "Fine. *Shut up*, Drew." Composing herself, she smoothed her hair, hitched her purse strap over her shoulder, and started over. Smile bright, she said, "Fran, Loren. Thanks for agreeing to see us."

Fran eyed Drew as he grumbled and rubbed his midsection. She had a difficult time pulling her gaze from him but finally managed to give Gillian her attention. "No problem. I wanted to speak with both of you anyway."

Loren coughed. "Why don't we sit down?"

Drew made a presentation of looking at Gillian for permission. He started to sit, paused, and asked, "Is it allowed? Or will you clout me again?"

Oh, she wanted to clout him all right. Her aplomb shot out the window. *"Sit."*

"Great. Thanks." He rubbed his hands together. "So . . . we're all sitting. Now what?"

Loren looked at Gillian. "I hope you can understand our dismay—"

Drew snorted. "You know you don't give a damn about any of this, Loren. It's just Frannie here who—"

Again, this time more calmly, Gillian said, "Shut up, Drew." She leaned forward. "As Drew pointed out, through no fault of your own, of course, you are now in something of a predicament. Certainly there may be a few news reporters who take issue with how Drew handles things. But more important than any small measure of censure, the fans *love* him. As is."

Drew aimed both thumbs at his chest, and mouthed, *Love me.*

Gillian tried to ignore him. "They don't want him to change. They support him as much as they support the fighters."

Fran crossed her legs. "The fact remains that he does antagonize important people, and in doing so, he ruins connections that we need."

"Oh, please," Gillian said on a deprecating laugh. "Through his management on every level of this operation, he's grown the sport at Mach speed. And let's face it, those who disapprove of him are mostly interested in pleasing the public. And the public has spoken. They want Drew Black."

Gillian could feel Drew watching her, but she didn't dare meet his gaze.

Into the silence, he said, "If that glowing praise doesn't win you over, then know that I have options." He held up a hand before Fran could speak. "Yes, Frannie, I'm prepared to go to the competition. Your competition."

"Under his leadership," Gillian added, "another organization will grow to rival the SBC. Don't doubt it."

Furious, Fran shoved out of her chair. "You're blackmailing us."

"Not at all." Gillian stood, too. "I can spin this so that no one will question your decision to keep Drew at the helm."

"How?" Fran pointed at him. "Look at him! He's so damn smug even now. He—"

"Generously gives of his time and money to help others," Gillian said.

Fran's mouth snapped shut. Loren grinned.

Drew's head swung around and, very slowly, he came to his feet. Maybe she should have forewarned him about her plan of attack. But . . . as loudmouthed and obnoxious as Drew liked to be, he was absurdly private about the good things that he did for others.

Fran looked back and forth between them. "What are you talking about?"

"Gillian," Drew warned.

She lifted her chin and continued. "Obviously you don't know him very well. Yes, he can be abrasive. No one would deny that. But he's also very giving."

"*Gillian.*"

Sighing, she stood up and faced him. "What's the matter, Drew? Are you afraid I'll damage your bad-boy reputation? Don't you think it's time to grow up a little and admit that you care about others?"

He jutted his chin forward. "Who and what I care about is nobody's business."

"It's *my* business," Gillian insisted.

"Well, yeah." He threw up his arms. "You're on the list of people I care most about."

Gillian mentally reeled. She could feel the heat of Fran's and Loren's stares. "I meant," she said around the shock, "that it's my business because I'm representing you."

He did that infuriating shrug thing again. "However you want to look at it, honey."

Fran waved a finger between them. "Are you two . . . ?"

"An item?" Drew snatched up Gillian's hand. "Yeah, we sure are."

"Engaged?" Fran specified. "Are you *that* serious?"

Gillian couldn't breathe. This was not the turn she'd expected. "Don't be—"

Drew squeezed her hand to silence her. "You want to go with us to pick out rings, Frannie?"

Fran put her hand to her chin as she pondered them both. "I see."

Gillian jerked her hand free. How dare he play these types of games? This was not the time, and she was not the woman, for such foolishness.

Before she could say a single word, Drew pulled her up to her tiptoes and kissed her. Despite their mute audience, he was quite . . . thorough.

When he let her go, Gillian barely restrained the urge to smack him good. Instead, she straightened her dress with several hard yanks that left no doubt as to her mood.

Drew said, "You are so hot when you're furious."

Gillian opened her mouth to lambaste him.

Fran spoke before she could, saying to Loren, "Let's talk a moment while these two . . . settle their disagreement."

Brother and sister left the room. The second the door closed behind them, Gillian turned on Drew.

"How *dare* you treat me like that, especially in front of them?" Her whole body trembled with her outrage and humiliation. "I am not one of your starstruck bimbos who will tolerate your ridiculous antics. I am a professional businesswoman. I am a—"

"Lady, through and through," Drew agreed. "A sexy lady." He whistled low to emphasize that. "And so damn smart and cunning."

"Cunning?" That sounded rather insulting.

Drew tapped his temple. "Damn right. You know just what to say and when to twist people around your little finger. I love it."

Gillian couldn't tell if he spoke with sincerity or sarcasm, and at the moment, she didn't care. Only by extreme effort did she keep her voice moderate. "What you just did is reprehensible. I told you that if you didn't behave, I'd walk away, do you remember that?"

He nodded, but said, "I love the way you pelted them with my good deeds. I'm sure you knew how I'd react to that, right? And granted, at first I was seeing three shades of red. But I think it struck the right blow, so I'm willing to let you slide on it."

Though his repeated use of the L word threw her, she still wanted to make a point. "You have no reason to be so closemouthed about your generosity to others."

"You have no reason to be closemouthed about our relationship." He touched her cheek. "But I figure we all have our reasons, right?"

Disbelief flattened her. "So what you did—that was *payback*?"

"Nope. I spoke the truth, and in case you didn't notice,

Frannie is all but salivating over the idea of me being a domesticated man. It gives her the out she needs to soften her stance against me, and it reassures her that someone is in control—namely you. And to her way of thinking, much better you than me, right?"

Good God, she couldn't believe the way his analytical mind worked. "Let me make certain I understand you on this. You actually *want* them to think that we're engaged?"

He stepped closer, crowding her, dissolving her anger with the warmth of his intent. "I want them to understand that you, Gillian Noode, have considerable influence over me. It's true, you know. I really do care what you think."

Gillian put a hand to her forehead, trying to sort out things. "You're insane, Drew."

"Actually," he whispered, sounding far too serious, "I'm—"

Fran and Loren stepped back into the room, interrupting whatever Drew might have said.

On edge, almost desperate to have him finish that thought, Gillian stared at him.

But Drew just winked.

Folding her hands together, Fran addressed Gillian. "I take it you have a game plan to highlight Drew's . . . heretofore unknown *finer* qualities?"

"Oh." Drawn back to the here and now, she withdrew papers from her briefcase. "Yes, I do." She handed the detailed file over to Fran and a duplicate file to Loren. "I'm sure you'll agree that, once we make certain facts wider known, we'll be able to counter most misgivings."

Her smile tight, Fran said, "I hope so."

Gillian took that as agreement. "I can start implementing everything in a press conference tonight."

Fran waved that away. "Let's give it another twenty-four hours."

Drew took offense at that. "Come on, Frannie, you know you're not going to fire me."

Shooting him a dirty look over the nickname, Fran

reluctantly agreed. "No, I'm not. But right now, everyone is enthralled over that business with the new fighter, Brett Bullman."

Confused, Gillian looked at Drew and saw his escalating apprehension and anger.

He looked from Fran to Loren and back again. "What are you talking about?"

As Fran moved to a chair and continued to peruse the file, she said to Loren, "Could you pull that up on my computer so they can see for themselves, please? Thank you."

His expression bemused, Loren went to her desk. Multimillionaire that he was, his sister was likely the only person who could issue him instructions. From what Gillian knew, even Loren's current wife—number three—didn't try to boss him around.

Loren typed in an address, pressed a button, and a giant monitor on the wall switched on.

Gillian's heart began to race as she read the detailed, malicious release. This was going to be trouble for Drew, she knew. Would Brett blame him?

"I wouldn't have done this," he said low, his rage palpable. "I would have made it about accomplishments and overcoming the shit life throws at you, not . . . not *this* insulting garbage."

Knowing how this would bother him, Gillian moved closer to Drew and touched his arm. "How did Ms. Christian find out about Brett's background?"

"I have no fucking idea, but that nutcase seems to know way too damn much." Drew shook his head. "And this time she's gone too far."

"Drew . . ." His lethal mood worried Gillian. She didn't want to see him take monumental strides backward when they were just getting back on track again.

"No fucking way am I losing Brett as a fighter." Dismissing everyone in the room, Drew pulled out his cell and started punching in numbers as he stalked out of the room.

Gillian had not a single doubt that he was calling Brett, and somehow he'd make it all work out.

With the perfect illustration to drive home her point, she turned to Loren and Fran. "There, do you see?" Neither of them did, apparently, but she had no problem explaining. "More than anything else, Drew cares about the fighters. That's a commodity you won't find in any other man. And that's why he's so invaluable to you."

Loren sat back in his seat with a grin. "Oh, I don't know about that, Ms. Noode. I think Drew has found someone that interests him even more than the SBC as a whole."

Fran glanced up from the papers to nod. "Settling down will accomplish the same thing—a grand transformation for Drew. It's about time. And lucky for us, he's found a wonderful woman like you. We couldn't be more pleased."

So now she was wonderful? Gillian fought the urge to roll her eyes. Weren't these the same people who had fired her just this morning? Not that their misguided assumptions mattered. Soon enough, Drew would set them straight.

For now, she wanted to make sure they understood one very important thing. "My God, you're both still missing the big picture. Drew doesn't need to transform. As he is, faults and all, he's one of the most brilliant businessmen you'll ever meet, and he's an outright wonderful human being, too."

Disinterested in that assessment, Fran went back to reading, but Loren looked behind her. He grinned.

Oh, crap. With dread, Gillian turned and found Drew standing half inside the door, his gaze speculative.

Feeling her face go red, Gillian asked, "Are you ready to go?"

"Yeah. I'm sorry to do this to you, but we're heading straight to the airport. I need to talk to Brett, and he's not answering, so I'll have to track him down."

Gillian said a quick farewell to Loren and Fran and rejoined Drew. How he kept up such a phenomenal pace, she didn't know, but it was his life, and . . . she wouldn't mind sharing it with him.

Maybe, once everything settled back to the normal chaos, she'd make him see just how perfect they could be together—for real, instead of simply as an illusion.

CHAPTER 17

WHEN Audrey returned to her apartment that night, her only thought was to see Brett again. In such a short time she'd fallen for him. Hard.

She had to let Brett know that she'd be delayed by the meeting with the other WAVS members tonight. It was important that she speak with everyone, to share her differing perspective on the SBC. But when she called Brett, he didn't answer, so she left a message.

Disappointed, she took a quick shower and redressed in jeans and a comfy, long-sleeved T-shirt. She was putting on her shoes when her cell phone rang.

Hoping it was Brett, she snatched up the phone and said a breathless, "Hello?"

Millie asked, "Have you gone to any of the MMA sites to check out my story?"

Actually, with Brett on her brain, Audrey hadn't even thought to look at the piece. She covered by saying, "I was getting ready to pull it up right now."

"Great." Millie snickered. "Thanks to you, I was able to . . . enhance it."

As her stomach bottomed out, Audrey squeezed the cell phone. "You didn't trash the publicist, did you?"

"Audrey!" Millie tsked in mock censure. "You asked me not to, so of course I didn't."

She relaxed, but not much. "Thank you, Millie. It was the right thing to do."

"Yeah, so you said. You can explain why tonight when we all meet. But in the meantime, let me know what you think about the piece after you've read it, okay?" Laughing, Millie hung up without saying good-bye.

Reminded of the dread she'd felt earlier, Audrey rushed over to her desk and started her laptop. Millie had been acting so peculiar lately, she didn't know what to expect. She also didn't know which MMA sites carried her blog, so she did a quick search using Millie's name.

With shock, Audrey watched the volume of sites appear. Millie had gotten a lot of exposure on this one.

Audrey sank into a chair and, filled with apprehension, clicked on one of the best-known MMA boards.

The article was right there at the top of the page, generating a ton of hits and some furious feedback from hardcore MMA fans.

Feeling sicker by the second, Audrey began reading.

SBC SCOOP, from Millie Christian of WAVS: Fighter escapes dregs of society, to do . . . what? Thanks to a tip from Audrey Porter, the MMA world can switch its focus from the disreputable performance of SBC president Drew Black to Brett Bullman, a fighter who has seen it all. After suffering emotional and physical abuse from his father, and drug addiction and prison for his mother, you'd think someone with that background would seek a better life to set himself apart from the violence and drug (steroid) use. But not Brett Bullman. He's making a life for himself as a brutal, bloodthirsty fighter in the SBC. One has to wonder if his drive to improve his deadly skills is inspired by his need to confront his father once and for all, or to defend his mother when she gets out of prison and goes back on the streets, selling herself for drugs.

Is Brett Bullman the caliber of man the SBC seeks? Are societal rejects, the abused and the downtrodden, perfect pupils to brainwash into a "sport" of viciousness? It would seem so.

It didn't take much digging to uncover details of Bullman's sordid life, including homelessness, despair, and then an obvious need to get even.

Even though she was sitting, Audrey's knees felt weak. As the article and all the repercussions from it sank in, her eyes burned with regret and shame.

She'd done this to Brett; throughout the article, Millie repeatedly gave her credit for the inspiration in the story. Why would Millie do such a thing to her? She had to know how Brett would react to this.

And Brett . . . oh, God. He'd be so hurt, and so angry. Rightfully so. The last thing he wanted was his life laid bare for everyone to analyze.

The majority of the responses to the news were outraged on Brett's behalf. But they were also filled with pity. She couldn't even imagine how a strong, independent man like Brett would feel about that.

He'd trusted her, and she'd inadvertently given Millie the initiative to go digging into his past. Millie had switched her cannon from the publicist to Brett with devastating and destructive effect.

She wouldn't call Millie back. No, Audrey would see her tonight at the meeting, and then she'd make her feelings known. Right now, she just needed to talk to Brett, to explain. But her call again went straight to voice mail, and her anxiety doubled. Was he ignoring her calls?

The idea of that tortured Audrey until she couldn't stand it anymore. The very least she owed Brett was a sincere apology. If he never wanted to see her again, she couldn't blame him. But she couldn't live with herself if she didn't explain to him and tell him how sorry she felt for all of it.

She glanced at her watch and decided to make a quick stop at the meeting first to get it out of the way. Her reign within WAVS was coming to an end. She couldn't be a part of a group that sought maliciousness over effectiveness, that used cruelty toward others for recognition.

It didn't take her long to drive to the meeting location. With early evening descending, the temperature dropped and a chilly breeze drifted in. Audrey pulled on her hoodie and, determined to enact some change, entered the room where the others had already gathered.

An expectant silence descended the second she stepped through the open doorway.

At the front of the room, Millie called out to her, "Perfect timing, Audrey. We were just discussing you."

Discussing her? Spine going stiff and straight, Audrey surveyed the once friendly faces of the women she'd considered friends. They looked at her with disapproval, distrust, and animosity.

Rather than be intimidated, Audrey went on the offensive. "What's going on here, Millie?"

Millie held out her arms to encompass the whole room. "We've been talking, and we've decided that you have a clear conflict of interest." She started toward Audrey. "After all, you insisted that I not break the story on that slutty publicist, even though we all know it would have had a great impact for our cause."

"That's nonsense and you know it! How would trashing Gillian Noode have furthered our objectives? She's not part of the SBC, and she's not a fighter."

"No," Millie agreed. "But Brett Bullman is, right? And still, here you are, all set to defend him, too."

Audrey clenched her fists. "I trusted you."

Millie got so close that she bumped into Audrey. "And we all trusted *you*. But now that you're screwing a fighter, you've turned your back on us, and our goals!"

Taking a step away to put some space between herself and Millie, Audrey scanned the faces of the other women. A few of them now looked sad for her, but most were nodding in agreement, ready to encourage Millie in her nastiness and aggressive posturing. Never had Audrey encouraged this type of behavior.

Why hadn't she seen the ugliness of it all before now?

Keeping her voice strong, Audrey addressed them all. "We were never about ruining lives. Our goal was to make others understand the possible hazards to this type of sport. That's all. Targeting individuals is wrong."

"Even Drew Black?" Millie sneered.

"Even Drew has the right to honest, fair, and professional treatment."

Millie almost snapped. She jerked forward to loom over Audrey, her face red, her eyes burning. "After what he did to me?" she screeched. "After how he maligned me for all the world to see?"

Undaunted, Audrey replied, "Mr. Black was unfairly harsh, but this can't be about getting even with him at all costs. Don't you see that?"

She tried to talk to the others, but Millie wouldn't let her. Each time she moved, Millie moved with her, belligerently staying in her face, challenging her with her attitude.

"You've chosen sides, Audrey. Accept the consequences."

"What consequences?"

"You're out. For good. No one wants a traitor here."

Audrey sighed, sad for her friend, but done with the group all the same. "Can't you see that you're stooping to the very behavior you object to?"

Snatching up Audrey's arm in a vicious grip, Millie jerked her toward the door. "You don't know anything. Now get out! We don't want you here anymore."

Stunned by Millie's maliciousness, Audrey glanced over her shoulder and saw varying degrees of shock on every other face. Yet they all just watched. No one said a word in Audrey's defense.

"Forget it," Millie said. "The meeting's over anyway." She put Audrey outside the door with a vicious shove that nearly knocked her to the ground.

Audrey regained her balance and faced her one-time friend. Something was very, very wrong with Millie. Why had she never seen it before? "You're out of control."

"Go to hell, Audrey." As she started away, she said,

"And you can take your boyfriend with you!" With her back already to Audrey, she paused, then looked over her shoulder with a smile. "Unless he gets there before you."

The way Millie said that, how she looked as if she knew a great secret, set off alarm bells in Audrey's head. But how could Audrey hurt Brett? He was a man more capable than most, and Millie, though filled with hatred, was no match for his strength.

Head pounding, Audrey went to her car and got in. While she sat there, deciding what to do, the others filed out of the meeting room. Some were solemn, some chatting. Millie outright laughed, as if enlivened by her contemptible attack. Audrey watched them all drive away with a sense of finality. She'd spent years building a group that had morphed from community concern into something ugly and malicious, spearheaded by a fanatic.

She'd never wanted that. But because of her, so many had been hurt.

Sick at heart, Audrey pulled back onto the road. She called Brett again with the same result. He didn't even want to hear her apology.

Maybe she should go see him, face to face. She had no idea where he'd be this time of the evening, but she could start at his apartment. He couldn't reject her more hatefully than her group just had.

But she knew, any rejection from Brett was going to feel a million times worse.

Cowardice urged her to wait until the morning to seek him out, but she couldn't abide that decision. She'd made the mistakes; she had to own up to them. She was within minutes of finding much-needed solitude in her own apartment when she decided to turn around.

If Brett weren't at his apartment, then she'd give up for the night.

But she would at least try to give him the sincere apology and explanation that he deserved.

At this time of year the sun set early. By the time Audrey reached Brett's apartment building, thick gray clouds darkened the night even more. It had only been a half hour since she'd left the meeting room, and she still felt frazzled, her hands shaking and her stomach in knots.

The thought of an ugly confrontation with Brett wasn't helping.

She pulled up to the curb in front of his building, drew several deep breaths, and opened her door. That was when she realized that people were clustered on the street, but she didn't know why.

Until she saw the smoke.

Her chest tightened and her heart pounded. Brett's building was on fire! And she didn't see Brett anywhere.

Audrey ran for the two-story, run-down building, but was stopped by hard hands. After Millie's manhandling, she was edgy enough to strike out. Luckily her automatic blow was blocked.

"Brett ain't in there," a young man told her as he released her and held up his hands. "He left a few hours ago for some bar."

Her knees nearly gave out with relief. She recognized the youth as one of the residents who had greeted Brett before they'd gone into his apartment. "What happened?"

"Some asshole did a drive-by on us," he said in disgust. "But instead of gunfire, he lobbed a gasoline-filled bottle right in through the big front window."

Good God, someone could have been seriously hurt or even killed. "You all got out okay?"

"Yeah." His expression darkened. "But we didn't see who did it. We were all inside, playing the new SBC fighting game. By the time we got out here, he was long gone."

Why would anyone do that? Audrey looked around and remembered what Brett had said about the area being rough and dangerous. This was likely a private dispute that had gone public in a big way.

But . . . she remembered that awful look on Millie's face, what she'd said about Brett.

"When . . . when did it happen?"

"Few minutes before you pulled up. The gas spread

over the porch and the front rooms so fast that it singed my damn eyebrows."

Relieved that Brett wasn't inside, Audrey asked, "Someone called the police or the fire department?"

He looked like she was nuts. "Uh . . . probably."

Audrey started to relax—and then it hit her. "Spice," she gasped. She looked back at the building. The fire wasn't that bad yet; it was mostly on the front of the first floor. But choking smoke could kill as easily as flames could. "Oh, my God, *Spice!*"

The young man gave her another funny look. "My name is Huckman. Friends call me Huck."

Panicked, she turned on poor Huckman. "Is there a way into Brett's rooms?"

His brows crunched down. "You serious, lady? You want to break in?"

"No . . . *yes.* Brett has a cat. Oh, please, Huckman. He loves that cat! We have to do something or she'll die."

Eyes widening, Huckman said, "Come on. I know how I can get you in."

As they ran around to the back of the building, distant sirens shattered the quiet of the night. Thank God, the fire department was on the way. But Audrey wasn't willing to wait. Would firefighters put the life of one cat above their own safety? How could they?

Huckman took her through a back alley for the building. One street lamp provided enough light for her to see dumped refuse and scattered garbage.

"The fire escape goes up to his kitchen. But you'll have to break the window yourself. I ain't getting in no trouble for a cat."

Audrey peered through the darkness in dismay. "I can't reach it." The fire escape ladder was raised and well out of her reach.

But that didn't slow down the young man.

Huckman dragged over a trash can, upended it without remorse, and, using it for added height, jumped up and snagged the ladder.

It came down in a clatter that, to Audrey, sounded like gunfire, adding to her jumpiness.

Even here in the back alley, the smoke was horrible enough to burn her throat and eyes. Poor Spice. She had to be frantic.

It was tricky, but Audrey managed to climb up the rickety metal ladder to the kitchen window. Never in her life had she deliberately broken glass. She tried opening the window first, but Brett had it secured.

She looked down and found Huckman still there, looking up at her, watching with a bemused and awed set to his face. "How do I do this?"

He said, "Use your elbow," and demonstrated with a quick jerking move of his arm.

Audrey nodded. Aligning her elbow with the window, she closed her eyes and mimicked his move. The glass shattered. Even as the sirens grew closer, she climbed over the jagged sill and into the apartment. She tried a light switch, but the electricity was out. Maybe the wires had burned. She could smell the stench of scorched fabric, wood, and paint. Smoke billowed around the room.

Making her way over to the kitchen doorway, she called out, "Here, kitty, kitty, kitty," as loudly as she could. "Here, Spice. Come on, kitty."

Audrey heard meowing seconds before Spice ran to her and twined around her legs. Luckily, the smoke wasn't as bad low to the floor. Scooping up the cat and hugging her, Audrey said, "Thank God you're okay."

It was even trickier going down the ladder while holding a cat, but Spice cooperated. At the very end, she leaped out of Audrey's arms, but Huckman grabbed her before she could get away. He held the cat in one arm and reached the other up to assist Audrey in getting down.

Once her feet were on solid ground again, Huckman asked, "You know where to find Brett?"

She hoped so. "I'll take the cat to my apartment first. I think she's been through enough."

Spice's eyes were huge and reflective in the darkness,

filled with wariness. When Audrey took her back from Huckman, Spice sank her claws into Audrey's arm. She just hugged the cat in relief, grateful that she was able to do this one small thing for Brett.

"If Brett shows up here, ask him to call me. Tell him that Spice is at my apartment and that I'm going to Roger's to look for him."

Huckman grinned. "You're all right, lady. You know that?"

After the night she'd had, his kindness brought tears to her eyes. Of course, he didn't know that she was a part of WAVS, and Audrey wasn't about to tell him. She'd had enough hatred spewed at her already. "Thank you."

"Brett's a lucky guy."

Smile sad, Audrey turned away. "Somehow, I don't think he sees it that way."

CHAPTER 18

DREW looked at Gillian and saw the dark shadows under her eyes. Tendrils of her sleek black hair had loosened to frame her face. Even the bright blue of her eyes seemed faded.

Exhaustion pulled at her, obliterating her edge of sharp wit, dulling her vitality. Beside him in the car, she was half slumped, lost in thought, all but asleep.

And still, she was the most beautiful, sexy woman he'd ever known.

What she'd said to Fran and Loren . . . did she mean it? Could her opinion of him still be so complimentary?

"Your apartment," he said, drawing her attention. "Is that your only place?"

His question amused her. "Unlike *some* people I could name, most of us don't have multiple residences to choose from."

"Should I take that bit of sarcasm to mean yes?"

"Yes, it's the only place I live." She put her head back against the seat. "I travel a lot with my job, so I've been all over the country, and on a few occasions, outside the country. But at the end of each assignment, I like to have one place to call home. The familiarity, the comfort of having everything just as I want it, that's what *home* means to me."

Her answer frustrated Drew. "So . . . you wouldn't want to live anywhere else?"

She gave him a questioning look. "I don't know. I haven't thought about it."

Trying a roundabout way to get the reply he wanted, Drew asked, "Do you have family here?"

"They're scattered. I have relatives an hour or so away, some that are out west, a few more to the south." She shrugged. "We're all resigned to traveling for visits."

"So . . . what do you think of Vegas?"

"It's great for gambling and live shows." She yawned. "But Drew, we weren't really there long enough for me to form any new opinions on it."

"Yeah." Frustration bit into him. "I'd meant to show you around a little. Dinner, a little nightlife, and then we could have gone to my house there."

She studied him. "I can see you fitting right in with Los Angeles or Vegas."

"I always thought so, too, that's why I have houses in both cities. I like L.A. more, though." And eventually, he did want to return there. "But it's not bad here. I came to visit because, well, the fighters seemed to be congregating here."

She laughed with him. "Once Havoc and Simon set up shop, the others followed?"

"Fighters will always gravitate to the best camps. I like to scope out new talent, so . . ." He shrugged. "Here I am."

"I'm surprised you bought a house."

"I like to be comfortable wherever I go."

"You're spoiled rotten." Her grin morphed into another yawn.

He reached for her hand. "I'm damned sorry you got dragged into all this."

Her smile was a pale imitation of her usual vitality. "I'm a big girl, Drew. I can handle it."

"But you shouldn't have to." Figures that the one time he wanted to impress a woman, he'd instead gotten her fired, brought a lunatic's revenge down on her, and run her ragged. They stopped at a light, and he turned to look at her. "I've been thinking about this mess."

One brow lifted. "Come to any conclusions?"

"Yeah. We need to do a phone conference."

The sooner he settled this bullshit, the sooner he could concentrate on getting Gillian enmeshed into his life—on a permanent basis. He didn't like leaving anything to chance. If he waited too long, she might make plans for moving on without him even knowing it.

"I want to tie in with my Internet guy, some reporters, maybe even ESPN. I want stuff posted all over the Web, in the papers, and on TV if I can manage it."

"When?"

"Soon as possible. Tonight sometime."

Slowly, Gillian straightened and turned to him as much as the seat belt would allow. "You can arrange it that quickly?"

He gave her a look. "Yeah, no problem."

She drew a tired breath. "Is this where I should remind you that Fran said no press conferences?"

"I know what she said, but she's wrong. The garbage thrown out there about Brett is wrong. The threats are wrong." He drew a breath. "I'm going to attack Millie Christian worse than she ever thought possible."

To his surprise, Gillian didn't shy away from that ferocious suggestion. She pondered it, nodding slowly, and then—she agreed.

"You want to draw her out, right?"

Damn, she was smart. Not much got by Ms. Gillian Noode. "And deflect the focus. If that crazy bitch thought I was harsh last time, she hasn't seen anything yet. But I won't lie, Gillian. Every damn word I say about her will be true. And it'll be enough to bring her to her knees."

"Or make her crack?"

"Exactly."

"With your particular spin on it, I don't doubt it." Gillian's mouth twitched. "You do have a way with four-letter words."

He gave one hard nod. "Release me from my promise to tone it down in public."

Gillian snorted. "Like that promise slowed you down anyway."

Very serious, Drew said, "What you think is important to me, so yeah, it slowed me down." He half grinned. "I did try, honey. If I wasn't always successful, well, you have to give me credit for effort."

Either she didn't get his sincerity or she chose to ignore it, because when the light changed to green, she went right back to talking about the press conference.

"If you want me to set up the conference call, I'll need some names and numbers."

Warmth filtered through Drew, helping to ease his anger at the current situation. Helplessness sucked, and that was how it all made him feel: helpless. He was a control freak and he knew it. He accepted it about himself. And as such, it wasn't easy for him to be around most people, especially when furious.

But Gillian . . . she not only softened his edge of rage with her mere presence, she sort of took him in stride and assisted where she could.

"Tell you what, we're still an hour from my house. Why don't you nap and I'll make the arrangements?" His phone was practically an extension of his body, but it was programmed to be hands-free in the car. He could easily drive and make calls at the same time.

"I can't nap while you do all the work."

He went from holding her hand to smoothing over her thigh. "I need you rested up."

"Why?"

His muscles tightened with the now familiar mix of burning lust and tender emotion. A potent combo, at least for his libido.

"Several reasons." *But only one that really mattered to him.* "Brett's not answering his cell, so I have to do a face-to-face with him. Just as the Powers That Be don't want me working for another fight organization, I don't want Brett fighting for anyone but us."

"He's that good?"

"Championship material, yeah. I want you with me when I hunt him down."

"Why?"

"Because I don't want you out of my sight until the danger is over. But also because you're a good influence."

She made a very unladylike sound of skepticism.

Drew let that slide. Later, he'd convince her of how she affected him. "It could take a few hours, depending on how pissed Brett is and how determined he is to cut out on the SBC and me. And I can't go looking for him until after we do the press bit, so it could end up being late."

"Afraid I'll be too muzzy brained to be of use to you?"

Oh, hell, she'd be of use to him, all right. Gillian had the unique ability to distract him from business. He wanted her enough that being with her could easily become a priority.

Drew curved his hand to cup more of her soft inner thigh. So hot and smooth . . .

"Actually, I'm afraid you'll be too tired to say yes when, after we iron out all this shit, I want to strip you naked and spend an hour or two making you scream."

"Oh. When you put it like that . . ." Gillian's blue eyes heated like the center of a flame. She drew a short, shuddering breath. "Perhaps I should nap just a little. After all, I take great pride in my . . . performance. I'll need some rest to be at my best."

With that sexual taunt thrown out there, she turned into the passenger door, got cozy, and closed her eyes.

But Drew saw the smile on her lips.

Yeah, Gillian was easy, all right. Easy to talk to, easy to joke with, to work with.

And very easy to love.

* * *

GIDDY with recent accomplishments, Millie sat at her desk and opened up the browser. She couldn't stop chuckling as she remembered the horrified look of shock on Audrey's face.

How dare that bitch choose Brett over her? Screwing the guy was one thing; she had nothing against that. A stud should never be wasted. Like that photographer loser . . .

He'd been so anxious to please, so titillated at the idea of joining her in her efforts to expose Drew Black for the bastard she knew him to be. But he'd proven too stupid to risk having around.

It was bad enough that he'd botched the bomb threat. But he'd almost let Drew catch him taking photographs, too. That was something she couldn't allow. Loose lips sank ships, and really, who'd miss that creep anyway?

It sucked that she hadn't gotten the photographs first, but eventually they'd be released.

For a little while there, Millie had considered Dickey Thompson as a possible conspirator. Even with his cauliflower ears, he was gorgeous, built like steel, and he looked like he could go all night long. After his girlfriend dumped him, he should have been easy pickings.

Unfortunately, the fool was all about the SBC and protecting the devil at the helm. She'd figured that out easily enough. So, fuck him. Dickey Thompson could go down with the rest of the organization, as far as she cared.

Millie first looked up news of the fire, but only found one small account. Apparently no one cared when a house in the slums turned into kindling. The report said that no one had perished, but that was okay. Brett would get the message anyway.

And so would Audrey.

She laughed again, imagining the fear that Audrey was starting to feel. She might even have some suspicions, but she couldn't prove a damn thing. This time, Millie had unfailingly covered her trail. No more anger-management courses for her.

Next, Millie pulled up the article she'd posted on Brett. How easy it had been to dig up the dirt from his past. Even his mother and father hadn't wanted him, but Audrey, damn her, chose to stick by his side no matter what. After all the work they'd done, all the work *she'd* done, to reveal the SBC and Drew Black as evil, blood-hungry, violence-mongering pricks, Audrey had still turned her back on them for a *man*.

And not just a man, but a fighter, their *enemy*. Stupid, stupid, stupid.

Audrey deserved whatever she got.

Hunkering in front of her laptop, Millie enjoyed all the comments from posters who wanted to support Brett in his time of need—something she knew he'd hate—when up popped a new headline.

The owner of the site encouraged everyone to check out a live news conference from Drew Black. Live? What was that demon up to now?

Millie read a follow-up comment from someone bouncing back and forth between the sites. It read: *Dude, he's destroying that WAVS chick. You have to check it out!*

More posts popped up in agreement, most of them thrilled by what was surely another unjustified attack against her.

Millie went cold inside. No, Drew wouldn't dare. Not now, not with his job gone and his whore exposed. Even an idiot would have enough sense to lie low, to ride out the storm without more public exposure.

Feeling numb, Millie clicked on the link—and reeled back in disbelief when Drew Black's voice came through her computer. He *was* doing this live, right now, despite everything.

She started breathing hard and fast. Humiliation and rage expanded in an explosion of emotion that blocked part of the garbage Drew Black spewed for all to hear.

But key words, like *fucking nutcase*, and *sick idiot*, and *pathetic loser out for revenge*, all seeped into her burning brain.

The fury built, boiled, until Millie snatched up the laptop and flung it across the room with a guttural scream of rage. The screen cracked and hinges broke.

Standing, panting, her hands in fists and her eyes burning, she focused on one thing. Only one.

Making Drew Black pay.

AUDREY was a mess, and she knew it. Her eyes were not only red from fighting tears, but because of the smoke. Her wrinkled clothes and tangled hair smelled of smoke, too. She looked like a walking disaster.

She'd taken Spice straight to her apartment and set her up in the kitchen with a makeshift litter box, a water bowl, and a soft bed of towels. Even though the cat seemed fine, she might need to see a vet. Reaching Brett was now more important than ever.

If he wouldn't answer her calls, she'd just have to go to him. If he went back to his apartment without knowing . . . She shuddered. He had to be told about the fire and where to find Spice.

She called again, and this time she left a message, saying, "Look, I know you must hate me right now, but I have to talk to you. It's important. I . . . I have Spice. She's fine. I just wanted you to know. I'll explain when you call me back or . . . I see you."

When she pulled up in front of Roger's Rodeo, she searched the lot and found what she thought was Brett's black truck. Her chest hurt at the thought of confronting him before a crowd. Not that she believed Brett would go out of his way to humiliate her. He wasn't like that. But a cold shoulder would accomplish the same thing.

After rubbing her tired eyes one more time, Audrey put a hand over her thudding heart and left her car. People glanced her way as she walked into the bar, making her even more self-conscious about her disheveled clothes and hair.

She was standing at the outskirts of the main room, working up her courage and conviction, when a big, handsome man stepped in front of her. After blinking fast, Audrey recognized him as the fighter Havoc Conor.

He tilted his head to study her with an unreadable expression, making note of her rumpled appearance. "You're Audrey Porter, aren't you?"

Her nervousness grew, but she wouldn't be driven away before seeing Brett. She nodded. "Yes."

He looked her over, shook his head at her appearance, and asked, "Looking for someone?"

"Brett Bullman."

"He's here," Havoc confirmed. Then he glanced behind her, narrowed his eyes, and took her arm. "Come with me."

He had her trotting along, moving between dancers, waitresses, and chatting throngs, before she finally found her voice. "Where are we going?"

As he wended his way through the crowds, he leaned down near her ear so she could hear him. "You want to see Brett, right?"

Her throat tightened. "Yes." She did, she really did, but the place was so busy . . . meeting him outside would be preferable. "Maybe you could just tell him to come out front?"

Havoc glanced behind her again. He had the advantage of much added height for a better view. "Brett's right over here."

He rushed her so that she almost tripped, and he had to right her.

Sounding apologetic, he asked, "You okay?"

"Yes, thank you." His eyes weren't mean, just curious and maybe . . . protective. But that made no sense at all.

Did he really think Brett would be cruel? She couldn't imagine that. Indifferent, yes. Even angry. But despite her role in all this, she couldn't imagine him cutting her down.

The farther they went into the bar, the more her anxiety grew. And then finally, they came upon Brett.

He sat at a table with two other men . . . and three women. Audrey stalled. She could barely breathe, so how could she talk?

"They're fans," Havoc told her with a hand at the small of her back, nudging her forward. "That's all. The guys are just being friendly."

"I . . ." Her heart suffered a crushing blow, but pride made her say, "He can see whomever he wants."

"Right." Havoc propelled her right up next to Brett.

Brett saw her, almost smiled, and then . . . didn't. Everyone at the table looked at her, and then looked at her again, giving her a disbelieving once-over.

Maybe she looked even worse than she realized.

Havoc broke the awkwardness by saying, "Someone here to see you, Brett."

Belatedly, Brett stood. "Audrey." Frowning, he studied her from head to toe. "What are you doing here?"

Havoc leaned in to him. "Drew came in right behind her. I, ah, thought it'd be better if she didn't run into him just yet."

One of the other guys stood, too. Audrey thought his name was Dickey something or other.

Eyes flared, he said, "Shit. Is she the one?"

Brett crossed his arms over his chest and regarded her as he spoke to the other fighter. "Audrey Porter."

The guy whistled. "Well, it'd be best if Drew has a day or two to cool down before he sees her."

"That's what I figured," Havoc said.

The fighter held out a hand. "Dickey Thompson."

Stunned at the courtesy when obviously they all knew who she was, and what she was responsible for, Audrey took his hand. Voice wavering, she said, "Nice to meet you, Mr. Thompson." She switched her gaze back to Brett. "I tried to call, but—"

"When?"

Audrey didn't understand him. He was distant, but not . . . furious. At least, he didn't seem to be. "Several times tonight. The last time was just a few minutes ago."

He frowned and fished out his cell. His mouth flattened. "It went dead. Sorry, I didn't realize."

He was apologizing . . . to her? Audrey shook her head, but couldn't get a single word out.

He shoved the phone back in his pocket. "I guess having my past up for discussion must've distracted me."

Big tears filled her eyes, and Audrey tried to blink them back. "Brett . . . it wasn't me. It was Millie. I told her not to post her story—"

"But she did anyway." He crossed his arms over his chest. "With a few new twists."

Her throat tightened. "I was trying to explain why it was so important not to attack Ms. Noode. I didn't mean to make things worse."

He nodded, and then his eyes narrowed. "What the hell happened to you?"

Oh, God, she'd almost forgotten about Spice! Thinking of the best way to give horrible news, Audrey licked her lips. "Everyone is fine, and Spice is safe at my apartment—"

"Spice?" Dickey asked.

"His cat," Audrey said, and then in a rush to Brett: "I'm so sorry to tell you this, but someone burned down the building you live in. Everything is ruined."

His arms fell to his sides. Seconds ticked by with him saying nothing. And then: "How do you have my cat?"

With each breath, she felt the lingering burn in her lungs. "The fire department wasn't there yet, and I knew Spice was inside your apartment. The smoke was so bad, and she's so small, that I didn't think she'd survive if I didn't get her out of there."

His expression darkened. "You went into the place for my cat?"

"One of those nice young men below your apartment showed me how to use the fire escape. When I got in the kitchen, Spice came right to me. I was only in there a few seconds, I swear."

"Christ, Audrey."

Now he sounded angry. She stared up at him, unsure what to think. "She seems fine, Brett, just as smelly with smoke as I am. But I thought you might want to have her checked by the vet anyway."

After a heartbeat of surprise, Brett cupped her face. He examined her red-rimmed eyes and used his thumb to smooth away a smudge of soot off her cheek.

She didn't know what to think. He was being so sweet to her. "Brett?"

As if her voice broke a spell, his brows came down, and then Havoc said, "Drew's moving in."

With all of them acting like Drew would have her head, Audrey should have been nervous. But the only one she'd really been worried about was Brett, and he didn't appear to hate her, so she could take on the world if need be.

"It's okay," she told everyone. "I plan to apologize to Mr. Black and Ms. Noode, too. Might as well be now instead of later. An apology won't change what's happened, I know, but I do feel terrible about things."

Brett's scowl eased, but not by much.

And then suddenly she found herself behind three fighters.

Brett said, "Hey, Drew."

Audrey gulped and her courage flagged. Was everyone so sure that Drew would verbally annihilate her with a roomful of witnesses? She closed her eyes and thought, *Yes, he definitely would.* Drew Black didn't care what anyone else thought. She sort of admired him for that quality.

And sadly, she couldn't blame him for being furious. Not after the terrible scandal that had erupted because of her group.

Her eyes snapped open when she heard Drew Black say, "Hiding something, Brett?"

Havoc snorted. "Leave it alone, Drew."

"But I'd like to talk to the lady."

A woman's voice said, "Now, Drew, I thought you wanted to talk to Brett."

"That, too. But since she's here with him, I might as well kill two birds with one stone."

Dickey said, "Still can't control him, Ms. Noode?"

Obviously unconcerned with possible repercussions, Ms. Noode laughed. "It's like trying to marshal a tornado. I can't be expected to work miracles." Then her voice firmed. "But I can promise there will be *no* killing."

Drew made a sound of exasperation. "For God's sake, I'm not going to hurt her."

None of the fighters moved. That they would defend her like this, attempt to protect her . . . well, Audrey was humbled by their gallantry. Her own group had turned on her, and yet these men, the men she'd labeled as barbaric, thought to shield her.

It wasn't easy, but she wedged between Dickey and Brett and stepped forward to present herself. "Mr. Black."

"Ms. Porter." His eyes narrowed on her. He looked a little surprised at the state of her condition. "What the hell happened to you?"

Ms. Noode elbowed him.

Audrey gulped and squared her shoulders. She would not be a victim in this. "Long story, but I'm fine." She nodded to the woman. "Ms. Noode."

Seeming friendly enough, the other woman smiled. "Hello, Ms. Porter."

"Please, call me Audrey."

"If you'll call me Gillian."

The men were all mute, which was somehow endearing.

Drew shook his head, collected himself, and said to Audrey, "It's past time we had a face-to-face, don't you think?"

"I had planned to contact you," Audrey confirmed. She forced herself forward another step and folded her hands

together to keep them from shaking. "I take full respon-
sibility for the posting Millie put online in the name of
WAVS. But I want you to know that I didn't approve it, and
I don't condone it."

Drew crossed his arms over his chest and regarded her.
"Is that right?"

Audrey felt Brett's hands settle onto her shoulders. She
appreciated his support more than he could know. "What
should have been a professional accounting of facts turned
into a vicious, personal attack."

Drew shrugged. "Similar to the attack I heaped on Ms.
Christian. Problem is," he said, "she went after the wrong
people."

Audrey flickered a look at Gillian. As Brett had told
her, that awesome woman didn't look like a victim in any
way. Audrey admired her poise. "My sincere apologies to
you, too."

Gillian waved that off as unnecessary. "I think we
should all talk."

Drew looked past Audrey to Brett. "Right now is good
for me. I'd like to clear the air and get all of this settled."

Audrey looked back in time to see Brett run a hand
through his hair. He'd been through so much already. But
she didn't know how to help him.

"Fine." Brett turned back to the table of women and
politely excused himself. They bade him farewell with no
clinginess in sight.

"Let's go outside where it's quieter," Brett said. "We
can all talk there."

Audrey glanced back at the women Brett left behind
and saw that they were thrilled when Dickey Thompson
rejoined them.

"Don't worry about it," Brett whispered in her ear, as if
he knew exactly what she was thinking.

"I didn't mean to interrupt." They trailed out of the bar
behind Drew and Gillian.

"You didn't." And to Audrey's surprise, he slipped

an arm around her shoulders and even gave her a slight squeeze for reassurance.

Somehow, she decided, they'd be able to work this out. She had to believe that, because she loved Brett Bullman more than anything.

CHAPTER 19

THE brisk night air gave Drew enough reason to pull Gillian into his side. Given that some patrons lingered on the walkway, Drew half expected her to move away. Public displays of affection were not her thing; she was too private for that.

But Gillian didn't budge. Instead, she curled into him and said low, "Be nice, Drew."

He rubbed his chin against the top of her head, feeling mellow now that they were making some headway. "Or what?"

She looked up at him with her blue eyes intent. "Or . . . I'll be disappointed."

He half smiled and then quickly kissed her lips. "Can't have that, now can we?" He led her toward the far end of the walk, away from the congestion of the front doors. "I'll ruin my reputation if I don't keep you satisfied."

She didn't reply, but Drew saw the small smile that curved her mouth.

It looked like another storm might be rolling in. Thick clouds obscured any sign of the moon, but street lamps and security lights from the bar kept the area well lit. Without the live band and elbow-to-elbow crowd, it was quieter out here, but not much more private.

Brett and Audrey came around next to them. Drew had no idea what was going on between those two, but Brett's little woman looked like she'd been through hell. From what he remembered in meeting her before, her idea of spiffing up meant dark jeans and something other than sneakers. But her current appearance was rough, even for her.

Drew asked her, "You're sure you're all right?"

Chagrined, Audrey nodded. "I'm sorry for the scent of smoke. It's been one heck of a night. After that awful report about Brett was released, I went to see him. Luckily he wasn't at home because someone had thrown a lit bottle of gasoline into his apartment building."

Drew's mind jumped ahead to possibilities on that one. So many strange threats, and now, right after thrusting Brett's life into the public forum, someone torched his apartment?

Brett looked grim. "You shouldn't have gone in there, Audrey."

"I couldn't just leave Spice," Audrey said. "I knew she had to be scared. And I know how much you care about her."

Perplexed, Drew asked, "Spice?"

"My cat." Brett kissed Audrey's temple. "Audrey saved her."

Gillian said, "My God. You went into the building after her?"

"It was mostly just smoke when I got there," Audrey explained. "The fire hadn't yet spread from the first floor." And then to Brett, "But I think everything was destroyed. All your possessions . . ."

"They're just things, Audrey. I can replace them."

Talk about a shitty day . . . Drew saluted Brett for his cool head. "Let me know what I can do to help, okay?"

Gillian beamed at him, making him say, "What?"

"You are so generous."

What the fuck. He didn't want her getting all moon-eyed in front of the others. "I have a vested interest in Brett's well-being."

"Of course you do." And it was plain to everyone that she was placating him.

"For the love of—"

Audrey said, "Brett can stay with me." And then, clearly flustered by her hopeful enthusiasm, she added to Brett, "That is . . . if you want to."

Brett's indulgent gaze warmed on her face, and he gave her a quick hug. "We'll see."

Huh. So maybe he needed to make nicey-nice with Ms. Porter, since it looked like she and Brett were an item.

He didn't have time to think about that much before Gillian said, "Drew, do you suppose—?"

"That the fire could be the work of a crazy little bitch, hell-bent on destruction?" He didn't have any doubts. "Fucking-A."

Brett scowled and, instead of warning him about his language, asked, "What are you talking about?"

"Ms. Millie Christian," Gillian announced. "You know the photographer who was lurking around Drew's house? Well, it was a stolen car that ran him down and killed him. The car was found torched near the river. And now some-one torches a building? That's a lot of coincidence."

Audrey paled, and Drew couldn't help but notice.

He sympathized with her. She obviously felt some sense of responsibility for all the trouble. "Sorry, Audrey, I know Millie is a friend of yours, but I think she's the one behind all this, including the bomb threat."

With a hand to her stomach, Audrey asked, "You really think Millie would do all those things?"

"Or have it done." Drew gave them all the facts he had, including Millie's rap sheet and history of violence. Things were fast spiraling out of his control. Fuck being calm. Drew knew he had to do something before someone got killed.

Gillian said, "She's the one who leaked the story on Brett, isn't she?"

Brett cupped his hand around Audrey's nape, but spoke to Drew. "I assumed it was you, Drew. You made no bones about wanting to sensationalize my past."

"If I'd done it, it wouldn't have been behind your back." He was not a chickenshit who couldn't face up to his own decisions. "But I told you I wouldn't, and I might not be Prince Charming, but I don't lie."

Looking dead on her feet, Audrey said, "That's my fault, too. I was only trying to make Millie realize why someone like Gillian shouldn't be singled out as a target. I wanted her to understand how hurtful that could be." She rubbed tired, red eyes. "I guess what I said was enough to make her want to start digging. I'm so sorry."

Brett lifted her chin. "You couldn't have known she was so . . . unwell."

Drew snorted. "I knew she was a fanatic zealot from day one. And a shitty reporter, too."

"Drew." Gillian slapped his chest, saying in a harsh whisper, "Knock it off."

He looked at Audrey, so downcast and guilty, and Brett, so disgusted at having his private life flung out there for the masses.

Shit.

It'd be best to get things back on track.

"So, Audrey, I was thinking we should call a truce with WAVS. Maybe work through our differences and all that. What do you say?"

"I wish I could." Mouth twisting with derision, she admitted, "I was . . . ah, *escorted* out of the meeting earlier today and told not to return. Millie sort of took over."

Brett propped his hands on his hips. "That organization is important to you."

She licked her lips. "Not as important as you."

Brett looked flattered, but Drew thought, *Screw that.* "The group isn't going away, and you now know that Millie's not rational, right?"

"Apparently not," Audrey said.

"So don't you think you should regain control of it?" Brett said, "It is *your* organization, Audrey."

She put back her shoulders and looked between Drew and Brett. "If I still run it, my goals would have to be the same."

"Meaning?" Drew asked.

"I'd want people to be aware of my objection to all violent sports."

Brett held her shoulders. "And like I keep telling you, no one minds that."

She licked her lips. "I'd want to lobby for extra precautions in all the fight clubs."

"The SBC already uses every precaution," Drew said. "But you should feel free to harangue other organizations."

She glanced between the men. "I'd want every effort made to keep the athletes safe, too."

"Guaranteed," Drew told her. "So if we get down to it, it's the personal attacks and distortion of facts that we agree are wrong, right?"

"Definitely."

Drew nodded. "Not a problem. With Gillian's help—"

Gillian looked startled. *"What?"*

"—I'll check things on my end." He hugged Gillian when she started to protest. "So what about you, Audrey? Can you get WAVS to stick to the facts?"

Brett brought her attention to him. "If you walk away now, you allow the group to stand as is, and that makes you no different from them."

Brows raised at Brett's vehemence, Drew nodded at him. "What he said."

"I'll do my best," Audrey promised.

"I know just how to get things started," Gillian said, jumping in to lighten the mood. "Join us on another press conference."

Since Drew wanted to take Gillian back to Vegas, not instigate more business, he wasn't keen on that idea. "Right now?"

She flapped a hand at him. "It's easy for you and you know it. You have incredible influence."

Drew smiled. "I've created a PR monster."

Gillian put her hand over his mouth. A bold move, but then, Drew liked it when she was bold.

"It's the easiest, most efficient way to convey accurate data," Gillian stated. "With Drew's connections, you could reach a lot of people, Audrey, including followers of your group, which will make it easier to reorganize. State your case with our blessing. We'll make it clear that we want to take your group's concerns into consideration and work with you on resolving them."

"We will?" Drew asked around her fingers.

He was ignored.

"All right. I'd like that." Audrey looked at Brett. "Because of my brother, this will always be an issue with me."

"I know. I get that." He smoothed back her hair. "Standing up for your convictions is an important part of you, Audrey, a part that I love."

Love? Damn, now both of Drew's brows shot up. So Brett was in love with the girl? He hadn't quite seen that one coming. The fighters rarely wanted for female attention. Most who were Brett's age cared more about playing the field.

But from the beginning, he'd known that Brett was different. More focused.

Audrey still stood there staring at Brett with enormous eyes and parted lips.

Drew leaned in toward Brett and said sotto voce, "I don't think she quite got it."

Brett grinned. "Then I guess I should be more blunt." He cupped her face. "I'm falling in love with you, Audrey."

She blinked hard and threw herself against him. "I'm already in love with you."

Drew nudged Gillian, but she made a point of studying her nails. Knowing she was never obtuse, he scowled.

Audrey said, "I'm so sorry, Brett. I had a lot of misconceptions on the sport, and the athletes."

He lifted her off her feet in a tighter hug. "We're all part and parcel with our backgrounds, honey. There's no separating it. There's only dealing with it."

"And we'll all deal better together." Gillian looped her arm through Drew's, clearly pleased with the outcome. "We'll create a united front to put a stop to the hostility before someone gets seriously hurt."

As Brett released Audrey, she smiled and turned to Gillian. "I would appreciate that very much. Thank you."

"Great," Drew said. "One down, one to go."

Brett put a hand on his hip, looked down at the ground, and waited.

Drew got right to the point. "I still think your circumstances make one hell of a draw, but only with your involvement and approval. I wouldn't go behind your back to do the story any other way. If you say no—"

"I say no."

Damn. But he'd expected no less, especially now that Millie Christian had thrown things in such a bad light. "Then that's it," Drew agreed. "Done. But I still want you at the SBC."

Brett let out a breath and shrugged. "At this point, no matter what organization I go to, someone is going to question my past. I might as well stay where I most want to be."

"Fair enough." Drew couldn't help but grin as he reached out for Brett's hand in a gentleman's agreement. "You should know that I did a press conference before coming here, and when someone asked about you, I stuck with one line, and one line only."

"What'd you say?"

"That you are one hell of a fighter and I was going to do my best to sign you with the SBC. You already know that won't stop people from asking, but I've never had a problem ignoring questions I don't want to answer."

Brett's smile was slow. "I'm sure you don't."

"But," Drew continued, "I want you both to know that the main purpose of the press conference was for me to rip Ms. Christian to shreds." He held up his hands before they could question him. "I figured it was the easiest way to draw her out and to get her focus back on me instead of you."

"Do you think it worked?" Audrey asked.

Drew opened his mouth—and a rifle blast sounded. Everyone jumped as a shot slammed into the brick face of the building, sending shards to pepper the air only inches from Drew's head.

Oh, yeah, he'd drawn her fire back on him—literally.

It'd be nice if he lived to tell about it.

GILLIAN gave a short scream as Drew dove on her, driving her down to the ground and covering as much of her body as he could with his own. The next bullet grazed his upper arm, making him curse in burning pain. He shoved Gillian's head down when she tried to raise up to check on him.

Fumbling, he half crawled, half dragged her over behind a parked car, leaving a trail of blood in his wake. With a hand on the back of her neck, keeping her pinned down, he fished in his pocket for his cell phone and finally got it out.

"What in the world are you doing?" Gillian gasped.

Into the phone, Drew barked, "Where the hell are you, Marcus?"

Sounding winded and excited, the investigator said, "I just conked her on the head with a fucking rock. It's all I had available. She's out cold now." He wheezed in a breath. "Everyone okay?"

Drew dropped to his back beside Gillian. God Almighty, that crazy bitch had nearly done him in.

Immediately Gillian crawled up and over him. "Drew!"

She sounded shrill and panicked and . . . concerned. "Oh, my God, you're bleeding!"

"I'm okay," he told her, but his fucking arm was fast growing numb.

She smacked him on his uninjured shoulder. *"Are you out of your mind?"*

Remembering, Drew jerked up and around and saw that Brett had Audrey caught down low against the building and was shielding her with his back. Thank God he hadn't been the target, because he was still fully exposed.

Drew yelled, "It's okay, Brett. My investigator has her now."

"Her?" Brett asked, not really moving much.

"None other than Millie Christian." And this time, she'd gone way too far. She'd finally be out of his life, once and for all. "Call the cops, will you? Ask for Officer Sparks."

Brett eased up from covering Audrey. He looked at Drew, saw the blood, and cursed. He was on his phone in a heartbeat, still keeping Audrey tucked behind him, just in case.

Drew went back to his call. "Cops are on the way, Marcus. Don't take your eyes off her. I mean it. Sit on her if you have to."

"Her head's bleeding real bad," the investigator said with a sort of disinterested observation. "I might've hit her harder than I meant to. It's dark as hell up here and I was trying to be quiet, when suddenly she started shooting. I had to lunge to reach her."

But thank God he had. "Don't worry about it, Marcus. You did what you had to do." Hopefully Millie would recover, because Drew wanted to see her sorry ass behind bars.

The only saving grace to any of this was that his ploy had worked: he'd been the target. Not Brett or Audrey and, thank God, not Gillian.

With an effort, Drew sat up more and, thinking of what could have happened, he tucked Gillian into his side with his uninjured arm. She fought him and got free enough to take off her wrap. Big tears swam in her eyes, but they didn't fall. Her face had gone pale, and when he'd tackled her to the ground, he'd knocked the careful chignon from her hair.

"Dear God, Drew," she mumbled in a shaky voice that still sounded pissed.

He held her off when she would have started messing with his arm. It hurt enough without her help.

"Where are you, anyway?" he asked Marcus.

"Half a block down, on the roof of a convenience store. I saw Christian climb up, and I figured she'd be spying on you or calling in another bomb threat or something, so I followed." He sounded almost admiring when he said, "She's a crack shot with a rifle."

Drew looked at his arm, now steadily oozing blood and throbbing like a son of a bitch. "Thank God she's not quite perfect, or I'd be dead." That sentiment brought the tears in Gillian's eyes spilling over. "Stay put, Marcus, you got that? I'll send the cops to you."

"We're not going anywhere."

Drew hung up, saw Gillian shaking like a leaf, and decided he'd better man up before she fell apart. "Calm down, Gillian. I'm fine."

"You are not fine, you are *shot*! What were you thinking to use yourself as a shield?"

"I didn't want you hurt," he told her simply. And he smoothed a long, silky tendril of hair away from her face.

Her mouth worked twice before words came out, all wrapped up in tears and hysteria. "You stupid, stupid man, you were almost killed!"

He knew it was the residual fear making her sound like a nag. Nodding toward Brett, Drew said, "He did the same thing as me. Why aren't you bitching at him?"

"Because he . . . you . . ."

Drew didn't quite plan it, but seeing her like this, knowing she damn well cared or she wouldn't be so upset, he said, "I love you, too."

She gasped so hard she landed back on her ass. When

Drew just grinned at her, she held her breath a second, then started breathing hard and fast. Finally she said, "Damn you, Drew Black."

"I love you, Gillian."

She sobbed once, hiccuped, and then used a sleeve to dry her eyes. "What are you doing to me?"

Very slowly, trying to pretend that fire wasn't burning through his arm, Drew leaned in and kissed her. "I don't know, but I want to do it for the rest of our lives."

She covered her face, nodded.

Drew waited, but when he heard the sirens approaching, he said, "Woman, I really wish you'd tell me that you love me, too."

Nodding hard, she dropped her hands. "I do." She touched his face with trembling hands. "I love you."

Feeling light-headed, Drew stretched out on his back on the ground. "Huh. That was almost worth getting shot, just to hear you say it."

OFFICER Sparks was on the scene, directing everyone with efficient authority. Brett slumped down on the ground next to Audrey. It had been one hell of a day. Not only had his past caught up to him, but everything he owned was now gone.

Except for his cat.

He closed his eyes and leaned his head back against a brick wall. When he thought of Audrey going into that old house . . . His hands curled into fists and his jaw tightened. The building had probably gone up like dry leaves, it was so old and so badly maintained.

Audrey sat silently beside him, still sad, probably exhausted. She, too, had been through the wringer.

Early in life, he'd learned how easy it was to walk away when things weren't to his liking. When his father left, he'd rejoiced. When his mom sank so low that she'd become a stranger to him, he'd blocked out any hurt and written her from his life. He'd worked hard to be the person he wanted to be, polite, educated, above the trash that had been his environment. But he'd never gotten so closely connected to another human being that he or she mattered. He'd never wanted to care to the point that he couldn't walk away.

With Audrey . . .

He turned his head to look at her. "You really don't mind if I stay with you?"

Burdened with uncertainty, she said, "I would like it very much."

Brett nodded. "Okay. Thanks." He stood and held a hand out for her. After he helped her back to her feet, he just stood there, looking at her, marveling at how she'd captured so much of him, so soon, when he'd never thought it possible.

He turned to look around at the chaos. Poor Roger was beside himself. Too much had happened at his establishment for his peace of mind. Simon Evans and Dean Conor stood talking to him. Off to the side, Gregor and his wife stood talking to Dickey Thompson.

It seemed no matter what, Roger's place would remain the hangout.

Both Drew and Millie were taken away by ambulance, Millie unconscious, Drew bitching up a storm. Gillian, bless her, was about to follow.

"Come on." Brett took Audrey's hand and hustled her along with him. Not for anything did he want to let her out of his sight. Bullets and fires and lunatics . . . he had to keep her close for his own peace of mind.

"Where are we going?"

He nodded toward Gillian. "She's a mess. She shouldn't try driving herself to the hospital."

Audrey agreed, and even freed herself from Brett to run ahead and catch Gillian before she got in her car.

Gillian's relief was palpable. She hugged Audrey and agreed. Even from a short distance, Brett could see her shaking, and there was no mistaking the mascara tracks left by her tears.

So that they'd all fit, they took Audrey's car rather than Brett's truck, but he drove. Gillian climbed into the backseat without a word, and then she fretted all the way to the hospital.

Brett glanced at her in the rearview mirror. "He'll be okay, Gillian."

She nodded. "I know. Thank you." As they pulled up to the hospital, she said, "Will you just drop me at the door?"

"We could come in and keep you company," Audrey offered.

But Gillian refused her. "You look as wiped out as I feel, and besides, Drew won't like an audience while he's not one hundred percent."

Brett figured she was right about that. "Will you call us if either of you needs anything?"

She smiled, wiped at her eyes as more tears seeped out. "I'm being ridiculous, I know, but if that bullet had done more damage . . ." She shuddered. "Even after I stopped denying how I felt, I didn't want to tell Drew. I thought if he didn't know, I could protect myself. But that was just plain foolish."

Brett pulled up in front of the main doors and put the car in park. "Looking back is a waste of time, Gillian. Believe me, I know."

Pausing in her exit from the car, Gillian tipped her head and studied him. "If we never look back, we might avoid dwelling on bad times, but we miss out on fond memories, too. It's always a balance." She reached up and touched Brett's shoulder. "But the most important thing is to face the future without letting the past get in the way."

And with that sage advice thrown out there, she got out of the car and came around to Audrey's window. "Thank you both again."

Brett watched her hustle into the hospital, shoulders back and stride proud, despite what she'd just been through.

After a second, Brett let out a breath. "She's right, you know."

Audrey nodded but didn't quite look at him. "I'm looking forward to a future . . . with you."

His heart damn near broke in two. Gillian made so much sense that now he saw how he'd almost let the past cheat him of a future. He caught Audrey and pulled her half over the console so he could kiss her.

The lingering scent of smoke wrenched him, reminding him of how easily he could have lost her.

With his forehead against hers, he whispered, "Before, when I said I was falling in love with you?"

She said nothing, just closed her eyes.

"I lied, Audrey. I fell a long time ago, almost from the first time you kissed me." He put a few inches between them so he could see her face. "I love you."

Her arms wrapped tight around him. "Let's go home, Brett. Spice is waiting for you."

THREE MONTHS LATER

DREW sat beside Brett after he'd achieved an impressive knockout the night before. Drew's arm had healed pretty fast and only a slight scar remained as a reminder of that awful night. Gillian was now officially his fiancée, and she'd already given up her apartment to live with him full-time.

Millie was still being evaluated, though how it could take so long, Drew couldn't fathom. Anyone could see she was loony. At least they kept her in a high-security facility while the court system worked it all out.

Brett and Audrey were now an item, too. The romance hadn't negatively affected Brett at all. He was the same hard worker, with the same dedication. But now, more often than not, he had Audrey at his side.

Surrounded by media, flashing lights, and fans, Drew gave a few statements about his plans for Brett in the SBC and then took questions.

Of course, as always, some asshole couldn't resist asking about Brett's background. They wouldn't give up on that and it drove Drew nuts. He'd already banned two persistent reporters who couldn't refrain.

Drew thought about what he wanted to say, knew Gillian and Fran would both be watching, and decided, what the hell? Sometimes a rough edge was needed.

Staring out at the crowd, Drew said, "Fuck the past. Fighters like Brett are the future of the SBC, and that's what we're here to talk about."

Brett leaned forward. "Let's put this to rest, okay?" Relaxed, sincere, and comfortable, he gave a brief accounting of his parents' woes and his dysfunctional childhood. He blew it off as it pertained to him, but then, while he had everyone's attention, he announced a new charity that he'd started to help abused and abandoned kids.

That inspired lots of personal questions, and Brett fielded them all with information on how others could contribute to help kids in need.

Once the questions died down, Drew covered the mic with his hand and said, "You sly dog. Well played."

Brett grinned. "It was my and Audrey's idea to start the charity, but it was Gillian's idea for me to announce it when the personal questions started again. It not only deflects off of me, it brings some publicity to kids in need."

He should have known. "Damn," Drew said. "Smart women are so fucking hot."

Brett laughed as he pushed back his chair.

Drew led the way out of the back of the press room. He was glad that Brett had finally come to grips with his past and was looking to the future.

"Love the charity idea," he told Brett. "I'll donate cash, of course, but let's have dinner with the ladies to talk about anything else you need."

"Thanks." Brett gave him a nod. "Gillian said you already support a boys' home. She figured you'd want in on this, too."

"Yeah, well, Gillian tends to see the best in me. It's thanks to her that I'm back in black." He clapped Brett on the shoulder. "The future couldn't look any better."

Brett agreed.

Following is a special excerpt from

Mad, Bad and Blonde

by Cathie Linz

Coming from Berkley Sensation
in March 2010!

IT was the perfect day for a wedding. Too bad the groom didn't show up.

Faith West shivered in the beam of May sunlight streaming through a small window in the bridal anteroom of the historical Chicago Gold Coast church. Fingering the rich white satin skirt of her wedding dress, she sat very still, unable to believe this was really happening to her. Alan Anderson, the man she'd agreed to marry, was late for his own wedding.

There had to be a reasonable explanation for Alan's absence—car trouble, a dead cell phone, maybe even an accident, heaven forbid.

Faith caught sight of herself in the large mirror on the opposite wall. A few wisps of her brown hair had escaped the confines of her upswept hairstyle, and her blue eyes appeared haunted despite her perfect makeup. Did she look like the kind of woman a man would leave at the altar? Possibly. She was certainly no raving beauty. She was just a librarian. A librarian with a rich private investigator father.

Faith's family flitted around her like a skittish school of fish, coming and going—offering help, offering suggestions, offering vodka. She remained calm in the center of all the chaos, strangely distant from her surroundings. The reality was she was probably going into shock and should accept the offer of alcohol purely for medicinal purposes.

The question was: what would Jane Austen do in this situation? Whenever Faith was in trouble, she looked to her favorite author for the solution. And Faith was armpit deep in trouble at the moment.

"I bet you scared the poor man away," Faith's pain-in-the-butt aunt Lorraine interrupted Faith's racing thoughts to declare. "A children's librarian whose father taught her how to shoot a gun. A big mistake."

Aunt Lorraine, also known as the Duchess of Grimness, was the bane of the West family's existence. With her demonlike black hair and Hellboy eyes, she was scarier than anything written by Stephen King. Not exactly the model wedding guest, but Faith's mom had insisted on inviting her.

For a wild second Faith wondered if Alan had stayed away because he was afraid of Aunt Lorraine, having met her for the first time at the rehearsal dinner the night before. Maybe *she* was the reason he hadn't shown up. Could Faith really blame him for wanting to avoid Aunt Lorraine's stinging barbs?

Hell yes, she could blame him! How could Alan leave her sitting here wondering what had happened to him? How could he be so cruel? How could anyone, aside from Aunt Lorraine, be that cruel?

Alan wasn't just anyone. He was her fiancé—a reliable and respectable investment banker she'd known for two years. They'd been engaged for the past eleven months. They were perfectly suited for each other, sharing the same interests, values, and aspirations. Neither one of them was blinded by passion or prone to wild behavior.

That's not to say that the sex between them hadn't been

good; it had been. Not great but good. She loved him. He loved her. Or so he'd said last night before kissing her.

Faith looked around. Someone had led Aunt Lorraine away. She was replaced by Alan's shamefaced best man. "Alan just sent you a text message."

"Where is he? Is he okay?"

Instead of answering her anxious questions, the best man hightailed it out of the room, heading for the nearest exit and no doubt the nearest bar.

"Where's my BlackBerry?" Faith asked her maid of honor, her cousin Megan, who was like a sister to her. Faith and Megan were born two days apart, grew up within a few blocks of each other, and had been known to complete each other's sentences. Their dads were brothers. Faith only had one bridal attendant and of course that was Megan.

"I'm sure Alan has a good reason for being late." Megan had always been the optimist in the family. "Maybe he was in an accident. Your dad is still checking the area emergency rooms."

Faith's überworkaholic father owned the most successful investigative firm in Chicago. If Alan wasn't in an emergency room, then her father would be tempted to put him in one.

"Where's my BlackBerry?" Faith heard the edge of hysteria in her voice but couldn't do anything to stop it.

"Here. It's right next to you." Megan handed it to her. Sure enough, there was a text message from Alan that had been sent two minutes earlier.

thought i wanted marriage. i don't. i need to find who i really am. i want adventure and excitement. don't want u. sorry.

Alan hadn't left her because she could shoot a gun. He'd left because he didn't think she was exciting enough. She'd scared him away by *boring* him to death.

"What did he say?" Megan demanded.

Her cousin was her best friend, but even so Faith was too humiliated to show her what Alan had written. Instead she turned the BlackBerry off with trembling fingers. "I've been dumped in a text message," she said unsteadily. "And not just dumped, but left at the altar."

"We never actually walked down the aisle."

"Close enough." Faith angrily wiped away the tears that were starting to stream down her face. "There are people waiting out there. Lots of them. And they're all expecting a wedding."

"They'll all be on your side."

That was cold comfort at this point. Faith welcomed the anger starting to surge through her. It kept the pain and humiliation at bay.

So much for her happy ending. Faith had continued to believe in her fairy-tale wedding even when Alan hadn't shown up for the pre-ceremony photographs, even when his best man had refused to look her in the eye, even when the minister had approached her privately to ask if she wanted to delay the proceedings.

"He'll show up," Faith had kept saying. "You'll see. He'll show up. And he'll have the lamest excuse for being late."

Her belief in Alan and her faith in a positive outcome had lasted longer than it should have and was now as tattered as the lace handkerchief she'd nervously shredded with her beautifully manicured fingers.

Last night he'd claimed he loved her, yet today he didn't want her. How did that work? Did Alan love her like he loved fine wine and the Cubs instead of the way you loved the person you were supposed to marry? Weren't Cub fans supposed to be the most loyal guys on the planet?

Faith was having a hard time thinking coherently and she felt cold enough to get frostbite. The man she loved didn't want her. She couldn't think about that or she'd dissolve into a sobbing mess. But she could think of nothing else.

Her parents burst into the anteroom. "I finally tracked him down," Jeff West said. His usually smooth brown hair was messed from him running impatient fingers through it. "The bastard took a flight to Bali an hour ago. One way."

Alan has gone to Bali searching for adventure and excitement, because he couldn't find any with me. So much for love and commitment. I guess those things don't matter to him. I don't matter to him.

What had she done to make him change his mind about marrying her? He couldn't have thought she was boring when he proposed. So what had changed?

Would Alan have stayed if he'd known she was a crack shot with a gun? Her dad had taken her to the firing range and taught her himself when she was ten. Faith had never told Alan about her weapons training because she didn't like to brag about the marksmanship awards she'd won. Maybe she should have. Maybe then he'd have thought twice about dumping her. Maybe then he'd have thought she was more exciting. A children's librarian who had a gun and knew how to use it. Yeah, that ranked right up there on the excitement scale with . . . what?

What *was* Alan's definition of exciting? Interest rates and the stock market? Sex in the middle of Wrigley Field? A blow job in Bali?

"You poor baby." Faith's mother, Sara, sat beside her and hugged her. "He seemed like such a nice investment banker."

"There was nothing in his background to indicate he'd bolt like this," her dad said. "I had him thoroughly checked out. Other than being a Cubs fan instead of a Sox fan, there didn't seem to be anything wrong with him. He wasn't seeing another woman, or another man, wasn't defrauding the bank or his clients."

"Maybe he just got a case of cold feet," Megan said. "He could still come back."

"And when he does, I'll beat the crap out of him," Jeff growled.

Faith would have thought that her fiancé would be smart

enough to figure out that dumping her at this late date meant there was no place he could hide. Not even Bali. Her father would track him down and make him pay . . . big time.

Only one person was more imposing than Jeff West and that was Aunt Lorraine, who was now trying to push her way back into the room.

"Get rid of her," Faith begged her parents.

"Gladly," her dad said. "Do you think I haven't wanted to make her disappear for years now? But your mother would never let me."

"She's my much older sister," Sara said apologetically. "She practically raised me."

"And she scares you shitless," Jeff said. "Believe me, I get it."

"She implied it was my fault Alan left," Faith said. It turned out the Duchess of Grimness was right. According to Alan's brief text message, it was obvious that he blamed Faith for being too dull for him.

"Your fault? That does it." Sara glared at Lorraine, who was still trying to get in the room but was being prevented by Megan. "She's gone too far this time." A curtain of fierce determination fell over Sara's face. "Don't worry, I'll handle her." She marched over and moved Lorraine out of the room.

Watching her mother's totally uncharacteristic behavior, Faith realized anything was possible. Anything but her wedding. There was no saving that now.

"What are we going to do?" Faith asked her dad. "All those people are out there waiting. We've got the wedding reception at the Ritz-Carlton. You paid so much for everything." Tears welled again but she dashed them away. Alan had said there were only a handful of people he wanted to invite. His parents were dead and he had no other close family. Since almost all of the guests were from her side of the family, Alan had been perfectly happy to have Jeff foot the bill, and her dad had done so with boatloads of paternal pride.

Again, what would Jane Austen do? She would take control.

"Tell the people in the church that due to circumstances beyond our control, the ceremony has been canceled," Faith said. "Tell them the reception is still on. Don't cancel it. You might as well enjoy it."

"That's my girl," her dad said. "We'll get our money's worth as a celebration of friends and family. And it makes good business sense since a lot of West Investigation's top clients are also in the audience and will be at the reception."

"Are you nuts?" her mom said, having rejoined them in time to hear Faith's request.

"Probably," Faith muttered.

"I was talking to your father." She turned to face him. "Your daughter is suffering and all you can do is talk about business and money?"

"I could put out a hit on Alan," Jeff growled, "but I'm restraining myself."

"I know people who could do the job," Faith's paternal grandmother said, speaking up for the first time. Her blue eyes and high cheekbones proclaimed her Scandinavian heritage while her gelled, spiky haircut revealed her rebel nature. "They're in the Swedish mob."

Jeff frowned. "I never heard of the Swedish mob."

"Of course not. They're very discreet. Not like the Finnish mob."

"I appreciate the offer, Gram, but it's not necessary," Faith said.

"Well, if you change your mind, the offer stands," Gram assured her.

"I'll keep that in mind."

"You do that." She patted Faith's hand. "I'm sorry things didn't work out."

"Thanks." She took a deep breath but felt the walls closing in on her. "Listen, you guys don't have to stay with me. Go on to the reception and please give everyone my regrets, but I just can't . . ." She shook her head, unable to go on.

"You have nothing to be regretful about," her mom said.

"Except regret at ever hooking up with Alan the Ass-hole to begin with."

"Are you sure you want us to go?" Her mom looked uncertain.

"Yes, I'm sure. Megan will stay with me, right?"

"Of course I will."

"See, I'll be fine."

"Of course you will . . . in time." Gram patted her hand again. "A year or two should do it."

When they finally left, Megan looked at her with concern. "Are you okay?"

"Not yet. But after a few mojitos I will be. Now please help me get out of this damn dress!"

FAITH woke with a hammering headache and the sound of intense roaring in her ears. Her eyelids didn't seem to want to open but she was able to sneak a peek through a narrow slit. The limited view was not enough to tell her where she was.

"This is your captain speaking. We'll be landing in Naples in about an hour."

Her eyes flew open.

"The flight attendants will be going through the cabin . . ."

Faith didn't pay attention to the rest of the announcement as the events of the day and night before came rushing back. Left at the altar. Humiliated, brokenhearted, angry. She and Megan downing several mojitos at a neighborhood bar before heading to Faith's Streeterville condo only to trip over Faith's suitcases just inside the door. A matched set of luggage packed with carefully chosen outfits for her dream honeymoon to the Amalfi coast in Italy.

Alan had wanted them to spend their honeymoon ele-phant riding in India because his boss at the bank had done that and raved about it. Personally, Faith was not that fond of pachyderms. Had he left her because of that? Because she didn't want to boogie with the elephants?

It wasn't like her choice was dull or boring. Who didn't like sunny Italy? Faith had longed to go to the Amalfi coast ever since she'd seen the movie *Under the Tuscan Sun* and watched Diane Lane swept off her feet in the beautiful town of Positano.

She distinctly remembered shouting at her living room wall the night before. "Alan ruined my wedding, but he's not going to ruin this, too! I refuse to allow him to mess up any more of my life! I'll show you exciting and adventurous! I'm going to Italy! Solo! Solo Mio!"

Faith spent the last two years trying to please Alan. This trip was one of the few times she'd stood her ground and refused to back down. Once he didn't get his way, Alan had completely lost interest and told her to handle all the arrangements. Gladly, she had—which was why she had possession of the nonrefundable tickets and the rest of the travel reservations.

Megan had been supportive as always. "Go for it! I'd come with you but I can't get away from work right now."

Sitting on the plane, Faith felt as if she'd just woken up from a long, drugged sleep. Unlike Sleeping Beauty, she hadn't been brought back to life by a kiss from a handsome prince. Instead she'd been brought back to reality by the handsome prince screwing her over.

The ironic thing was that Faith was usually a worst-case-scenario specialist, always prepared in case things went wrong. One of her dad's favorite mottoes, which she'd imbibed, was "Expect the worst, and if it doesn't happen, you'll be pleasantly surprised." Her relationship with Alan was the one time she'd allowed herself to believe . . . and look what happened.

She ended up on a flight to Italy. Alone. Her first solo trip ever. But it was better than moping in her condo crying her eyes out. She'd taken action. She'd left the mayhem behind in Chicago, calling her dad and telling him she was fleeing the country.

There was no time to reflect further on her actions as the flight attendants prepared for their landing. Her arrival in Naples went smoothly as she cleared customs with no problem. Two aspirins and a bottle of Pellegrino water took care of the headache. Her rental car was ready . . . and so was she.

She *was* ready, right? She wasn't going to let fear hold her back, right? She could do this. She *would* do this.

Faith plugged her iPod into the sound system and moments later the Gnarls Barkley song "Crazy" blared out of the sporty little red Italian convertible's speakers. She'd had to put her smaller suitcase in the passenger seat next to her since it didn't fit anywhere else.

The instant she hit the road, all the other drivers seemed determined to *hit* her. She refused to let them. She'd handled rush-hour traffic in Vegas, not to mention on the Kennedy Expressway in Chicago during construction season. The crazy Italian drivers didn't scare her. Being alone on her honeymoon scared her if she thought about it. So she refused to think about it and instead stepped on the gas, cranked up the sound system, and sang along with her favorite Bon Jovi CD, *Lost Highway.*

CAINE Hunter had his instructions. Keep an eye on Faith West, keep track of her actions, and report them back to Chicago. He knew a lot about her already—children's librarian, jilted bride, handy with a gun. Her team from the library in Las Vegas where she'd worked two years ago had come in second place in the city's Corporate Challenge, an event where organizations compete in various sporting events. She'd aced the shooting event.

Caine was only mildly impressed. She still seemed like a spoiled little rich girl to him, with her fancy wedding in one of the most prestigious churches in Chicago, a fancy banker fiancé, and a condo in Chicago's trendiest Streeterville neighborhood. Not that the wedding or the fiancé had panned out for her in the end. Too bad, so sad.

No one had ever accused him of being the sentimental type.

He'd say this for Faith West, she didn't drive like a
librarian . . . more like race car driver Danica Patrick.
Driving in Italy, especially around Naples, was not for
wimps.

Yet here she was, weaving in and out of traffic, music
blaring. Was she really that reckless or just plain stupid?
Hard to tell at this point, but Caine aimed on finding that
out . . . among other things.

FAITH'S knuckles were permanently white by the time
she reached the small town of Positano. The infamous
"road of a thousand curves" on which she'd been traveling
clung precariously to the steep cliffs and was narrower
than her parents' driveway at home. That didn't stop huge
tour buses from barreling around the blind curves, hog-
ging the entire road, and making her fear for her life and
her sanity.

But she'd done it. She'd made it here. Alive. In one
piece. Jane Austen would be so proud.

"Welcome to the Majestic Hotel, Mrs. Anderson." Huge
terra-cotta urns filled with flowers bracketed the reception desk adorned with colorful majolica tiles. The lobby,
with its antiques and artwork, was a study of understated
elegance. "We have the honeymoon suite all ready for you
and your husband."

Her stomach clenched. This was no honeymoon and she
had no husband. But she did have sunshine, breathtaking
views, and the scent of citrus blossoms in the air. "It's Ms.
West. Faith West. Not Mrs. Anything. I called ahead to
explain the change . . ."

"Oh, yes, I see the note here. I'm sorry for the confusion, Ms. West. If you could show me your passport,
please." The concierge raised his hand and a uniformed
bellman immediately appeared with her luggage. "Paco
will take you to your room."

She'd spent hours during the past winter poring over guidebooks and surfing websites trying to decide where to stay—the Grand Hotel in Sorrento or the Capri Palace Hotel on the island of Capri? But Positano had held her under its spell and, while she planned on visiting both Sorrento and Capri during her stay, this was her ultimate destination. The room didn't disappoint, with its private terrace displaying a colorful bougainvillea-framed view of the pastel sunlit town hugging the rugged cliffs that plunged down to the blue waves of the Mediterranean.

John Steinbeck was right. This place was a "dream."

The dream was interrupted by the sound of her stomach growling. She needed to eat something and fast. The hotel dining room was serving for another hour, Paco the bellman informed her in a sexy Italian accent, his liquid brown eyes gazing at her with Latin approval.

Faith was starving. But not for male attention. She handed Paco his tip and showed him the door.

She barely had time for a fast bathroom stop, where she looked at the thick towels and large tub longingly before hurrying down to eat. Knowing that nearby Naples was the birthplace of pizza, she quickly ordered a pizza margherita.

And waited. And waited. Other diners were seated on the sunny terrace dining area. Two guys in particular made a point of staring at her sitting all alone. She wasn't pleased to see their food arrive before hers. They hadn't even ordered Italian, but steak and fries. The skinnier of the two men gave her a leering look. He poured ketchup onto his plate and then dipped a fry into it, holding it up and taunting her with it before he chomped into it with gusto.

Normally Faith would have looked away and ignored him, but she wasn't feeling very generous toward the opposite sex at the moment.

Faith gave the man her best withering librarian look.

He responded by smacking his lips at her.

She made an *Ew, yuck* face.

He dipped another fry in the ketchup and waved it at her before sucking it into his mouth in one go. An instant later the man grabbed his throat and started turning red then blue.

Before she could react, another man smoothly moved past her and gave the choking man the Heimlich.

Faith sank into her chair. She felt guilty that while trying to impress her, the idiot had ended up choking and nearly killing himself. Was there some kind of Italian curse that was reserved for brides who came to the Amalfi coast without their grooms?

Then all thought went out of her head as she got her first good look at the rescuer. Dark hair, dark eyes, stubble-darkened cheeks and chin. A dark knight. A man meant to get a woman's juices flowing.

He stopped at her table and stared down at her before saying with amusement, "I'll say this, you sure know how to make an impression on a guy."

And now a special excerpt from

Something About You

by Julie James

Coming from Berkley Sensation
in March 2010!

THIRTY thousand hotel rooms in the city of Chicago, and Cameron Lynde managed to find one next door to a couple having a sex marathon.

"Yes! Oh yes! YES!"

Cameron pulled the pillow over her head, thinking—as she had been thinking for the past hour and a half—that it had to end *sometime*. It was after three o'clock in the morning, and while she certainly had nothing against a good round of raucous hotel sex, this particular round had gone beyond raucous and into the ridiculous about fourteen "oh-God-oh-God-oh-Gods" ago. More importantly, even with the discounted rate they gave federal employees, overnights at the Peninsula Hotel weren't typically within the monthly budget of an assistant U.S. attorney, and she was starting to get seriously P.O.'ed that she couldn't get a little peace and quiet.

Bam! Bam! Bam! The wall behind the king-size bed shook with enough force to rattle her headboard, and Cameron cursed the hardwood floors that had brought her to such circumstances.

Earlier in the week, when the contractor had told her that she would need to stay off her refinished floors for twenty-four hours, she had decided to treat herself to some much-needed pampering. Just last week she had finished a grueling three-month racketeering trial against eleven defendants charged with various organized criminal activities including seven murders and three attempted murders. The trial had been mentally exhausting for everyone involved, particularly her and the other assistant U.S. attorney who had prosecuted the case. So when she'd learned that she needed to be out of her house while the floors dried, she had seized on the opportunity and turned it into a weekend getaway.

Maybe other people would have gone somewhere more distant or exotic than a hotel three miles from home, but all Cameron had cared about was getting an incredibly overpriced but fantastically rejuvenating massage, followed by a tranquil night of R&R, and then a brunch buffet in the morning (again incredibly overpriced) where she could stuff herself to the point where she remembered why she made it a general habit to stay away from brunch buffets. And the perfect place for that was the Peninsula Hotel.

Or so she had thought.

"Such a big, bad man! Right there, oh yeah—right there, don't stop!"

The pillow over her head did nothing to drown out the woman's voice. Cameron closed her eyes in a silent plea. *Dear Mr. Big and Bad: Whatever the hell you're doing, don't you move from that spot until you get the job done.* She hadn't prayed so hard for an orgasm since the first— and last—time she'd slept with Jim, the corporate wine buyer/artist who wanted to "find his way" but who didn't seem to have a clue how to find his way around the key parts of the female body.

The moaning that had started around 1:30 A.M. was what had woken her up. In her groggy state, her first thought had been that someone in the room next door was sick. But quickly following those moans had been a second person's moans, and then came the panting and the wall-banging and the hollering and then that part that sounded suspiciously like a butt cheek being spanked, and somewhere around that point she had clued into the true goings-on of room 1308.

WhaMA-WhaMA-WhaMA-WhaMA-WhaMA-WhaMA . . .

The bed in the room next door increased its tempo against the wall, and the squeaking of the mattress reached a new, feverish pitch. Despite her annoyance, Cameron had to give the guy credit, whoever he was, for having some serious staying power. Perhaps it was one of those Viagra situations, she mused. She had heard somewhere that one little pill could get a man up and running for more than four hours.

She yanked the pillow off her head and peered through the darkness at the clock on the nightstand next to the bed. 3:17. If she had to endure another two hours and fifteen minutes of this stuff, she just might have to kill someone—starting with the front desk clerk who had put her in this room in the first place. Weren't hotels supposed to skip the thirteenth floor, anyway? Right now she was wishing she was a more superstitious person and had asked to be assigned another room.

In fact, right now she was wishing she'd never come up with the whole weekend getaway idea and instead had just spent the night at Collin's or Amy's. At least then she'd be asleep instead of listening to the cacophonous symphony of grunting and squealing—oh yes, the girl was actually *squealing* now—that was the current soundtrack of her life. Plus, Collin made a mean cheddar-and-tomato egg-white omelet that, while likely not quite the equivalent of the delicacies one might find at the Peninsula Hotel buffet, would've reminded her why she'd made it a general habit to let him do all the cooking when the three of them lived together their senior year of college.

Wheewammawamma-BAM! Wheewammawamma-BAM!

Cameron sat up in bed and looked at the phone on the

nightstand. She didn't want to be that kind of guest that complained about every little blemish in the hotel's five-star service. But the noise from the room next door had been going on for a long time now and at a certain point, she felt as though she was entitled to some sleep in her nearly four-hundred-dollar-per-night room. The only reason the hotel hadn't already received complaints, Cameron guessed, was due to the fact that 1308 was a corner room with no one on the other side.

She was just about to pick up the phone to call the front desk when, suddenly, she heard the man next door call out the glorious sounds of her salvation.

Smack! Smack!

"Oh shit, I'm cooommmminnnggg!"

A loud groan. And then—

Blessed silence. Finally.

Cameron fell back onto the bed. *Thank you, thank you, Peninsula Hotel gods, for granting me this tiny reprieve. I shall never again call your massages incredibly over-priced. Even if we all know it doesn't cost $195 to rub lotion on someone's back. Just saying.*

She crawled under the covers and pulled the cream-colored king-size down duvet up to her chin. Her head sank into the pillows and she lay there for a few minutes as she began to drift off. Then she heard another noise next door—the sound of a door shutting.

Cameron tensed.

And then—

Nothing.

All remained blissfully still and silent, and her final thought before she fell asleep was on the significance of the sound of the door shutting.

She had a sneaking suspicion that somebody had just received a five-star booty call.

BAM!

Cameron shot up in bed, the sound from next door waking her right out of her sleep. She heard muffled squealing and the bed shook against the wall again—harder and louder than ever—as if its occupants were *really* going at it this time.

She looked at the clock. 4:08. She'd been given a whopping thirty-minute reprieve.

Not wasting another moment—frankly, she'd already given these jokers far too much of her valuable sleep time—she reached over and turned on the lamp next to the bed. She blinked as her eyes adjusted to the sudden burst of light. Then she grabbed the phone off the nightstand and dialed.

After one ring, a man answered pleasantly on the other end. "Good evening, Ms. Lynde. Thank you for calling Guest Services—how may we be of assistance?"

Cameron cleared her throat, her voice still hoarse as her words tumbled out. "Look—I don't want to be a jerk about this, but you guys have *got* to do something about the people in room 1308. They keep banging against the wall; there's been all sorts of moaning and shouting and spanking and it's been going on for, like, the last two hours. I've barely slept this entire night, and it sounds like they're gearing up for round twenty or whatever, which is great for them but not so much for me, and I'm kind of at the point where enough is enough, you know?"

The voice on the other end was wholly unfazed, as if Guest Services at the Peninsula Hotel handled the fallout from five-star booty calls all the time.

"Of course, Ms. Lynde. I apologize for the inconvenience. I'll send up security to take care of the problem right away."

"Thanks," Cameron grumbled, not yet willing to be pacified that easily. She planned to speak to the manager in the morning, but for now all she wanted was a quiet room and some sleep.

She hung up the phone and waited. A few moments passed, then she glanced at the wall behind the bed. Things had fallen strangely silent in room 1308. She wondered if the occupants had heard her calling Guest Services to complain. Sure, the walls were thin (as she definitely had discovered firsthand), but were they *that* thin?

She heard the door to the room next door open.

The bastards were making their escape.

Cameron flew out of bed and ran to her door, determined to at least get a look at the sex fiends. She pressed against the door and peered through the peephole just as the door to the other room shut. For a brief moment, she saw no one. Then—

A man stepped into view.

He moved quickly, appearing slightly distorted through the peephole. He had his back toward her as he passed by her room, so Cameron didn't get the greatest look. She didn't know what the typical sex fiend looked like, but this particular one was on the taller side and stylish in his jeans, black corduroy blazer, and gray hooded T-shirt. He wore the hood pulled up, which was kind of strange. As the man crossed the hallway and pushed open the door to the stairwell, something struck her as oddly familiar. But then he disappeared into the stairwell before she could place it.

Cameron pulled away from the door. Something very strange was going on in room 1308 . . . Maybe the man had fled the scene because he'd heard her call Guest Services and was abandoning his partner to deal with the fallout alone. A married man, perhaps? Regardless, the woman in 1308 was going to have some serious 'splaining to do once hotel security arrived. Cameron figured—since she already was awake, that is—that she might as well just sit it out right there at the peephole and catch the final act. Not that she was eavesdropping or anything, but . . . okay, she was eavesdropping.

She didn't have to wait long. Two men dressed in suits, presumably hotel security, arrived within the next minute and knocked on the door to 1308. Cameron watched through the peephole as the security guards stared expectantly at the door, then shrugged at each other when there was no answer.

"Should we try again?" the shorter security guard asked.

The second guy nodded and knocked on the door. "Hotel security," he called out.

No response.

"Are you sure this is the right room?" asked the second guy.

The first guy checked the room number, then nodded. "Yep. The person who complained said the noise was coming from room 1308."

He glanced over at Cameron's room. She took a step back as if they could see her through the door. She suddenly felt very aware of the fact that she was wearing only her University of Michigan T-shirt and underwear.

There was a pause.

"Well, I don't hear a thing now," Cameron heard the first guy say. He banged on the door a third time, louder still. "Security! Open up!"

Still nothing.

Cameron moved back to the door and looked out the peephole once again. She saw the security guards exchange looks of annoyance.

"They're probably in the shower," said the shorter guy.

"Probably going at it again," the other one agreed.

The two men pressed their ears to the door. On her side of the door, Cameron listened for any sound of a shower running in the next room but heard nothing.

The taller security guard sighed. "You know the protocol—we have to go in." Out of his pocket he pulled what presumably was some sort of master key card. He slid it into the lock and cracked open the door.

"Hello? Hotel security—anyone in here?" he called into the room.

He looked over his shoulder at his partner and shook his head. Nothing. He stepped farther in and gestured for the second guy to follow. Both men disappeared into the room, out of Cameron's view, and the door slammed shut behind them.

There was a momentary pause, then Cameron heard one of the security men cry out through the adjoining wall.

"Holy shit!"

Her stomach dropped. She knew then that whatever had happened in 1308, it wasn't good.

FROM *NEW YORK TIMES* BESTSELLING AUTHOR

LORI FOSTER

MY MAN MICHAEL

"Foster writes smart, sexy, engaging characters."
—CHRISTINE FEEHAN

On the verge of a shot at a title match, fighter Michael "Mallet" Manchester is injured in a car accident. And just as quickly as his career was taking off, it's over. Then Kayli Raine appears, offering him a second chance at becoming whole. Even though Mallet thinks it's the pain medication talking, he accepts her challenge. And on an extraordinary journey with Kayli, he'll get the chance to fight again—to save the woman who has saved him.

M571T0909

Lori Foster writing as
L. L. Foster

SERVANT
THE KINDRED

Gabrielle Cody is a paladin—God's enforcer on earth. But she's not sure she can endure the life of a holy warrior. Her relationship with Detective Luther Cross is under constant strain already—and it's going to get worse.

There is a monster feeding off of human blood, flesh, and souls, and Gaby must stop him. But her passion for Luther distracts her from the terrible connection she has with her quarry—and the creature's desire to devour her.

M575T09

The darkest hour is before the dawn...

OUT OF THE LIGHT

INTO THE SHADOWS

New York Times Bestselling Author
Lori Foster

National Bestselling Authors
L. L. Foster

and

Erin McCarthy

Embrace the darkness and experience the light in this all-new anthology filled with touching stories of happily-ever-after alongside smoldering tales of irresistibly dangerous, otherworldly passion. From bewitching emotions and untamed desires to dazzling romance and tantalizing sensuality, these novellas explore the complex facets of the human heart—both the light side and the dark.

penguin.com